FORBIDDEN DESIRE

Miranda looked into her daughter's wide eyes, mirrors of delighted wonder, and felt a deep frisson of fear. What was she doing? This was wrong. Utterly crazy. She had lain awake last night in bed, replaying the terrifying adventure in the park over and over, trying to convince herself that she was analyzing it to figure out who wanted to kill her.

But all she truly thought of was the way her body had felt pressed so closely to Brandon Caruthers's hard frame. She could recall every nuance of his scent, even the smell of blood on his hand . . . his ungloved hand with its long fingers and powerful tracery of veins, even the light sprinkling of golden hair on the back of it. And he was her daughter's suitor! One day he would be her son-in-law.

How could she bear it?

REBEL BARON

SHIRL HENKE

LEISURE BOOKS NEW YORK CITY

For Ann Milenovich,
Bookseller Extraordinaire,
for all your support through good times and bad.

A LEISURE BOOK®

April 2004

Published by

Dorchester Publishing Co., Inc.
200 Madison Avenue
New York, NY 10016

ISBN 0-8439-5242-3

The name "Leisure Books" and the stylized "L" with design are trademarks of Dorchester Publishing Co., Inc.

Printed in the United States of America.

Visit us on the web at www.dorchesterpub.com.

Prologue

Spring 1865, America

Everything he had lived for now made him want to die. Brandon Shelby Caruthers stood before what had been the most elegant plantation house in Fayette County, Kentucky, one of the most elegant in all the vast bluegrass country. Where wisteria once vined lovingly on russet brick chimneys and gleaming white pillars supported a two-story white veranda, only blackened ash remained. His fine plantation and stud farm lay in smoldering ruins.

The only things left standing were a few charred walls that even fire could not topple. All the outbuildings—everything from the paddocks for his prize thoroughbreds to the neat rows of cabins where the trainers and other farm workers lived—everything had been put to the torch. Not even the dairy cellar or icehouse had been spared.

Once he had crested the rise at the edge of his property and saw the dense stand of burr oaks bare-leafed, their trunks blackened by fire, he felt a gut-deep fear displacing

1

hope. The dream of coming home to River Trails had kept him alive through the hellish months in a Yankee prison in Chicago, kept him walking across Illinois and Indiana, fording the spring flooding of the Ohio until his feet were once again on Kentucky soil.

The whitewashed rail fences had been down, of course. After being away at war for four years, he'd expected that. Fields of wild rye and bluegrass were trampled and muddy, crushed by the countless men, horses and wagons of Federals and Confederates alike. He'd expected that, too. But some tiny compartment hidden deep in his heart had refused to relinquish the vision of River Trails' magnificent Georgian outline silhouetted against the backdrop of rolling fields and the cool, swift waters of the Kentucky River. He'd envisioned it waking and sleeping, while he fought and especially when he lay rotting in prison.

Slowly, like a man sleepwalking through a nightmare, he dismounted from the skeletal gelding he'd been given by a distant cousin in Louisville and started to walk around the well-worn brick path to the rear of the burned-out house. The place was utterly deserted. Nothing larger than the birds trilling in a stand of blue ash trees remained. Two years ago, his mother and sister had moved to Lexington where their Aunt Agatha lived. He was grateful neither of them had witnessed the destruction of their ancestral home.

He walked into the center of what had been a huge vegetable garden and, seeing a few bright green onion sprouts peeping out of brown weeds, squatted down to scoop up a handful of dirt and tiny white bulbs, inhaling the musky pungency.

"You always were a fool over this place, but sniffing dirt's for blue tick hounds, not people," a lazy voice drawled in a distinctive British accent.

Brand jumped up and whirled, opening his arms to envelop the slightly built man of mixed race who thumped his back as they embraced. "Sin—damn, man, I thought you were carried off by the Federals!"

Gideon Hercules St. John, who insisted his last name be given the proper English pronunciation, "Sinjin," had worked hard during his fifty-odd years to live up to its first syllable. "In spite of the martial sound of my given names, the Federals found my stature, not to mention my age, less than imposing," he replied, straightening up to his full five-foot height as they broke apart. "Also my attitude."

His curly black hair was now liberally flecked with white and wrinkles creased his light brown face as he grinned at his friend and former employer. Returning the grin, Brand had never been so happy to see anyone in his life. "Twenty-five years in Kentucky and still you sound like an Englishman. That's probably why the Yankees didn't trust you. And, knowing you, you insisted on no less than captain's bars."

Sin's dark eyes danced as he stroked his pencil-thin mustache. "Why, dear fellow, I'd never settle for less than colonel. General Kilpatrick did not take it well when I broached the subject." He paused, studying Caruthers's weary countenance. "Hell, Brand, I could scarcely chance encountering you on a battlefield. I would've had to shoot you."

"And what makes you so sure I wouldn't have come out the winner?" Brand replied, falling easily into their old one-upmanship.

Sin snorted. "You rather conveniently forget that it was I who taught you to shoot. Besides, you lost the war, didn't you?"

"Yeah, we surely did, Sin . . . we surely did that." His eyes swept across the desolate ruins of his dreams. "I always figured we would. But I didn't expect to lose

Mama and Barbie . . . and then come home to this." He raised his hand to gesture toward the half-standing wall of the smokehouse, then let it drop.

"The cholera took hundreds of fine folks in the city, none finer than your mama, Brand. I spoke without think-ing—"

"No, you only spoke the truth. You warned me not to go riding off with Morgan and leave River Trails unpro-tected."

"You did what you felt you had to do."

"I did what Reba wanted me to do." There was a bitter edge to Caruthers's voice. "Did she marry her banker?"

Miss Reba Cunningham had been the most sought-after belle in Lexington and Brand's fiancée before the war, but when the tide of battle turned against the South, she'd broken their engagement and taken up with the son of a wealthy pro-Union family from Frankfort.

Sin nodded, knowing what a blow to Brandon Caruth-ers's pride that had been. "She and Earl Wilcox spoke their vows last spring, but gossip has it that their rela-tionship is not precisely one of connubial bliss."

Brand gave a mirthless laugh. "I should be grateful to the fool. He saved me from myself. I don't regret Reba anymore . . . but . . ."

"You couldn't have stopped Barbie even if you'd been here, Brand. She was young and fancied herself in love. One might even hope it will work out."

"He's a riverboat gambler, for God's sake, Sin. What kind of life is that for a girl like my baby sister?"

"Barbara Caruthers is stronger than she looks. We each have to make our own mistakes, Brand," Sin said gently.

"Like me joining the Rebs?" A faint trace of a grin played about his mouth, then vanished as he looked around him again.

"Mayhap I have just the medicine for your melancholy,

old chap," Sin replied, gesturing toward the blue ash grove on the rise. "Come along, now. There's a good fellow."

As the two men walked through the spring bluegrass near the trees, a soft whickering floated on the breeze. Brand's long strides speeded up in response. Sin was forced to break into a trot to keep pace and he still fell behind, coming up breathless as his friend gazed in rapt wonder at a coal-black stallion and two chestnut broodmares pacing nervously inside a small corral.

Brand walked around the rough-hewn wooden railing, approaching the stallion as if he were a ghost. The horse pawed the ground with excitement as his master stroked his muzzle. "Midnight Reiver, you beauty, you! I was sure you'd ended up in General Kilpatrick's remuda. And your ladies are here, too."

"Between them, the two armies managed to appropriate the rest of the livestock, but I hid your favorites in the canebrakes down by the river each time I received word of approaching soldiers. Mathias was my eyes and ears. The lad's off gathering firewood. He'll be about soon and thrilled to see you've returned unscathed." Mathias was a thirteen-year-old mulatto who had worked for Sin as a stableboy before the war.

"I owe you both more than I can ever repay," Brand said, his throat tightening with emotion.

"Tut," Sin replied dismissively, his dark eyes gleaming. "You'll repay us handsomely—and remake the Caruthers fortune in the process. The house and outbuildings may be gone, but you still own the land. And, the finest race horse in the Bluegrass. The track in Lexington's still open. As well as lots of others across the state. Even that infernal Yankee wilderness of Cincinnati has been known to hold a horse race or two."

"And place a bet or two?" Already Brand's mind was

whirling with the possibilities for racing Midnight Reiver, standing him to stud and breeding the two prime mares he already owned.

The men discussed plans as they strolled to the cleverly hidden cabin where Sin had survived the incessant marauding of Northern and Southern armies who fought the length and breadth of the divided border state. Inside the rude shelter, St. John broke out a jug of corn whiskey and they shared the contents, taking turns sipping with the heavy container slung over the shoulder the way Brand's father had taught them.

"We can do this, Sin. We can rebuild River Trails better than ever. Damn the Federals and the Confederates both to hell if we won't!"

Chapter One

Spring, two years later, London

"I thought you and Abigail Warring were going for a ride in Hyde Park," Miranda Auburn said to her daughter Lorilee. Smoothing back a tendril of dark red hair that had worked its way free of the tight cluster of braids at her crown, she walked over to the window where her only child stood silhouetted in the pale light straining through the curtains. The heavy forest-green brocade valance and side draperies made a perfect foil for the seventeen-year-old's pale golden beauty. Every time Miranda looked at Lori she could scarcely believe that a plain wren like herself had given birth to such delicate perfection.

Lori's pale lips trembled as she turned toward her mother with a forced smile. "Oh, we decided the weather was too beastly for riding out."

Miranda studied the girl. In spite of being occupied much of the time with business matters, she knew her daughter well. "It is a bit rainy and damp, but our new

Victoria would keep you nice and dry with the top pulled up." In fact, Lorilee had begged her mother for the expensive new slipper carriage with its collapsible top for just such exigencies as rainy days. Miranda knew there was a good reason her daughter was not showing off her new toy. "What is it, dearheart?"

The misery was apparent in Lori's eyes, but she continued smiling in spite of it. "I fear Abbie has had a better offer. Her footman came half past the hour to deliver this." She handed her mother a small piece of expensive stationery with the Easterham crest embossed on it.

The message was brief and to the point. Abigail, whose father was a baron, had been invited to tea in the exalted presence of a countess. "Why, you had made an engagement with Abbie last week. How very rude of her to break it at the last moment just because she must fuss for hours over her toilette to impress that dreary Belford clan." Miranda knew how such a rejection must sting her sensitive daughter.

Lori's smile wobbled for an instant before she raised her chin stubbornly, a trait inherited from Miranda. "Oh, Mother, only you would call the Earl of Varley's family dreary."

Miranda took her daughter's hand and patted it. "Well, it is nothing but the truth. They're vapid and exceedingly self-centered. The earl has the brains of a squirrel. All he's concerned with is riding to hounds and drinking at his club. And as for his wife, she lives only to collect jewelry and attend court functions."

"You're saying that because the countess told you she thought Her Majesty was exceedingly witty," Lori said, the smile at last spreading to her eyes.

"Her Majesty is a fine, upstanding woman, but Mr. Disraeli winds her about his little finger." Miranda sniffed

8

with disgust, both for women prone to flattery and Tory politicians likely to give it.

"You're Whig to the core," Lori replied as she studied her imposing mother.

Miranda Stafford Auburn, courtesy of her own ingenuity, industry and perseverance, sat on the boards of iron foundries, banks, shipping firms and railway companies. In the cutthroat circles of Britain's leading businessmen she was accepted, albeit sometimes grudgingly, with considerable respect. Her acumen in investment and ability to foresee expansion into new areas had taken the modest fortune of her late husband and multiplied it many times over.

If only she would agree to dress her hair properly and wear some flattering clothes. Lorilee studied her thirty-six-year-old mother's crisp but unadorned gray wool dress and that hideous bun of braids into which she insisted on torturing her hair. "Perhaps we could go to Madame Celeste's this afternoon. She has some of the loveliest new fashions—"

Miranda shook her head regretfully. Not because she had the slightest interest in fashion, but because she could not take the time for her daughter. "I'm ever so sorry, dearheart, but Mr. Minton from the National Bank is coming for tea. We're to discuss the new railway investment." At Lori's look of disappointment, she countered, saying, "I have it. How would you feel about the opera tonight? Adelina Patti is performing. Sarah Beverton told me anytime I wished, we could join them in their box."

Lori's expression brightened. "That would be wonderful! Did you know that Adelina Patti is considered the foremost coloratura soprano in all of Europe? It's true. I read it in *The Times*."

"Well, if you read it in *The Times*, then who am I to doubt?" Miranda said, returning her daughter's smile.

*   *   *

Lorilee insisted on selecting a gown for her mother that evening and had their personal maid Tilda fix her hair. Wanting to please her daughter, Miranda acceded although she always felt as if she were mutton disguised as lamb whenever she wore low-cut, brightly colored clothing. As for having her hair dressed in an upswept cascade of curls, well, that was more suitable for young misses making their debuts.

Girls such as her own beloved daughter.

But Lori's debut was sadly restricted. Commoners whose families engaged in trade, no matter how wealthy they might be, could not be presented at court. Lori had endured this sort of snubbing all her life. In spite of everything that Will and Miranda had been able to do—spending a small fortune on governesses and sending her to the finest schools—she was still the daughter of a jumped-up merchant from Liverpool.

Will Auburn had never cared for the fine opinions of Society, nor had his wife, who came from less than sterling bloodlines herself. But Will had insisted Lorilee be educated as a lady since he had toiled so long to amass the fortune to which she would one day be heir. Unfortunately, such an education led to mingling with the peerage, and that often led to heartbreaks and snubs such as the one today.

Miranda's own success in multiplying her child's inheritance only complicated matters, for unlike her utterly practical mother, Lori was a dreamer, a gentle girl who longed for a handsome young man to sweep her off her feet.

"You look splendidly handsome, ma'am," Tilda said as she finished looping the myriad tiny jet buttons down the back of her mistress's evening gown. It was a deep pewter shade of velvet which brought out the color of her gray eyes. At least, that was what her longtime maid and companion said, although Miranda knew Lori would think the color far too drab.

"Thank you, Tilda," she replied absently as she tried to breathe in the nasty corset which was necessary with an evening gown such as this.

"You look all the brown study. What's troubling you—besides having me lace you tighter than you prefer, that is?" Tilda asked with the familiarity of a servant who had attended her mistress since Miranda had been twelve years old and the East Indian a girl of sixteen.

"Nothing's wrong. I was just wondering if Geoffrey Winters will be at the opera tonight."

"Pelham's youngest?" Tilda's tone indicated what she thought of the third son of Viscount Pelham. "A pretty one. He might be quite a catch if not for the gambling vowels he cannot pay . . . and other vices no lady dare mention," she added beneath her breath. "You're worried that he'll pay court to Miss Lori?" Her shrewd brown eyes studied Miranda, who nodded.

"He's already approached me."

"I trust you sent him packing," Tilda replied indignantly. "He hasn't a shilling to his name, nor will he ever. Gossip is that Pelham's cut him off completely for his dissolute ways."

"Gossip in this rare instance is quite correct, not that the viscount's family has all that much of which to deprive him," Miranda replied dryly. But still she worried. "I did indeed refuse his request to call on Lori, but he's been appearing at social events and accidentally encountering her in spite of my wishes. She'll hear nothing ill spoken of him."

"Young love is quite painful, but that's the strength of the young—they can survive it," Tilda said gently.

"You're a love yourself, Tilda." Miranda smiled at the

tall, thin woman with ink black hair and smooth, light tan skin.

As the bedroom door softly closed, Tilda shook her head sadly. "If only you'd had the chance for such foolishness as Miss Lori does."

Just outside Cincinnati, Ohio

The racetrack was crowded. Throngs of people, from tattered ruffians to dandified gambling men, with a sprinkling of women of a certain reputation, set up a roar as the horses neared the finish line. When the big black pulled ahead of the gray who had been neck and neck with him for the past dozen yards, cheers and curses erupted simultaneously. Brand and Sin exchanged grins and prepared to collect their money.

Afterward, they strolled away from the muddy track toward where Mathias stood with Midnight Reiver. The lad was beaming from ear to ear. Although only fifteen and small for his age, his mentor, the great racing genius Mr. St. John, had trusted him as jockey for the first time. And he had not let them down.

"I tole him I cud do it, didn't I, Major?" he asked Brand.

"That you did, and you were right."

"He eased up on the reins too much around the first turn. The inattentiveness of youth," Sin said with a world-weary sigh that belied his own pride in his charge.

"In-tent-what?" Mathias asked. "Whatever that means, it must be good."

"You haven't been keeping up with your studies," Sin scolded.

"Considering how busy we've kept him on the racing circuit this spring, that's hardly his fault," Brand said. Turning to the young jockey, he warned, "Just don't start thinking that you can make your way as a jockey without an education, or the grifters who hang around racetracks will steal you blind."

"I knows—er, know, Major," Mathias corrected himself. "And I promise to finish that primer before we head on home to River Trails."

"See that you do. I shall quiz you on it," Sin interjected sternly, but he allowed Mathias one of his rarely seen genuine smiles.

"Lord, after six weeks I've all but lost track of the states, not to mention the towns, we've been through," Brand said as they walked the spent horse slowly toward the barn where Mathias and Sin would cool him down. "It'll be good to put my feet back on Kentucky bluegrass."

Sin snorted. "You just have an aversion to Federals, that's all."

"Don't have an aversion to taking their money. None at all," Brand replied with a chuckle. Then his expression turned grim. "Damnation, what's she doing here?"

"Intent on making trouble, that I can predict," Sin murmured.

Reba Wilcox sashayed toward them, twirling a frilly pink parasol. One gloved hand held up her skirts daintily so the hem did not touch the muddy grass. Her golden curls were piled high beneath a straw bonnet trimmed with pale pink roses that matched her gown. For daytime, it was cut scandalously low, revealing more creamy flesh than current fashion approved. But Reba had never wanted social approval. Only money . . . and Brandon Caruthers.

"Why, imagine finding you here, Brand," she exclaimed ingenuously, batting thick golden lashes against her subtly rouged cheeks. "I was visiting my second cousin once removed—you do recall me mentioning the Cincinnati Cunninghams, don't you? Well," she continued without giving him a chance to reply, "Cousin Stephan suggested we come to the race and you know how horse-mad I've always been. However could I resist?"

"Ladies don't attend this sort of race, Reba," Brand said, crossing his arms over his chest and giving her a look that clearly indicated what he thought about her presence at the track.

"Now don't be rude," she scolded with a mock pout, reaching up to take his arm, tugging it to indicate that they should walk. When he did not move, she said, "We need to speak privately, away from your darkies." The moment she said it, she could feel Brand's muscles stiffen beneath her fingers, but she ignored his anger and bestowed a blinding smile. "Please, Brand?"

Darkie! Not half as dark as the space between your ears! But Sin's face remained expressionless. Since returning to America from Britain where his English father had taken him to be educated, St. John had learned to curb his bold tongue around the flower of Southern womanhood—even if this particular flower was actually a weed.

"Why don't you and Mathias see that Reiver is cooled down? I'll be along directly," Brand asked his friend with a weary sigh.

Wordlessly, Sin nodded. He and the young jockey led the horse away. Brand turned back to Reba, making no attempt to stroll with her or allow her to put her hands on him again. "Say what you have to say and be done with it."

"Don't be cross," she wheedled. "After all we meant to each other—"

"We no longer mean anything to each other, *Mrs.* Wilcox. You made your bed with Earl. Now lie in it—if there's room enough after he flops onto it."

Reba stamped her foot, then looked up at him with

crystalline tears gleaming prettily in her cornflower-blue eyes. "What would you have had me do, Brand? Sleep in a dirt-floor cabin with slaves?"

"River Trails never owned a slave, Reba." His voice was flat. "But as to your sleeping in a rude cabin, I can't imagine it under any circumstances. That's why you chose your banker. Quite a fancy big house he has in town. Hear his daddy in Frankfort has one even bigger he'll inherit one day. You should be overjoyed."

She twisted the handle of her parasol and let several plump teardrops trickle down her cheeks. "I'm not. I'm utterly miserable because I still love you, Brand. Earl is just a boy." She gave a delicate shiver. "And he's fat."

Brand laughed, realizing that his misplaced affection for this girl-woman was completely gone. He thanked whatever powers were in charge of the firmaments that he had not married her before going off to war. He could well imagine the living hell he'd have faced upon returning to a wife forced to endure the hardships of rebuilding River Trails with him. "Earl's been fat ever since we were children, Reba. I'd think you could get him frisky enough in bed to shake off forty pounds."

She raised her hand to slap him but he caught it, holding her wrist as she hissed at him, "The war's made you crude and cruel, Brand. How dare you say such a thing to me after I've bared my heart to you! You're going to be sorry." She yanked her hand free and massaged her wrist, looking up at him with a crafty expression on her small, catlike face. "Maybe I'll forgive you one day . . . or maybe I won't."

The next two weeks passed in a blur as they moved from track to track on the racing circuit. Reiver faced the best and fastest horses everywhere, from rural outposts in southern Indiana to prosperous sporting events in St.

Louis. Everywhere they went, they won. Sin kept control of the money and hid it in Mathias's shabby knapsack. Any racetrack sharpies looking to steal from them would never think to examine a black youth's meager possessions—even if they got past Brand's .45 caliber Remington.

As they sat around a campfire after their last race before heading home, Sin wrote in his precise script, recording the day's receipts. "Those St. Louis Germans may know their beer but they're sadly deficient in judging horseflesh," he said with relish, stuffing the last of the currency—all of it good Federal banknotes—into a pouch.

"If only we have enough to satisfy that damnable vulture Wilcox," Brand said, sipping from a tin cup of bitter chicory coffee.

Sin added the day's winnings to the running tally he'd kept in his head over the past months. "We're within a few hundred dollars. When we win in Lexington, we'll have the whole of it."

"We'd better," Brand replied grimly.

Rebuilding the burned-out stud farm and purchasing new stock had taken longer than either Brand or Sin had realized it would. Much of the backbreaking work of cutting timber and erecting stables and corrals they had done themselves. Brand had hired freedmen who knew horses and were willing to pitch in doing what horse trainers normally considered menial labor. But if the major himself was willing to grow calluses with a hammer and saw, they were willing to join him.

Midnight Reiver won almost every time he raced, but the purses in these hardscrabble times after the war were frequently meager. If not for their heavy winnings in St. Louis, they would not have found the trip worthwhile.

Brand's hope was to be able to afford more broodmares

soon and raise a host of Reiver's colts for sale. A handful of wealthy pro-Union racing enthusiasts were willing to purchase them. In a good economic climate the prices would have gone far to bring River Trails back to its old prominence. But knowing that the proud "secesh" Caruthers was struggling, the buyers took delight in offering less. In time, as the magnificent horse's reputation spread across the lower Midwest and further east, Brand was counting on that to change.

His biggest problem in the short run was paying his taxes. Brand had been expecting his taxes to reflect how much less his land was worth because of the destruction of the war. Instead they were higher than ever. And back taxes kept compounding interest, making it almost impossible to pay off the debts. The Kentucky Unionists were as guilty of squeezing every penny out of former Confederates as were the carpetbaggers in those states that had seceded. Kentucky had remained in the Union, but her people had been evenly divided in their loyalties. Now those who had been Federal supporters sat in the catbird seat. In Fayette County their leader was his former fiancée's husband, Earl Wilcox.

Brand had been forced to endure the double humiliation of seeking a loan from a Union bank and from the man to whom Reba had sold herself. The terms were usurious but the only ones he was going to get, and Brand had taken them. So far, he'd kept up with payments. Barely.

They arrived at River Trails on a warm afternoon, tired but happy to be home. Before Brand could dismount, Ulysses, their cook, came running out of the log cabin the men were sharing, skillet in his hand, forgotten in the excitement.

"Major, sir! They're fixin' to sell the place. Right this

afternoon!" The old man continued babbling, practically in tears as Brand strode toward him.

"Whoa, Uly, who's fixing to sell what?" Brand asked, with a hot knot of dread tightening in his gut. "Slow down and start at the beginning."

In moments he was up on Reiver, riding hell-bent for Lexington. Sin followed at a no less dangerous pace on the mare Silky. The ride from River Trails to town took nearly an hour. Brand galloped up to the steps of the courthouse and jumped from the lathered black's back. The obedient horse stood with reins dropped on the ground as his owner pushed his way through the noisy crowd toward a wooden podium obviously brought from inside.

Judge Harkins was banging a gavel, trying to quiet the men and women as they yelled boisterously. This was the most excitement in Fayette County since the last time Colonel John Hunt Morgan had ridden home with his infamous raiders. Dogs barked and men spit great lobs of tobacco while jugs of corn whiskey were upended all around. Some were celebrating, others consoling themselves over the end of an era. Gradually the noise level subsided as people recognized Major Brandon Caruthers. Mostly, they stepped back respectfully. A quiet hum of whispering filled the late afternoon air.

"What's he gonna do now?"

"Whut kin he do?" a companion responded.

"Crock of shit if'n yew ask me."

"Aw, Billie, who'd ever ask yew anythin', even 'bout shit?"

That sally was greeted with a bit of laughter, which quickly died as Brand stood in front of Judge Harkins. Every eye in the assembly stared at them with a mixture of horror and fascination.

"I understand you intend to auction off my land without

so much as a by-your-leave, Judge," Brand said.

The judge tried to meet the fierce gaze of Colonel John Hunt Morgan's favorite officer, but could not. At the moment he was damn grateful the "Thunderbolt of the South" was cold in his grave, although he felt some trepidation about Morgan's ghost rising up to smite him. "Now, Major Caruthers, you know you've been delinquent with your taxes—"

"I've got the money, Judge. Right here." Brand raised his fist, filled with Federal currency.

"It's too late, son," the judge said, casting a nervous glance toward where Earl Wilcox stood with a smirk wreathing his plump features.

"The deadline for making a tax payment isn't for another two weeks," Brand said, stepping closer to the judge, who seemed to shrink inside his fancy new black suit.

Beads of perspiration broke out on Asa Harkins's leathery face, dripping into his heavy eyebrows and beard. "That's not strictly true, Major."

"Oh, and what is 'strictly true,' then?" Brand asked through gritted teeth. He could feel Wilcox's eyes on him.

Harkins swallowed hard and tried not to look at the banker. "The regular deadline applies only to current taxes. You're paying on back taxes."

"Me and half the folks in Kentucky! Damn, Judge, most of the folks in Fayette County are behind in their taxes. We were off fighting a war."

"A war that you unfortunately lost." A clear, high-pitched voice rang across the wide stone steps leading up to the courthouse. As if waiting for the most dramatic moment to make his appearance, Earl Wilcox strolled toward the podium. He was a short man, running—no, dashing—to fat. His skin was soft and as pale as buttermilk, owing to the hours he spent inside the marble

19

interior of his father's bank, the only one in the Bluegrass to remain solvent after the war.

"I might've known you'd be behind this, Wilcox," Brand said tightly, crossing his arms over his chest to keep from seizing that flabby white neck and wringing it like Uly would a chicken's. "What does the war—whatever goddamn side I was on—have to do with my taxes?" The dangerous light in his eyes dampened Wilcox's smirk a bit.

"Why, nothing at all. It's just that you borrowed quite a sizable amount from my bank. Our investors have the right to worry about recovering that loan when you can't pay your back taxes." He paused to lick his thick lips in nervous anticipation.

"So you went crying to the judge here. Just to 'protect your investors.' "

"By putting River Trails up for public auction, the county recovers what it's owed and the bank loan is repaid by the new owner," Wilcox replied with a pompous smirk.

"Oh, and just precisely who is that new owner?" With a twisting gut, he knew. He also knew he was going to choke the life out of Earl Wilcox.

Casting a furtive glance around to see that the sheriff was nearby, Wilcox replied, "My wife has always fancied being mistress of River Trails. Now she will be."

When Brand lunged at him, Wilcox squealed like a pig hoisted for slaughter. But St. John slipped through the crowd and jumped on his far larger friend's back as he would leap atop a large thoroughbred. He whispered, "Easy, old chap. Squeeze him too hard and we'll drown in grease." By the time he pried Brand's hand from Wilcox's throat, the elderly sheriff had placed himself between the two men and faced Caruthers while Earl's clerk thumped the banker on his back until he quit coughing.

Sheriff Cy McCracken's rheumy eyes gazed sadly on

the younger man, whose father had been a close friend. "Sorry as kin be 'bout this here mess, Brand, but law's on his side—even if he is a fat lazy hawg," he added in a low voice, eliciting sniggers from the crowd, most of whom thoroughly disliked the Wilcox family but also owed its bank money. "They ain't a thang I kin do. Damn shame."

By now Sin had released his hold on Brand. "We'd better go before there's more trouble." He waited to see what would happen next, praying Earl Wilcox had enough sense to keep his mouth shut while he was still breathing.

Fortunately, Wilcox backed away in silence, a petulant look of triumph written all over his face. The sheriff kept an uneasy watch on the two antagonists as Sin steered his friend down the steps.

I wonder if he knows his wife still fancies Brand.

As if giving voice to Sin's thought, Brand said, "She told me I'd be sorry. We should've headed straight home from Cincinnati."

"Without the money we made in St. Louis, we could not have paid the taxes in any case. The land is gone, but you still have Reiver, the mares and colts." Weak words of consolation, even to Sin's own ears. He knew that losing the Caruthers birthright, land that had been in his family for generations, was a stunning blow to Brand.

"We'd best get back to River Trails and round up the stock before Wilcox takes it into his mind to have my broodmares held for ransom with the land," Brand said.

As they made their way through the crowd, many well-wishers offered the major condolences, even places where he could stable his horses free of charge until he got back on his feet.

St. John followed Brand, remaining silent as his companion thanked friends and neighbors for their kindness. They did not acknowledge the small man of mixed race.

21

In this class-conscious society, much as it had been in England, he was a man no one understood. Few felt easy around him. To the Kentuckians he was a foreigner, his father an Englishman and his mother a Jamaican.

The two men mounted wearily and rode up Main Street at a far slower pace than they'd ridden down it earlier. Just as they were turning the corner onto Broadway, Asa Harkins's voice echoed after them. Brand reined in and waited as the old judge, riding in his little black buggy, approached. He clutched a letter in one hand, which he was waving at Caruthers.

"In the excitement earlier, I almost forgot this. It came while you were away racing Reiver. Since . . ." Harkins's voice faded awkwardly for a moment before he regained his composure. "What I mean to say is that since there was no way to leave it at River Trails, the new postmaster asked me to hold it until you returned. It came all the way from London, England."

Sin watched as Brand bent down and took the dog-eared missive from the judge, who watched in rapt fascination as the major began to open it. *It might as well have come from the moon,* Sin thought, silently amused at the older man's provincial curiosity.

As Brand read, a look of bemusement replaced the weary resignation of moments earlier. "Well, I'll be damned," he said softly to himself, passing the letter along to Sin.

As he started to read, he knew the judge was irritated that he could do so and that a white man had been willing to share such a confidence with a man of color. But that consideration was pushed to the back of his mind by the time he'd skimmed the second paragraph. Sin whistled low and gave Brand a mock bow.

"Well, Rushcroft, I suppose congratulations are in order. Mr. Gideon H. St. John, your obedient servant, m'lord."

Chapter Two

"Isn't he quite the dashing one?" Mrs. Horton whispered behind her fan.

Miranda, preoccupied in watching Lorilee dancing with Geoffrey Winters, had not taken note of her companion's interest. She scanned the crowded ballroom as the elderly widow blathered on while beating the stuffy air with her fan.

"The scandal sheets call him the Rebel Baron. He was one of those Confederate soldiers during their recent war, you know. Inherited the Rushcroft title, but little else is known about him."

Miranda's gaze fixed on the subject of Elvira Horton's discourse. "My—a mere American and he received an invitation to the Moreland ball. Of course, he is a peer and we're but commoners," Miranda said dryly. The way society segregated people had always offended her sense of fairness. She knew that if she had not been wealthy enough, Lady Moreland would never have deigned to invite her. Nor would she have come in any case if not for Lori.

"At least we're of good solid English blood. Heaven only knows how his might have been contaminated," Elvira said. Her eyes remained fixed on the tall stranger standing at the opposite edge of the large room. "He is a handsome devil, I'll give him that."

Finding herself studying the new Lord Rushcroft, Miranda was forced to agree. She could make out little of his facial features at this distance as the gaslights were turned low, flickering romantically over the assembly. But his body was lean and erect, and his elegant black cutaway coat and trousers flattered broad shoulders and long legs. He carried himself like a man to the manor born.

But he was as restless as she, Miranda sensed, bored with the gala, standing off to one side, evincing no particular interest in what those around him were saying. His hair appeared to be some shade of dark blond, slightly curly and cut longer than was the fashion. He was clean-shaven, and that, too, went against fashion. Perhaps he was vain about his appearance, but for some reason that eluded her, Miranda did not think so.

His profile was striking, she had to admit—long, straight nose, high brow and firm jawline. Then he smiled in response to Georgette Mayer's flirtatious hand on his arm. Forward hussy. The Widow Horton echoed Miranda's thoughts when she spoke.

"That gauche woman is desperate to enter the peerage . . . or for some peer to enter her! With all the money old Mayer left her, she'll doubtless succeed."

Miranda laughed. "Elvira, dear, don't be vulgar. And do give the devil her due. Georgette is accounted a great beauty."

"If only the same high compliment might apply to her morals," Elvira snapped.

Miranda was surprised when a sudden wave of disappointment swept her as the new baron bowed with an elegant flourish before Georgette. Then the couple moved gracefully into the strains of a waltz that had just started. As they drew nearer the secluded box where the older women not in the marriage mart were seated, Miranda was drawn to study his face. Although finely chiseled and exceedingly handsome by any standards, it was hard, even dangerous-looking. His expression seemed to hint that he had seen more than a man of his years should have been called upon to witness.

She'd heard stories of the incredible carnage the Americans had wreaked upon each other, brother against brother in that tragic, fratricidal strife. Miranda had volunteered nursing the wounded brought back from the Crimea and had seen that same look in their eyes. Then she saw Rushcroft's scar. It was a thin white line stretching across his right cheekbone down to his jawline. Odd that he would not grow a beard to conceal it. But then perhaps, being one of those Southern cavaliers whom the press loved to romanticize, he wore it as a badge of honor.

Who knew? Why should she care? Miranda forced her gaze away from the American and scanned the room for Lori, but before she could locate her daughter and Winters, Elvira once again distracted her.

"Georgette will find him easy pickings or I miss my guess. Rushcroft hasn't a shilling. His family seat is crumbling to ruins. The Caruthers men always ran to excesses. Small wonder the English branch died out, leaving an American to claim the title."

"Really, I've heard nothing of the family."

"Oh, pish, I know you're too busy running banks and shipyards to bother with Society. The only members of the peerage who interest you are those who owe you money." Her scolding tone hid the fact that Elvira was in awe of a woman who dared to enter the male world of business.

But Miranda's attention was now absorbed by her search for her daughter, who had apparently vanished from the room. "If you'll excuse me, Elvira, I must collect Lorilee. The hour is growing late, and I have appointments early in the morning."

"A pity. You really should hire some man to oversee your affairs so you could spend more time out in Society," Elvira replied.

"I prefer to handle my late husband's businesses myself. It is quite stimulating . . . and no one will ever take advantage of me."

As she bade her companion good evening, she worried about why Lorilee had disappeared—and with whom.

"Please, Geoff, I really must go back. We've been alone far too long. Tongues will wag," Lori said breathlessly as her suitor pressed another ardent kiss on her cheek. She had already allowed him shocking liberties, and only when his mouth opened over hers had she come to her senses and realized she might compromise herself beyond redemption if she were not careful.

"Never say you find my attentions unwelcome," he pleaded, slowly releasing her, satisfied when he felt her trembling.

"No—that is, yes, I welcome your suit, but we must take care. You are the son of a viscount and I—"

"You are the woman I intend to wed," he interrupted, watching in satisfaction as her eyes widened and her mouth formed a small "O."

Before Lori could gather her wits to respond to his declaration, she heard her mother's voice and noted a fleeting look of annoyance mar Geoff's face. But she quickly dismissed it as a trick of the light. After all, he was the soul of gentility and had always been utterly charming to her mother. He was quite the most wonderful young man she'd ever met, so witty and sophisticated. Her very own handsome young prince who had at last declared himself.

"Will you do me the very great honor of marrying me, Miss Auburn?" he blurted out suddenly, as if to get the words said before fate intervened.

"Oh—"

Before she could get out the "Yes" she wanted to shout to the rooftops, her mother slipped past the hedge and bore down on their hiding place in the shadows beneath the gazebo in the Moreland formal gardens.

Miranda did not like the looks of what was transpiring. However, she pasted a smile on her face and nodded to Pelham's youngest son. "Mr. Winters, good evening," she said in a perfunctory manner. Then dismissing him, she turned to Lori, who seemed crestfallen at her mother's interruption. They both began to speak at the same time.

"Mother, Geoff—"

"Lorilee, we must—"

Miranda carried the day. "I fear we must be going," she said firmly. "I have an appointment quite early tomorrow morning." She gave her daughter a quelling look, which elicited a guilty one in exchange. According to decorum and her mother, Lori knew she was not to be alone in the shadows with any young man—from Miranda's viewpoint, most especially this one.

"But, Mother—"

"Mrs. Auburn, if I might—"

"No, sir, you might not. We shall speak privately at a later date, Mr. Winters," she replied in frosty dismissal, as dread of what he had just said to Lori seeped deep into her bones. *The little jackal! He's asked her to marry him!*

Taking Lori's arm, she steered her daughter toward the sounds of music and glitter of gaslights.

"You did not tell him yes, did you?" she asked, then could have bitten her tongue as soon as the words escaped her lips.

"How did you know?" Lori asked incredulously. Then, reading the tight set of her mother's mouth, she sighed. "You gave me no opportunity, nor Geoffrey to ask your permission."

"Oh, Geoffrey, is it? And, it's marvelous that he would deign to bother with my permission since he's already taken liberties with my daughter, for which he should be publicly horsewhipped!" At the stiffening in Lori's body, Miranda once more cursed her lapse of temper. Normally, she was under so much better control. In fact, as a woman in the male-dominated world of business, she had always prided herself on how well she held her emotions in check.

"Mr. Winters," Lori replied primly, "has taken no liberties which I have not allowed." Strictly speaking, that was not true, but Lori was hurt and bewildered by her mother's intransigence regarding her charming young suitor. "You were quite rude to him."

"Yes, I was. But at least he still has skin on his backside."

Lorilee gasped but knew better than to make a retort when her mother was in this mood.

They entered the press of the crowd once again. Both women were forced to smile and pretend nothing was amiss. Miranda had to pause and bid this friend and that business acquaintance good evening as they made their way toward where Lady Moreland stood in the entry hall, saying farewell to another group of early departing guests. "Lori, please ask the footman to fetch our wraps while I thank our hostess for the evening," Miranda instructed.

Obedient if not cheerful, Lorilee hurried toward a servant dressed in gaudy yellow and blue livery. So intent was she on her frustrations, she did not see the tall stranger who materialized from a doorway, cutting directly into her path. Her slight frame bounced off his hard-muscled body, and she might have stumbled backward if he had not caught her, steadying her balance, then quickly releasing her.

"My deepest apologies, miss," he said, bowing gracefully and bestowing a smile. "I was not watching where I was going."

"It is I who should apologize for being so clumsy. If not for your kind aid, I would've made a spectacle of myself tumbling onto the floor," Lorilee said, returning his smile curiously. He spoke with a soft, drawling accent unfamiliar to her.

From her vantage point across the entry hall, Miranda observed the brief exchange. He was courtly and charming, young enough and titled . . . *Of course, he was American,* she thought wryly, recalling Elvira Horton's snide remarks. Miranda was appalled to even be thinking of such a wild scheme, but she knew her daughter. For all her gentle ways, Lorilee Anna Auburn could be as stubborn as a balky dray horse and she had set her mind on that fortune hunter Winters.

Already she'd spurned several far more suitable matches, both wealthy commoners and even the heir of a marquess, in favor of Pelham's boy. Miranda thanked heaven Gretna Green was no longer a haven for runaway lovers, but still, Lori could ruin her reputation if she continued to be led on by Winters. That was his game, to force her to permit the marriage after he'd destroyed Lori's chances for happiness elsewhere.

I shall simply have to spend more time with her, my business obligations be damned, Miranda vowed, dismissing the fanciful idea of matchmaking between the "Rebel Baron" and Lorilee. London was, after all, the center of the civilized world, and within its five million odd inhabitants there would be the right husband for her daughter. All Miranda need do was steer her away from those who would take advantage of her.

As they rode home, Lori sat in martyred silence until her normally bubbly nature overcame her pique. "How did you know Geoff—Mr. Winters had asked me to marry him?"

Miranda's lips curved wryly. "Call it mother's intuition, dearheart."

"But then, surely you can see his intentions are honorable."

"Perhaps, but I do not believe you would suit," she replied gently. "I want you to marry a man who will be kind to you as your father was to me."

"Kind. What a weak word that is. I know yours was not a love match, Mother, but I do not intend to marry a man only to fulfill family obligations." The moment the words escaped her, Lori wanted desperately to call them back, but it was too late.

Miranda felt them pierce her heart like daggers of ice. "Yes, I married your father for duty, but my father took great care in assuring that Will Auburn would never do me a hurt. And he did not," she said stiffly, suddenly overcome with a ridiculous and selfish longing to have the world of choice that lay before her daughter. A world forever closed to her.

What is making me think this way? Visions of a tall, elegant man sweeping across the ballroom floor with a shadowy redheaded woman in his arms flashed into her mind, and she caught her breath. The sheer audacity of it—the utter folly. What madness had taken hold of her! Lori's words of apology did not register until her daughter had crossed the carriage seat and sat sobbing on her mother's shoulder.

"There, there, I know you did not mean to hurt me, dearheart," she crooned, taking Lori in her arms. "Nor have you. I've had a full and worthwhile life. Please don't cry."

But as she sat consoling her only child, Miranda Stafford Auburn fought the overwhelming urge to cry herself. Her life had indeed been one of wealth and privilege as well as duty and work.

But never had she known love.

"What do you mean, there is no money! I'm heir to a huge manor house and thousands of acres and have not a cent—a pence with which to maintain it?" Brand leaned over the solicitor's desk, fists planted on the gleaming walnut surface as he glared at the austere man seated behind it.

With calm deliberation, Herbert Austin Biltmore stared down his pinched nose at the documents spread out before him. "Please be seated, Lord Rushcroft. I understand you Yankees can be excitable, but—"

"I am *not* a damned Yankee," Brand gritted out in a menacing tone that had made grizzled sergeant majors run for cover.

Solicitor Biltmore did not so much as flinch. "Very good, Anglo-American, then," he replied without missing a beat. "There is no need to raise your voice. Please take a seat so we can proceed."

Brand backed off, but did not take the seat he'd just vacated. Instead he paced the confines of the book-lined office, combing his fingers through his hair. He'd been living at Rushcroft Hall, which was in only marginally better condition than River Trails had been after the war. But the Hall was several centuries older, and its poor condition was due to neglect, not fire. It could be restored, as could the fertile lands surrounding it. With enough money.

He had immediately made an appointment with the executor of his distant cousin's will. Biltmore was the attorney—blast it, "solicitor"—from whom he'd first received the summons to England. Brand had dozens of plans for refurbishing the Caruthers ancestral estate when he walked into Biltmore's office. Until the terms of dear old Cousin Mortimer's will were read to him.

"Now, as I was saying"—the solicitor returned his eyes to the page—"the taxes are due by midyear, as are the rents—"

"But the rents are ten thousand pounds less than the taxes and other debts owed."

The solicitor enumerated the precise amounts, adding dryly, "You are quite astute with figures, m'lord."

Brand fought the urge to laugh insanely. "This is a jest of cosmic proportions—you do realize that, don't you? Of course not. I lost my family's home in Kentucky because I couldn't pay back taxes."

"Well, you need have no fear of that. As a peer of Her Majesty's realm, you are heir to an estate which cannot be sold or broken up in any way. The laws of primogeniture hold Rushcroft Hall and its lands in perpetuity for the direct line of male descendants of the Caruthers family."

"So I can sit and mold on the land but I can't sell it. Just watch it fall down around my ears. And what of the taxes and debts?"

The solicitor shrugged. "Most of the peerage is in arrears on taxes. Since you have no other properties to secure, there's nothing the county warden can seize in lieu of payment."

Thinking of his horses, Brand started to sweat. This

could turn out even worse than he had just imagined. He'd had to sell a splendid colt for less than its worth just to pay for his and Sin's passage to England, but he'd never dreamed that once he claimed the title, there would be no money. What if the government or his creditors took Reiver and his broodmares? He would have no way of earning a cent . . . pence. Stranded in bloody old England, panhandling with the beggars in Whitechapel!

With visions of himself and Sin sneaking the horses aboard some lug bound for France in the dark of night, he barely registered the solicitor's droning voice at first. But the word "marriage" finally penetrated the miasma surrounding him. "What did you say?"

"I said," Biltmore reiterated disdainfully, "if you were to wed a woman of means from amongst the carriage folk, her dowry might solve your pecuniary difficulties."

"You mean marry for money?" The words left a sour taste in his mouth as visions of Reba Cunningham flashed through his mind. "If so exalted a person as a peer of Her Majesty's realm were to do so," Brand replied, parroting the solicitor's pompous diction, "why not wed a peeress?" Was there such a word as peeress? Damned if he knew. These people didn't even speak English!

Biltmore looked down his nose again. "Everyone is aware that the late baron was without means and deeply in debt. So, for that matter, are many of the peerage. But there are ever so many men in trade who have plump pockets and want nothing so much as to marry their daughters into the aristocracy. You would be well advised to take advantage of that fact."

The solicitor's manner indicated quite clearly that he believed the crass American's blood was far enough removed from blue that sullying it by wedding a commoner should be no great sacrifice. Brand wanted to choke the life out of him.

In this case, he resisted the urge. Sin was not present to rescue him from the hangman's noose. "Save your advice. This American usurper is not for sale."

"As you wish, m'lord." Biltmore's expression oozed an irritating combination of disdain and pity.

Brand turned on his heel and quit the office, wondering if they did indeed hang peers of Her Majesty's realm. The punishment would almost be worth the satisfaction of shaking Biltmore's arrogant certainty.

Miranda sat at her desk, staring at the papers in her hand, trying to digest the implications . . . and possibilities. As the major shareholder of the largest bank in London, she reviewed all loan applications for amounts in excess of ten thousand pounds. "My, the baron is truly as destitute as Elvira Horton indicated," she murmured to herself as she scanned the inventory of Caruthers's holdings.

The preceding baron had been a gamester, as were all of his ancestors. Unfortunately for Brandon Caruthers, his cousin Mortimer's luck was the poorest of the lot. He had sold off every scrap of the family possessions he could before his untimely death. In addition, he had taken not the slightest interest in the running of the family seat in Surrey, which was now in utter chaos. Virtually all the tenants were in arrears in paying rents, due in no small part, Miranda surmised, to the absence of the lord of the manor, who cared nothing about making repairs or seeing to their welfare.

Would the new baron be any different? His application for a sizable loan outlined ambitious plans for making improvements, not to the manor house itself, which she would have expected, but rather to the land. Much of it was lying fallow now, but apparently he'd inspected it and felt it would suit quite perfectly for raising and training horses. He had experienced some notable success, if the report appended to the loan application was to be believed, in breeding thoroughbred stock and racing his prize stud, Midnight Reiver. He even had aspirations to run horses at Ascot next year.

Once when Lori was a baby, Miranda had attended the races with her husband and some business associates. She thought the exorbitant bets placed between members of the nobility were quite appalling. And now this man wanted her to lend him money—her and Will's very hard-earned money—so he could cavort at racetracks!

She felt a sudden flood of righteous indignation that smacked of the Queen's puritanical philosophy, and grimaced. This was business. The morality of gambling had nothing whatever to do with it. If the stud farm Major Brandon Caruthers proposed could produce the income he projected, she should approve the loan.

But Miranda had another idea in mind—if the Rebel Baron came up to her exacting standards. She walked briskly to the heavy walnut door and summoned her secretary, Herbert Timmons. "I have an investigation that requires the utmost discretion, Mr. Timmons. Here is what I wish you to do . . ."

"Who the hell does this woman think she is? Queen Victoria herself?" Brand fulminated as he glared at the letter in his hand, then passed it to Sin as if it were a live snake.

Quickly perusing it, Sin chuckled. "It would appear to be a royal summons indeed—in this case, the royalty being not of the peerage but rather the industrial elite. The Widow Auburn not only owns controlling interest in the bank from which you have requested a loan, but a shipyard, an iron foundry and so many other ventures, I fail to recall them all."

"Unnatural female. As bad as those crazy Yankee women demanding they be allowed to vote."

"I hate to break it to you, old chap," Sin said with a chuckle, "but they're making the same demands here in England."

Brand shuddered. "Women should stay home and tend to their families. Leave the running of government—and industry—to men."

"You and Her Majesty are in complete accord on that issue." Sin's voice had taken on a decided hint of irony. "You were turned down by every other bank in London. At least the Widow Auburn deigns to grant you an interview Tuesday next."

Brand muttered a vile oath and paced across the narrow carpet runner, now quite threadbare, that was one of the few remaining adornments of the Caruthers city house. Every painting, sculpture and piece of furniture that could be sold had been, leaving the library in which they sat devoid of all but a pair of scuffed, creaking leather chairs in front of the fireplace and moth-eaten velvet drapes in a hideous shade of puce. Even the built-in mahogany bookcases lining the walls had been denuded of their contents, save for a few cheap editions of popular fiction Mortimer had been unable to sell.

"You'd best go, hat in hand, and charm the lady, son," St. John said, ignoring the baron's restless pacing. Although disappointed that Brand's windfall had proven chimerical, Sin was not surprised. He had spent enough time in Britain to know the vices of the aristocracy. His own father, second son of a squire from Kent, had escaped by fleeing to Jamaica one step ahead of his creditors.

Brand poured himself a generous portion of brandy, which he detested. "Damnable island. A man can't even buy bourbon here." He tossed down the alcoholic libation like medicine, then said with resignation, "Here's to charming an old woman. I bet she's a veritable hag."

Chapter Three

Miranda took a swallow from the glass of water and replaced it on the massive, ugly Gothic Revival table across from her high mahogany desk. Although she detested the ornate heavy furnishings with which her late husband had filled his office, she had kept them. They imparted an aura of masculine power, and she had learned to make herself comfortable within it. Right now she needed all the courage she could muster if she was going to lay her bold proposal before Lord Rushcroft . . . Major Caruthers.

Dared she do it? It smacked so closely of the arrangement her father and husband had made eighteen years ago. *No, it is nothing like that. I only want Lori's happiness.* Was her logic faulty, motivated by her fear of Geoffrey Winters? While her daughter had been out riding with Abbie, Pelham's boy had arranged "accidental" encounters twice in Hyde Park, all within the space of a week. He had managed to sit next to her at the Southingtons' musicale on Friday afternoon and danced twice with her at the Hortons' ball Sunday night. The last event had really started tongues wagging. One more waltz and they would be all but engaged. Or Lori would be ruined.

She could send her daughter to Liverpool to visit Will's distant cousins, but that seemed cruel in the midst of Lori's first London season. And who was to say Geoffrey Winters would not sneak across country after her, with dire consequences? The boy seemed bent on making trouble in spite of her clear warnings to him regarding his suit.

No, this was a better solution—if she and the baron could agree on terms. Summoning her courage, she rang for Timmons to show him into her office.

In the waiting room, Brand took note of the opulent furnishings. Thick Brussels carpeting in a deep maroon and green floral design covered the floor, accented by the dark green wall covering. The heavy rosewood Gothic Revival desk and chairs dwarfed the anemic, mousy-looking man who rose at the sound of a tinkling bell. *Like a lap dog,* Brand thought scornfully as the great lady's secretary scurried into her lair, closing the massive walnut door behind him.

Here he was in the heart of "the City," as London's central financial district was known. This was his last chance. If this old crone refused his request for a loan, he would toss back his claim to the barony and return to America on the next ship before the tax collectors got wind of his cache of valuable horses and confiscated them. He had tried every means at hand to lift his estate from disaster, but it was impossible without an infusion of cash.

He and Sin had broken their backs for the past month at Rushcroft Hall, working side by side with his tenant farmers to plant an oat crop. But tariffs no longer protected grains from foreign competition, and cheap grains from the damn Yankees poured into Britain. The profits from the harvest would be so meager that his few re-

maining tenants faced starvation. Brand had neither the
heart nor stomach to take his portion from them.

But he did have a plan that could rescue them all from
perdition. All he needed was money. A great deal of it . . .

"Mrs. Auburn will see you, m'lord," the office mouse
said deferentially.

He might be impoverished but he was still, by God, a
bloody baron and he'd act the part to the hilt. Maybe he
could bluff this female into doing what none of the male
bankers had been willing to do. He strode toward her office as if he owned half of Kentucky and the whole of
Surrey.

And froze in the massive doorway. Brand was barely
spared the indignity of having his backside shoved into
the office when the secretary closed the door. He had
imagined a harridan similar to the portraits of hatchet-
faced Yankee suffragettes he'd seen scowling from flyers
posted on public buildings from Cincinnati to Saratoga.

But Miranda Auburn was not an old hag. Far from it.
Oh, she was no raving beauty, to be certain, dressed as
she was in somber dark gray. The two-piece business suit
was fitted crisply to her tall, slender body, although the
high neckline and square-cut loose jacket seemed designed to hide any womanly curves. Her hair was pulled
severely back into some sort of highly unflattering bun.
The color was dark red and might have been quite arresting if the tresses had been arrayed more softly. It was
obvious to him that she intentionally denied her feminin-
ity. Some gut instinct warned him that that denial meant
trouble.

Always good at assessing people, he tried to decide
how to handle her. Her face was more strong than con-
ventionally pretty, but quite striking in spite of its lack of
artifice. A pair of perfectly arched eyebrows and thick
lashes were a shade darker than her hair. She had high

cheekbones and a firmly developed jaw presaging stubbornness. The slightest of smiles indicated straight white teeth and displayed a generous mouth innocent of lip rouge. Eyes a peculiar shade of silver-gray assessed him in return. He could sense the shrewdness in them as she rounded the desk and glided toward him.

Yes, she's going to be trouble, he thought as he recovered from his surprise and minded his manners, bowing smartly.

"Lord Rushcroft," she said in a husky, cultured voice.

She surprised him by extending her hand for a firm shake rather than allowing him to press a discreet kiss on its gloved back. Brand disliked being a supplicant to anyone, especially a female. He liked it even less that this female approached him as if she were a man.

And his equal.

What was he to make of such an unnatural woman? Bestowing his most winsome smile, he replied, "My pleasure to make your acquaintance, Mrs. Auburn."

"Please have a seat, my lord," she said crisply, gesturing toward another of those ugly leather chairs, this one placed in front of her monstrous desk. She immediately turned her back on him and walked around the desk, taking her place behind it. An obvious power ploy if he had ever seen one, and every officer serving under General Wheeler's command had.

Brand smiled, waiting until she was seated before sinking into the devouring depths of the hellish chair facing her. "Since you arranged this appointment, Mrs. Auburn, I assume you have had the time to consider my proposal," he said in his most disarmingly genial voice.

Miranda was struck by his grace once again, the self-assurance with which he moved. But there had been something hesitant, which he had covered very smoothly, when he'd first entered her office. No doubt he'd been led to

40

expect an ancient ogre. She would've allowed herself an inward smile if not for the seriousness of this meeting.

That sense of leashed danger buried deep inside him was hidden by a smile that could melt a glacier. She had been unable to discern the color of his eyes before, only their hardness. Now she could see they were gold and black . . . tiger's eyes. Not for the first time, she wondered if hers was a wise plan.

"I hope your decision will be in my favor, ma'am."

And his voice—she had not been prepared for the low, rich timbre of it, or for the slow, drawling accent which held none of the affectation of the English aristocracy. The odd lilt was quite at variance with the speech of other Americans she'd dealt with. Of course, they weren't from the Southern states, she reminded herself.

He's trying to charm me. "I have given a great deal of thought to your rather detailed proposal for the improvements you envision on your estate," she began very carefully. Best to tread slowly and take his measure further. "You intend to turn Rushcroft Hall into a . . . stud farm," she said, glancing down at the papers in front of her.

"That is my plan. It's prime grassland, and I've brought with me the finest thoroughbred racehorse and brood stock in Kentucky."

She knew that he was not boasting, merely stating a fact. "You also intend to race this Midnight Reiver, is that not so?"

"Yes, I do. In fact, Reiver's already won several purses at Epsom and Sandown," he said with pride.

"It would seem a rather risky venture, basing all your hopes for the future on winnings from such a capricious sport. What if your horse loses?" she asked, playing devil's advocate just to see how he'd respond.

As Sin would say, "just bloody lovely." She's a damn

straight-corseted Puritan. Brand smiled over his disgust. "Reiver seldom loses, ma'am."

"Reiver—what an odd name. Is it American?"

"It wouldn't appeal to a fine, upstanding Englishwoman such as you, Mrs. Auburn," he said with a slow grin. "The origin of the word isn't American. It's Scots, and it means a member of a raiding party who swoops down from the hills to steal whatever isn't nailed down, then vanishes like a lightning strike."

His smile was infectious and infuriating at the same time. She could sense the defiance behind it. *He hates having to ask anyone for help.* This foreigner with the molasses accent affected her in ways no other man with whom she'd transacted business ever had. Of course, she'd never considered making to any of them the offer that she might make to the Rebel Baron. That was the difference—the only difference, she hastened to assure herself before continuing, "I'm not at all certain the image of thievery is one you should mention while discussing business with a banker."

The bit of dry wit took him by surprise. *So the lady has a sense of humor.* Perhaps all was not lost. "I'm not so certain, given the character of some American bankers I had the misfortune to deal with. Still, reiving isn't in my plans for Rushcroft Hall. Neither is merely winning races at the tracks."

"Pray enlighten me." She steepled long, tapered fingertips together and gazed at him with those cool silver eyes.

He knew damn well she'd read his very detailed explanation in the application. Was the woman toying with him? The urge to get up and walk out swept over him again, but he quashed it. "As I wrote in the proposal"— he gestured at the neat stack of papers before her—"I intend to breed and sell horses. I'll begin with the racing stock I have now—winning at the tracks around London has already attracted several potential customers for Reiver's colts. In the long run, that's a great deal more important than the purses we collect."

"But much as the British aristocracy is horse mad—and it surely is—there is hardly demand for thoroughbreds to justify such a large loan," she countered.

"Once I have my breeding program established and barns, stables and fencing in place, fields planted for fodder and men trained to harvest and dry it, then I'll be ready to branch out, to purchase new breeding stock. How many carriages cross over London Bridge every day?"

Miranda blinked at the unexpected question. "Quite a few, I would hazard."

"Nearly thirty thousand. Every jumped-up bookkeeper and tradesman aspires to join the 'carriage class' and stable his own horse or team of horses, whatever he can afford. Then there is the matter of draft animals for drayage and agriculture. I've investigated the costs of purchasing Scots and Flemish stock. A prime team of Clydes can command a handsome price."

Miranda nodded. She'd been stalling, taking his measure as he spoke. The light that burned brightly in his eyes now indicated the passion he felt for his plans. With sufficient capital behind him, she was certain he'd succeed. When she had shaken his hand, it felt firm and strong. He was no idler who hired others to do his work for him. Another good sign.

"In all of this, you've not written or spoken of the Caruthers family home. Surely as the new baron, you would like your seat refurbished. I'm given to understand it was one of the loveliest manor houses in Surrey."

Visions of River Trails's burned-out shell flashed into his mind for an instant, overlaid with images of crumbling neglect at Rushcroft Hall. "Eventually, I would enjoy having a gracious home once more, but that is a luxury

I'll forgo for the present," he replied guardedly.

"Most gentlemen of your class would think possessing a splendid manor house—and city house—the most pressing needs."

"I am not most gentlemen," Brand replied levelly. "Holding balls and galas never held much appeal for me."

"But you do take pride in your family heritage."

"I took great pride in the Kentucky land that had been held by my family for generations. By English standards, four generations may seem a laughable span, but in Kentucky, it is a very long time. My great-grandfather cleared the land and planted the first crops himself."

"But he used slaves."

Ah, now we get to it, he thought with a grim smile. "He did. But as I suspect a well-informed woman of business such as you knows, slavery's been abolished in America."

"You have never owned a slave," she stated, glancing down at the papers on her desk, sorting through a report which had nothing to do with his finances . . . and everything to do with whether or not she made him her offer.

"You have me at a disadvantage, ma'am, knowing everything about me while I know nothing about you. And yet I'm the wily foreign adventurer and you're the widow lady. Shouldn't it be the other way about?"

Miranda felt a smile tug at her lips and permitted it. "Touché, my lord. Perhaps it is time to explain my position." She took a deep breath for courage, happy that Tilda had not laced her at all tightly this morning. "You are in need of a large amount of money to rebuild your ancestral estate and restore it to profitability. I am in need of a husband for my daughter." Baldly put, but there it was. She studied his reaction as she added, "I believe we might discuss a mutually satisfactory way for both of us to achieve our goals."

Brand sat frozen in the clutches of the damnable leather

monstrosity of a chair, too amazed to bolt to his feet and storm out of the room. This was the very last contingency he could have imagined. "Seeing as how I lost everything in the war, then came here to find myself with an empty title, you believe I can be bought." In spite of his lazy drawl, icicles dripped from every word.

"Not you."

"But my title?" he snapped.

As he stood up, preparing to storm out, she hastened to add, "It was not my intention to insult you."

"It may not have been your intention, ma'am, but you surely did. My solicitor has already made the suggestion that I wed a wealthy heiress to recoup the Caruthers family fortune. I told him to go to the devil. My mother would rise up in her grave if I said the same to a lady, but I believe our business is concluded."

"Wait, please, Lord Rushcroft. Please allow me to explain," Miranda said as calmly as she could when his hand reached for the massive brass doorknob.

There was something in the tone of her voice, a desperation that he'd heard often during the war . . . when women pleaded for their homes to be spared, for food, or for the lives of their children. What would make a woman like this one plead? He sensed it was not in her nature, any more than it was in his, to beg for anything. She was proud and self-sufficient. And not in the least maternal. Brand turned around, curiosity warring with humiliation.

"Pray, enlighten me," he said, throwing her words back at her.

He stood stiff as a board, rigid with anger. How could she blame him? He was a proud man who had lost everything in America and now stood to lose again after crossing an ocean in search of a second chance. She moistened her lips nervously, feeling his eyes on her. She met them and said, "You are precisely the kind of man I want for Lorilee."

"One with a title? If that's all you require to sell your child, there are a surfeit of impoverished peers." She flinched, and he almost wished he had not said it.

"I don't care a fig about your damnable title, Major!"

His eyebrows rose expressively but he said nothing, merely stood like some restless jungle cat, waiting for her to continue.

"I am not looking for an entree to the drawing rooms of the aristocracy. My money has already gained me that. I have no interest in Society."

"But your daughter does?" He was beginning to see the picture of a spoiled little rich girl and he did not like it.

"My daughter fancies herself in love with a man who wants only her money."

"So you offer her to another man in exchange for money. The logic of that escapes me."

"I know Geoffrey Winters. He will hurt Lori. I do not believe you would."

Again, he raised his eyebrows. "And why is that? What do you know about me other than that I fought on the losing side of the war, have a bankrupt barony, and my American antecedents were slaveholders?"

"Actually, quite a bit. I've had your personal life and family background as well as your financial situation investigated."

"Really." She met his eyes steadily, although he knew it could not be easy for her to do it.

"Yes. Before the war you were forced to take over your family estates when your father became ill. As a boy scarce out of knee britches you made a vast plantation prosper. You—"

"I had help."

"Yes, Mr. Gideon Hercules St. John," she said, glancing down to read his name from the report. "Quite interesting. He's here in London with you. He was your mentor after your father became incapacitated." How well Miranda could understand such a bond. "His mother was Jamaican, father an English expatriate in the islands who sent him to England to be educated, in spite of his being born on the wrong side of the blanket."

"Don't forget his mother was *black* Jamaican. That didn't set any better here than it did on the other side of the Atlantic."

"Point taken, my lord. The English may in principle wish those of other races to be free, but we do not readily admit them to our society any more than do Americans. But that is a separate issue."

"You're the one who had Sin investigated." He shrugged. "Why?"

"Only because of your unique relationship with him. I believe it reveals a great deal about your character."

A slow smile spread across his face, mocking her. "Good or bad?" She was an abolitionist, no doubt about it. He already knew the answer, but it angered him that this woman dared to sit in judgment on something as sacred and personal as his friendship with Sin. It was an invasion of his private life. And of his friend's as well.

"I want a man of strong moral character, a man who is not concerned about what Society says, only what he believes is right."

So prim and self-righteous. "As long as what he believes is right agrees with what you believe is right."

"Quite well put," she replied honestly. "When I received your application for the loan, I had already been considering you along with several other gentlemen, but none of them measured up."

"And I do? If I didn't feel like a stallion at a stock auction, I imagine I should feel honored. But what does your daughter have to say about the matter?" He watched her flush slightly at his vulgarity, surprised she didn't rise to the bait. But then she suppressed a sigh, enabling him to draw his own conclusions before she answered.

"She is infatuated with Pelham's son and has refused all other suitors. You must understand that I did not start out to arrange a marriage for her—although that is certainly not an inappropriate thing to do. My own marriage was such, and it worked out quite amicably."

"But she wants a love match. Even if I were willing to go along with your *business proposal,* I'd never force a woman to marry against her will," he said angrily.

"That is precisely the quality I have been looking for, don't you see?"

"Nothing about this makes sense to me," Brand admitted. "If she fancies herself in love with another man, there is nothing either of us can do about it."

"You're mistaken. You could make her see that Winters is a callow boy. I did not ask you to explain your plans for the Rushcroft seat because I was too lazy to read your application papers, I assure you."

"You wanted to see if I was desperate enough for the money to accede to your proposal."

"Just the opposite. I feared your reaction might be as it was. But what I have learned is that you have a sense of honor and of industry. Your passion for the land and what you want to do with it came to life when you spoke—in ways that mere words put to paper could never convey. You'd never waste my daughter's inheritance on debauchery or gamble it away."

"Are you certain of that? You were quite concerned about my racing Reiver." A little of his anger began to dissipate.

She shook her head. "No, Major, you would be a prudent financial manager. And, equally as important, you could win over my daughter."

"Permit me to doubt that, ma'am," Brand said dryly as visions of his former fiancée flitted through his mind. "I'm a horse breeder, not a courtier. A scar-faced soldier is hardly the stuff of a young girl's romantic dreams."

Miranda studied him frankly, and a frisson of heat danced down her spine. Forcing herself to ignore the disquieting sensation, she said blandly in her best negotiator's voice, "The scar is scarcely a disfigurement. And you're older, sensible enough to guide a girl of Lorilee's impulsive and generous inclinations. You must be aware of your good looks. Half the women in London are swooning over them. They call you the Rebel Baron."

Brand scoffed. "I never put much stock in what gossips print in newspapers."

"Neither do I. That's why I had you investigated so thoroughly. You must admit, when you came to my bank for a loan, it did seem a fated coincidence."

Brand smiled sardonically. "No, ma'am. Yours was the only bank in London that hadn't already turned me down, but I expect you know that, too."

Miranda nodded. "My daughter is quite a lovely young woman. She'll turn eighteen in a fortnight. This is her first season," she said as she picked up a photograph from her desk and extended it to him.

He took it from her as if it were a live viper, holding it at arm's length as he studied the youthful, smiling girl. She was utterly beautiful. *Just like Reba.* "I can see why she'd have many suitors. She'll find someone she wants if you're patient."

"My patience is infinite, my lord. However, being eighteen, Lorilee's is not. She's being manipulated by an utterly ruthless scoundrel who has already proven he'll stop at nothing to compromise her. I cannot take that chance.

If you will not court her, I shall have to find another who will."

Her words were clipped, yet he could sense tension underlying them. Miranda Auburn was hardly a woman he would call maternal, but he was willing to concede she cared for her daughter's happiness. "And if I don't court her, will you still consider my loan?"

"No," she replied flatly. Gray and gold eyes locked. She was calling his bluff, and they both knew it. What would he do? Miranda held her breath, wanting to sweeten the bargain by explaining the very generous dowry she would provide for Lori; it was far more than he had requested to borrow. She wanted the manor and city houses restored as well as the lands, since Lori would be in residence. But her instincts warned her that if she made any further efforts that he might construe as bribes, he'd turn and stalk out. She held her piece.

Brand weighed his options. All were wretched. He and Sin could make a run for home, or more easily, France, but he would not put it past this enigmatic woman to send the Peelers after them to confiscate their horses. He turned the matter around in his mind, growing more frustrated with every passing second. And she, the icy queen of industry, stood waiting without so much as a twitch. He could see how she'd managed to run her late husband's many holdings.

She probably eats ballocks for breakfast. "I won't agree to court your daughter yet, but I will agree to meet her. If she's willing."

"I'm certain she will be." Miranda tried very hard not to gloat.

Chapter Four

Miranda was certain of no such thing. For all she knew, Lori would lock herself in her room and sob her heart out until her face was so red and puffy Tilda would be required to soak it with ice cloths to reduce the swelling. On the long carriage ride home from the City to the enormous house Will had built in Kensington Gardens, Miranda was preoccupied with how to broach the subject of a new suitor with her daughter. Lori would immediately infer that this was an arrangement between the baron and her mother.

How could she convince an idealistic young woman filled with dreams of true love that Geoffrey Winters was a fraud and that a man such as the baron was far more honest about his motives? Caruthers was young enough and quite handsome, a quixotic figure of romance who should appeal to Lorilee, indeed had already appealed to a great many other young debutantes. He had them all aflutter.

Just then her driver opened the box and called down to

her, apologizing because they were stalled in a traffic snarl involving an overturned fodder cart and a racing gig that had collided with it. That shifted her thoughts to Major Caruthers's business acumen. He was right on the mark about the need for prime carriage horses. The man had definite potential.

Now all she had to do was convince Lori to abandon Pelham's wastrel son.

The situation resolved itself far more easily than Miranda could have imagined. She had no sooner set foot inside the entry hall of their three-story home than Lorilee came rushing down the long flight of stairs with such haste that Miranda feared she might take a tumble and injure herself. Without uttering a word, she flung herself into her mother's arms, quaking like a leaf in a summer storm. Miranda steered her toward the closest sitting room and closed the doors behind them.

"What is it, dearheart? What has happened to you?" she asked, leading Lori over to take a seat on a Rococo Revival settee facing the mantel. Miranda did not like the pallor of her daughter's normally rosy cheeks, nor the wooden stillness in this young woman who was always filled with life.

Lori kept her head bent downward as she replied in a whisper so low Miranda had to strain to make out the words. "You were right about Mr. Winters, Mother." She twisted her handkerchief in two small white hands, wringing it until the lace edging ripped, but still not looking up. Nor did she weep.

Mr. Winters. My, what has that bounder done? Miranda had known her soft-hearted daughter to cry uncontrollably over a stray puppy run over by a dray wagon, even over the young tweenie she'd been forced to discharge for pinching silverware last month. Now Lorilee sat with her back rigidly straight, her head bowed, silent as a Greek statue.

"How did you find out that my judgment of him was correct?" she asked gently.

"At Murcheson's musicale this afternoon I was in the ladies' retiring room when I overheard Gretchen Lieder and Thea Murcheson discussing him."

Miranda nodded. Mrs. Lieder and that ancient Murcheson baggage were the worst gossips in all of England, but they knew everything that went on in Society. She waited patiently as Lori gathered herself to continue. Already she could feel a killing anger at Winters boiling through her veins. The rotter had hurt her daughter!

"The Earl of Falconridge's daughter Varinia has been compromised by him and they are to be wed by special license within the week. The scandal is spreading across London. The earl at first wanted to call him out, but his countess prevailed upon him to allow the marriage instead. Mr. Winters expected a large dowry. The earl refused. Instead, he has provided them with a very modest allowance. If Mr. Winters does not mend his ways, he will be banished to America to work in the offices of a shipping firm owned by the earl's family."

Miranda could not resist an inward smile. Ah, the splendid irony of it. She would have laughed aloud but for her daughter's distress. "I have had business dealings with Cameron Beaumont. Given the chance, he will work Geoffrey Winters very hard indeed."

"All he wanted was my money, and . . . all the while he was courting me, he was still . . . searching for a wealthy woman of his own class." Lori's eyes finally began to swim with tears, but she met her mother's gaze, refusing to break down.

She's growing up. Miranda hated the brutal blows which all too often accompanied maturity, but it was for the best. What if his scheme to entrap Varinia Beaumont had snared her Lorilee instead? What if her beloved daughter had been the one to be compromised and forced to wed a man who had used her thus?

"I know this must be very painful," Miranda began carefully, feeling as if she had spent the entire day walking over eggshells. First the prickly baron, now her wounded daughter. She took Lori's hands in hers, massaging the tight little fists until they released their deathlock on the shredded handkerchief. "Geoffrey Winters is young and callow, too wrapped up in his own selfish schemes to see your worth. That is no reflection on you, my dear. You're beautiful, intelligent and warmhearted, all any gentleman of breeding could wish in a wife. Only think of how many suitors you've already turned away—and how many," she hastened to add, "you have yet to meet."

"But Geoff—Mr. Winters," she coldly corrected herself, "was the only one whom I fancied. And now he has turned out to be just like all the rest. Men are only interested in my money, not in me."

"You know that's not true. Several of the young swains you spurned were rich as Croesus. Ralph Condon certainly did not need your money, nor did Leander Fleming." Both were heirs of wealthy industrialists, albeit, Miranda was forced to admit, rather dull sticks. Perhaps a rakish charmer such as the Rebel Baron would prove just the tonic for Lori. But not so soon. She would require time to lick her wounds.

Miranda remembered how bitterly disillusionment could hurt. And she'd been given less than a week to accept Will Auburn's marriage proposal . . .

"I want to marry for love, not make a business merger, Mother." Upon seeing the tiny flinch Miranda quickly hid, Lori was instantly contrite. "I'm sorry. That was most unkind of me. I know that you and Father—"

"I regret that you did not have enough time to appreciate what a fine man William Auburn was," Miranda said softly. "But I promise you will find a man far closer to your age who will cherish you just as he did me."

"Perhaps," Lorilee replied in a despondent voice, gripping her mother's hands as if they were a lifeline in a storm-tossed sea.

Sin was busily humming his second chorus of "Froggie Went A Courtin'" when Brand threw the boot he'd been polishing at his friend's head. Unrepentant, Sin merely ducked, then returned to mending the halter he'd been working on for the past quarter hour as Brand prepared for his first meeting with Miss Lorilee Auburn, heiress.

"I know you don't approve, and I can't say I'm the least bit enamored of the scheme myself, but it's the only way we can survive, dammit," Brand snapped, attacking the other boot with enough zeal to rub the fine leather to the thickness of gauze.

"No estate is worth leg-shackling, old chap." St. John shuddered. "I've avoided connubial bliss for well in excess of five decades and have never regretted the decision. Need I remind you of the mistake you nearly made with Reba Wilcox?"

"I'm not signing any marriage lines just yet. Only going to meet the young lady . . . who, if her likeness was any indicator, is very beautiful."

Sin grunted, putting down the tack. "And what if she has the disposition of a treed bobcat? Or the mind of an imbecile? I say we take the horses and make a run for it."

"There's nowhere to run, Sin," he replied wearily. "If Miss Auburn does not find me appealing, then I'll have no recourse but to approach her mother for the loan once again. The widow has shrewd business sense; I'll give the devil her due. She made no attempt to hide her interest in my plans for Rushcroft Hall."

"You really feel a tie to the old ruin, don't you?" Sin asked rhetorically. Brand had walked the land with a gleam of hope in his eyes. After the loss of River Trails, St. John had feared that hope was gone forever.

Brand laughed self-consciously and resumed polishing the boot. "Perhaps it's bred into Caruthers men to covet land. Or maybe it's because I was born on English soil."

"Pure happenstance, that. If your parents had not been returning from their grand tour of the Continent when your mother was ordered abed carrying you, you'd have been born in Kentucky just as your forebears were."

Brand chuckled. "Father was furious at the inconvenience. It was the opening of racing season back home."

"A far more important event than your entry into the world," St. John said with a rich chuckle. "But here you are, sitting in the House of Lords."

"I'd far prefer a business arrangement to a marriage alliance, believe me," Brand said grimly as he thought of the interview coming up that afternoon.

Sin's eyes swept over Brand's elegant features and tall, lean body. "Give me leave to doubt the girl will spurn you. Need I remind you the ladies of London Town are fairly swooning over the Rebel Baron? Why should this chit be any different from the rest? She's from a family in trade, and you're a peer."

"An American peer. An utter barbarian according to some lights," Brand said, unconsciously rubbing the narrow white scar on his cheek—and marking it with a smear of bootblack.

"Keep applying that and you'll be in no danger of attracting the young miss—nor will you get your bank loan," St. John said wryly.

Caruthers looked over to the opposite wall where the

room's sole mirror hung, one so chipped and ancient as to be unsalable. He applied a matching streak of bootblack to his other cheek. "Perhaps I can frighten Miss Lorilee Auburn away and then deal with her mother. What say?"

Sin grinned, happy to see his friend's old sense of humor reassert itself. When he'd returned from the solicitor's office, Brand had been in a killing rage, his pride so affronted he'd all but called the man out. But oddly, after receiving a similar suggestion from this formidable widow at the bank, he had simply ridden back to his ancestral land and resumed planning for the future. One way or the other, Brandon Caruthers intended to hold on to what was his.

If that included taking a simpering slip of a girl to wife, would he be able to go through with it? St. John had known Reba Cunningham was a dreadful choice. He doubted the Englishwoman would be any better. Of course, he was a confirmed misogynist who felt it his duty to find some way for Brand to escape this marriage trap. He stroked his chin, considering options. . . .

"You've done splendidly." Miranda squeezed her daughter's hand as she inspected Tilda's handiwork. The handsome older woman fussed with last-minute touches to Lori's golden ringlets.

"Thank you, Tilda," Lori said with a tremulous smile. She turned this way and that, inspecting her new sprigged muslin gown, trying to take her mind off the prospect of meeting the dashing American. She was a bundle of nerves. Would he find her attractive? More importantly, would she find *him* attractive? She scarcely remembered him from their brief collision at the Moreland ball.

Her mother had explained that the baron required money with which to restore his estate—money that would come from Lori's inheritance. Not precisely the stuff of dreams. But Lorilee was becoming resigned to what she knew most other women of her station accepted. A marriage alliance between families. Her only consolation was that if she detested him, her mother would not force her into the match.

"Don't fret. You look quite perfect, dearheart," Miranda reassured the nervous girl. She had given her daughter nearly a month to recover after her deliverance from Winters before even broaching the subject of Lord Rushcroft. After a round of outings to musicales, balls, regattas and other social events, Lori showed no particular interest in any young man. Overall, that was a good thing, for many of them were every bit as irresponsible and mercenary as Pelham's boy.

Perhaps Lori was at last putting aside girlish dreams and could evaluate a man's ultimate worthiness more maturely. Miranda devoutly hoped so. Not only would Caruthers not squander Lori's inheritance, but he would also provide the social recognition that her insecure and often slighted daughter so dearly wished. As a baroness, she would be presented to Queen Victoria.

Let Abigail Warring choke on that! Miranda thought with a sudden surge of vitriol. Lori would have a dashingly handsome peer for husband while Abby would be saddled with Varley's ogre of a son. Although heir to an earldom, Jonathon Belford picked his nose. Miranda suppressed a chuckle of triumph and said, "I do believe I hear the baron arriving."

Lori could not resist peeking out the window at the street below, where the sound of hoofbeats clattered to a halt in front of the iron gate enclosing their small front yard. A groom took the reins of a magnificent bay gelding as the rider dismounted with casual ease. "He's taller than I remembered," she said breathlessly, straining to see his face, which was obscured by a wide-brimmed hat not at all in fashion.

Looking over Lori's shoulder, Miranda noted the same thing, but could not help thinking the plumed headgear suited him. "A veritable cavalier," she murmured dryly.

"You did say he was a soldier for the Confederates. I suppose that is part of their uniform," Lori remarked uncertainly.

"And the frock coat? Somehow I doubt it, considering it's cut in the latest fashion. Fresh from Bond Street or I miss my guess." Miranda knew he'd won a sizable purse at Epsom two weeks ago and surmised he'd invested in some new clothing, but she did not feel it prudent to share that bit of information with her daughter. "Come, let me introduce you to the baron."

Brand stood at the foot of the stairs, ignoring the servant who was holding open a wide oak door into the parlor in favor of observing the two ladies descending the steps. She was as lovely as a siren, he had to admit, but he could sense no air of sophistication to go with her striking beauty. Perhaps that was a mark in her favor. Lord knew, Reba had been aware of her power over men from the time she'd learned to walk.

Lorilee Auburn's hair was pale gold, her complexion like milk and rose petals. She was slightly shorter than her mother, who was tall for a woman. Her slender figure was accented fetchingly in a day gown of light blue muslin sprigged with darker blue flowers. Most appropriate for a young miss in her first season.

Every feature from her huge cornflower-blue eyes to her little red bow of a mouth was quite perfect . . . and perfectly untried. There was nothing . . . formed about her yet. A woman to mold any way he chose, if that was his pleasure. A vague sense of uneasiness mingled with his anticipation. He'd grown up around complaisant women who employed only soft wiles to influence their men, deferring to them in all matters of importance. But that was the South . . . half a world away from here.

This was England, where a woman sat upon the throne. Brand didn't much care for the idea. Were all Englishwomen as strong-willed and self-assured as Her Majesty . . . and Miranda Auburn? His eyes moved from Lorilee to her mother. There was nothing untried whatever in those cool silver depths. Those eyes belonged to a woman who had seen much of life and was fooled by little of it. And to think he'd once dreaded Alvira Cunningham. Comparing Reba's coy, manipulative mother to this woman was like comparing a tabby cat to a tigress.

He nodded and smiled at the widow, then returned his attention to her pride and joy, her only child. Lorilee held her skirts like a princess entering a throne room. She bestowed a hesitant smile on him, and again he was struck by how young and insecure she looked.

Brand felt like a money-grubbing carpetbagger taking advantage of a girl little more than half his age. He knew damn well he was a supplicant before Miss Lorilee's cool and elegant mother. And he did not like it. But nevertheless, he gave them a blindingly white smile and bowed, flourishing his hat as grandly as Colonel John Hunt Morgan himself.

When the women reached the bottom of the stairs, Miranda immediately took charge, greeting Brand and making introductions. "Lorilee, may I present Brandon Caruthers, Lord Rushcroft."

When Brand took her hand, he could feel a faint tremor. After pressing a brief and most properly executed kiss on its back, he raised his head and noted the way her eyes fastened on his scar, then instantly skittered away. Many women found it romantic, but he was certain this one did not, judging from the slight flush of embarrassment staining her cheeks. In the dim light of Moreland's cloak room, she must not have noted it.

"Your servant, Miss Auburn," he said with a smile which seemed to warm her the tiniest bit. Turning to her mother, he paused, asking, "Am I allowed to observe the amenities in your home, or would you prefer a handshake?"

Arching one eyebrow sardonically, Miranda presented her gloved fingers for him to salute. "That is reserved for the world of business, not social calls, Major," she said wryly. He bowed smartly over her hand. No tremor there, but he'd expected none any more than he did a missish blush.

The widow turned and glided toward the door held open by a deferential servant who seemed to blend into the oak panels. The room they entered was enormous for a city house and filled with expensive but, to his taste, garish Rococo Revival furniture. If possible, the intricately carved oak pieces covered in dark blue brocade were even uglier than the more massive Gothic decor in the widow's banking offices.

It said little for her taste if she'd made the selections. But, overall, he found the taste of the British as boorish as that of the noveau-riche Yankees who'd flooded into the South after the war, buying up gracious homes and refurnishing them like emporiums overflowing with costly bric-a-brac.

Miranda noticed the way his gaze swept the room. She could sense that he did not like the ostentatious display of wealth. Neither did she. But Will had been so proud of his home that she had done little to change it after his death. "Please, be seated, my lord," she said, gesturing toward a large chair facing the settee.

Brand waited for both ladies to sit down before he complied. They took the settee, perching with starchy spines not touching the back cushion, a study in contrasts. Lorilee dressed in youthful pastel, her mother in a dull green day gown which was no more flattering than the gray suit she'd worn at the bank. *Lordy, I've seen better-dressed squirrel hunters.* He supposed she had no time for fashion with an empire to run.

"Lori, will you pour?" she asked her daughter as a maid deposited an immense tray laden with a silver teapot, Sevres china and the rich, heavy foods so favored for late afternoon repasts in England.

Obediently the young woman leaned forward and picked up the elegant teapot, filling the first of three cups. Her hands trembled ever so slightly, but she performed with perfect decorum as she'd doubtless been drilled to do by a succession of governesses.

"Cream or lemon, my lord?" she inquired.

All so very proper. "Just a touch of sugar, thank you, Miss Auburn," he replied, wishing fervently for a good strong cup of black coffee. He hated tea. Smiling at her, he searched his memory for what other skills and interests young women of her class might possess. "Do you by any chance paint, Miss Auburn?"

"Yes, watercolors, but not very well."

"Nonsense. Your work is lovely," Miranda pronounced, encouraging Lori with a smile. "She took a red ribbon at the West End art fair only last month."

"What subjects do you favor?" he asked dutifully. *This is going to be a long afternoon.* He eyed the leaden scones and pallid watercress sandwiches and could already feel their sticky mass congealing in his stomach. Often, while riding through the night on raids with Colonel Morgan, he'd have given a silver dollar for any morsel of food. The irony of his situation now did not escape him.

In response to his polite inquiry, Lorilee set her teacup aside and replied, "I've always preferred to paint animals.

My most recent was of Calico's new litter."

"Calico?" he echoed.

"Yes, our mother cat. She has six of the most playful kittens you could ever imagine. I dote upon them."

Her eyes sparkled with more animation than he'd seen yet. Unfortunately, it was over cats. "Have you ever painted horses?"

"Why, yes, I have." Lori warmed to her topic, a safe subject with which she was familiar. "I've done several of our carriage horses—one pulling my new Victoria and my favorite of all, Taffy, my mare."

"You ride?" Brand took heart.

"Oh, yes. My friends and I take a turn in Hyde Park most days, weather permitting, of course."

"Tell me about your mare," Brand encouraged.

Lori was only too happy to oblige, going on about the pretty little buttermilk-colored filly and how much she loved feeding her sugar lumps and apples. Miranda sat back, quietly observing the interchange with satisfaction. The baron seemed to know how to draw out a shy young woman like Lori. She recalled from the dossier on him that he had a younger sister around Lori's age, but nothing was noted regarding the young woman's current status. Miranda assumed Barbara had been wed before the misfortunes of war befell the Caruthers family.

Just as she was congratulating herself on how swimmingly well their first meeting was progressing, a movement at the corner of her eye distracted her. The heavy oak door of the parlor was opening a small bit. A minuscule squeak accompanied it, and Miranda made a mental note to have the downstairs maid oil the blasted thing.

Then all hell broke loose.

Six balls of orange, black and white fur flew into the room and launched themselves at various pieces of the furnishings. One raced for the pulled-back velvet draperies while its companion swatted at the sheer curtains across the window, then both began scrambling up them in a race to reach the cornice at the top.

A third batted at the tassel of the bell pull, while two others sank their little claws into delicate brocade uphol- stery to reach their goal—the tea service on the table in front of the settee. After a quick dive, one stood drenched in cream from the overturned silver pitcher, while the other attacked the edge of a scone with sharp little teeth.

The last one deliberately climbed the ottoman beside Brand's chair and used it as a springboard into his lap. While he remained frozen in amazement, the multicolored bit of fluff sank its tiny needlelike claws into places never even whispered about in polite society. He could hardly get out a decent yelp of protest before it was climbing his chest.

Two pairs of gold eyes stared raptly at one another— the kitten's round with curiosity, Brand's round with sheer horror. Within a heartbeat, the second kitten bounded from the tea service up his chest.

Miranda scooped up the kitten on the bell pull with one hand, saying, "You've saved me from summoning the tweenie who was so negligent as to let you escape from the kitchen."

She'd no more than uttered the words when said servant dashed contritely into the room, undecided whether it was more prudent to curtsy to the mistress first or to begin rounding up the escapees. "I'm that sorry, mum," the tan- haired girl said in a thick Irish brogue, abbreviating the curtsy in favor of making an unsuccessful grab for a kitten who swept by her feet heading for the fire screen in front of the mantel.

She and Lorilee were scrambling about the parlor, try- ing to corral the rest of the kittens, when a loud yowl sounded. An enormous dark yellow tiger-striped cat with well-chewed ears stalked into the room.

"Oh, Major, my deepest apologies," Miranda said.

"Oh, my," was all Lori could muster, for Marmalade commenced to chase the kittens about the room, overturning vases of flowers and small gilt-framed pictures from tables. One ornate pedestal table toppled when his solid twenty-two-pound bulk gave it a none-too-gentle nudge as he swatted the rump of a fleeing kitten. Then, like one of the fabled "town tamers" from American dime novels, he turned his attention to the large chair occupied by their honored guest and two small, uninvited ones.

That was when the women realized that the baron had not moved a muscle since the chaos descended. Brandon Caruthers sat stock-still, his neck seemingly elongated and posed at a most peculiar angle, stretching away from the two small orange, black and white felines sniffing at his face.

Major Brandon Caruthers, fearless raider and much decorated veteran of the Confederate States of America, scourge of General Kilpatrick's Union Cavalry, was terrified of cats.

Chapter Five

Not that he had ever admitted it. Unfortunately, Brand knew his day of reckoning had finally arrived when he stared at the grizzled old tom who was eyeing the two kittens perched at his throat as if they would make a tasty luncheon—or *he* would. The kittens were bad enough, but the dark green eyes of the ancient feline studying him with unblinking interest were enough to make Brand wish he were back in the thick of battle. Surrounded by Yankee cavalry. With their new Spencer repeating rifles.

Breaking the spell, Miranda calmly scooped up the tom. "Back to the kitchen with you, you impenitent rascal," she said. As if comprehending Brand's utter humiliation and wishing to compound it, the tom gave her face a big lick and nuzzled her chin, eliciting a rich, throaty laugh. She handed the huge squirming beast to the serving girl, saying, "You've created enough havoc for one afternoon."

Then she turned her attention back to the baron. A wisp of a smile played about her mouth as she pried loose a tiny set of claws from his shirt front. Lori approached his

person with considerably more trepidation and pulled the
second kitten away, cradling it in her hands as if *he* intended *it* harm!

By this time the butler and two other servants, kitchen
help by the looks of them, were all engaged in the feline
roundup, which took only moments but seemed like hours
to him. Then while Brand struggled to regain his composure, the servants quickly set the room to rights and
cleaned up the overturned tea tray. The Irish maid promised to bring a fresh service out immediately as she
backed from the room.

Brand swallowed and tried to take a deep breath without seeming to do so. His smile was a rictus that would
have looked at home on a battlefield corpse, but it was
the best he could manage. His mind went utterly blank.
He blinked, trying valiantly to summon his wits as mother
and daughter gazed at him.

"Oh, I do so apologize, my lord," Lori said, fingertips
pressed to that tiny bow of a mouth. Her cheeks were
pink with embarrassment . . . and her eyes alight with a
blend of unease and curiosity.

Miranda waited a beat for him to reply. When nothing
was immediately forthcoming, she said smoothly, "Marmalade is quite a devil. I fear he's learned to turn the
knob on the kitchen door when the cook isn't paying attention and slip down the hall to my sitting room." She
gestured across the way to a cozy little room with a large
bay window piled high with throw pillows.

He must suffer from a phobia of cats. Miranda was
amazed. After reading of the man's battlefield exploits,
she'd been convinced he was absolutely fearless. Perhaps
it was good to find that even the most invincible warrior
possessed one chink in his armor. The proud aristocrat
was human. Then again, Lori seemed taken aback by his
bizarre behavior, and that was not good.

"Marmalade would be that great yellow brute?" Brand finally managed, proud that he did not shudder visibly.

"He favors sleeping in the window of Mother's room on sunny days," Lori explained nervously. "Then once the door is open, Callie's kittens come tumbling out in search of adventure."

"They certainly appear to have had one," he replied with a more natural smile.

Miranda noted that the color that had leached from his darkly tanned face was once again returning.

"Now that they're getting larger and can move quickly, Marm loves to chase and play with them. But when they were newborns, we had to watch him closely. He tried to eat them. Can you imagine—his own young!" Lori blurted out.

"If you ever met my cousin Horace's hellions, the idea of eating one's young might hold more appeal," Brand remarked dryly.

Lori gasped, shocked that she had made such a gaffe, speaking of a tom eating his kittens, but even more appalled by the baron's reply. She flushed pinkly, not at all certain how to respond, but her mother surprised them both, emitting a hearty chuckle.

"My late husband's cousin had just such a brood. You do recall Wilfred's children, Lori? Dear Cousins Lucy, Lemuel and Lymon?" Amusement danced in Miranda's eyes.

Lori nodded, still uncertain. "Yes. They were . . . rather accident-prone as I remember it. Especially the boys."

"You are most charitable, my dear," Miranda replied archly. "Lymon once dumped an entire bowl of raspberry compote on your white Easter dress."

"It was an accident . . . I think," Lori said thoughtfully. She had never realized her mother knew the nasty boy had done it on purpose.

"You only said that to keep Wilfred from taking a strap to the lad." Miranda turned to the major and added with a hint of warning in her voice, "Lorilee has a very soft heart, sometimes too much so for her own good."

"A weakness you most obviously do not share." The light of a dare danced in his eyes now.

Miranda's smile was cool. The arrogant American was offended by her business acumen. The devil with it, so were most men. "No, I have not had that luxury," she replied, thinking with satisfaction of the many business associates who had already learned precisely how hard a bargain she could drive.

Just then the maid bustled in, bearing the heavy tray, and placed it on the table. Lori once again leaned forward to begin pouring tea. The silence thickened for a moment before Brand broke it. "Perhaps," he began carefully, "I should explain my . . . er, rather bizarre reaction to old Marmalade and his band of tiny raiders."

"Oh, no! That is, I'm quite certain it was nothing. Why we hardly . . ." Lori's voice faded, and the teapot hit the silver tray with a clank.

Miranda rescued her, interjecting, "You have a phobia of cats. There is nothing rare in that. I've read that people fear all sorts of things—heights, closed-in spaces, spiders—"

"Ugh," Lori said, shivering. "I'm terrified of spiders."

"Ah, but you're a young lady and that is quite acceptable. A bit less so for a man of my years to freeze at the sight of small house pets."

"You need not speak of it, my lord," Miranda replied.

"I believe I must, ma'am," he said with a decisive nod toward her. "When I was a tadpole, er, between three and four years of age, I was placed in the bathtub by my elder cousin Tim, who was supposed to see to it that I ended up with less creek mud on me than when I'd been brought into the bathhouse. Then my aunt Crystal was called away and her elder son Sam slipped into the room. He and Tim thought it might be fun to drop a sack of half-grown cats in the water to see if they could swim."

"Oh, my," Miranda said, beginning to imagine what happened next.

"Yes," Brand said grimly. "Sam and Tim had a devil of a time getting the burlap sack opened, with all the clawing and yowling inside, but after a couple of tries slapping it against the side of the big old tub, the cats came tumbling out. Never did figure out just how many there were. When they landed in the water, all teeth and claws—and used me as a ladder to climb out—I commenced to doing some yowling myself and lost count. Even at that tender age, I knew how to add," he said dryly, for the first time seeing a bit of humor in what had been a debilitating problem for all these years.

"You must have been clawed to bits," Lori exclaimed.

"My cousins didn't intend to hurt me, but it took a month of Sundays before I had more skin than scabs. Ever after I've kept my distance from felines, who were mercifully kept busy handling mouse problems in the stables."

"Did you never have any pets?" Lori asked.

"My daughter could not imagine life without her menagerie," Miranda said with a smile.

"Besides my horses, I had a pair of bluetick hunting hounds named Betsy and Bitsy. Best coon dogs in Kentucky."

"Coon dogs?" Lori echoed.

"I believe it's an American way of saying 'raccoon,' dearheart."

"You mean you hunted raccoons? Whatever for?"

Brand shrugged, knowing he had just dug himself a deeper hole. "I'm afraid folks eat raccoons in Kentucky, Miss Auburn. In fact, we never hunt an animal unless we intend it for our table." His dislike of fox hunting had prompted the latter comment, but now he could see the girl was taken aback by what he'd said.

Miranda knew he fully intended to sell thoroughbred hunters to the squires and peers who were avid fox hunters, but she decided pointing that out would be less than politic. Heavens knew the afternoon had not gone exactly swimmingly thus far. Instead, she suddenly found a way to change the subject. Her expression shifted from tart irritation to mocking solicitude as she said, "It would appear you'll have cream with your tea whether you prefer it or not."

Brand followed her eyes, looking at the right lapel of his immaculate new frock coat. The black wool bore a clear set of cream-drenched paw prints. He bit back an oath, knowing he could not afford to replace the obscenely expensive garment. He also knew that Miranda Auburn was aware of the fact, and it galled him.

Lori saved the day, interjecting, "I've observed our housekeeper Mrs. Osbourne using a sponge soaked in vinegar to remove oily stains from wool."

Miranda nodded briskly, rising to give the bell rope a tug. "Quite true. She saved one of my favorite jackets from just such a fate. Of course, Major, I apologize for your being forced to depart reeking of vinegar."

"Being a horse breeder, ma'am, I'm used to far worse odors, believe me. And as to the remedy for this small matter"—he brushed the lapel with his hand dismissively—"my valet can attend to it. Please don't trouble Mrs. Osbourne." His smile was broad and charming as he asked Lorilee, "Do you, perchance, enjoy horse racing?"

"I have only attended one. Ascot on Gold Cup Day is quite wonderful."

"All the ladies turned out in their finery was what interested you," Miranda said, teasing Lori. "Their hats were so large they obscured the racetrack."

Brand gave Lori a gentle smile. She was young and without artifice, utterly unlike her clever, hard-headed mother. He liked the girl. Not a bad beginning in spite of the fiasco with the kittens and that thrice-damned tom. "A new acquaintance, Lord Mountjoy, has invited me to join him in his box this Gold Cup Day. I may bring any guests I wish. Would you ladies do me the honor?"

Lori looked toward her mother first. Miranda nodded, then replied, "We would be pleased to accept your invitation, Major."

"Good. I only hope we can see the racecourse for the hats."

By the time he arrived back at the Caruthers city house on St. James Square, Brand's spirits had revived quite a bit. The first meeting had not been a total disaster. Lorilee Auburn would be putty in his hands if not for the presence of her overprotective mother. The widow utterly doted upon the child. It was a miracle that the girl was not spoiled rotten as he had feared. She was really quite sweet.

After all, she loved horses and dogs—yes, and cats. Oddly, after he spoke of his—what was the starchy widow's word for it—"phobia" regarding felines, he had unaccountably felt better. He'd never explained why he avoided them to a living soul before. Of course, he'd never been forced to, since back in Kentucky cats earned their keep mousing in the outbuildings, not destroying furnishings indoors. As he walked into the parlor, he vowed that his future baroness would have to keep her pets more carefully confined.

"And, under no circumstances will 'Marm' be allowed to accompany his mistress to Rushcroft Hall," he murmured to himself as he poured a cup of strong black coffee and laced it generously with brandy from the sideboard.

"I'm afraid I have some distressing news, my friend," Sin said as he entered the room without knocking.

One look at his grave expression made Brand clutch the decanter tightly as he raised it in silent inquiry. Sin nodded, and Brand poured the golden liquid straight into a cup and handed it to him. "The horses? Reiver?"

"He's unharmed, but it was a near thing." St. John gulped the brandy, then continued, "Someone left an open jug of kerosene in the straw and it was kicked over. Sullivan caught the smell of it just before he tossed his match on the ground."

"I've warned him about smoking in the mews," Brand said with an oath. "Bad enough to have him tossing hot matches near dry straw without having it soaked with flammables. Why in the hell did someone leave the kerosene uncorked?"

"That is the disturbing part," St. John replied. "It was not our kerosene jug. The stableman is quite careful to fill the lanterns out on the cobblestones, not inside with the straw. He'd not left it. And when Sullivan arrived at the stable this afternoon, he said he heard footfalls out the door leading to the house . . . very swift footfalls."

"Someone was running, interrupted before he could fire the straw?" Brand supplied as the cold certainty settled deep in his gut. "Were any of the horses injured?"

"They are all basically unharmed. I checked them myself when Sullivan sent Mathias to fetch me. They were restive. The stench of that much kerosene, combined with the presence of a stranger, was more than enough to send Reiver into fits. He bruised his right front fetlock kicking at the stall bars, but Mathias is poulticing it now. I believe there'll be no permanent damage."

"Thank heavens for that." Brand began pacing, combing his fingers through his hair as he polished off the coffee and took a straight refill of brandy. "Why would anyone try to burn down the mews? To destroy my horses?"

"To insure the success of their own? Or perhaps to hedge a bet already placed on another animal?" Sin replied.

"It might do to see who's bet heavily on our competitors," Brand said thoughtfully.

The Rebel Baron's big black had already acquired quite a reputation around the London tracks. Sin and Mathias investigated who stood to gain if Reiver did not run, checking the betting rumors. Several days passed as they ferreted out information. Meanwhile, the horses remained under twenty-four-hour guard.

Brand was timing Kentucky Sunrise, one of Reiver's best two-year-olds, at the Sandown track early on the fourth morning after they discovered the attempted arson. When Sin handed him the list they had compiled, Brand curled his lip in disgust as he read the name, Hon. Geoffrey Winters, scrawled near the top.

"Quite a large bet. I imagine he'll make short work of his new bride's dowry," Brand said in disgust.

"Cost me a few quid, but worth it to obtain the information." The older man had bags beneath his bloodshot eyes owing less to age than to the late hours and smoky alehouses surrounding the betting parlors of London. "The young Winters is quite a high flyer about the tracks. Mostly he loses. Frightful horse sense." Sin shook his head as if that were the most unforgivable transgression of all.

"For the time being he has money enough to throw away." Brand looked at the rest of the notes, written in

74

St. John's precise hand. "King Arthur! He wagered a thousand pounds on that wretched beast!"

"I said he had no horse sense, did I not? The beast belongs to the Earl of Falconridge, his father-in-law. Perhaps he was only being politic with his new relations."

Brand snorted. "I doubt, considering the circumstances of his marriage, that placing a bet—no matter how dear—on Falconridge's 'beast' will in any way endear him to the clan." He thought of sweet Lorilee and the rumors he'd overheard regarding young Winters's pursuit of her. Miranda had proven a far better watchdog than the earl and his countess. He was grateful, not only because it afforded him the opportunity to court the girl himself, but also because she'd been saved from a wastrel such as Winters.

She was too innocent and sweet to be victimized by a fortune hunter. *But what are you?* an inner voice accused him. Was he any better than Winters? Miranda Auburn had made the mercenary nature of his courtship abundantly clear when she proposed it to him. But he would be kind and faithful to the girl, and break his back making a success of his stud farm. His uneasy reverie was interrupted by Sin's low whistle of incredulity.

"Never in my worst nightmare did I imagine to see that baggage again," St. John muttered.

Eyes fixed firmly on her quarry, Mrs. Earl Wilcox picked her way across the muddy grass at the edge of the track. Although it had rained during the night and the ground was a veritable quagmire, the mud did not deter Reba, who held her skirts up, revealing a shocking amount of trim ankle and dainty foot encased in elegant kid slippers with impossibly high heels. Revealed, no doubt, for the baron's appreciation. She was resplendent in a day gown of deep violet silk trimmed with bits of black lace. Her golden ringlets glistened from beneath an elaborate straw hat of matching violet, trimmed with all manner of fantastical flora and fauna.

Brand watched, dumbstruck at seeing her here. *She doesn't fit*, a small part of his mind judged as he stood waiting. She waved at him, smiling like a cat whose outstretched claws have just sunk into the wing of a sparrow poised for flight. But he'd escaped her in Kentucky and flown all the way across an ocean. There was no chance he'd fall prey to her now.

"You're a long way from Lexington, Mrs. Wilcox," he said in a level voice when she stopped in front of him.

Completely ignoring St. John as if he were part of the fence railing, she smiled up at Brand and said, "That is scarcely the greeting I was expecting after making such a long and arduous journey." Her lower lip, always plump and kissable, jutted out in a mock pout.

Without his saying a word, St. John's expression spoke volumes to Caruthers. Then he turned and walked to the track, where Mathias was sliding from Kentucky Sunrise's back. Brand watched them lead the animal into the stables for a rubdown, ignoring Reba as she had ignored his friend. He could see her foot tapping petulantly on the ground for a couple of beats before she quelled her impatience.

"You always did care more for your silly ole horses than for me." The voice was forlorn and little-girl sad.

And it no longer affected him. He wondered how it ever had. "Sunrise almost broke the record Reiver set last week." He placed the watch back in his pocket and looked at her. "Where's your Earl, Mrs. Wilcox? He know you're out here traipsing around after a mere baron?"

Reba let out a long, slow sigh. Her voice was flat when she replied, "Earl's dead."

"Impossible, darlin'. Only the good die young. Earl should live to be a good ninety." He eyed the violet gown and matching hat ensemble. "I can see how deeply you grieve for him."

"Purple is the second stage in mourning." She brushed a black lace ruffle at her wrist. "I'm observing the conventions, Brand, darlin'."

"The 'conventions,' as I recall my mama instructing me, require black for the first year," he said with a hint of bitter mockery. "Last time I saw old Earl he was hale and hearty, and that was only six months ago."

"Poor Earl was, as you pointed out, always fat. He developed an infection from his gout and died of blood poisoning while on a business trip to Philadelphia."

"How convenient for you. You're a rich widow now, I imagine . . . or did his daddy see that you were cut out of the will?" He really didn't give a damn.

Reba stiffened and stifled a sob. "I never did love him, Brand. He knew that when he married me, but he wanted me anyway."

"Just to get back at me for beating him at childhood games?" His tone was scoffing. Once her tears would have moved him, but that was a lifetime ago.

"Something like that, but I made certain old Cal Wilcox couldn't get his greedy hands on my share of Earl's estate. I am a rich widow, Brand . . ." She let her voice trail away suggestively. "All alone here in London."

"And now you want a genuine earl, not just a rich country boy. I hate to tell you this, Widow Wilcox, but I'm just a lowly baron who's barely got a shilling to his name."

"I have the money. And I'd be willing to settle for a lowly baron . . . providin' he's the right one."

"Well now, I reckon I'm just not the one," he said with a slow grin.

Angrily she whirled in a flurry of violet silk and perfume and walked swiftly toward the elegant new spider phaeton sitting at the side of the road. *She must have known I was going to refuse her overtures.*

What good would it do to try to resurrect a long-dead love? One that she herself had killed. Brand cared nothing for her but worried about the trouble she might cause between him and the Auburn family. He'd put little past her. Once Miss Reba Cunningham set her sights on anything or anyone she wanted, the devil could take whoever got in her way.

One of the servants working at the track waited by her vehicle to assist her up. Without taking time to arrange her skirts in the small open phaeton, she cracked the whip over the matched grays and drove off, wheels churning mud.

"You must've said something inappropriate, old chap," Sin remarked dryly as he strolled back from the stables.

"Woman always did drive like hell on wheels."

"Everyone who's anyone in London drives that way. She'll do smashingly well here," St. John replied.

"No matter her money, the sort of people she wants to impress won't give a damn. She'll always be an ignorant American overreacher."

"You scarcely sound regretful," Sin said with a chuckle, relieved that Reba's spell over his friend had been well and truly broken. "Just so long as she doesn't impress you."

"No, she doesn't impress me," Brand said softly, thinking of Earl Wilcox dying alone in some Philadelphia hotel room while Reba counted his money. The idea that he might be anything like her made his skin crawl with self-loathing.

Miranda sat staring at the telegram, then rubbed her eyes wearily and reread the message, which was exciting in content. Kent Aimesley, her factor in America, had just arrived in Liverpool after profitable discussions with the transcontinental railway directors. He would be in London within the week with the agreements drawn up for her review and signature. She should be elated but was not.

Mr. Aimesley had once been the love of her youth. The penniless son of a vicar, Kent had asked Miranda Stafford, the daughter of a prosperous merchant, to marry him. But that was a lifetime ago.

"I see Mr. Aimesley is in town," Lori said with a small frown marring her smooth brow.

"How did you . . . ?" Miranda smiled at the knowing look on her daughter's face. "All right, don't be so smug." She knew Lori had interpreted her expression when she opened the telegram. "Actually he's in Liverpool now."

"Are you going to see him, then?"

"How can I not? He has just arranged one of the largest ventures in which I've ever been engaged—and," she quickly emphasized before Lori could suggest she find a new factor, "he is quite irreplaceable. It would be neither prudent nor fair to discharge him because of the past."

"Would Father have offered him work if he had known about the two of you?"

A good question. Miranda had often wondered about it herself. "There was little to know. We were very young and naïve. We would not have suited."

Lori could tell by the tone of her mother's voice that the topic was closed. "So you wed Father instead."

Miranda did not reply. Instead she removed a sheet of stationery from her desk drawer and began writing instructions for her secretary to wire Mr. Aimesley.

Another message arrived that afternoon, this time from the baron. He had just uncovered an invitation to a musicale at Lady Tottingham's the following afternoon, which he'd accepted weeks ago, then most regretfully forgotten—until rummaging through a stack of correspondence. Would Miss Auburn and her mother join him to hear a string quartet play Mozart?

Augusta Tottingham was a fabulously wealthy dowager baroness and one of the social arbiters of the day, dividing her time between London and Bath. The old lady still took the waters. Given her great age, she was doubtless a veritable walking or at least creeping advertisement for them, Miranda thought wryly as she penned an acceptance. Lori would be delighted to mingle with so many of the "best people." And she adored Mozart.

Brand's carriage arrived promptly for them at one. Giving her reflection in the mirror one last inspection, Lori asked Tilda nervously, "Do I look well in this shade of blue?"

The maid sighed at her charge, decked out in the palest aquamarine mull with matching slippers and a parasol for the open carriage which the baron said he was bringing. "You've changed gowns four times already and His Lordship is waiting downstairs. Even if you looked faded as a ghost—which you most certainly do not—there would be no time for another change. You're lovely. Go and enjoy," she admonished, throwing up her hands.

Miranda stood smiling at the doorway. "As usual, Tilda is quite right. You're a confection. Come, we mustn't keep the baron waiting."

"Or Lady T," Lori said in awe. "Abbie was positively green when I told her where we were going."

Brand was standing near the door as the women entered the small sitting room, the one favored by Marmalade. He was keeping an escape route handy in case the great orange brute shoved open the kitchen door again. Mercifully, he'd seen neither hide nor hair of a feline.

"Ladies, you are both visions," he said with a bow.

"And my rescuers from Lady Tottingham, who I've heard eats barons for breakfast."

Lori giggled as Miranda replied, "If you had not put in an appearance, Lady T just might do precisely that. She is quite formidable, Major."

"Then I shall endeavor to be on my best behavior," Brand replied as he escorted them to the waiting carriage.

They passed the ride discussing the weather, the upcoming races at Ascot and other innocuous topics, both Brand and Miranda attempting to draw Lori into the conversation. However, since she was too nervous about her first meeting with the legendary dowager to say much, the conversation turned to politics and the current battle in Parliament to enlarge the suffrage.

"You of all people should support Mr. Gladstone. After all, he supported recognition of the Confederacy during the late war."

"And you, a Liberal admirer of that gentleman, are staunchly abolitionist. How do you reconcile those conflicting points of view?"

"I was merely offering a reason for you to appreciate him, even if he was wrong on that one issue. Politics is an art of compromise, after all. Mr. Gladstone's position on voting reform is more moderate than that of the Conservatives. We Liberals do not wish to see unpropertied men voting on a par with those who have made this nation the richest on earth. It would lead to civil disorder."

"And the spread of trade unionism?" he countered with a cynical smile.

She stiffened. "Yes, and look what chaos that has wrought wherever it is instituted. I pay my employees fair wages, but I can scarcely have them dictating to me how I run my foundry, shipyard or bank."

"Heaven forbid. I do agree, however, that the Conservatives only want to broaden the franchise so they can recapture control of Commons. They haven't held power since '46. What better way to do it than by stealing Gladstone's thunder?"

"My, you are quite astute regarding English politics," Lori finally interjected. "I have no idea who holds power today, much less that many years ago."

"In time you'll come to understand these matters," Miranda replied. "You need to read *The Times*. That's why I bring it home each evening from my office."

Lori made a face, but Brand grinned and said, "Your mother would see women with the vote . . . possibly even unpropertied women. I'd wager on it." He raised an eyebrow in mock dismay, smiling encouragingly at Lori.

"You would win," she replied softly, glancing at Miranda.

He chuckled. "I knew it. Well, Miss Auburn, I will agree with your mother. If you're to vote, you must learn for whom to vote."

"Oh, I do not wish to vote . . . ever. But Mother does."

"And perhaps even stand for a seat in Commons?" he could not resist adding.

Miranda became agitated. How could a man charm and infuriate at the same time? "Men *and* women of property should have the franchise, not those of the lower classes," Miranda stated firmly. "We have not yet been able to sufficiently educate them to vote responsibly. That will occur over time."

"So will the Second Coming, but I don't hear any echo of trumpets yet," Brand replied as their driver pulled up in the queue of carriages disgorging passengers at the estimable Lady T's front steps.

"How cynical you are, my lord," Miranda said as he assisted them from the carriage.

"I've led that sort of life, I fear," he murmured, then

added in a lower voice for her ears only, "as I'm sure your reports made clear."

Once again Miranda felt herself vexed by his charm.

The musicale was a crush with over a hundred people taking the seats assigned them by the beady-eyed Lady T, who held her lorgnette over her nose as if ready to swat flies with it . . . or anyone who displeased her.

Just as they were passing into the room where the quartet was tuning up, a honey-dripping voice broke into their conversation. "Why, I do declare, if it isn't my old and dear friend from Lexington. How are you, Brandon?"

The woman was decked out in a silvery shade of gray silk trimmed with black lace. The glimmering color was flattering, although she wore pearls at her throat and ears, a gauche display for an afternoon entertainment. She advanced toward them with a distinguished older man in tow. Miranda recognized him as the head of a rival banking firm in the City. The blonde had eyes only for the baron, and judging by her drawling speech and familiar manner, she was his countrywoman and well acquainted with him.

Brand cursed inwardly as he forced a smile. There was nothing for it but to make introductions. "Ladies," he said, turning to the Auburns, "may I present Mrs. Wilcox, late of Kentucky." Damned if he'd call her a "friend," dear or otherwise!

"Charmed, I'm sure," Reba said after he introduced the redhead and her vapid little daughter. "Oh, this is Mr. Harold Grimsley. He's in banking, just as my late husband was."

Miranda nodded as he bowed. "Mr. Grimsley and I are acquainted. You remember my daughter, Lorilee?" she replied breezily, turning the tables on the lascivious younger woman by ignoring her.

Lori made her curtsy to her mother's friend, all the

while noting the subtle currents between the beautiful widow and the baron. Inexperienced as she was in society, she intuited that they had more in common than being from the same town in America.

Moving closer while her escort and Mrs. Auburn chatted about some boring old banking matters, Reba tapped Brand on the arm playfully, saying, "You always detested Mozart, Brand. Why on earth are you here?"

"I'm enjoying the company of two lovely ladies," he replied, casting a smile at Lorilee. "The better question is why you're in England at all." His tone indicated he didn't care a whit if Reba had swum across the Atlantic.

"London is far more exciting than Lexington." She raised her other hand to the heavy triple strand of pearls at her bosom and fingered them delicately.

"I thought grieving widows were supposed to shun excitement," he replied, removing her hand from his arm. "After all, Earl's barely cold in his grave."

"You know I never gave a fiddle what folks think," Reba said with a smirk at Lorilee, who had emitted a tiny gasp of shock at Brand's last words.

"Your dress and presence here make that attitude abundantly clear," Miranda said cuttingly, making it obvious she found the behavior of Mrs. Wilcox utterly unacceptable. She had worn unrelieved black for Will Auburn for two years.

Just as Reba opened her mouth to make an angry retort, Brand interjected, "I believe the musicians are ready to begin. We must take our seats. A pleasure, Mr. Grimsley," he said, nodding to the banker, but completely ignoring Reba as he turned and took Lori's hand.

In spite of the noise of the crowd, he was certain he could hear Reba Cunningham stamp her foot.

Chapter Six

Brand hated opera. But Miranda and Lorilee adored it. What was a dutiful suitor to do but escort the ladies to see *The Marriage of Figaro?* The production was considerably more amusing than he had feared. At the conclusion of the performance, he joined them in hearty applause.

As a servant held the velvet curtain at the door of their box for them, Miranda murmured to him, "Was it less painful than you'd anticipated?"

Could the woman read minds? He smiled, offering an arm to her and her daughter as they descended the wide, curving staircase from the box seats. "It was more enjoyable than a tooth extraction, although I'd far prefer a good Shakespearean play to either one. I understand Mr. Osgood's troop will do *Romeo and Juliet.* May I invite you to attend Tuesday next?" He looked first to Lorilee, than to Miranda. She nodded.

"I believe that would be agreeable, don't you, my dear?"

"It sounds exciting. I've seen *A Midsummer Night's Dream*, but never a tragedy," Lori replied.

"Well, the tragedies are a bit more, er, vigorous than the comedies," Brand ventured, thankful that Osgood wasn't doing *Titus Andronicus* this season.

"Just so you are not disappointed in the ending, perhaps it would be best for you to read the play first," Miranda suggested dryly, exchanging a fleeting look of amused understanding with the baron.

Again he was possessed of the uneasy notion that she knew what he was thinking. Ridiculous. He must surely be imagining things. "Are you familiar with the play, ma'am?"

"I read the complete works of Mr. Shakespeare when I was young. I found the histories to be particularly instructive."

Brand could not help wondering about her background. Her manners and education indicated one born to wealth, but why would such a pampered woman decide to run her own businesses? Before he could puzzle more over it, her daughter spoke.

"I have always found history quite boring, I fear," Lori confessed. "But I do enjoy reading poetry."

"Lord Byron?" he asked hopefully.

"Mr. Shelley is more to my taste," she murmured.

"Of course. Far more suitable for a young lady's sensibilities," he agreed.

"Byron was a scoundrel," Miranda interjected firmly. "My daughter's tutors set her to reading fine literature appropriate for a young lady."

Unlike you, who read what you pleased, Brand thought.

Had that sort of unstructured upbringing enabled her to become such a formidable woman? Brand squelched his curiosity about a young Miranda secreting forbidden books from her father's library. *Concentrate on the daughter. Forget the mother,* he reminded himself. Still, he could not help wishing that Miss Auburn's education had been broader. But that was unreasonable. After all, she was fresh out of the schoolroom and, from what he knew of governesses and tutors for the wealthy classes, education was as deficient for women in England as in America. Perhaps more so.

"It's not fair to confuse Byron's personal life with his literary work, which should stand on its own merits." He could not resist continuing the argument. By this time they stood outside the theater beneath the flickering gaslights, waiting as carriages queued up to pick up the elegantly dressed crowd of opera lovers. Those of lesser means who hired hansom cabs departed from doors on the next street.

"*Childe Harold* is a frivolous piece compared to *The Rime of the Ancient Mariner,*" Miranda replied. "Mr. Coleridge teaches an excellent moral lesson as he entertains."

"Ah, but Mr. Coleridge was an opium eater," he countered.

Lorilee placed her fingers over her mouth, uncertain whether to gasp at the baron's audacity or giggle because he had gotten the best of her mother. In all her observations of her mother's verbal exchanges, this was a first.

Before Miranda could make a reply, the footman who worked for the jobmaster from whom Brand had engaged his carriage came dashing down the street toward them, his natty livery wrinkled and askew, crying out to the baron, "I'm that sorry, Yer Lordship, but they're after old 'arry, they are. Won't let 'im go, but 'e's usin' 'is whip on 'em right proper, 'e is!"

"Calm down, man. What are you saying?" Brand demanded as the out-of-breath footman stood panting before him and the women. The last of the theater patrons gave them curious looks as they climbed into their carriages.

Then, before the frightened man could elaborate further, the carriage came careening around the corner from the alley where it had been parked. Harry was indeed engaged in a battle with three toughs who were attempting to climb aboard the driver's box, apparently intent on stealing the expensive vehicle. Harry lashed out from side to side with his whip to good effect, eliciting curses and snarls of pain. Then one of the fellows, a large hulk of a man with matted filthy hair obscuring half his face, swung one brawny leg over a horse and yanked on the harness with brute strength.

The footman took off at a dead run, heading around the corner and vanishing from sight before Brand could tell him to summon help. Perhaps he would, but the look of stark panic on his face gave Caruthers little hope.

"Get back inside the theater," Brand instructed the women, seeing no one around now to come to their aid. The street had suddenly become as deserted as a graveyard at midnight. He reached for the fastening of his opera cloak and let the expensive garment fly in a maroon satin whirl, cursing the loss of yet another article of clothing he could ill afford to replace.

Miranda seized hold of Lori and turned toward the heavy brass handlebar on the theater door, only to find it locked tightly. She began to pound on it with one hand while protecting her terrified daughter by sheltering her with her arm wrapped around her.

The carriage stopped about a dozen yards down the street as the team of horses neighed furiously, rearing up on their hind legs in terror. Two of the brigands yanked cruelly at the horses' mouthpieces. The third man was engaged in a battle to the finish with Harry, who still held on to his whip. But now his assailant was on the box beside him. In such close quarters he could not use his weapon effectively.

Brand cursed his lack of firearms, but attending the opera with his bulky Remington had hardly seemed appropriate. Fortunately, he never went anywhere without his "Arkansas toothpick" in his boot, a holdover from his days as a raider. Now he was glad for it as he bent down and pulled it into his hand. He moved to intercept the first man, who had stepped away from the horses and was advancing toward the women.

The gleam of avarice in his eyes chilled Miranda to the bone. She felt his slitted gaze fasten on the ruby pendant she wore. She'd give him the antique ruby earrings and necklace, and Lori's favorite aquamarine jewelry as well if only the bounder would leave them unharmed. Pulling off the jewels, which had been Will's wedding gift, she threw them at the squat man's feet, but he ignored them, advancing with an ugly grin twisting his round face.

Then the baron stepped in the thief's path. A long, wickedly gleaming blade suddenly materialized in his hand to match the one the thief held. Miranda covered Lori with her cape as the girl clung to her, not wanting her daughter to witness what was happening.

But Lori would not look away. She and her mother watched the way the baron moved, like the great jungle cat Miranda had first thought him. He lashed out with one clean, sweeping arc that left the thief gurgling in disbelief as his hands flew to his stomach where a river of gore suddenly gushed. The thief crumpled to the pavement, gutted. Caruthers stepped around him with no more thought than he'd give a puddle of water, advancing on the remaining two men.

One was still engaged with the driver, but the other, the large brute with long hair, raised an old Blanch four-barreled pistol he'd yanked from his belt and fired at his opponent. Lori screamed, holding her hands over her ears while Miranda cried out for a Peeler in a strong, clear voice, all the while yanking off the rest of her rubies. "Take off your jewelry," she whispered hoarsely to Lori.

The girl did as she was asked, but her eyes remained fixed on Brand.

The thief fired at Brand and missed. Before he could rotate the barrel cylinder for a second shot, the baron dodged, then came in low, butting his heavier opponent in the stomach, taking him to the filthy gutter, where they rolled and thrashed. Brand had one hand wrapped about the thief's hand which held the gun. In turn, his other hand was grasped by his foe to keep him from wielding his knife. The big brute came up on top and tried butting his head into Brand's, but only grazed it when the baron moved.

The pain was almost enough to make Brand lose his grip on his knife, but he held on and used every ounce of his strength to roll them over again. He stared down into the blood-crazed eyes of a madman who growled, "Ye killed Maury, ye bloody bastard!"

He was back in the war again. All he could see before him was a blue coat and a pistol. *The enemy. Kill the enemy.* This was hand to hand, just as he'd done so much of his fighting over those hellish four years. As he'd done to escape the filthy hole of a Yankee prison near the war's end. With a roar of rage, he was swept away in a tide of crimson to a place he prayed nightly never to visit again. Although he did often, in his nightmares . . .

Miranda and Lorilee watched as the baron wrenched free his hand and plunged his dagger into the throat of the man below him, then jumped up to face the third fellow. The thief had finally overcome their driver, who lay crumpled on the seat of the carriage.

"Let's see 'ow ye likes a taste o' the whip," the thug snarled as he lashed out with the weapon.

Instead of ducking away, Brand took the blow. The heavy carriage whip wrapped around his shoulders and bit deep through his jacket and shirt. Yet he stood. As the bloody whip uncoiled, he suddenly grabbed it in his hand and yanked hard, throwing his assailant off balance so he toppled forward. Just then the shrill of Peelers' whistles rent the night stillness. The thief tossed the whip handle toward the baron and tried to make a run for it, but Brand overtook him and smashed his fist into the man's narrow, grizzled face, crushing his nose to a pulp.

He was still beating the insensate man when the Peelers pulled him away. "There, sir, please, he's done for," one pleaded to the dazed gentleman.

"Damned bluebellies. Come to kill us," Brand muttered, seeing only the policeman's blue uniform, not registering where he was or who the officers were.

" 'E's a Yankee, Jackie," the second Peeler said, as if that explained Brand's crazed behavior toward them.

Now restrained by two strong men who held him carefully, Brand felt the red haze of battle start to lift. He was in London and these were officers of the law . . . and they'd just called him . . . "I'm no damned Yankee," he snarled, shoving free of their grasp.

"American, then, sir?" came the uncertain reply.

"He is Brandon Caruthers, Lord Rushcroft," Miranda said as she approached them. "I am Mrs. Auburn."

The Peelers were in awe of the famous Rebel Baron and also the lady standing so calmly before them. They knew she was a very wealthy widow from Liverpool who'd made an additional fortune all on her own here in London. As Brand and Miranda answered their questions regarding the incident, a third officer attended to Harry, who had been dealt a terrible blow to the head but was still breathing.

Lorilee stood staring numbly at the carnage surrounding

them. Although the whole incident had taken at best two to three minutes, it seemed to go on and on in her mind, replaying over and over. She looked at the disemboweled thug on the sidewalk, the huge brute with the slashed throat in the gutter, the third fellow with his face beaten to an unrecognizable mass near the carriage. Had the elegant man standing beside her mother actually done such violence?

She could scarcely have credited it if not for witnessing it with her own eyes. Then suddenly her mother was touching her cheek gently, saying soothing things to calm her as the baron's footman climbed aboard the carriage and pulled the skittish horses to a halt directly in front of the theater.

"Now, dearheart, let's go home," Miranda said, guiding Lori to the carriage.

But when the baron attempted to assist her into it, Lori flinched, reacting to his battered face and torn, blood-soaked evening clothes. Good heavens, the smell of him! He reeked of the gutter, and the hard, cold light in his eyes sent icy ripples of renewed terror shooting down her spine.

"My apologies for my appearance, Miss Auburn," he said gently, giving her a concerned smile as he waited, hand outstretched to her.

Lori looked down at his hand. Somehow during the fight he'd even lost his gloves, and his fists were bloodied, the knuckles swollen from beating that poor ruffian nearly to death. Perhaps he, too, was dead like the others. At her mother's urging, she climbed up the steps into the security of the enclosed carriage, hating the feel of those hard, naked hands on her arm.

But even more she hated the cold penetration of his eyes, piercing her as if they knew how much he frightened

her. He was a stranger and a killer . . . and her mother
wanted her to marry him!

"Er, these be yers, Mrs. Auburn?" one of the Peelers
said, pointing to where her rubies winked by gaslight, as
red as the blood flowing in the gutters. Close by, Lorilee's
aquamarine necklace and earrings were barely visible. The
other officer gathered up all the jewelry and handed it
deferentially to her. "Sorry, ma'am, but an officer'll be
calling on ye in the morning."

"Thank you," Miranda replied, nodding her understanding as she stuffed the jewels into her pocket. She cast a
worried glance toward her daughter, then climbed into the
carriage after her.

Brand leaned inside but made no attempt to enter. "I
think it would be best if I rode with our driver," he said,
then tried to reassure them with a smile. "I'm hardly fit
company for ladies in this condition." He glanced down
at his filthy, blood-smeared clothing, now partially concealed by his cape, which after having been cast on the
ground was muddy and torn.

Miranda nodded. "I believe that would be wise, my
lord," she said coolly.

With a terse nod, Brand climbed atop the carriage,
where the nervous driver was barely in control of the
horses. "Give me the ribbons, man," he said wearily. After
surviving three cutthroats, he was damned if he'd see
them die in a carriage accident.

The driver made no protest, handing over the reins. As
he coaxed the still nervous horses into a slow trot, Brand
considered what had just happened. He'd seen the "thief"
ignore Miranda Auburn's rubies when she tossed them
practically at his feet. She'd tried to throw away every
jewel they were wearing. Normally, such presence of
mind would have saved the wealthy Englishwomen's
lives.

Somehow, he guessed it would not have worked this time. He vowed to add a pocket pistol to his arsenal. Brand had a feeling he might have need of it on the streets of this, the wealthiest and most civilized city on earth.

"Try to get some sleep now," Miranda coaxed, taking the half-empty glass of warm milk from her daughter's hands. She'd laced it generously with brandy, but Lori had made a face and refused to drink the whole of it.

Lying back against the pillows piled high on her Louis XV bed, Lorilee Auburn shivered in spite of the covers pulled up to her neck and the heavy linen night rail she wore. "I'll be all right, Mother," she said softly. "You look as though you could use some rest yourself. You were ever so brave."

Miranda gave her cheek a swift kiss, then climbed off the edge of the bed. "Nonsense. I was just as frightened as you. Now, try not to think of it. It's over and done, and none of us has been injured except for the baron's poor driver, and I was told he will recover."

Once the door closed softly, leaving Lori alone with the tiny flicker of a lone gaslight turned down low, she closed her eyes and rubbed her temples, trying to do as her mother had asked. But visions of that awful scene appeared instantly in her mind. She sat up in bed, hugging herself, unconsciously rubbing the place on her elbow where the baron had touched her with his bare hands as he'd helped her into the carriage.

He'd been kind, solicitous even, but the danger still lay coiled deep inside him. She had been able to sense it through the heavy folds of her satin opera cloak and long white kid gloves. There was a coldness bred into him that had disturbed her even when she'd seen him standing at the foot of the stairs in their foyer on his first visit.

Oh, he was fine-looking enough, she supposed, if one

ignored that awful scar. Some women found such marks dashing rather than disfiguring, signs that a man had proven himself on the battlefield. But the very lean elegance of his hard body, the pantherish way he moved, like a cat stalking a bird, made her wish only to retreat from his presence. He had fought in a long and bloody war, for a cause that even her mother did not approve, although she had explained to Lori about his not owning slaves himself.

She did not understand him or the faraway place from which he had come to claim his place in England's peerage. And he was so much older than she. He'd read books and understood politics and made jokes that often mystified her. But her mother approved of his business acumen and felt assured that he would not waste the fortune which she and her husband had labored so hard to accumulate for their daughter.

Lori had learned from bitter experience with Geoffrey Winters that her money was indeed a far more potent enticement than any charms she possessed. At times such as this, she wished to be an impoverished peeress, one for whom some perfectly agreeable younger son of the aristocracy would offer without expectation of anything but herself. Even a young man in trade would do, if he truly loved her.

The baron did not. Above all, that was the unvarnished truth and it tore at her heart's youthful dreams. "Oh, Mother, how were you strong enough to do what you did?" she murmured as her eyelids grew heavy. Then the brandy and warm milk did their work and she slept.

"So, the summons has arrived. You expected it, did you not?" Sin asked as Brand threw the heavy piece of velum onto the scarred old desk in his office. It was embossed with the Auburn monogram.

The baron cursed, then sighed. "Yes. I expected a dressing down after the fiasco last night, but damnation, to be summoned like a schoolboy who's been caught scrapping on a bloody playground . . . summoned!"

St. John listened to his friend mutter something about high-handed, unnatural women, then commenced to pace the length of the room. He cleared his throat and said, "I have a bit of interesting information regarding the wager young Winters placed on Falconridge's horse."

That brought Brand from his angry reverie. "Go on," he said, intrigued in spite of his wrath toward the widow.

"Winters has not fared quite so profitably as he'd hoped with the earl's daughter. It would seem Falconridge stole a march on him. His daughter's dowry is being doled out by his none-too-generous hand. Oh, he sees that they have a decent house in town and pays for its upkeep. One must see to appearances, after all," Sin said dryly.

"How very British of you," Brand shot back.

Unperturbed, St. John shrugged. "You're the bleeding baron, not I, old chap. My father was the son of a mere squire, and I born not only on the wrong side of the blanket but from the wrong color of mother as well." If he felt any rancor over that fact, Sin did not reveal it. Instead, he continued, "The point is that Winters has not a sou of his own with which to wager."

"Who would be fool enough to lend him money for any enterprise, least of all that sort?" Brand asked, mystified.

"That's the oddest part. The rumor has it that an old . . . acquaintance of mine is involved. One Dustin O'Connell from County Cork."

"The trainer? I've heard of him. A shady sort, by all reports."

Sin grinned. "Quite so. My misspent youth has proven useful from time to time. It seems Dusty is employed at

Epsom currently, but he could never earn enough to afford placing a thousand-pound wager—and that is the amount, so rumor has it, he gave to the Winters pup, who placed it in his own name."

"With Reiver out of the race, King Arthur might have a chance to win, although I still think he'd do well to place at all. Hmmm. Where do you suppose O'Connell got the money? And why use Winters as a cat's-paw?"

"All good questions. I shall work hard to provide answers. By the by, please endeavor not to get your throat cut in some back alley while I am not about to protect you."

Brand snorted. "The Royal Opera House is scarcely situated in an alley. Just watch your backside while you're unraveling this mystery at the racecourses."

Sin's eyes traveled to the creamy sheet of paper with the large bold handwriting on it. "Speaking of backsides, you'd best look to your own when you do battle with the mama bear."

By the time he was ushered into Miranda's office, Brand was seething. He'd been kept waiting since half past the hour while she conducted some sort of business with a tall, anemic-looking stranger who had just walked past him without so much as a glance. The officious secretary held the door open for "the changing of the guard." Brand firmly took the heavy brass knob and closed it in Timmons's face.

"I apologize for the delay, Major, but Mr. Aimesley had a matter of pressing importance to discuss with me before his ship sails for New York."

Miranda did not appear the least bit penitent, Brand thought, but he bit back his retort and nodded, only taking his seat after she took hers. He noted that there was no foolishness about handshakes this time. "You summoned me, Mrs. Auburn," he said levelly.

Those gold tiger's eyes pinned her to her seat. Although not cold and deadly as they had been last night, they still unnerved her—and she was considerably stronger than Lori. "My daughter and I thank you for the flowers you sent by this morning."

"A note would've sufficed for that," he replied, waiting her out. The damned roses had cost a goodly portion of his winnings from yesterday's race; he had no idea how he would cover the loss of his opera cape and the evening wear he now had to replace at Bond Street's exorbitant prices.

"You were quite bold to take on three such ruffians singlehandedly. We owe you our lives," she said stiffly.

"Why is it, ma'am, that I hear a qualification in your voice?" he asked, mustering the most charming smile he owned.

"Surely you realize how the sight of such carnage affected a young woman of my daughter's sheltered sensibilities. Perhaps if you'd simply allowed me to give them our jewelry—"

He shot out of the chair and leaned over her desk. "A most level-headed gesture if it had worked, but since the first fellow paid not the slightest bit of attention to a set of rubies flung at his feet, I suspect his compatriots would've been no more easily distracted. They intended us harm. To put it bluntly, they were going to kill all of us in cold blood."

"So instead you killed the three of them." By this time she was standing across the desk, her palms flattened on the polished surface.

"The third one is still alive, but I have not given up hope," he snapped, his hands balling into fists which he planted on the desktop.

"You beat him into a bloody trifle in front of my daughter and terrified her out of her wits!" She leaned forward until their faces were within a foot of each other. Gold and silver eyes glared at each other, neither blinking.

"How rackety these Americans can be! Would a proper English gentleman have stood by and allowed that scum to slit your throat in front of your daughter—then drag her off in the carriage?"

Miranda's breath caught. She had negotiated with some of the most arrogant and infuriating captains of industry and never lost her temper, yet here she was, screaming like a Billingsgate fishmonger at a member of the peerage! She sat down abruptly, gathering her scattered thoughts. "Dear lord, do you think he would have . . . could have . . . ?" Her words trailed away as visions of Lori being carried off to an unthinkable fate flashed before her eyes.

Brand realized how badly he'd lost control just now, not to mention the preceding night when the rage of battle overtook him again. He had gone to a place he never wished to go again, and it had cost him dearly, but he would never admit that to a living soul, not even Sin. Certainly not this haughty woman. *Haughty, yes, but incredibly brave also*, a voice admonished. And he was forced to admit it was nothing but the truth.

"You were quite level-headed last night. Most women would've swooned or become hysterical. It was a good idea to try distracting them with the jewels," he said as he, too, took his seat once again.

Miranda shook her head to clear it. "I . . . I witnessed a robbery once many years ago. A wealthy woman in Liverpool refused to give over her ermine cloak and pearls to a street thief. In the struggle that ensued she was killed. Senseless. No possessions are worth one's life."

"Spoken like one who's never done without them," he

said dryly. He was curious about this enigmatic woman who might yet become his mother-in-law.

Miranda was taken aback by his unfair assessment. What did he know of the sacrifices she'd been forced to make? She would damn well not enlighten him. Her past was too painful. "My father owned an iron foundry and I had a comfortable childhood. But all of that was long ago and quite frankly none of your business. Lorilee is my concern and should be yours as well—*if* you would make her a suitable husband."

The threat hung between them. She could withdraw her offer of a marriage with her daughter and he would be ruined.

Chapter Seven

The baron said nothing for a moment and Miranda feared she'd overplayed her hand. Last night's brush with death must have addled her wits. She'd never in her life used such language as the vulgar words she'd spoken during their exchange. In spite of Lori's upset, the gentleman had risked his life to rescue them. But before she could offer an apology, he spoke.

"I can imagine how a young girl would react to what happened—to what I did. I offer my deepest apologies to you both, ma'am," he said stiffly.

"You would understand, wouldn't you?" Miranda's voice softened. "Your sister must have been younger than my daughter during the American war."

"Barbie survived. Southern women had no alternative. And that was long ago and quite frankly none of your business." He echoed her words with the faintest of smiles curving his lips.

Miranda felt the deftly delivered setdown. In spite of it, she could not help noticing the way his mouth was sculpted so beautifully when he smiled. But when he was angry . . . the cold, killing rage of last night flashed before her eyes once again, and she wondered if she was making a mistake. Would it be better to break off this courtship before it went any further? He seemed to guess her thoughts.

"If you no longer see me as suitable husband material, I quite understand, Mrs. Auburn," he said, starting to rise.

He was a proud man, and she had summoned him here to humble him. After he'd saved her daughter's life. What was wrong with her? "No, wait, please, Lord Rushcroft. I . . . I did not mean to pry, nor to insult you. You are right. Lori and I owe you our lives and I owe you an apology."

"Handsomely done, ma'am."

He nodded, still standing with that rakish hat in his hand, which was now discreetly gloved. She could imagine the swollen knuckles hidden by black leather. Injuries he'd received because of them. "Why do you think we were chosen for . . . whatever those awful men intended to do with us?"

Brand shook his head. "I have no idea. Do you have business enemies who might have reason to want you dead?"

"One or two over the years," she replied dryly. "But no one dangerous or desperate enough to hire someone to kill me. Of that I'm positive . . . in spite of my formidable reputation, about which I'm certain you've heard."

He paused for a moment, debating whether to say anything. Then he plunged ahead. "I don't know if this has any bearing on last night, but someone tried to burn down my mews."

Miranda gasped, knowing what his horses meant to him. "Was it serious?"

"Could've killed Reiver and several other fine horses,

but thank heavens my groom foiled the attempt before things went that far. It was certainly not like last night . . ."

"Yet?" Miranda prompted.

"Geoffrey Winters bet heavily on a horse that wouldn't stand a chance unless Reiver was out of the race."

Miranda looked as if she'd just tasted something rancid.

Brand went on. "It could be nothing, but he hasn't the quid—I believe that is your English expression—to place a thousand-pound bet. A shady character my trainer knew from his old days in racing was involved. Dustin O'Connell." At her blank look, he remembered she knew nothing of the racing circuit.

"And you believe this Mr. O'Connell gave the money to Pelham's boy?"

"That's what Sin is looking into now."

"You rely on Mr. St. John quite a bit, don't you?"

He grinned. "He's a most reliable man . . . and my best friend."

"You do break all the rules, do you not, Major?" she asked, returning his smile broadly this time.

"Every chance I get, ma'am."

Miranda breathed a sigh of relief. She was not making a mistake, and her imperious summons had not botched her hopes for the baron and Lori. "My daughter and I shall look forward to this weekend . . . that is, if your gracious invitation still stands?"

When she tilted her head that way and smiled, she looked almost beautiful, much younger than he'd imagined the first time he met her. If only she'd wear dresses that flattered her and do something softer with all that heavy red hair. He could imagine it floating like a flaming mantle around her shoulders. What the devil had made him think of that! Fixing Lori's golden ringlets firmly in his mind, he replied, "I shall look forward to escorting you to Ascot."

And he would. But whose company would he enjoy? The lovely daughter's . . . or her formidable mother's?

On his way out of her office, Brand was too preoccupied to pay particular attention to the somber fellow who had been in conference with Mrs. Auburn earlier. He was once again pacing agitatedly in the outer office. Timmons immediately ushered him inside after seeing the baron to the door.

"Mr. Aimesley, I thought you were on your way to the docks. Is something amiss?" Miranda asked.

Kent Aimesley was tall and cadaverously thin with wispy brown hair and pale, lashless eyes. His body had been robbed of the vigor of youth by a bout of consumption which nearly took his life when he was twenty-two. Years of toiling for Will Auburn, working his way up from mere clerk to chief factor for the vast Auburn holdings, showed in the careworn lines of his face. Although he was only two years older than Miranda, he looked nearer fifty than forty. He was thirty-eight.

"In all my rush, I neglected to have you sign the bids for the railway equipment." He rummaged through a sheaf of documents extracted from the well-worn leather case opened on the edge of her desk.

After Will had hired him, Miranda had become somewhat uncomfortable with Kent Aimesley. But in those early days she'd been a young mother who had nothing to do with the operation of her husband's foundry and other diversified interests. Since taking over the businesses, however, she had become acutely aware of Aimesley's feelings for her—feelings she no longer returned.

He had always been more than discreet, and only well

after her period of mourning for Will had he made an overture to her. She had explained that he was a good friend and valued employee upon whose expertise she relied, but that was all he could ever be to her. He had acceded to her wishes with the utmost grace.

But he had never married.

Somehow, Miranda had always felt guilty about it. Perhaps because of this, she had asked him to go to the United States to investigate investments in railway building. With the triumph of the Union forces during the war there, the promise of westward expansion had become a lucrative reality. And Kent Aimesley had become her right hand, making the arduous journey from Philadelphia to London and back regularly.

"Everything is in order with our offer of capital for the Union Pacific . . . the shipping of iron tonnage is here . . . manifests for the two steamers out of Liverpool," he murmured to himself as he deftly double-checked documents until he was satisfied all were in order and only the one bid for railcars and locomotives remained incomplete.

Miranda took the bid from him and signed her name after scanning it again. "How ever did we both miss such an obvious thing?" she asked with a smile as she handed it back.

"This is the largest American business venture you have ever undertaken, Mrs. Auburn," Will replied in his deliberate manner. "If the directors of Union Pacific accept our offer, we stand to make an incredible return on shipping the iron alone, not to mention the long-term profits from being major stockholders. Small wonder, with so much to consider, that you overlooked one signature. However, that does not excuse me."

"You caught the mistake, and for that I thank you. It would scarcely do to arrive at Dr. Durant's office with papers I had neglected to sign. I'm quite certain these

American entrepreneurs would have their opinions about a woman dabbling in business confirmed."

"Only because they do not know you, Mrs. Auburn," Aimesley said as he tucked the document into his case. He hesitated for a moment, clutching the old leather to his chest as if prepared to ward off a blow.

"What is it, Mr. Aimesley?" she asked with apprehension. This was not like him at all.

"If . . . if you will forgive my presumption . . . that is, I saw that Rebel Baron as I was leaving earlier and . . ."

Miranda stiffened but said nothing, waiting him out.

"Well," he stammered, red-faced now. "That is, I hope you aren't considering a business investment with a former secessionist, even if he has become a member of the peerage." He pursed his lips and stood as if fully expecting a tongue-lashing for his presumption.

She held her temper, reminding herself that although any interest in her and Lori's personal lives would be most improper, he was only making an inquiry about business matters and that was within bounds. "No, Mr. Aimesley, I am not entering into any horse-racing ventures, if that is your concern."

Her reply was to the point, if not altogether truthful. Ultimately, she would be turning over everything she and Will—and Kent Aimesley—had worked for to Brandon Caruthers. But she was not investing in his horses . . . precisely.

Aimesley nodded with hooded eyes which revealed nothing. After he was gone and she sat alone in the big ugly room where she had spent so many hours of her life over the past fifteen years, Miranda wondered if he knew something about Brandon Caruthers's life in America that her investigators had missed. She had come to understand, even pardon, the carnage at the opera. But what of the nasty encounter with Reba Wilcox at the musicale?

Would the baron marry Lori and then make the voluptuous American widow his mistress? Lord knew, most of the peerage had such liaisons. No, everything she'd learned about him, including the way he had fended off Mrs. Wilcox, indicated that he was a man of honor. But Reba Wilcox possessed not a shred of honor. Of that she was certain and the knowledge troubled her.

The following morning, Miranda took the opportunity to sleep later, a luxury she seldom allowed herself. Just before nine she awakened and rang for morning tea. When Tilda came in, bearing the tray along with the day's post, the mistress of the house was sitting at her dressing table, brushing her hair briskly.

"Here, let me do that. You always get it tangled," the maid said, adding, "It would do no harm for you to eat two or three of those scones Cook just baked while I'm working on this hair. You're too thin and you work too hard. Hoped you'd sleep until at least ten."

Tilda's bossy manner was endearing to Miranda. The prickly Indian woman was far more confidante than servant. "I never sleep to ten and you know it," she replied, humming with pleasure as Tilda ran the heavy ivory-inlaid brush through her waist-length hair, massaging her scalp expertly.

"You have such lovely hair," Tilda said.

"It's red," Miranda replied flatly.

"And what's that supposed to mean? Golden blond isn't the only lovely color the good Lord created to grace a woman's scalp. All you need do is let me fix it the way I do Miss Lorilee's—"

"I'm scarcely a girl in the bloom of youth. Just braid it and put it up as usual so it's out of my way."

"It's too heavy to be worn that way. It's why you get those headaches of yours, mark me."

"Very well, leave it down until after I go through the mail," Miranda relented, tearing into the pile of letters beside her breakfast tray. She sipped tea with lemon but ignored the rich scones and raspberry jam.

As Tilda began laying out her mistress's clothing for the morning and seeing to the drawing of her bath, she fussed aloud about stubborn women who didn't know what was best for their own health. Miranda ignored her and concentrated on her reading. After a couple of invitations to various soirees which Lori might enjoy and she would endure, an envelope with the Rushcroft crest caught her attention.

Frowning, she asked, "When did this arrive?"

"Just before you rang. Hand-delivered by a young American lad."

"Since you never deign to speak with footmen, how would you know he was American?" Miranda asked, amused.

"I have eyes. He was black as a spade in a deck of playing cards," she harrumhped.

"Mathias," Miranda murmured to herself. The baron had mentioned the young jockey fondly. She read an invitation from the baron for a ride in Hyde Park at one that afternoon. He was going to make certain his stallion's injury was healed and wondered if Miss Auburn and she would do him the honor of accompanying him. "Is Lori up?" she asked Tilda.

"Still abed with her nose in one of those Sir Walter Scott romances," Tilda said with disapproval. She had been raised on the classics and considered popular fiction a waste of time.

Miranda chuckled tolerantly. "Please ask her to come here."

Lorilee was less than enthusiastic about the invitation but smiled dutifully and agreed that it was indeed a lovely day for a ride. She quickly left her mother's room, saying she would have to select a riding habit, an excuse that she knew Miranda would believe. Though it was a warm June day and the sun beckoned everyone outdoors, and though she loved riding her mare along Rotten Row to see and be seen, she did not look forward to the prospect of spending time with Brandon Caruthers.

If only she could find a way to explain her feelings without seeming childish or ungrateful. The baron had saved their lives at no small risk to himself, she reminded herself. But his violent actions left her shaken. So did his bizarre reaction to Marmalade and the kittens, not to mention the encounter with that dreadful American woman.

Perhaps what bothered her most of all was the way she felt left out of the conversation whenever he and her mother talked, no matter how much they tried to include her. She felt too young, too poorly educated, too . . . unsophisticated, she supposed. Why, even compared to the flirtatious widow, who was quite ill-mannered, Lori felt socially maladept. How easily Baron Rushcroft and her mother had handled the brazen woman. All she could do was stand like a stump and gape.

She had never felt such discomfort with other younger suitors. She dismissed Geoffrey Winters from her mind, recalling many other eager young men who had attempted to woo her. Although none took her fancy, neither had they made her feel in any way wanting, as did the baron.

Lorilee knew he was considered one of the catches of the season, a mysterious and dashing cavalier whose Southern cause had been lost in a desperate conflict. Many of the debutantes swooned over the romance of it all. Newspapers were filled with stories about the Rebel Baron. Gentlemen who were racing enthusiasts spoke of his marvelous blooded stock and how often his small stables took large purses.

Now he was hailed as a hero for foiling an attempted robbery and possible kidnapping. No, she would have to go riding this afternoon and attend the Ascot with him. And pray as the summer wore on that it would become clear to the baron and, more importantly, to her mother that they did not suit. And, too, if she was seen with such a celebrity, there would be more opportunities for her to find that young man of her dreams.

Out of the blue, a thought occurred to her. The baron needed a wealthy wife to redeem his family estates from the ill repair into which they had fallen. What if she could find such a candidate for him? One older and more sophisticated than herself. That would solve both their dilemmas.

With that plan fixed firmly in her mind, Lori smiled to herself and went to her clothes cabinets to select a riding habit.

"She has a good seat," Brand said to Miranda as they watched Lorilee jump a low hedge with considerable grace, then turn her little buttermilk-colored mare back toward them. "Are you certain you don't want to learn to ride? It's simple and fun."

Miranda shook her head. She had driven Lori's slipper Victoria to the park. "I have mastered the ribbons for one horse, safely situated inside a well-sprung carriage. That will suffice for the social graces of horsemanship as far as I'm concerned." She could tell he was incredulous by the look he gave her.

"How is it you never rode? Your family obviously stinted nothing on the rest of your education."

"We were of the merchant class, my lord. Running an iron foundry in Liverpool scarcely required skill in riding to hounds. Nor did my father have the leisure for such indulgences."

110

"Spoken like a true Puritan. Are you certain you're Church of England, not a Calvinist?" he said with a teasing glint in his eyes.

When he smiled at her that way, something inside her turned over, something warm and vaguely frightening. Still, she could not resist returning his smile. "We are staunchly Establishment. As to riding, perhaps I'm afraid of taking a fall."

"You're not afraid of anything," he replied, his expression suddenly grave. "I remember how you behaved at the theater. So calm and resourceful."

His eyes made Miranda flush like a girl Lori's age before she looked away. "I've told you how frightened I was . . ." She hesitated then, wanting to share with him a bit of her past. He would be part of their family one day. But no, not yet. She was not ready. Perhaps she never would be. Only Tilda knew the whole of it.

"Something happened to your family." He held up his hand. "I know, it's none of my business . . . only it is if we're to be kin one day."

It was as if he could read her mind, she thought, not for the first time. But there was genuine concern, not idle curiosity, in his voice. Haltingly she said, "My father had a prosperous business until the financial crash in the forties. Then he had to struggle to hold the foundry together."

Brand wondered what Miranda Auburn had been forced to give up when she was poised on the brink of womanhood. From what he'd gathered, Will Auburn could not have been a young man when he wed her, for he was well into his sixties when he died and they'd been married for less than five years.

Together they watched as Lorilee reined in her mare and spoke with two other young women, obviously friends of hers. Then Brand broke the silence. "You were

111

forced to marry for money, too, weren't you?"

She gasped as if he'd struck her. "That is a matter between me and my husband. You have no right—"

"I'm doing the same thing. I think it gives me every right." His voice was anguished, yet at the same time gentle.

She sat back against the cushions, breathless as she studied his face. "Yes, I suppose it does," she replied at length. "My father was facing utter ruin when Mr. Auburn offered for me. We developed . . . a rapport over the years. He was . . . very kind." She swallowed back the tears that suddenly and inexplicably burned her eyes.

Kind. What a weak and pitiful word that was for what was supposed to be the closest relationship possible between a man and a woman.

"And you want so much more for your daughter," he said quietly, wondering what else he could honestly say to reassure her. "I promise I will be very kind to her . . . but I cannot promise to fall in love with her. After all I've been through, I doubt I know what love is, if I ever did."

She looked up at him, and that awareness hummed between them once more. "Perhaps there is no such thing as the romantic love written about in books. I don't know. Once . . . long ago, I believed in it, but found it chimerical. Marriages are far safer based on practical considerations."

"If you want to be safe." He shrugged, cursing himself for saying that, uncertain just why he had. Or what he meant by it.

Lorilee, who had bade adieu to Abbie and Marian, trotted Taffy across the soft grass, approaching her mother and the baron. She noted that they appeared to be in some sort of intense conversation. Her mother was looking up at him strangely. And he appeared bemused, for want of a better word. As soon as they heard her draw near, whatever spell had held them was broken and they greeted her with smiles which she felt were forced.

"You're a natural rider, Miss Auburn," he said smoothly.

"I only wish I could convince Mother to join me, but she's a stick about horses."

"I can barely control one carriage horse and she wants me bouncing on the back of a spirited riding mount," Miranda exclaimed. "One might believe my daughter wishes me to break my neck."

The teasing light in her mother's eyes kept Lori from vehement denials. "You can do anything to which you set your mind," she replied instead.

"I second that," Brand replied, but Miranda shook her head.

"I am content to watch the two of you ride." The implication was clear. If they were seen on the Row together, it could only mean that he was courting her with her mother's blessings.

"Will you show us how that great black beast wins so many purses?" Lori asked him with a sunny smile. "Perhaps we can have a race before we get to the Row . . . if you will handicap a lady?"

He touched the brim of his hat. "My pleasure—and Reiver's, isn't it, boy?" he asked, patting the stallion's neck. The big black raised his head as if nodding assent. "I'll give you forty yards. The race is to the hedges by the pond and back. Agreed?"

With that, Lorilee was off, leaning gracefully forward over the little mare's neck.

Brand waited longer than the agreed-upon forty yards before kneeing Reiver into a graceful gallop across the wide-open field before them.

Miranda watched him hold back the powerful stallion so Lori could win the race. The thought struck her that they had made no wager, which made her sad. If Lori were smitten with a young swain, she would most certainly have made some flirtatious bet. Miranda had been out enough in society as her daughter neared the age of debut to know how such things were done. Lori knew, too.

But this is no game of flirtation and romance. It is a sensible arrangement, she reminded herself. A tightness began forming in her chest, and almost as if sensing her restiveness, the carriage horse suddenly shied.

"Whoa," she commanded, tightening her hold on the reins as the horse began to nicker and rear up. "What the devil—" She got out no more than that when the beast suddenly bolted off, heading for a ditch some hundred yards distant, surrounded by trees. Miranda yanked frantically on the reins, only to find them abruptly loosen in her hands. The horse had nothing holding him back! She could see the useless ribbons caught up in the harness, flapping around his legs, only adding to his inexplicable terror as he ran.

The ground beneath her carriage wheels was a blur of greens and browns as the strong young gelding picked up speed at an alarming rate. The carriage was light as a feather and offered no resistance to his run. Thoughts flashed through her mind with lightning speed as the trees and ditch drew closer. Better to jump than risk crashing into a massive oak trunk or overturning in the ditch? But what if she jumped and her ballooning skirts caught in the wheels? She'd be pulled beneath them and crushed!

Brand and Lorilee had already made the turn at the pond and were headed back. Lori was still in the lead when Brand heard Miranda's cries for help. Fortunately, because he'd played the gentleman allowing his lady to win, he was nearer to the carriage. Wheeling Reiver about, he headed in a direct course to intercept the runaway.

His head bent over the black's neck, he urged his mount on in earnest now, racing flat out. Winning the Ascot Gold Cup paled in comparison to winning this contest. Miranda Auburn's life was at stake.

She could hear the pounding of hoofbeats behind her, faint over the rush of the wind and jingle of the harness. And most of all, the furious pounding of her own heartbeats. She leaned out of the carriage and saw Brand, saw the grim desperation on his face as he spurred Reiver recklessly faster.

Then she turned to where he was looking and her pounding heart froze in her chest. The horse was racing directly toward the trunk of a huge gnarled oak tree.

Chapter Eight

Brand could see her white face as she leaned out of the carriage and turned back toward him. He was five yards from the carriage and the carriage was five yards from the tree as the horse veered frantically at the last moment to avoid the obstacle in its path. There would be an even finish unless Reiver could beat the odds.

The black responded to the desperate challenge. With one mighty lunge he leaped forward as Brand yelled, "Miranda! Jump!"

She cried out something indistinct to him as the vehicle began to spin in a sickening arc toward the tree. His body leaned toward her, arms outstretched. She leaped, her body seemingly suspended in midair for a breathless instant, arms reaching for his neck.

He swooped low and caught her to his side. Reiver veered sharply to avoid disaster as the light slipper Victoria smashed into the tree. The sounds of wood and leather being ripped apart and the screams of the gelding struggling to break free filled the air. The horse lunged over and over with crazed strength until the last pieces of the harness snapped. Then it bolted away as if shot from a cannon.

Neither Brand nor Miranda noticed. Reiver, lathered and winded, slowed to a walk, then stopped with his sides heaving. The baron's shocking breach of propriety in using her Christian name was a faint memory teasing the periphery of her mind. Her skirts were spread across the stallion's flank and her body molded to his as he held her in his arms. Unthinking, she buried her head against his neck, inhaling his scent, the essence of life from this man who had saved her yet again.

She could smell the elemental maleness of him, the faint musk of his skin, the slight rasp of a heavy beard already starting to grow so early in the afternoon. Never had she been so aware of a man's body. How hard it was, how different from her own. Her husband had not, even in the intimacies of the marriage bed, inspired such feelings. Certainly Kent Aimesley had not. If such thoughts had been conscious, she would have died of embarrassment, but in the aftermath of a harrowing escape from death, they remained deeply buried.

She clung to him.

And he held her fast.

Lori had seen the runaway carriage from a distance when the sound of Reiver's hoofbeats had caused her to look over her shoulder. Terrified that her mother was going to die, she had turned, too far behind the baron to catch up. All she could do was pray he would be in time to prevent an unthinkable tragedy. Tears of sheer terror blinded her as she drew nearer.

She blinked them away, watching the scene unfold—the carriage splintering a bare instant after he swept her mother from the jaws of sure death; Reiver carrying them past the thrashing gelding while the baron's strong arm held Miranda against his side. As Lorilee drew nearer, she observed the way they clung to each other. Then they slowly broke apart. He lowered her mother to the ground, quickly dismounting, his hands supporting her lest she faint. But Lorilee knew Miranda Auburn had never fainted in her life.

Still the two of them stood looking into each other's eyes. Although a respectable space was visible between them now, neither of them relinquished the hold on the other's arms. Instead, they slowly slid their hands down until they were joined together like two dancers at the start of a country reel. Suddenly Lori could picture them that way—see her mother as a young woman with a dashing partner, eager to begin . . . what?

Surely not a courtship. After all, her mother had recently turned thirty-six! To one barely eighteen, that seemed a formidable age. The baron himself was thirty, according to a story she'd read in *The Times*. Her suitor was twelve years her senior, and she'd felt that age difference keenly even though she knew it was hardly an unusual one. Indeed, it was far less than the forty-two years that had separated her own parents.

But her mother and the baron were only six years apart, even if he was the younger of the two. Was such a thing acceptable? She looked at them again and decided it just might be.

They shared an understanding of business matters and were both tirelessly hard workers. That was one of the reasons her mother had hand-picked him to marry her. They also laughed at jokes and argued about political matters she did not comprehend. The only thing they did not have in common was a love of horses. Suddenly Lori realized that was the sole interest she and the baron did share.

Yes, it could work!

She reined in Taffy and jumped down just after they broke apart. Her mother fussed with straightening her dress, something she normally never did. The baron turned his attention to his horse, patting Reiver's neck and murmuring to him. She could tell that both of them were shaken—not only by the brush with death, but also by what had passed between them immediately afterward. Something neither of them wanted to acknowledge.

"Are you all right, Mother?" she asked as Miranda rushed to her and embraced her.

"Yes, dearheart, I'm fine . . . just a bit shaken." She attempted a jaunty smile that wobbled.

"I was so frightened. How did you lose control of Bally that way?"

"She didn't," Brand answered for her. He held up one of the reins and showed them where it had been cleanly cut just over halfway through before it broke. "If the other ribbons have been tampered with the same way, someone deliberately intended grave harm for one of you." He and Miranda exchanged a telling glance. He knew she was recalling the thief in front of the opera house.

Lorilee blanched, but Miranda said more calmly now, "Bally jumped and reared up very suddenly. That's when I yanked hard on the ribbons. When he began to run out of control, I felt them snapping."

The implication was clear. If the horse had been deliberately spooked so it would bolt, then whoever did it knew that Miranda, not her daughter, would be the victim.

"Let's just see what might have made Bally react so violently." Brand swung back on Reiver and trotted after the carriage horse, who was now grazing peacefully down in a swale about a hundred yards away.

He returned, leading Bally. By this time a small crowd was gathering, inquiring solicitously about Miranda's well-being and gawking at the smashed ruins of the carriage.

Miranda assured everyone that she was unharmed, and gradually the curiosity seekers dispersed. Lori's friends Abbie and Marian were torn between offering assurances that their mothers would have been prostrate after such an adventure and exclaiming about how positively dashing it was of the baron to have rescued her.

While Lori tried to soothe her agitated companions, Miranda watched as Brand pulled off his riding gloves and began to examine the gelding. He stopped in the midst of checking the horse's right front leg, then held up his bare hand. She could see a smear of blood on it.

"Something, a stone or sharp missile, hit him, hard," he said with grim certainty.

"I thought . . . perhaps I heard a slight hissing sound just before he screamed and reared up," Miranda said, although she did not sound positive.

Brand looked around the park. People were scattered here and there, some on horseback, some in carriages or strolling afoot. Most were fashionably dressed, but shabby vendors and other less savory sorts were sprinkled among them. Trees and shrubs could have hidden someone who had a good aim with a slingshot. Perhaps even a blowgun of some sort.

Wanting to see what her mother and the baron were discussing, Lori bade her friends farewell and hurried over to them. He was bare-handed, just as he had been that night at the opera. The sight bothered her. But not nearly as much as the blood he'd wiped from Bally's foreleg, which was beginning to swell. "Someone is trying to kill you," she whispered incredulously to her mother.

"We don't know that for certain," Miranda replied.

Brand backtracked over the wheel ruts and returned a few moments later with the other ribbon. He held it up for their inspection. "Yes, we do," he replied. "Mrs. Auburn, although I know you're loath to ever mount another horse—and at the moment I scarcely blame you—we must get you home. Will you ride with me?"

"Well, it's obvious that Lori's small mare can't hold both of us, and the sidesaddle would not permit it in any case, so I have no recourse but to accept your kind offer. I'll send a footman back for Bally."

Her smile was tinged with a wariness that Lorilee could sense. But after assisting her to remount Taffy, Brand swung up on Reiver and reached down for her mother. At least he'd put his gloves on again. Miranda allowed his strong arms to lift her in front of him.

Lori knew full well that they could have asked any of the gentlemen in the park to drive them home. Several had made the offer earlier and Miranda had graciously declined, sending them on their way. Riding beside them, she smiled inwardly. Plans began to buzz in her mind. It would all be quite perfect . . . if not for the person who wished harm to her mother. But perhaps even that could be turned to good advantage. . . .

After all, the baron had already appointed himself her protector, and he was quite good at the job.

"Will you help me, Tilda? Oh, please say you will." Lori's voice took on the wheedling tone she'd employed with such good results since she was a little girl. She held up the deep turquoise silk gown like an offering.

The Indian woman studied her young charge with shrewd dark eyes. Since coming to England many years ago, she had learned every trick that Miranda and now Lorilee used to bend her to their ways. "Why this sudden interest in your mother's manner of dress?" she asked suspiciously.

Lori sighed impatiently. "You yourself have chided her

since my earliest memories for wearing such drab, ugly clothes. I'm merely agreeing with you."

Tilda knew that Miss Lorilee had just neatly evaded answering her question, but she was not about to argue the point. "Your mother says her clothes are suited for business and she has no time for fashion. This would not have anything to do with the baron, now would it?"

Drat the woman's perceptiveness. Lori would have to chance confiding the truth. "Well . . . yes, it does. What would you say if I suggested . . . that is . . ." She struggled for the best way to word it.

"That your mother suits the baron better than you do?"

Lori blinked. "H-how did you know that?"

Tilda only smirked. "One of the mysteries of the East."

"You left India when you were a girl. Don't try to fool me with such nonsense. You're just very intelligent!" Lori said, exasperated. "If you knew what I was about, why didn't you save us both time and just say so?"

"Perhaps I wanted to plumb the reasons why you feel as you do," Tilda said dryly. Then her expression grew serious. "No more mooning about Lord Pelham's son?"

Lori threw up her hands. "Heavens, no! I've learned my lesson. Perhaps I'm too young to settle down and marry—yet," she hastened to add. "Why, I might take a year or two or even more to find just the right man. What if I'd been deceived as Falconridge's daughter was?" She shivered at the thought, then looked abruptly puzzled. "Odd, but I was so hurt at first, I thought my heart would break."

"Young hearts mend quickly," Tilda said with the wisdom of experience.

Lori dismissed that, caught up in her own thoughts, which she voiced aloud. "Now . . . I don't know how to explain it. I feel . . . free. I don't have to marry the baron or anyone else if I don't choose."

"What makes you so certain your mother will agree to this rather unorthodox switch in plans?" Tilda asked, ever practical.

Lori noted that Tilda's voice no longer sounded dubious and took heart. "Oh, you should have been there yesterday. Seen the way they held on to each other when he scooped her from the carriage just before it crashed."

She described the scene in detail so minute it would have made Miranda's face burn with embarrassment, had she been aware of how scandalously she'd acted. But Lori did not think it was scandalous at all. Merely romantic. And an indicator of how much her mother was drawn to the baron and he to her.

Tilda took it all in, nodding but making no comment until Lori breathlessly ran out of words. Then she cautioned, "You may be right, Miss Cupid. However, I don't know that your mother will appreciate your acting as a matchmaker. You'd best be careful not to reveal too much to her."

"Oh, I plan to continue accepting the baron's suit," Lori said airily. "Mother won't have any idea that we've reversed roles. I'll be the chaperone." Here she paused and giggled. "Only I'll not be a very good one."

"There is one problem. Your mother will feel horribly guilty when the baron begins to pay more attention to her than to you," Tilda said thoughtfully.

"Well, at some point I'll tell her that Lord Rushcroft and I simply do not suit—but not until she sees for herself which way the wind blows."

Tilda nodded with approval. Her young charge had surprised her by exhibiting such insight. They would have to keep Miranda from guessing what they were about at first, lest she put a period to the whole courtship immediately. But if she could justify her interest in the baron as being only for her daughter's sake, it just might work.

"We'll begin by arranging for her to wear this gown to Ascot," Tilda said, spreading the vibrant silk skirt across the bed. "I remember when last your mother wore it . . . to a ball given by one of your father's business associates."

Lori's expression turned wistful for a moment. "I remember it, too. I thought she was so beautiful—like a fairy princess." Then she frowned. "But isn't it out of fashion now?"

Tilda shrugged. "We have no time for new clothes before Gold Cup Day. A few minor changes. I'll take some of the fullness from the skirt and catch it up in the back using this trim." She held up a roll of cream-colored lace. "I think I'll add a bit of it at the sleeves and neckline, too."

"What about a parasol? And a hat? She must have a hat for Ascot," Lori pronounced.

The conspirators set to work on their plans, beginning with disposing of the drab tan dress Miranda had selected to wear to the race.

"Mutton disguised as spring lamb," Miranda said, shaking her head as she looked at herself in the tall mirror. The color was far too bright, and the way it fitted, revealing every curve, was too brazen for her taste. She blushed, imagining what her business associates would say if they could see her now. *If the major could see me . . .* Where had that thought come from? She quashed it and said quickly, "Honestly, Tilda, I don't believe—"

"Oh, Mother, it's quite perfect!" Lori exclaimed. "Tilda stayed up all night sewing just to finish it in time. After all, you have nothing else to wear, and it is such an important day."

"How could my new tan poplin have been stained that way? I was positive the last time I wore it that I hadn't spilled coffee on it. I rarely drink coffee," she added suspiciously.

"Well, someone stained it and this is what you'll have to wear. It's really far more appropriate for Ascot anyway. Remember, Mother, this is where all the ladies of Society go to see and be seen—not some stuffy old shipping office."

"The hat won't fit." Miranda tried again, fighting against something she was afraid to name.

"Yes, it will," Tilda said through a mouthful of pins as she picked up a hairbrush. With that, she began fashioning her mistress's heavy hair into a soft roll, allowing wispy tendrils to fall around her face.

"I'll look like a girl."

"Only because you still do. Best to worry about that when you only *think* you do," Tilda replied wryly.

"I trust you'll tell me when that day arrives," Miranda scolded.

Tilda nodded calmly, her deft fingers continuing to perform magic with the masses of heavy red hair. Finally she positioned the wide-brimmed aqua straw hat at a jaunty angle on Miranda's head and pinned it in place, then stood back to admire her handiwork.

Lori said not a word, gazing raptly at her mother as if seeing her for the very first time. With trembling hands, she offered the matching parasol to her mother, who now more closely resembled a sister than a parent.

Miranda looked into her daughter's wide eyes, mirrors of delighted wonder, and felt a deep frisson of fear. What was she doing? This was wrong. Utterly crazy. She had lain awake last night in bed, replaying the terrifying adventure in the park over and over, trying to convince herself that she was analyzing it to figure out who wanted to kill her.

But all she truly thought of was the way her body had

felt pressed so closely to Brandon Caruthers's hard frame. She could recall every nuance of his scent, even the smell of Bally's blood on his hand . . . his ungloved hand with its long fingers and powerful tracery of veins, even the light sprinkling of golden hair on the back of it. And he was her daughter's suitor! One day he would be her son-in-law.

How could she bear it?

Miranda stiffened her spine and swallowed hard, pushing back her fears. After all, one look at Lori's delighted face made her realize that she would sacrifice anything for her daughter's happiness. Even the major. Most particularly the major. "Very well. I suppose I shall have to wear this ensemble to Ascot."

"And you shall require a whole new wardrobe in order to fit into Society, Mother. Please don't say no," Lori added. Then she played her trump card. "Remember, you're not conducting business with stodgy old men in trade now. You're strolling among the ranks of the peerage."

"I shall make an appointment with the dressmaker," Tilda said before Miranda could protest.

"Why do I feel as I did after Lionel Wingate bought the Wrexham Iron Foundry right out from under me?" Miranda asked rhetorically.

Perhaps if she had not been so preoccupied with her own guilt and the pain of self-sacrifice, she might have noted the conspiratorial grins Tilda and Lori exchanged behind her back.

Brand sat on the hard, uncomfortable railway seat with Lori by his side for the short trip to Windsor. From there they would travel by carriage to Ascot, but his mind was far from horse racing now. Mrs. Auburn and her maid Tilda shared the small private car, sitting directly across from them. Mother and daughter talked of the splendid weather, such a delightful break from the incessant rain which had quite spoiled the spring of that year.

"I feared our whole summer season would be ruined if the rain didn't stop," Lori said.

"Far more than the social season still remains in jeopardy. Crops are rotting in the fields, and the economic consequences of that could be dire indeed," Miranda chided.

"Mother always turns any conversation to business," Lori said to the baron.

"Your mother is right," Brand replied, nodding to Miranda. "My own crops will be a total loss if the rain returns." He didn't care a fig about that dilemma at the moment. All he could think of was the way she returned his gaze. The way she looked. He tried not to stare, certain that he had made an ass of himself when he arrived to pick them up for the ride to the station.

He still could not believe the transformation. Miranda had gone from cold, drab, no-nonsense business woman to this elegant, strikingly alluring female who sat next to her exotic East Indian servant. If Tilda had the slightest trace of a smirk on her face, he was too preoccupied with her mistress to notice.

Was it the color of the sea-blue gown or its fit? Was it the new soft hairdo with burnished curls surrounding her face, or the large hat swathed in lace perched atop her elegant head? Her eyes glowed like silvery waters, and her smile . . . somehow that had changed, too. It had always been radiant when turned on Lori, but now it seemed open for the whole world to admire. She appeared truly younger now. He'd caught the illusion of youth earlier, in brief flashes, but now he could see that she must have wed and borne her child at a very early age. Yet she hid behind a facade of clipped severity and ugly clothing.

Why?

The question tantalized him, and he vowed to solve the riddle that was Miranda Auburn. Lorilee's question broke into his thoughts, making him feel guilty for paying so much attention to her mother when it was the girl to whom he should be attentive. But the subject of her discourse only made matters worse.

"Is not Mother's new gown simply smashing?" she asked ingenuously.

"Yes, it is," he said with what he hoped was a neutral smile. The problem was he could not stop talking at that point. "Blue flatters you, ma'am."

"Oh, it isn't merely blue," Lori exclaimed. "Why are men so color-blind? It is the most brilliant deep turquoise."

"I stand corrected," he said with a grin for Lorilee, but quickly found his attention drifting back to her mother.

"That shade brings out the highlights in Mother's hair. It flatters her complexion and turns her eyes a silvery color."

Brand could not have said it better himself. Miranda's hair was a burnished halo surrounding her face, which glowed with youthful color. And those eyes . . . He gave himself a mental shake when Miranda broke into her daughter's recitation.

"I, for one, believe gray is more appropriate for me, but I was overruled," she said.

"Now, why do I have the feeling that seldom happens?" he responded with a glint in his eyes.

"Never in matters of business," she replied flatly, daring him.

"It's good that you're willing to take advice . . . from time to time."

"Only in regard to unessential matters, such as fashions." Casting an amused look from her daughter to her maid, then back to him, Miranda said, "I can be influenced . . . up to a point. But gray *is* more practical for business."

"Perhaps. But this isn't business. Today is the Ascot," Brand countered. Were her drab clothes necessary for the sort of work she did? He doubted that, but she appeared to believe it. Or perhaps that facade made her feel safer in the world of men. It seemed to him that looking as she did now would make her associates do anything she asked without question. But somehow he knew that Miranda Auburn would never do business using feminine wiles. She'd think it was contemptible.

"Everyone who attends Ascot simply must dress festively. Why, Abigail Warring and I spent hours and hours deciding what to wear and how to coordinate slippers, reticules and parasols. And, of course, our hats. One has to be ever so careful to select just the right accoutrements . . ."

As she continued to prattle about fashions, Lori pretended oblivion to the way the baron was studying her mother, but winked quickly at Tilda. Things were going just as they had hoped.

Uncomfortable with Caruthers's gaze on her, Miranda decided to shift the conversation in more suitable directions. Lori was babbling with uncharacteristic loquaciousness. What the devil had gotten into her shy daughter? This must certainly be off-putting for a man of the major's background. Perhaps if she could steer Lori to their mutual passion, horses? More easily said than done.

Normally a sharp and witty conversationalist and downright keen debater in business matters, she found herself almost tongue-tied when she opened her mouth to speak. If only the major would stop looking at her the way he did. She felt mesmerized by those intense gold tiger's eyes, immobilized like a butterfly skewered by pins. "Do the Americans hold horse races similar to Ascot, my lord?" she finally managed.

"Across the border states where I grew up, folks always loved horse races, but they're not grand like the Ascot."

His slow, lazy drawl seemed to mock her ever so subtly, as if he were aware of the effect his attention had on her. "Really?" was all she could manage in response.

He shook his head. "No fashion shows, no box seats or places where the better sort can keep from mixing with riffraff."

"Riffraff? So much for your vaunted American democracy," Miranda jibed.

"But your drab gray clothes would fit right in there in the backwoods," Brand jibed right back.

"You mean there is no royal box?" Lori interjected ingenuously before her mother could launch a retort.

"No president's box either," he teased. "We don't even have fancy painted fences to keep the crowds under control. Often they run right onto the track and fights break out."

"It sounds like quite an adventure," Lori said melodramatically.

"I fear you wouldn't like it. The race courses are muddy or dusty depending on weather, and often cover rough terrain. Men bet large sums of money on their stables, but society isn't organized around elegant events like the Ascot. Kentucky planters did form a Jockey Club back in 1797."

Miranda could not help raising one eyebrow and smiling wryly. "That long ago? Imagine!" she murmured.

"I realize by English standards, a mere seventy years is nothing. I suppose three hundred years is considered uncouthly recent for a title," Brand parried, knowing full well the Rushcroft barony had been in his family for over twice that. And he knew that Miranda knew it.

She smiled. "I sometimes wonder, Major, of which you are more proud—your title or your horses."

"Of both, I expect. Without my horses, I have no hope of proving myself worthy of the Caruthers name in England."

"But you're the baron. You don't need to *do* anything," Lori said, genuinely puzzled by this enigma of a man. Far better that her mother deal with him than she.

"Ah, but Lord Rushcroft was raised with an American work ethic," Miranda said archly. Her eyes danced as she added slyly, "Now who's the Puritan, Major?"

"I strive never to allow it to interfere with pleasure," he drawled, eliciting a flush from Miranda.

Although Lori didn't understand the allusion, she knew the two of them were flirting. And that was exactly what she wanted. She would have rubbed her hands in glee if she could have. Tilda merely sat back and smiled as serenely as a mysterious Indian goddess.

Chapter Nine

When they arrived at the train station, a slightly built, light-skinned man of mixed race waited on the platform. His short-cut nappy hair was liberally flecked with gray, but there was an ageless quality and a keen zest for life in his lithe step and open smile when he responded to Brand's greeting.

So this was the remarkable Mr. St. John, Miranda thought, but her eyes quickly shifted back to the tall, whipcord-lean body of the baron. It was a pleasure to study him while he was not looking and the others were engaged in conversation. She had not been altogether happy to see Abigail Warring and her new fiancé, Jonathon Belford, Varley's heir, arriving with the whole of the earl's overbearing family. But Abbie was Lori's good friend, and now that Lori had secured a titled gentleman as a suitor, she was once more in the good graces of the little snob. Miranda detested such shallow behavior, but if her daughter could forgive Abbie, so be it.

She returned her attention to the major, wondering what

he and his friend were discussing so earnestly. Whatever it was, it surely must be more interesting than anything being discussed by the others.

"I've investigated the bets placed, and your guess was right. Winters is burning money he does not have," Sin said to Brand.

"Any idea where he continues to get the funding for his folly? What of O'Connell?"

St. John shrugged. "He appears to have dropped from the face of the earth. Nowhere to be found about the race-course."

"I wish we knew what's afoot here. I'll need you to help me keep an eye out for Mrs. Auburn's safety. The crowds at Ascot will be large, and there could be another attempt on her life."

"From the looks of that maidservant, I doubt our services as guards will be required. If looks could kill, she'd skewer any man alive who laid a hand on her charges."

"Tilda?" Brand echoed, looking across the platform to where the women stood, chatting with Lorilee's friends. The Indian woman stood like a sentinel towering protectively over the Auburn women.

"So that's the long Meg's name." At Brand's puzzled look, he explained, "An archaic term for a maiden lady, but particularly apropos in this case. Tilda appears as formidable as a Valkyrie."

"More like Kali, given her ancestry." Brand had never thought of the quiet woman as formidable. "Don't tell me you're smitten?"

St. John stroked his chin consideringly. "I always did fancy tall women. So she's Indian. Tilda, hmmm . . ."

As if she knew they were discussing her, Tilda turned her head and stared at St. John with penetrating dark eyes. Her expression was unreadable.

"I think you have your work cut out for you," Brand said with a chuckle.

"So do you," his friend replied, noting the way Mrs. Auburn studied the baron out of the corner of her eye. He made no further comment.

The Mountjoys' private box was situated so as to give the best view of the horses as they came into the homestretch, but the ladies were more immediately concerned with seeing and being seen as they paraded around the seats greeting old friends effusively. Parasols twirled, fans fluttered, and huge hats so top-heavy they should have sent their diminutive wearers tumbling to the ground bobbed up and down like dinghies at high tide.

A sea of bright colors swirled beneath the glorious midday sun as emerald silks vied with violet linens, interspersed by the more demure pastels and whites of the young debutantes on the marriage mart. The ladies bussed cheeks and hugged each other, exclaiming in delight over the latest fashions. Gentlemen in dark coats and tall hats exchanged jovial handshakes and studied racing programs, making personal wagers and discussing the merits of various entries.

"Will you have an entry next year, Rushcroft?" the Earl of Varley asked Brand. A large man outrunning portliness in favor of fat, the earl had ginger hair going gray and a perpetually sour expression.

Brand found him pretentious and boring, but since he was a fellow Conservative in the House of Lords, the baron was pleasant, smiling as he replied, "I have several possibilities. Whether I will attempt to qualify depends on my trainer's decision."

"Eh? That blackamoor we saw at the station? Was he one of your slaves from America?" Varley asked, his mouth frozen in a downturn, as if he perpetually sucked on a prune.

"Mr. St. John has always been a free man, and he's English, not American," Brand replied with a lift of his eyebrows.

Standing with the countess and several of her intolerable friends, Miranda eavesdropped on the conversation across the box, smiling faintly as Brand explained about his friend's background and invaluable skills.

Lori took time from critiquing the fashion show when the royal carriage procession began. As she sat in awe of the pomp and circumstance, she noticed her mother's attention once more surreptitiously drifting toward the baron. She would have been pleased if Geoffrey Winters had not just taken a seat in the adjoining box with his new bride.

Mrs. Winters was plain as a wren with mousy tan hair and a plump face. Her narrow, shrewd eyes missed little. Lori turned her back when Geoffrey looked over toward her and dared to nod as if they were casual acquaintances. Then while everyone's attention was fixed on Her Majesty's procession to the royal box, Lori was handed a note by one of Mountjoy's footmen.

Opening it, Lori suppressed a gasp of indignation, feeling Geoffrey Winters's eyes on her. It was written in his hand, offering her the exalted honor of becoming his mistress.

"What is it, dearheart?" Miranda asked, leaning over to her daughter to be heard over the noise of the crowd.

Without a word, Lori showed the missive to her mother, noting with satisfaction the way Winters blanched. Could he have been that sure of her? That arrogant? That *stupid!* Before Miranda could say a word, Lori snatched the note back and stood up.

"Now, Lorilee, do not do anything—"

Before her mother's words of caution could delay her, she made her way calmly to the velvet-trimmed railing dividing their box from Falconridge's. Leaning over, she waved to Mrs. Winters and said in a clear voice, "Your husband sent this to me by mistake, I'm quite certain. Perhaps you need to straighten out the misunderstanding?"

Almost grudgingly, the earl's daughter motioned for one of her servants to fetch the missive from Lori. Meanwhile, her husband quickly made his way from the box, red-faced and muttering curses beneath his breath.

Smiling beatifically, Lorilee Auburn returned to her seat.

"That wasn't quite in the spirit of charity . . . but it's precisely what I would've done," Miranda said with a chuckle.

"I hope she has her father cut off every farthing to the rotter," Lori said with a grim smile.

Miranda was relieved. Her daughter was well and truly done with that bounder.

Brand, too, had observed the sequence of events and put two and two together. It might do to keep a very close eye on young Winters.

Several boxes down, Reba Wilcox watched the exchange with interest. Young Winters would always be a skirt-chaser. But more interesting yet was the way Brand treated his young lady fair. He was polite and deferential, but Reba remembered how different it had been when he'd courted her. Why, he was paying more attention to the mother than the daughter! And Mrs. Auburn was aware of him in a way no prospective mother-in-law should be.

A slow smile spread across Reba's face. Surely it couldn't be . . . but she believed it was true. The girl bored him, which didn't surprise her. Nor did it seem unreasonable that the rich widow would be smitten by his charms. Those circumstances would work perfectly into her plans if she played her cards with care. Unlike Geoffrey Winters, Reba was a very good gambler. . . .

"Isn't that your countrywoman, Mrs. Wilcox?" Miranda asked Brand when Reba's vivid red dress caught her eye.

"Leave it to Reba to end up next to the royal box. She always picked winners," he said with cynical amusement.

"You were more than friends back in Kentucky, were you not?"

He gave her a sardonic lift of one eyebrow. "You know we were engaged to be married . . . before the small inconvenience of the war intervened. Reba doesn't like to be inconvenienced."

What Miranda really wanted to know was whether he'd ever bedded the witch, but there was no way on earth propriety would allow her to ask that! She was shocked she even dared to think it, much less imagine the two of them in a torrid embrace. Miranda had never been jealous in her life. The emotion took her utterly by surprise. Why, oh why, had she ever brought up the subject of that hateful woman? Before her wayward tongue could stop, she found herself saying, "I can scarcely credit Lady Ashworth inviting her here. After all, she's been widowed less than a year."

"And dressed in red," he added, knowing how it offended Miranda's sense of decorum.

"Ah, but with that touch of black lace to signify how much she mourns her loss."

He grinned at her. "Naughty lady, sheathe those claws."

She resisted returning the smile, appalled by her own lack of charity, not to mention other more grievous sins. "I fear I must warn you, Major, that my daughter shares my vindictive nature." She knew he'd relish the set-down Lori had given Winters, so she described it in detail. After all, it was her role to promote the happiness of her child, not steal it away.

As if she could divert the attention of an eligible young peer such as Caruthers from a beauty like Lori!

They spent the afternoon watching the races and cheering for the horses in Mountjoy's stables and other favorites upon whom the gentlemen had placed bets. Many racing enthusiasts among the aristocracy spoke with the baron about his now famous Midnight Reiver and when they might purchase his stud services, as well as discussing which of his get would be entered in next year's races at Ascot.

By evening, everyone was hoarse, sunburned and quite exhausted as they returned to the railway station. The Belfords, who had come from their country seat, were now returning to London and invited the Auburns and the baron to join them in their car. Sin, who had spent the preceding day around the track, rode in the servants' car with the aloof Tilda. Brand watched the two of them disappear down the narrow corridor and smiled to himself. Although slender, she was strong and wiry, nearly a foot taller than the diminutive former jockey. "A challenge for Sin indeed," he murmured to himself as he entered the Varleys' ostentatious accommodations for what he knew would prove an interminably boring ride to London.

In the servants' car things were far from dull.

Tilda Shankhar watched the baron's dandyish little horse trainer approach her the way she would view an invasion of army ants.

Sin bowed before Tilda with a rakish elegance that would have made his English father proud, sweeping his bowler hat to his chest with a flourish. "Gideon Hercules St. John, at your service. I am Lord Rushcroft's trainer and stablemaster. May I have the honor of taking that seat?" He motioned to the seat adjacent to her. There were quite a few unoccupied in the car.

"I am aware of your position, Mr. St. John. It is, after all, far shorter than mine." She turned her head and gazed out the window, dismissing him.

"In terms of nearness to the heavens, I would most certainly agree, but here on earth . . ." He shrugged. "You are a ladies maid and I an entrepreneur who has won great prizes. My size has been a considerable advantage over the years . . . in more ways than you have yet to imagine."

Tilda arched her spine in affront and fixed him with a steely glare. "For all your fancy airs, you are a vulgar rascal without proper regard for a lady."

"Show me a lady and I'll show proper regard."

"You are rude as well as bawdy!"

"You were the one who was first rude. But no matter," he said, taking the seat anyway, "for I prefer my women like my horses, with spirit."

"If your head stood as high as your opinion of yourself, you would be seven feet tall! How dare you, you gnattish creature, to presume that I'd ever take up with racing riff-raff?" She looked around the car, but no one appeared to be paying any mind to her angry outburst.

"You took my meaning clearly enough, did you not? That's how I dare." He grinned at her, revealing a set of dazzling perfect teeth.

Tilda scooted against the window. He made no move to crowd her but left the space between them on the seat. "Go away," she gritted out.

"And deprive you of information vital for the safety of our employers? That would be remiss of us both. We should work in tandem, I think."

She harrumphed at the last bawdy remark, but turned to him, curious in spite of her temper. "What information?" she asked with a suspicious glint in her eyes.

"Someone intends harm to Mrs. Auburn."

"Nonsense. She merely had a carriage accident."

"Oh, and what of the attempted robbery at the opera?"

She looked around to see if anyone was near enough to overhear them. Satisfied of their privacy, she turned back to him. "Very well. What do you know about it? And no more nonsense about my becoming your... woman."

As he began explaining, he knew he had her... in more ways than one.

On the ride back to the city, Lori knew that her mother was watching her as she babbled on about the ladies' hats at Ascot and how grand the carriages had been and all the other frivolous matters with which young girls unwittingly tortured their suitors. Her chatter was, however, quite deliberate. She showed little interest in discussing the horses that had run. She intended the baron to realize how hopelessly mismatched they were. But not before he also realized how well matched he and her mother were.

This would have been far easier if her mother did not know her quite so well. Miranda was suspicious about why Lori had suddenly overcome her natural reticence and become so garrulous. There was also the danger that if she overplayed her hand, Lord Rushcroft might just cry off in disgust. She needed to discuss how to handle this with Tilda as soon as possible.

That very evening, Miranda cooperated by going to her office to review the cables from America which Mr. Aimesley had sent while they were in the country. Still dressed and sitting up in her bed, surrounded by dozens of puffy pillows, Lorilee schemed and waited for Tilda, who entered the room sporting a frown.

"You look as if you'd just stepped on something Marm brought in," she said curiously. "What's wrong?"

Tilda muttered beneath her breath, something about arrogant stablemen not knowing their place as she laid out Lori's night rail and robe.

"Oh!" the girl exclaimed. "It's that man who works for the baron, the horse trainer, Mr. St. John, isn't it?" She knew how zealously Tilda cherished her independence, swearing never to marry again since narrowly escaping death by suttee when her elderly husband had died in India. "You rode with him in the servants' car."

"The longest railway ride of my life," Tilda said darkly.

"The baron believes him to be the finest horse trainer in all of England or America. And he's exceedingly well educated. I rather hoped you would find him charming," Lori teased.

Tilda harrumphed and gave an innocent pillow a fluffing that nearly caused it to rupture. "Matchmaking for your mother is quite sufficient, young lady. You don't need to concern yourself with me. If I ever *would*—and mark me when I stress the conditional tense—consider another marriage, it certainly would not be to an arrogant popinjay such as that one."

Lori knew when a change of subject was judicious. "Speaking of matchmaking, I think Mother is becoming suspicious of my antics. We need to find a way to keep them together before my magpie imitation drives the poor man to distraction."

"Or your mother figures out what you're about." Tilda calmed down and took a seat in a delicate rocker as Lori changed into her nightclothes.

"Perhaps we could hold a dinner party and invite some of the baron's political friends," the girl called out from behind her dressing screen. "They would talk politics and forget about me."

"Perhaps. But you must speak to His Lordship soon."

Lori reached for the glass of warm milk Tilda had

brought her, a nightly ritual since she'd been a tot. "What do you mean, 'speak to him'?"

"You need to explain the truth to him and enlist him in our deception so that he can win your mother."

Lori made a most unladylike noise when milk backed up in her throat and nose. Coughing, she finally got out, "Tell him the truth? You mean that I don't want to marry him but my mother does!"

Tilda rocked calmly. "Just so."

"B-but . . . how can I . . . what will he . . . oh, dear." What had been an amusing game of wits suddenly promised to become a very daunting face-off with a man who still half frightened her.

"Yes, 'oh, dear,' " Tilda echoed dryly. "You must do so quickly." Her amusement with Lori's predicament turned to concern as she thought about the danger to Miranda that that dreadful St. John had outlined for her. "It is imperative that the baron or someone in his employ accompany your mother at all times when she goes out."

She explained what Sin had told her about the relationship between the incident at the opera, the attempt to burn the baron's mews and the carriage crash. White-faced, Lori sat on the edge of the bed, listening with growing horror. "Lord Rushcroft was certain someone had tried to harm Mother that day in Hyde Park. So was I. Who could be behind this whole monstrous thing?"

"That is what the baron and his stablemaster are trying to find out. They suspect Geoffrey Winters may be involved," she added, studying the girl's reaction.

"I would not be in the least surprised," Lorilee replied coldly.

Brand discussed the voting reform proposals being debated in Parliament with Lord Pell and the Honorable Mr. Reed, M.P. They were joined in the Auburn parlor by several other members of Lords and Commons. Two of the gentlemen he had met since arriving in London, but the other three were business associates of the widow's. Liberals outnumbered Conservatives, and the debate was quite lively.

While the men argued, their wives and daughters clustered at the opposite end of the large room, looking through an enormous volume of photographs. Lori, as usual, was the center of attention, giggling and laughing as she described the pictures. Miranda had not yet put in an appearance, owing to an unexpected business emergency. Brand found his attention drifting from the debate as he watched the door for her.

Which would she be tonight? The cool, no-nonsense woman of affairs, or the warm, vivid creature who had bewitched him at Ascot? Guiltily he turned his eyes back to Lori, sitting surrounded by the other women—the youngest of the lot by far. *Too young for you.* He sighed, knowing it was true.

What a conundrum his life had become. He had given his word to Miranda Auburn to court her daughter. Made a verbal agreement that would affect the security of hundreds of people who were depending on the new baron. It was a good thing, he thought wryly, that peers could not be placed in prison for debt. Perhaps he could make enough on the racing circuit to hold his ancestral estate together. He had met a few men at Ascot who would pay exorbitant stud fees for Reiver.

But that did not solve the dilemma of Miss Auburn. It was his duty to go through with this marriage. Crying off after escorting Lorilee to so many public functions would humiliate an innocent young woman who believed in his honorable intentions. He could not hurt Lorilee. But he couldn't marry her either. It would not be fair to him or her. She must be the one to break off the courtship before they became formally engaged, an event Miranda had indicated she would announce within a few weeks.

But how the devil could he arrange it without devastating an innocent?

Across the room, Lori hid her nervous anxiety behind a facade of bubbling enthusiasm, laughing over pictures her mother had insisted she pose for from the time she was a small child. The note she had labored over so long seemed to burn through the thin silk of her gown. Tonight was the night she had to speak with the baron alone and tell him that she did not wish to marry him . . . and all the rest.

Even if he did prefer her mother, how the devil could she explain without offending his male vanity?

Just then Miranda entered the room, offering profuse apologies for keeping her guests waiting. She had already done so to the kitchen staff, who were struggling to keep an eight-course meal the proper temperatures after an hour's delay. At once she felt the baron's eyes on her. He stood beneath the massive crystal chandelier, and the light played lovingly in his dark gold hair. Ever the rebel, he still ignored convention, wearing it longer than was fashionable, curling slightly at the snowy collar of his lawn shirt. His face remained clean-shaven in a room filled with beards.

She liked that, just as she liked the way the tailored severity of his black dinner clothes molded to his lean body so perfectly. Most of the gentlemen looked as if they'd slept in their suits, their plump, dumpy bodies swathed in bulky woolens with jeweled stickpins and cuff links gleaming opulently to proclaim their positions. The only jewels apparent on the baron were two amber eyes that met and held hers for a moment frozen in time.

Brand had his question answered. She was utterly smashing in rich bronze brocade. The gown was cut severely, without the ruffles and furbelows so in vogue for a formal dinner party. But it suited her quite perfectly. The shade provided a striking complement to her coloring, setting off her dark red hair with brilliant highlights. The formidable Tilda must have worked her magic with it, for it was styled in loose curls and looped atop her head, accenting her high cheekbones and softening her determined jawline. At her neckline and ears, fire opals sparkled in antique settings, bringing out the silvery fire of her eyes.

But in spite of her new outer appearance, he still saw beneath the surface a woman in hiding. Was there the faintest hint of a flush to her cheeks as she averted her gaze from his and made her way across the room to greet the ladies? He reined in his wild imagination and concentrated on how he was going to speak to Miss Auburn, reminding himself that once he'd done so, Miranda would despise him. That would put an end to it . . .

Whatever *it* was.

No doubt she would make a formidable enemy. But she also had formidable enemies and someone was trying to kill her. He simply could not leave her before getting to the bottom of that dangerous tangle. This was going to be a long night indeed, he concluded as Miranda announced the pairing-up of ladies with their escorts and the order in which they would proceed into the dining room.

He, of course, was assigned to offer Miss Auburn his arm. Lord Pell, being the ranking peer, was first and Miranda's escort. The widower was seventy if he was a day. Brand watched the old goat's balding head bend close to hers as they chuckled over some joke. What was it about men so much older than she that seemed to draw the confounded woman?

While the servants were clearing the table between the fish course and the main entrée, a huge rack of spring lamb and a venison saddle roast accompanied by multitudinous vegetables, Lori fingered the note in her palm, working up the courage to slip it beneath the table to Lord Rushcroft, who was busily engaged in a heated discussion on tariffs with Miranda and Mr. Baggins.

Brand's hands were occupied in gesturing as he explained the negative effect of foreign competition on home-grown grains. Good heavens, what if she touched his . . . limb when she passed the note! Or some place even worse! Seizing her wineglass, which the thoughtful footman Charles had just refilled with a fine claret to accompany the red meat, she took a deep swallow. No, she would have to wait until dinner was over. But that was the time when the ladies would excuse themselves and allow the gentlemen to remain at table with their port.

Then an inspiration came to her. She would have one of the footmen give the note to the baron. Of course, why had she not thought of it before? *Because you have been so terrified, you haven't even had the courage to confess it to Tilda*, she admonished herself.

She took another swallow of wine. The room was growing rather warm in spite of the cooling breeze from the windows opening onto the garden. She looked down at the slices of pink lamb surrounded by creamed turnips and fresh peas. Lori smiled gratefully at the footman Charles, who knew she detested venison.

Charles! She must give the note to him and instruct him. Once the baron had read it, they could slip away while everyone else was occupied in the parlor. When Charles returned to take her plate, virtually untouched although she'd emptied her wineglass, Lori slipped the note to the infatuated young servant. She murmured instructions over the cover of laughter at an amusing anecdote her mother had just finished telling.

Charles nodded ever so slightly. He had been smitten

with her from a distance since coming to work here two years ago. As the next course of plover's eggs in aspic and a mayonnaise of pheasant was served, she watched him slide the note beneath the baron's plate. When Rushcroft took it surreptitiously and slid it inside his jacket, she breathed a sigh of relief . . . and took another swallow of wine.

Charles was such an attentive dear.

By the time the ladies left the gentlemen, Miranda could see that her daughter was quite tipsy. Lori had never done such an unthinkable thing in her life. Her mother would have excused it as a case of nerves—if she had not observed the passing of Lori's note to the baron via that young fool Charles. She would speak to him about such antics, not to mention the way he overattentively refilled her daughter's wineglass.

In the meanwhile, she had to see that Lori retired before social disaster befell. As they made their way down the hall to the parlor, she took her daughter's arm and, begging the other ladies to pardon them and proceed, guided her into the nearest sitting room.

"You are unwell and must immediately retire to bed. I shall make your excuses," she said crisply as soon as the door closed behind them.

"I . . . that is, what . . ." Lori's tongue suddenly seemed to trip over itself. Forming a coherent thought became inexplicably difficult.

Miranda continued, "You have had too much wine and I fear you'll disgrace yourself. And that is not accounting for the note to the baron."

"You saw it!" Lori squeaked. Suddenly the room began to spin about her.

"Where did you intend to meet him? In the garden?" Miranda asked, torn between anger at Lori's uncharacteristically scandalous behavior and sheer amazement that her shy child would have the nerve to set up a tryst. Something was definitely amiss here.

In the back of her mind a thought hovered like a vulture waiting to pounce: Was she concerned about Lori's reputation . . . or was she jealous? She suppressed the absurd idea. She was Mrs. Will Auburn, unshakable woman of business who never lost her calm sense of direction. "I will deal with the baron if he dares to tryst with you. You will go to bed at once," she said to the befuddled Lori.

But her daughter was not quite so addled as Miranda presumed. One thought flashed into her aching head: her mother and the baron alone . . . in the garden. Perhaps things would work out in spite of her incapacity. With a sickly nod of acquiescence, Lori murmured, "As you wish, Mother."

Brand reread the note for the tenth time as he stood in a dark corner of the library, inhaling the fragrance of a fine Cuban cigar. As if he did not have enough on his mind, that damnable Callie, mother of the army of attack kittens, sat quietly on the mantel. Sneaky beast. How had she slipped away from her assigned quarters? Across the room, none of the other gentlemen paid her any mind. She stared at Brand with basilisk eyes, as if mocking him for flinching when he saw her.

Just to show her who was the human in charge—and to put off deciding what to do about the note he had just read—he walked back to the cat. Taking a deep breath, he reached up and gave her a pat. She stood up, arching her back. Brand almost jumped out of his skin. He leaped away, praying the other gentlemen would not notice. Then he realized she had begun to purr. She wanted him to pet her some more.

Callie looked at him with an expression that indicated

precisely how dense the superior feline race felt mere humans could be. Dare he take another stab at detente? Stepping up to the mantel again, he ran his hand down her back once more as she bowed up and preened. Growing bolder, he scratched her behind one ear and she nuzzled his hand affectionately, then ran her raspy tongue across his fingers. Amazing! Cats reciprocated affection just as dogs and horses did.

Emboldened, he gave her several more strokes before one of his companions called out to him. They were discussing how excellent Mrs. Auburn's choice of cigars was. The luxury was often frowned upon in polite society because Her Majesty disapproved of smoking. Congratulating himself on his first bold step in overcoming a lifelong fear, the baron deserted Callie and strolled back to rejoin the conversation. But in spite of his triumph, the note he'd received continued to burn a hole in his pocket.

He had seen the footman slip it beneath his plate, but who the devil had it come from? It was written on the expensive velum letterhead of the Auburn family, but unsigned. He could not imagine the timid Lorilee asking him to meet her in the garden unchaperoned. So, he concluded, it must have come from her mother. How amazing. What could she want to discuss that couldn't wait until tomorrow? Perhaps she had learned something regarding the attempts on her life.

He would meet the formidable widow and find out.

Chapter Ten

When the ladies and gentlemen reassembled in the parlor, Miranda made Lorilee's apologies, saying her daughter had taken suddenly ill with a headache. However, their hostess insisted that the party should continue. Brand tried catching her eye as he edged toward the door, but Mrs. Frobisher, the elderly M.P.'s wife, cornered him before he could make his escape to the garden unnoticed.

Thank heavens the woman was myopic. When he excused himself to have a word with her husband across the room, she could not see that he slipped out the door instead. He expected Miranda to join him as soon as she could get away, but several moments passed and still she did not appear. They had to be discreet, so he understood the delay.

He strolled through the garden, which was cool and dimly lit by a couple of gaslights gleaming dully through the lush foliage. Lacy shadows swayed with the gentle summer breeze. Several marble statues of execrable taste were scattered about the elaborate topiary. Will Auburn had designed this garden to impress everyone with his wealth. Brand was certain of it. The same was true of the house and its interior. Auburn's home was a monstrosity of neo-Gothic architecture and massive, garishly carved furniture that literally made the floor groan beneath its weight.

It was as if, like their Yankee counterparts, the British noveau riche had to be absolutely certain everyone knew just how wealthy and, hence, how powerful they were. And the only way to do this was through a display of sheer mass. Even a sterling table knife weighed as much as a claymore, Brand thought contemptuously. But he was certain that Miranda Auburn had not chosen such vulgar ostentation. Her own spartan taste in clothing revealed her preference, whether she was dressed to conceal her beauty or to reveal it. No, the late Mr. Auburn was responsible for this mausoleum and all its trappings.

He wondered why she had never changed anything. Most women lived to refurbish their homes. Yet she left everything intact here and at her place of business, formerly her husband's place of business. Brand was growing more than passingly curious about the relationship between young Miranda and the husband who had been more than twice her age when he wed her. What hold from beyond the grave did he have on her?

Dare he ask such a personal question? In the past whenever he became too familiar, she'd given him firm setdowns, but he wanted to understand why such a beautiful woman had sequestered herself behind office walls. A widow of her wealth could have remarried and spent her life in a giddy social whirl. Then he smiled to himself. Miranda was hardly the social sort, much less giddy.

He could tell that she detested the protocol of pairing up dinner partners in order of rank. She'd looked bored to tears by the time the last tablecloth was stripped and the desserts served. If not for the political arguments, which some of the guests found unseemly, she would have nodded off during the soup course. So would he.

Lorilee, on the other hand, loved parties and had bubbled on about fashions, balls and the latest gossip with glee. How could he explain why he could not marry her without crushing her? Oh, he had no illusions that she fancied herself in love with him. She had been too wary and prim to indicate a girlish infatuation whenever they were in close proximity. The preceding week when he'd waltzed with her at the Mountjoys' ball, she had been as tense as a tightly wound watch spring.

But he was, after all, he thought bitterly, a fair catch on the marriage mart for a rich tradesman's daughter— her entrée to the aristocracy. If she lost him, there would be gossip and speculation, the very worst thing for a debutante. He paced back and forth, searching for a way to untangle a Gordian knot, knowing that direct severance was not an option.

A tiny mew distracted him from his troubling thoughts. One of Callie's kittens stood at his feet, poised to climb his pantleg. Emboldened by his luck with the mama, he felt the kitten to be no threat. Its round-eyed little face looked incredibly appealing and innocent in the moonlight. He scooped up the furball and began petting it as he paced. Again he was rewarded with the fierce vibrations of purring. Perhaps he was cured of his phobia of cats, he thought with a small smile. Then again, there still was Marm to consider.

Miranda stood hidden in the shadows of a willow, amazed as she watched him with the kitten. She knew there was little time to dawdle. With Lori already retired, she would be quickly missed. So would the baron. But she could not take her eyes off the way he cradled the small animal so gently in the palm of one hand . . . that scarred hand with its long, elegant fingers. *I cannot think such thoughts!*

What a shambles this whole evening was becoming! She should be furious with her daughter for sending the note and using Dutch courage in order to do it. But instead she forced herself to blame Brandon Caruthers. How dare he respond to such an improper request and endanger Lori's reputation! Fueling herself with righteous indignation, she stepped from the concealment of a willow tree and approached him.

Brand gently set the kitten down. Without turning, he said, "I wondered if it would be you or your daughter."

Caught off guard, she blurted out, "How did you know it was I?" What had made her say such a stupid thing? As his eyes met hers in the moonlight, her breath caught and she fought the instinct to take a step back.

"Your scent," he replied.

She did take a step back. "I do not wear perfume," she replied in as frosty a tone as she could muster, although the moment she said it, she knew that was not what he meant.

His smile was as lazy as his drawl. "I know. It's your essence. Unique. Miss Auburn wears a lovely, light floral perfume. You don't require any artifice besides the lavender you rinse your hair with." Without realizing he was doing it, Brand took another step toward her, closing the distance between them.

This time she stood her ground. "I did not come out here to discuss scents, but sense—as in common sense. And propriety. What ever made you respond to my daughter's request to meet her here? It was ill advised of her, but she's young and inexperienced in such matters. You should know better."

"First of all, since the note wasn't signed, I wasn't sure which of you—"

"You thought I'd arrange a tryst with you in the moon-light?" she practically hissed. The idea that he had come here to meet her was a possibility she did not wish to consider.

"Well," he chuckled, "I confess it didn't seem likely. But I didn't think your daughter would want to 'tryst' with me either. Miss Lorilee isn't exactly starry-eyed with infatuation over me, in case you hadn't noticed. Thinking about it now, I expect that's why she had to work up her courage with all that wine before she could face me."

Miranda groaned. "You noticed her overindulgence. I suppose everyone else has, too. I don't know what's gotten into her."

"She didn't tell you why she sent the note, which I assume you saw me receive."

Miranda shook her head. "Yes . . . that is, I saw that footman—who *is* infatuated—with *her*—pass you the note. Unfortunately, she was in no condition to explain it."

"Then wouldn't it have been wiser to let me stew out here after you sent her to her room?"

The question was quite reasonable, but at the moment, Miranda was feeling anything but reasonable. "I felt you deserved a proper dressing down for taking advantage of an innocent."

"As I said, I doubt that your daughter's intent was ro-mantic. I merely wanted to see who'd show up . . ." He let the words trail away as his eyes moved slowly down her neck to the soft pale flesh voluptuously revealed by her evening gown. The sudden urge to reach out and trace his fingertips across her collarbone took him utterly by surprise. So much so he nearly did it. "Miranda . . ."

"I have not given you permission to use my Christian name, Major! And I find your behavior most offensive." She brought her hand up to her throat, as if to conceal the pounding of her pulse. "You are my daughter's suitor, not mine," she said, as much to remind herself as to remind him.

"I apologize, ma'am. You're quite right," he said softly.

"I believe our agreement may not be working out to my expectations." She struggled for icy hauteur but managed only breathless wariness.

"Miss Lorilee is as skittish as a colt around me," he agreed thoughtfully. *So are you.* "Do you think she's changed her mind? That could be what she wanted to tell me tonight."

It made sense, but Miranda was in no condition to think straight with those hot tiger's eyes watching her. Yet she stood rooted to the ground like the damned willow tree, unable to move as he stepped closer and raised his hand, then lowered it when she finally managed to get out, "Yes, it might be that. I . . . I shall have to speak with her."

The world spun and her heart pounded as if it would burst from her chest. She was acting like a moonstruck girl! He was years her junior and an utter rogue. Had she imagined that he had nearly touched her—in a most improper way? Or, worse yet, was it just her own foolish fantasy?

Suddenly a voice called out into the darkness, "Mrs. Auburn?" It was Fitzsimmons, the butler.

"I shall be in momentarily, Mr. Fitz," she managed to reply as she turned away from Brand.

He let her go. Every fiber of his being ached to touch her, but he knew that to do so was folly. Instead he called after her softly, "Miranda . . . 'Oh, brave new world that has such creatures in it!'"

She spun around. "Your recall of Shakespeare is faulty. The proper line is 'O, brave new world that has such people in't.' Miranda is speaking to Ferdinand, not he to her," she snapped. Then she vanished into the house.

Well, he'd truly jumped into the hog wallow now. Damn, what was he thinking? There would be no money to rebuild the Rushcroft estate if their agreement was broken. He stood to lose everything. But he'd been thinking all evening of nothing but a way to let down Lorilee Auburn gently. Why had he not simply explained that to her mother?

But no, he had practically stalked Miranda Auburn as if he intended to seduce her in the moonlight. As if a woman like she would allow such an outrageous thing! Brand walked around the willow, combing his fingers through his hair as he struggled to make sense of what had just happened between them. When the kitten reappeared, he picked it up without thinking. Stroking its soft fur soothed his troubled thoughts.

Ever since Ascot, he had been struck by Miranda's surprising beauty. But even before that, something . . . elusive had attracted him to her. And, unless he was misreading all the signs—something he seldom did where women or horses were concerned—she was equally attracted to him.

Where might it lead? *Madness!*

Brand prayed that his sudden insight into what Lorilee had wanted to say to him was correct. She was the wronged party in this whole mess. The last thing he'd ever intended was to hurt her. Then he smiled ruefully. With a protective mama bear like the widow looking out for her welfare, Miss Lori would emerge unscathed. He only wished he could say the same for himself.

"Ooh, my head," Lori whimpered as she clutched her stomach, doubling over so her throbbing skull rested between her knees. She was huddled wretchedly in the middle of her bed. "I'm afraid I'm going to die," she moaned.

"Never worry. In a bit you'll be more afraid that you're

going to live," Tilda replied briskly, propping pillows behind the girl.

"What would I do without your tender sympathies?" Lori croaked as the older woman gently helped her lean back.

"Here, drink this."

"Ugh," Lori turned her head from the toxic-smelling brew in the cup. "What is it?"

"An old remedy the Sergeant Major used to mix up when he'd overindulged in gin." The Sergeant Major was Tilda's English guardian, the man who'd saved her life in India and brought her to England when he retired from the army.

"Will it help?" Lori asked dubiously, taking a tiny sip.

"I don't know. You drank wine, not gin, but I imagine it's worth trying, wouldn't you say? I would if my skin were as green as yours."

Lori swallowed down several more sips, pulling an awful face as she did so. "Anything to relieve my head and my tummy."

"What on earth possessed you to do such a foolish thing? You don't even *like* wine, for pity's sake." Tilda asked.

"Has Mother inquired about me?" Lori asked, eyeing the door nervously.

"She received an urgent transatlantic wire from Mr. Aimesley and had to meet with her associates in the City early this morning. I imagine she'll be 'inquiring' as soon as she returns home," Tilda replied dryly.

Lori polished off the rest of the foul concoction in one gulp. "Then I must use this time to my advantage since I made such a botch of matters last evening. Did Mother mention anything about the baron when she was retiring last night?"

Tilda was the one to look dubious as Lori climbed from

the bed and stood unsteadily. "No, she did not. What botch last evening?"

"Send for a bath and help me select my clothes while I explain," Lori replied.

She still looked a bit green about the gills, but the Sergeant Major's remedy appeared to work better on wine than gin. It had never worked all that well for the dear old man. Perhaps Lori's recovery was due to the resilience of youth.

Tilda listened as Lori explained about the note and her lack of courage which resulted in . . . she was not exactly sure what. "So, you see, I think she went to the garden in my place to give him a set-down . . . or . . ."

Tilda appeared thoughtful. "Knowing your mother, I'd rather lean to the set-down than to anything romantic. Although, heaven knows, she is attracted to the man. Now that I think of it, she was rather tense and uncommunicative last night, and then that wire arrived before anyone but the kitchen staff was up. As soon as I delivered it to her, she was out of here in a flurry."

"That may not give us much time."

Tilda's slim black eyebrow arched. "Us?"

"Why, yes. I can hardly go to the city house of a bachelor unaccompanied, can I?"

Sin opened the door at Brandon Caruthers's townhouse. As an economy, they had let go all the staff except for a tweenie, a footman and a beastly cook who insisted on boiling every morsel that came into his kitchen. Both of St. John's eyebrows arched in amazement when he beheld the statuesque Miss Tilda standing on the stoop.

"You," was her greeting.

"Good morning to you, as well, my Indian Goliath," he said, sketching a bow.

She harrumphed and asked, "Is His Lordship receiving?"

"That might depend on who's calling."

Just then, overhearing them, Brand walked into the foyer. "Miss Tilda, please come in. Is something amiss at the Auburn household?"

"Oh, something's amiss all right," she replied as she stepped inside. "And she's waiting in the carriage to speak with you." Before Tilda could turn around, she heard the soft scampering of Lori's footsteps as the girl dashed from the unmarked hansom they'd hired and up the steps to the door.

"Is there a place where we could speak privately, my lord?" she asked nervously.

He gestured to his study. "My honor, Miss Auburn. Does your mother know you're here?" He knew damn well Miranda Auburn would skin them both if she did.

"Of course not," Lorilee replied as if he were as dense as Manchester iron. She stepped inside the study, resolved to speak her mind and straighten out the tangle they'd all three created.

"Sin, if you'd be so kind as to entertain Miss Tilda?" Brand said to his friend. "I believe the cook has some coffee on the fire." He closed the door, leaving the two antagonists facing off in the hall.

"Probably as thick as the silt on the banks of the Thames by now," St. John replied, turning to the woman in question.

Quite literally looking down her nose at him, Tilda said, "I don't suppose anything as civilized as a cup of good English tea is available." It was not a question.

"I rather imagine the cook, whatever his deficiencies, can manage tea." Sin added beneath his breath, "Whether or not it's *good* is highly conjectural." He gave her a mocking smile. "If you'd be so kind as to follow me?" He led the way into the front parlor.

Tilda stood rooted to the floor, aghast. "You'd dare to entertain someone in His Lordship's parlor?"

St. John shrugged. "Well, I apologize for it's being a bit on the tatty side, but one does what one can."

"This is highly irregular. What kind of a servant are you? I thought those of your race in America were until very recently enslaved."

Entering the parlor as if fully expecting her to follow, he turned and stood arrogantly by the bell pull, yanking on it to summon the cook. "I am not a house servant but Brand's horse trainer and master of his stables, a position I held for many years prior to the late conflict in America. As to your second remark, neither am I American nor have I ever been a slave. Now please have a seat."

She entered the room but continued standing, obviously uncomfortable. "You're still in the baron's employ and have no right to assume such airs."

"Before he was even in knee britches I was wiping 'the baron's' arse. He'd be the first to tell you."

Tilda blinked. "I see your crudity has not abated since our first encounter. Upper servants ought to know how to conduct themselves with gentility."

He walked closer to her, his cocky stance belying what he said. "Oh, I know the way things are done in jolly old England, and it's pretty much the same way it's done in America. The color of one's skin determines who's in charge. My father had me educated as a white man, but I learned that my *erudition*"—he paused to emphasize the word ironically—"as well as my father's fine family pedigree, gave me not the slightest entrée into Society. Or even into your class of 'upper servants.' Tell me, Miss Tilda, do the white house servants treat you as their equal?"

Before she could reply, the cook, red-faced and belligerent, wearing a greasy apron, appeared in the doorway. "Whot do ye need?"

"A fresh pot of tea and some cream, preferably not curdled, old chap," St. John replied genially.

With a surly nod of acquiescence, the cook departed, muttering imprecations to himself.

Sin turned to Tilda and said, "If he possessed the slightest culinary skills, he'd quit and find other employment."

"Because of you." It was not a question.

"Most assuredly. I overturn the order of the cosmos, don't you know?"

"You'd overturn the patience of a saint," she shot back.

"Are we to continue this sparring match standing? It will prove awkward to manage our tea at the same time."

"You only want me to sit down because my height gives me the advantage." In spite of her words, she perched on the edge of a threadbare settee.

"You may need it," he replied with a grin.

Inside the study, Lorilee had been only too happy to take a seat, simply to keep her knees from giving way beneath her. She'd used up every ounce of her courage by the time the door to the baron's study had closed the two of them inside. Alone. She had never been unchaperoned before—except for those brief stolen moments with Geoffrey Winters, memories that did not soothe her case of nerves. But somehow, she felt this was too private a matter for even her beloved Tilda to witness.

The baron did not ease her discomfort in spite of offering to share the coffee and scones with jam on the breakfast tray at his desk. The very thought of food left her stomach roiling. He had disquieted her from the first moment she'd seen him standing at the foot of the stairs as her suitor. In truth, everything about him frightened her—his arrogant stride, those fierce tiger's eyes, his harshly handsome face disfigured by battle scars from a war she could not even imagine.

Yet she knew her mother did not share her aversion at all. Miranda found him alluring in a way Lorilee could not explain, but then the heart offers no reasons. She clung to that thought and tried to formulate the words for her shocking proposal.

Brand studied the skittish girl. She was like a colt being haltered for the first time. He felt the need to help her. "Do you want to break off our courtship, Miss Auburn?" he asked gently.

She cleared her throat before replying. "No. Quite the contrary. I would ask that you continue calling."

He raised his eyebrows. This certainly wasn't the answer he was expecting! Leaning forward in his chair, he tried to read her expression, but she kept her eyes demurely downcast, fidgeting with her reticule and rearranging her skirts. "Do you fancy marrying me, then, Miss Lorilee?" he asked, holding his breath.

Her head jerked up and their eyes met. "Heavens, no! That is . . . I mean . . ." Her face turned crimson. This was not going at all well!

He threw back his head and laughed in pure relief, then realized he'd offended the shy girl. "Please forgive me. I wasn't laughing at you but at my own arrogance—and confusion. If you don't want to marry me, then why should you not cry off the arrangement? After all, it was your mother who made it for you, not you. I shall make no scandal, but dutifully play the part of a rebuffed swain."

"That would do no good at all. Then how would you and Mother continue to see each other?" Lori blurted out.

The breath seemed to rush from his lungs. His thoughts

scattered to the four winds as his muddled brain tried to analyze their bizarre conversation. This green girl could not have an inkling of the sexual attraction he felt toward her mother . . . could she? Lordy, he certainly hoped not.

"Why would I want to continue seeing your mother if not for you?"

"Do not play the dolt, my lord. It ill becomes a man of your vast experience."

Her exasperated tone set him back. "And my vast age?" he added dryly.

"You are far closer in age to Mother than to me, you must confess." She was warming to her topic at last, sensing that she had the upper hand. The poor fellow simply had no idea that he was in love with her mother. But he would find out soon enough if she had her way. "If you call on us and escort us to social functions, you shall have the opportunity to continue your courtship of my mother."

"Whoa!" he exclaimed. "My courtship of your mother? You're confusing this poor Kentucky lout, baron though I may be."

"Under no other circumstances would she permit you to woo her," Lori continued, undaunted. At his dazed expression, she sighed and pressed on. "Do you think just because I am young that I am also blind?"

He shook his head, as much to clear it as to respond to her. "Miss Auburn, do I understand you correctly? You believe I should use our . . . er, arrangement as a pretext to court your mother?"

"For a 'poor Kentucky lout,' you catch the way the wind is blowing quite well," she replied brightly. "Of course you are attracted to her and she to you. That has been apparent for some time."

"Perhaps to you," he said, feeling a very unaccustomed heat stealing over his own face now. Miranda and he shared a physical attraction, yes, he could not disagree.

But to an innocent like Lorilee that translated to marriage. The very idea that the calculating and highly independent widow would ever consider matrimony again—least of all to him—seemed beyond the improbable.

"I fear I've embarrassed you, my lord, and that was certainly not my intention," Lori said, worrying her lower lip with her teeth as she struggled to convince him of the rightness of her cause. "You were both quite obvious the day of the carriage crash, the way you held on to each other long after it was necessary . . . or, strictly speaking, proper."

"Was that when you conceived this idea?" he asked. Marriage had not been in his plans when he'd come to England. Only when faced with the prospect of utter ruin had he agreed to Miranda's terms regarding a malleable young girl. Marrying the mother was quite another matter. How to explain this tactfully to her daughter, sitting so earnestly across from him?

"I'm not certain when it really began to sift together. Perhaps it was the evening at the opera when . . ." Her words trailed awkwardly away.

"When my violent nature frightened you half to death?" he said quietly. "Being in a war . . . does something to a man."

She met his eyes levelly now. "You and my mother have shared adversity in ways I cannot imagine, nor do I want to. But such bitter experiences have shaped you into people who are naturally attracted to each other."

Brand had always wondered about Miranda's relationship with her husband. She had stressed that he was a kind man, but from all reports of his ruthless business dealings, the baron wondered if that was the truth. "Do you remember your father?"

"Very little, I'm afraid," she replied with a sigh. "I was quite young when he died. He was seldom at home until he fell ill. Then I was kept from his sickroom. Mother was ever so brave, dividing her time between us so I should not be neglected."

"And you'll grow to be just like her some day. All this time, you played the frivolous giggling belle without a thought in her pretty head except fashions and gossip, just so I'd see how much more admirable your mother is than you. Am I right?" He grinned at her, and she nodded.

He read a great deal between the lines of what she'd said about her parents and decided that he wanted to learn more. Not because he harbored any illusions that the widow would allow him to court her. However, there was the matter of the attempts to kill Miranda. But when he started to explain what he and Sin had pieced together, she interrupted.

"Mr. St. John and Tilda have discussed it, and she's explained the connections to me. All the more reason for you to remain close by my mother's side," she cajoled earnestly.

"I'm not at all certain your mother would ever consider marrying me, but until we sort out this whole tangle, I'll continue keeping an eye on you both," he agreed.

"My mother and I are greatly in your debt, Lord Rushcroft," Lori said. She was smiling gamely when they left the study.

She was her mother's daughter, after all.

Chapter Eleven

"I understand a hansom nearly ran your carriage down. It almost overturned. You could've been trampled in the evening traffic." Brand stood in the doorway of her sitting room, glaring accusingly at Miranda, who sat with that huge orange tom on her lap. The battle-scarred beast blinked at him as her hand stroked over his scruffy fur. Brand was too angry to care about the cat.

"As usual, my lord, your information is quite accurate. It was merely one of those mishaps that occur during the press of people, when everyone's rushing madly to get out of the City at day's end—nothing to be upset about," Miranda replied calmly, placing Marm on the chair cushion as she stood up to face her antagonist.

"Nothing to be upset about!" he roared, advancing into the room. "After all that's happened, you surely can't believe it was just another traffic tangle." Brand felt like seizing her and shaking her. After his disconcerting conversation with Lorilee this morning, he suddenly wondered if he actually *was* falling in love with this woman.

Absurd. Then why had he grown icy with fear when Sin had told him about the incident on the Strand? Why had he rushed directly here to assure himself that she was unharmed?

"How could anyone have arranged such a chaotic mess?" she asked reasonably, although her temper was beginning to simmer at his arrogant manner. "A dozen vehicles were involved. I doubt their drivers all wished me ill."

"It would only take one clever man who knows how to sabotage a harness and spook a horse to start the melee. I've seen what bedlam the Strand is at that time of day. We know full well that someone has already tried this sort of 'accident' once before. From now on, you're going nowhere without a guard."

She looked at him as if he'd just proposed she frolic naked in front of Temple Bar. "I beg your pardon?" she said, her temper rising another notch. "I will come and go, and conduct my business as I please. I am not a member of your regiment, Major. In the increasingly unlikely event you ever become a member of this family, you still will not give me orders. I give the orders around here."

"Not to me you don't," he snapped.

The two of them stood glaring at each other until the big tom jumped from his seat and wended his way toward Brand. When the baron stepped aside to let him through the door, Miranda smiled. "He won't take orders either."

"Then we're even." Brand raised his hands in frustration, then sighed and ran his fingers through his hair as she once again sat down on the large overstuffed chair. "All right, I apologize for my peremptory behavior, but you might have been killed. Is it so much to ask that you keep at least an extra footman about when you drive to your office in the City? And wouldn't it be far safer to conduct business from your home until we find out who's behind this?"

"That's ridiculous." Then noting the tightening around the major's mouth, she tried a more conciliatory tone. "I cannot simply stay here and bid people keep me informed of what is going on as if I were the queen holding court. Besides, I'm right in the midst of negotiating an important American railway venture right now."

"The transcontinental that Durant, Stanford and the rest of those damn Yankees are funding?" he asked, then immediately added, "I apologize for my language, ma'am. I can't seem to say the word *Yankee* without the appropriate adjective modifying it."

She nodded with a slight smile. "Well those . . . Yankees, whatever their status with heaven, require quite a bit of help funding the railway, not to mention supplies such as iron rails and heavy equipment."

"I'm suitably impressed." He was. Brand had been following the newspaper accounts about the railroad planned to stretch from the Atlantic seaboard all the way to the Pacific Ocean. British capital would be a determining factor in American success.

"As well you should be. If my factor in the United States can win the bidding war for contracts, Auburn Iron & Steel will stand to make a fortune."

"Not to mention Auburn Shipping," he added with a grin.

She found herself returning it. "You're quite the thorough investigator yourself, aren't you, my lord?" He nodded, still smiling. When he looked at her that way, she could feel her heartbeat trip. *I'm behaving like a schoolgirl*, she scolded herself, but she was unable to stop smoothing her gray silk skirt. The outfit was dull and tailored for work, not something Lori and Tilda would have her wear for a social occasion.

But it was her daughter, not she, who needed to worry about pleasing the baron. Why did she have to keep reminding herself of that? It was hardly as if he'd consider an older woman as marriage material. Horrified at the way her thoughts kept straying into forbidden territory when he was around, she said coolly, "Other than upbraiding me for being involved in a carriage accident, do you have some purpose in being here, Major?"

Back to her Queen Victoria mode. Brand smiled wryly. "As a matter of fact, yes. I know Rushcroft Hall is in ill repair, but the staff there assures me they have things well enough in shape for guests. I'm extending an invitation for you and Miss Auburn to join me this weekend. It's a celebration of sorts, since two of Reiver's mares have foaled and from the looks of them, they'll be prime racing stock in a couple of years. I thought Miss Auburn would enjoy the outing," he added as an inducement, recalling her highly unorthodox visit and her schemes.

"I'm not certain I can break away just now . . ." Miranda thought about the wire from Mr. Aimesley naming another bidder, whose offer was holding up the completion of her deal.

"There is a telegraph office in Dorking. I can vouch that it works."

"Lori would love to see the foals," she equivocated, knowing how delighted with such a prospect her horse-mad daughter would be.

"And how about you? After all, you might be investing in my stud farm one day."

"Is manipulating people with such charm an American trait, Major?" She could not resist his sunny smile.

"When it's done properly, ma'am, it is a Southern trait."

How could she say no? "Very well. I shall ask my

daughter, but I believe we both know what her answer will be."

"I'll be here to escort you to the railway at five on Friday. I've reserved a car for us."

"Are you always this sure of yourself, Major . . . or is it only with women?"

"Now, that's a question packed too tight with black powder for any Southern gentleman to answer," he replied, reaching for her hand before she could stop him. He raised it to his lips, kissed it lightly and bowed.

As he walked out of the room, Miranda held to her lips that hand, scandalously bare since she had been working on accounts, and felt the heat of his mouth transmit to hers.

Bitter pain unexpectedly choked her.

As they rode up the long circular drive to Rushcroft Hall, Brand felt considerable trepidation about the Auburns' reaction to his shabby home. As if their opinions were not worrisome enough, he'd been cajoled by Lorilee into inviting her friend Abigail Warring and her fiancé, Varley's son Jonathon, who was an utter snob. The Pelham family seat was adjacent to Rushcroft, and Jon had just informed the party that Geoffrey Winters and his wife were in residence that weekend. Bloody lovely.

The entourage took three carriages from the railway station, one for the guests, one for the servants and one filled to overflowing with an incredible mountain of trunks and baggage. How many changes of clothing did a lady require for a mere two days in the countryside, anyway?

The roses were spindly and diseased, and the goldfish pool in the gardens was so murky the fish could only be seen if they floated to the surface dead, an event he'd witnessed on his last visit. Brand hoped the yardman had managed to clean the water, at the least. He could see that the overworked fellow had hacked down the worst of the weeds and vines, but the lawns were bare of grass and muddy in many places, and what had once been ornamental shrubbery was now a more or less shapeless mass of boxwood and barberry all grown together.

The Hall itself had once been quite splendid. Unfortunately, that had been in the Elizabethan era. It commanded a stunning view of the countryside from the top of a gently rising hill backed by a magnificent stand of walnut and oak trees. Although expanded over the generations, with wings added on in the seventeenth and eighteenth centuries, the main house was a rustic English manor of cleanly cut limestone, softened by sun and wind over time.

Large leaded-glass windows seemed to welcome visitors and bid them enter. Upon closer inspection, the cracked and broken panes and rusty hinges holding together the scarred oak door made the promise of hospitality appear thin indeed. At least the maids had washed what remained of the glass until it gleamed in the twilight.

"I said it was badly in need of repair. I may have understated the case," Brand said dryly as the carriage slowed, nearing the front steps.

"Oh, I can picture it refurbished in the Gothic manner with a tower there and arched windows placed just so," Lorilee said, pointing enthusiastically to her vision.

Brand struggled not to shudder. Was the girl playacting or was her father's execrable taste inherited? But it was Miranda who remonstrated for him.

"Why, I'd never ruin the simple lines of the architecture. It isn't a medieval church, dearheart, it's a country manor house. All it needs is a bit of polishing up to bring out the charm of it. Look at the way the light spills from the windows. It's enchanting."

"The first time I saw it, I thought of River Trails," Brand said.

"Your plantation home in Lexington?" Miranda asked as Lori and Abbie argued about how the exterior of the Hall could be refitted for modern sensibilities.

"Yes. It was white frame, a neoclassical structure. New by English standards, but beautiful. I loved its simplicity."

"So tragic it was destroyed during the war," she said gently.

He nodded. "When I first saw this place, I thought . . . not that they're anything alike architecturally, but this was . . ."

"Home," Miranda supplied for him.

"Yes. The furnishings—what the late baron did not sell off to pay gambling debts—are in poor repair but similar to the Greek Revival pieces my family had in Lexington."

"Quite unlike the monstrosities in my city house," Miranda said with a teasing smile.

Brand grinned back at her. "I confess the Wanstead sofa in your parlor does come to mind."

"I've bruised myself on those hideous griffins affixed to the ends of it so often, I've considered having it chopped up for firewood."

"The house is obviously not to your taste. Most women with the means would leap at the opportunity to redecorate, if not sell it outright and purchase one they wanted. Why haven't you?" He was treading a dangerous path here and knew he should let the matter drop, but he wanted to know.

Miranda felt as if the two of them were alone in the large open carriage. When he looked at her, the laughter of the young people, even the strident voices of Tilda and St. John in the carriage behind them, all seemed to fade away. But still, she could not give him an honest answer. Did she know it herself?

She moistened her lips and said, "My business affairs require too much attention. I haven't the time or inclination to search for another home or suffer the intrusion of painters, plasterers and the like."

"Well, here we are," Jonathon Belford, the next Earl of Varley, said with disdain, curling his mustachioed lips as he looked at the house. The expression would have been more effectively insulting if his beard were not quite so sparse. The bare spots about his mouth made him look like a mangy sheepdog.

Ignoring the steps the footman had pulled down, the baron jumped lithely to the ground and issued instructions for stabling the carriages once the baggage was unloaded. Grateful for the interruption, Miranda stood to alight. Courtesy demanded that she allow the baron to assist her. She could feel Brand's gaze still fixed on her, almost daring her to take his hand. Thank heaven they both wore gloves.

Still, it did not matter when the warmth of his fingers pressed into her palm. She was relieved when Lori and her friends followed, providing distraction for her most troubled thoughts. Miranda forced her attention from him to his home. It had once been lovely and could be again.

But it would never be hers. She'd lied about why she'd never redecorated her house. It had been Will's pride and joy, no matter how garish it was. And it was his only child's birthright. Just as this rambling country house would be for Brand and Lori's children. She tried to think of grandchildren with joy, but somehow the image would not come clear in her mind.

Miranda's disturbing thoughts were put aside as the party entered the spacious foyer, which had obviously been scrubbed and polished. The oak parquet floors bore the grooves and dips of great age but also revealed exacting craftsmanship. As did the gracefully curving staircase leading to the floor above. Fresh bouquets of wildflowers adorned a pair of spindly tables, but the walls above them, once covered with facing mirrors, were stripped bare.

"As you can see, I was not jesting about my predecessor's penchant for selling whatever was worth a farthing, but I'm assured the beds have been fitted with clean linens and there is a table upon which we may dine."

Lori turned to Brand with a smile, saying, "Then all's well for tonight, but tomorrow the first thing I wish to do is see those darling foals. Then perhaps, if this lovely weather favors us, we could have a picnic."

"I say, do they play croquet in America?" Belford asked Brand. "My man has brought the equipment, which he could set up—with your permission, of course."

"They call it lawn balls down where I come from, but yes, Jon, it's played. Awfully good of you to think of it," Brand said with a smile. "I'm certain the ladies would enjoy it, but I was hoping we could find something a bit more challenging. Say, shooting? I've had my man pack a pair of matched self-cocking Adams Conversion revolvers. How about early tomorrow?"

Knowing when he'd been outmaneuvered, Belford harrumphed his assent. He had heard of the Rebel Baron's reputation as a crack shot.

As everyone dispersed to his or her assigned room to rest and freshen up before dinner, Miranda murmured to Brand, "That was a low blow indeed." She chuckled. "Belford could not hit the Tower of London if he were standing directly in front of it."

He winked at her. "I know. But I couldn't drive a wooden ball through one of those cursed little hoops if my life depended on it."

Lori watched the two of them laughing and smiled to herself. She had some planning to do for tomorrow's picnic. That was why she'd invited the boorish Jon Belford, not to mention her erstwhile friend Abbie.

"That . . . that man is the most insufferable, rude, opinionated, jumped-up—"

"Do you not like Mr. St. John, Tilda? Tell me true, now," Lori teased as Tilda fussed over the girl's hair.

Miranda laughed as she observed Tilda's thunderous expression, made even more fierce by the hairpins in her mouth, around which she was muttering. "The argument between the two of you very nearly frightened the horses on the ride from the station," she said, having overheard parts of it. "Mr. St. John appears smitten with you, Tilda."

"He's far too full of himself to have any interest in me." She paused to jab the last pin in Lori's hair, then continued, "Even if he did, I'd certainly not return the regard of a racecourse gamester such as that one."

"He is a bit short of height for you," Lori said thoughtfully.

"Ha! That's like saying Temple Bar is shorter than the Tower of London." She inspected Lori's curly head and nodded with satisfaction. "Now it's your turn," she said to Miranda.

"Just braid it and put it up out of my way."

"Oh, no, Mother! Tilda and I have selected the gold tissue gown for dinner, and you simply must have your hair curled and piled up so its highlights will show by candlelight."

An argument ensued. Miranda, as usual, lost to the combined forces of Lori and Tilda. She hadn't even known that the scandalously sheer gown was among the clothes the maid had packed. Lord only knew what else would materialize from the clutch of trunks scattered about the bare room!

When they came down for dinner, Lori was pleased

with the way the baron stared at her mother, not even aware for a moment of what he was doing. As the ranking members of the entourage, he and Miranda were paired up for dinner, with a bit of skillful manipulation by her daughter. She sat between Jon and Abbie, whom she knew were appalled by the shabbiness of the country house. *If only they could see the city house, this would appear a palace by comparison!* She wisely kept that bit of information to herself, knowing that to reveal it would betray that she'd been there under less than proper circumstances. Even worse, it would be a betrayal of the baron, and she was developing a genuine affection for him.

During the long and rather dreary courses of the meal, Lori managed to chatter inanely with her friends about the regatta at Henley and what the ladies had worn to cheer on the crews. Knowing the conversation was boring in the extreme to Caruthers and her mother, she kept an eye on their discussion of political matters pending in Parliament, a subject upon which they could argue seemingly endlessly.

"Why can't you understand that giving votes to unpropertied men is foolish in the extreme? What stake do they have in society?" Miranda asked in exasperation.

"Keeping their families from starving?" Brand supplied helpfully. "Laissez-faire economic theory is all well and good—in theory. However, in practice it works only to the advantage of the rich. The leaders of industry can set any prices and pay any wages they wish. Factory workers must put their wives and children to work just to earn bare subsistence from their combined incomes. That, my dear lady, is the stuff of revolution."

"And all this time I believed it was the highly educated planters and propertied merchants of America who rallied about the cry of 'no taxation without representation,' " Miranda replied dryly.

"I was thinking more along the lines of the bloodbath in France in 1789," Brand said. "In America, as in England, leadership has fallen to landholders and merchants, but because of the abundance of free land on the frontier, and concomitant opportunities for small businessmen to flourish, those with 'a stake in society,' as you put it, are vastly more numerous. Here, in the richest nation on earth, you have literally millions of people trapped in an endless cycle of poverty. Look at the conditions in places like Seven Dials."

"And you'd give the cutpurses in the rookeries the vote?" she asked sweetly.

"Not at present. But the government can educate and provide opportunities for those poor devils before they rise up and burn the whole of London to the ground. Don't think I haven't seen what can happen when human greed runs unchecked," he said with a grim set to his mouth.

"I thought the war in America was about black slavery," Jon interjected snidely.

"It was about many of the same issues plaguing England, the chief of which was the unchecked greed of Northern industrialists—and," Brand conceded, "the evil of slavery, an institution that many Southerners never condoned."

"Did you not own slaves?" Jon's tone made it an accusation; he was certain that a major in the Confederate Army must surely have done so.

"No," Brand replied flatly. "My family paid fair wages to everyone at River Trails, white and black."

"As I pay fair wages to those in my employ," Miranda said, wanting to divert the conversation away from a topic she knew was painful for the baron and about which Jon Belford knew nothing. "It only makes good business sense."

"Touché," Brand replied as he raised his wineglass to her. "I could not agree more, but that still does not address the issue of what we're to do about the measures being considered in Parliament."

His comment set off another spirited exchange between her mother and the baron. Lori took a sip of water, having declined any stronger libation, and smiled to herself. The evening was going just as she'd hoped.

After dinner, they adjourned to the music room, where Abbie attempted to coax a tune from an ancient and sadly neglected pianoforte. Since the gentlemen were to have an early go at shooting in the morning, everyone retired shortly. After seeing that her mother had gone upstairs, Lori followed Brand out into the garden, where she could see he was lighting a cigar.

"Everything went swimmingly tonight," she whispered, catching him as he took a light puff.

"You think so, eh?" He appeared dubious.

"I know so. You and Mother have so much in common!"

He threw back his head and laughed. "If she'd been born in America, she'd have beaten every captain of industry in New England from old Jake Astor to young Jay Gould. Our political views are diametrically opposed."

Lori dismissed that with a wave of her hand. "No matter. She really does treat her workers well, you know."

"Yes, so I've heard," he replied thoughtfully. "She is associated with Mr. Mundella from Nottingham, isn't she?"

"He's quite a progressive reformer—and a Liberal M.P.," Lori replied with a cheeky grin.

Brand smiled at her. "You play the air-headed miss very well, but there's quite a brain busily at work behind that pretty face, isn't there?"

178

"If I know anything at all, I know it because I've learned from watching my mother."

"You've had a fine example to follow. I only hope you don't have to pay the cost she did for her knowledge," he said softly.

"You've learned about why she married my father?" Lori herself knew little but had always wanted to learn more. It was a subject Miranda always deflected by explaining that William Auburn had been a fine and upstanding man of whom Lorilee should be proud. End of story.

He shrugged. "A little. One day, when you're older, I'm certain she'll tell you about it. But it's for her to tell, not me."

"You want her to tell you about it, too, don't you?"

"Girl, you are a wonder," he said with a grin. "Your mother could not ask for a finer daughter."

Suddenly, looking at him this way, she could see Brandon Caruthers, Lord Rushcroft, not as the violent older stranger who had frightened her, but rather as the male relative she'd never had and always wished for. Impulsively she leaned over and planted a light kiss on his cheek. "And she could not ask for a finer husband either, I think."

Standing at the bedroom window, Miranda looked down on the tender exchange below. It was scandalously bold and highly improper for Lori to be alone with Brand, but they were young and would soon be affianced. She could see them laughing and smiling at each other . . . hear the soft, deep drawl of his voice and Lori's clear, crisp English soprano carrying on the summer breeze, although she could not make out what they were saying.

And then Lori kissed him before turning and dashing inside.

Miranda gasped with the sudden pain of it, remembering how she'd held her hand after his lips had touched it. What would it feel like to place her lips to his beard-roughened cheek? *Foolish, foolish old woman*, she berated herself, riven with guilt. Her heart throbbed with a sorrow so deep it seemed to crush her very soul.

Soon Lori would be up to bid her mother good night. How could Miranda face her daughter when she was in love with her child's husband-to-be?

Chapter Twelve

"This shall be ever so exciting," Lorilee exclaimed as the ladies made their way across the open field where Brand was offering Jon his choice of weapons for their contest. "I understand Lord Rushcroft is quite famous for his marksmanship."

"Considering how many men he must've killed in that barbaric war, I don't doubt he's a crack shot," Abbie said sourly, clearly displeased that the women had been forced to take a carriage such a distance from the house for something as boring as a shooting contest.

"A man tested on a battlefield is ever so romantic, don't you think, Mother?" Lorilee asked.

"From what I've read about modern warfare, marksmanship has little to do with victory," Miranda replied. "The objective is simply to overpower one's foe, usually by throwing more men into the field, regardless of casualties. That is one reason why the Union forces were able to defeat the Confederates. Their war was as senseless a bloodbath as ours in the Crimea."

It was not the reply Lori had hoped for, but she could still turn it to her advantage. "You and Lord Rushcroft understand history so well. I'm certain Abbie and I never will."

"Nor do we wish to," Abbie added with a flippant toss of her curls. Then she smiled sweetly at Lori and asked, "Oh, would you mind terribly if Jon accepted an invitation from Mr. Winters and his wife for tea tomorrow . . . now that you're practically affianced yourself and all?"

Miranda could have pulled Abigail's artfully coifed hair out by the roots. The petty girl knew how Geoffrey Winters's betrayal had hurt Lori. "I'm not certain—"

But her daughter surprised her, shrugging with seeming indifference. "I would be happy to meet the baron's new neighbors. Since Pelham Manor is adjacent to Rushcroft Hall, it would be impolite to decline, wouldn't it, Mother?"

Unsure, Miranda nodded. Was Lori so taken with Brandon Caruthers that all thoughts of Pelham's worthless son had been banished? That would be wonderful. *It would,* she repeated to herself.

"I understand they have a houseguest visiting them from the baron's home . . . someplace called Kentuck, I believe."

"That is Kentucky," Miranda corrected the girl, whom she was growing to dislike more by the moment.

"Mother knows so much more of the world. Just as the baron does. I've never been interested in geography or politics, much less warfare," Lori said with an ingenuous smile.

Miranda wondered at that odd pronouncement; her daughter had always been a bright and curious student. But before she could consider it further, they were hailed by the men. Brand wore a simple hunting coat and riding breeches that emphasized his broad shoulders and long, powerful horseman's legs. He looked quite ruggedly masculine compared to Jon Belford's dandyish appearance in an expensive woolen suit with high starched collar. The baron's face was darkly tanned, burnished by sun and wind, while the younger man's pale complexion indicated that he spent a good deal more time in drawing rooms than he did outdoors.

To any proper Englishwoman, the earl's son should have been far more pleasing, but Miranda perversely found herself admiring Brand's lazy drawl and sunny smile as he greeted them. His sun-bleached hair tumbled across his forehead and he combed it back carelessly with one hand. She swallowed a sudden lump in her throat and willed her heart to slow its rapid beat.

Even that scar adds to his appeal. Damn the man! Guiltily she looked at Lori to gauge her daughter's reaction. If the girl was smitten, she concealed it well, making her curtsy to the gentlemen with equal charm and indifference.

I'm seeing what I wish to see.

"Well, now, I'm delighted you ladies are interested in our humble masculine pastimes," Brand said, winking at Miranda. She looked utterly fetching in a simple day gown of moss green cotton, which contrasted dramatically with the richness of her burnished red hair. He forced himself to turn his attention to Lori and Abbie. "I promise, we won't take long,"

"Mother was explaining about marksmanship and warfare. I imagine it's quite romantic," Lori said.

"Not really. Target shooting and hunting for game one plans to eat is well and good, but war . . . well, that is another matter altogether, and I can assure you it isn't romantic in the least," he replied gently.

"You were on the losing side, I understand," Belford said, as if that explained the baron's aversion to war.

Insufferable pup. Yesterday afternoon, Brand had regretted daring the young fool to a shooting contest. He'd been angered by the boy's arrogance and wanted to take him down a peg, but in the clear light of morning, the gesture seemed petty. He had decided to play the gracious host and lose gracefully—until just now.

"Yes, we lost the war. If not for that, I wouldn't be here," he replied curtly.

"You cannot mean you'd have turned down entering the peerage to remain a Kentucky horse farmer!" Abbie exclaimed disbelievingly.

"I fear he would have done precisely that, impossible as it is for you to imagine," Miranda said dryly. When she turned to the baron, she had a gleam in her eyes.

He returned the look before asking Jon Belford briskly, "Shall we begin?"

He motioned to the tin dishes suspended from tree limbs at intervals between twenty-five and seventy-five yards distant and indicated Varley's son should choose his target.

In spite of the breeze that would make the shots more difficult, Jon chose the farthest one. And missed. He tried again on a closer target with the same result, biting his lip and clenching his jaw in frustration. "My weapon appears to be a bit off," he said stiffly.

"I'll check it . . . with your permission?" Brand asked, extending his hand for the pistol.

"Certainly," Jon replied, handing over the gun.

Brand opened the cylinder and examined it, then snapped it closed and aimed with negligent ease. He smoothly pulled the trigger and hit the closest mark dead center. Without hesitating, he fired a second round at the next target, then the farthest one. All three tins spun like tops. "No, I don't believe the weapon is malfunctioning. Perhaps you're more accustomed to longarms, shooting moving targets such as deer or grouse. During hunting season, we'll have to give it a go."

"I shall look forward," Belford replied, red-faced.

"Mother, a thought just occurred," Lori said with a bright smile. "Since you insist on going to the City alone on business, perhaps learning to shoot a pistol would be a wise precaution. What do you think, my lord?" she asked, turning to Brand.

"I'd be delighted to give you instructions, ma'am," he said with a lazy grin, daring her before she could refuse. "After all, with so many unpropertied creatures about, a propertied female must know how to protect herself and her possessions."

"Well, my ears are aching from the noise, and that awful smell of gunpowder gives me a headache," Abbie declared, oblivious to the interplay between Mrs. Auburn and the baron.

"I shall be delighted to take you back to the house, my dear," Jon replied.

"I'll join you," Lori chimed in, looking at her mother. "You and Lord Rushcroft can meet us in the drawing room for luncheon." She gave Miranda a quick peck on the cheek before seizing Abbie and Jon by their arms and setting a brisk pace back to their carriage.

"I have two fully operational Adams revolvers. You have my word they're not defective in any way," Brand said to Miranda as the younger trio set off.

"The only thing defective here is Varley's impertinent son—and the chit he plans to marry," she blurted out before realizing how improper such a pronouncement was. But before she could retract her rash words, Brand threw back his head and gave a hearty laugh.

"I was going to let him win until he made that ugly remark about the war."

A grudging glint of amusement danced in her eyes as

she replied, "Considering he could not hit a single target, I doubt that would've been possible, unless you contrived to shoot your own foot off. A stretch for even the most charming of Southern gentlemen." She mimicked his drawl almost perfectly.

Brand convulsed with laughter. "Believe me, I'm not that charming," he replied, stepping closer to her. She smelled faintly of lavender. Quashing an insane urge to pull the pins from her gleaming mass of hair and bury his hands in it, he offered her the second gun, butt first.

Miranda stared down at the weapon. No, not the gun, but the lean, elegant hand holding it. He was without gloves once more. She could see several small white scars and fine tufts of gold hair on the backs of his long fingers. "I—I don't know . . ."

"Here, don't be afraid of it," he murmured, curving her fingers around the grip of the Adams. "I'll guide you, and I promise 'pon my honor not to shoot either of our feet off."

"But I might," Miranda murmured breathlessly as he stood behind her, guiding her to raise her arm and point the pistol to the closest target.

"Now place your index finger on the trigger . . . just so, and line up the sight on the barrel with the rear notch. See?" His hand held hers as he helped her aim, looking over her shoulder.

Miranda could smell the clean essence of male, shaving soap and sunshine that she always associated with him. Biting down on her lip, she forced the thought aside and concentrated on following his instructions. If only she did not feel the heat of his body, the pressure of his larger hand curving around her smaller one, the warmth of his breath whisper soft against her ear.

I will *do this.*

"Now squeeze gently," he murmured.

She did, and the tin dish went spinning with a small hole in it. "I can't believe I hit it!" she cried with a whoop of joy.

"You're a far better shot than Varley's cub, and this is only your first try," he said with a beaming smile.

She looked up at him with mock indignation. "Considering how abysmal he is, that is a poor compliment indeed. Besides, you guided my aim, so I can scarcely take credit."

"Not true. You're too modest."

"Now there's something my business rivals would deny vehemently," she replied, backing away a step. His nearness made her dizzy. Or was it merely the ringing in her ears from the shot?

"Let's try it again," he suggested, once more moving close to her and guiding her aim.

Miranda tried to pay attention to what he was saying, but it was difficult when she was so keenly aware of his body close to hers. She'd never realized quite how tall he was . . . or how hard his muscles would feel when he touched her, however innocently. She focused on the second dish and forced herself to take a steadying breath before firing.

Once more the tin pinged. "I did it again!"

"You're a natural," he said with a grin. "Here, let's try—"

Before he could say more, another shot rang out from the woods across the field.

"Down!" Brand cried out, pulling her beneath him as he rolled to the ground. At that same instant a second shot whistled directly above them.

Miranda lay on the warm earth with his long body covering hers protectively. She was breathless, crushed by his weight yet oddly comforted at the same time. For all his leanness, he was surprisingly heavy. She could feel the muscles in his arms and legs, the rise and fall of his chest as he breathed much more rapidly now than when they were standing. She grew very still.

"Are you hurt?" he whispered.

"Only out of breath from . . . no, no, I'm not hurt," she quickly amended.

"We have to keep that tall grass between us and whoever is shooting." As he spoke he slipped a cartridge into the chamber of his pistol. "At least we have two guns and some ammunition."

"You don't think whoever that is will come closer, do you? Surely someone will hear the shooting."

"Since we're here with pistols to fire at targets, I doubt anyone will pay attention." His eyes traveled along the edge of the woods, searching the treeline in the distance for any sign of movement. "But our enemy is obviously using a rifle. If Sin or the old gamekeeper hear it, they'll know something's wrong."

"And if they don't?" she whispered.

"Then we're in considerable trouble." Brand knew that if they remained lying on the ground out in the open, the man trying to kill them could circle closer and finish the job. He could see nothing moving in the direction from which the shots had come, but that only indicated their enemy knew the territory and was experienced at this sort of thing. Hardly reassuring.

Feeling Miranda's soft curves beneath him was distracting him, and he could not allow that. Spying a small shed about fifty feet across the field where the yardman kept his tools, he said to her, "We're going to make a run for that shed. When I pull you up, I want you ahead of me. Pick up your skirts and run like hell, Miranda. No time for modesty. All right?"

When his face loomed above hers, so close that she could feel the warmth of his breath on her mouth, Miranda could scarcely focus on what he was saying, but somehow she managed to croak, "No modesty. Yes."

With that, he stood up and pulled her in front of him, shoving her toward the shed door, which, as in so many of the Hall's outbuildings, sat ajar on rusted hinges. She grabbed her skirts in both hands and took off, hearing his footsteps directly behind her. When she almost stumbled on a rock, his arm shot out and grabbed her elbow, urging her onward. Another shot, this time closer, whizzed by them.

He could be killed by a bullet meant for me! As she ran, she prayed, practically diving through the door with Brand on her heels.

"Stay down," he commanded as he shoved the door almost shut and peered out of the crack. When he heard the sound of voices and Sin yelling for Fergus the gamekeeper to check the woods, he turned to Miranda with a grin. "I think we've been rescued."

"Thank heaven," she breathed.

"I didn't know English ladies played at sports. You sprint like an Olympian goddess."

Miranda felt suddenly light-headed now that the danger had passed . . . or had it? She stared into Brandon Caruthers's fierce tiger's eyes and shivered.

"Wait here." With that, he was gone, calling out to St. John to guard her as he joined Fergus in a search of the woods.

They found nothing but a set of footprints that quickly vanished in thick field grass at the opposite side of the stand of oaks and dense underbrush. That field lay on Pelham land, and Geoffrey Winters was in residence over the weekend. For once, Brand would be happy to pay a teatime visit.

Within the hour, the formal invitation from Pelham

Manor arrived requesting the honor of their presence for tea, just as promised. The note indicated the Winters, too, had a weekend guest. Such a neighborly gesture, Brand thought cynically as Jon and Abbie exclaimed in delight. He wondered how Lorilee would feel about socializing with the woman for whom Winters had deserted her and decided to ask Miranda's advice.

But she had been skittish when he returned from the fruitless search of the woods and had avoided him since. Wanting to speak with her alone, he learned from Lori that she'd retired to a small sunroom off the main parlor. Bright golden light shone through the newly washed windowpanes and set her dark red hair aflame with brilliant highlights. He stood in the doorway, silently staring at the heavy mass of it, caught in a loose chignon at her nape. He wondered what it would look like falling freely down her back.

She sensed his eyes on her and looked up from the book she was reading. Her expression mirrored his. Startled. Bemused. Hungry.

Blinking to break the spell, she said, "Good afternoon, Major. I trust you're feeling well."

Needing to break out of his dangerous reverie, he put on a lazy grin and answered, "As well as a man who's narrowly escaped death ever does. The more important question seems to be, how are you faring, ma'am?"

"I'm fine, thank you. Oh, I took the liberty of borrowing a book from your library." She held up a moth-eaten volume.

He strolled casually into the room and glanced at the title on the spine. "Shakespeare again. No wonder you can quote the bard so well. The selections left in the library leave little enough choice. I'm happy you found something to your liking."

They stared into each other's eyes in silence, she looking up at him, he down at her. Finally Miranda broke the quiet connection by asking, "Is there something in particular you wanted, Major?" The moment she spoke the words, she knew heat was stealing into her face. The man made her commit gaffes she never would with anyone else! His slow smile revealed his understanding of her unintentional double entendre.

"Yes, as a matter of fact, there is." He took his time ambling over to a small sofa covered in faded chintz, taking a seat directly across from her.

His knees almost touched her skirts. She fought the urge to gather them up like armor against the masculine invasion of his presence and waited for him to speak his piece.

"I missed you at luncheon. Since you failed to take breakfast either, I worried that you might be falling ill."

"I never breakfast, except for taking a cup of tea."

He shook his head in mock reproval. "That's bad for a body. Back home, folks take breakfast quite seriously. Fried ham, grits, eggs. From what I've seen since arriving here, Englishmen take it even further—kippers and pastries, all sorts of fowl and even red meat along with the eggs."

"English men—not women. If I ate like that I'd weigh more than the Queen." At once Miranda clapped her hand to her mouth and stifled a laugh. "I simply cannot believe I said that!"

"*Lèse majesté.*" He tsked, shaking his head as he grinned at her like a fool. "But be careful. I doubt Her Majesty would forgive you." His chuckles blended with hers, then subsided. "I was hoping we could speak before it's time to go to Pelham Manor." He was in deadly earnest now as he continued, "It's quite apparent that someone wants to kill you. I'd hoped being away from the city would provide protection, but it appears quite the opposite. Which brings up the matter of—"

"The coincidence that Geoffrey Winters is in residence?" she supplied.

"I had wondered if your interference with his courtship of your daughter might have made him your enemy."

She had to smile at that. "I very much doubt that, Major. Mr. Winters is an utter coward as well as a cad."

"That would not preclude his hiring someone else to do the deed," he countered.

"In my opinion, merely taking the risk of hiring someone would be beyond his capacity. Besides, what would it serve him now that he's saddled with Falconridge's daughter?"

"I recall the insulting offer he made to your daughter at Ascot. He might feel you had influenced her to act as she did."

"He's petty, but even if he had the courage to seek revenge, I suspect he'd be inclined to attack Lori, not me." She considered that troubling thought, then dismissed it. "No, I simply don't believe he could be a threat."

"I'm inclined to agree, but I'll take his measure again when we attend his little tea party." He paused. "Will Miss Auburn be troubled by seeing Winters and his wife?"

"I might have thought so before the incident at Ascot, but now, no. I rather imagine it will be his wife who will find the situation untenable. I can't imagine whatever possessed them to invite us." Miranda's expression was decidedly vexed.

"Winters's friendship with Belford, for one thing. And, glutton for punishment that the young fool is, perhaps he intends another go at insulting your daughter. I'll deal with him if he does anything amiss. Or, if she prefers not to attend, that will be no problem either."

"Lori's well and truly over her infatuation." Miranda forced herself to smile and look him in the eye as she said, "I believe you have much to do with her change of heart."

It was his turn to shrug. "Don't give me too much credit. The girl has inherited much of your common sense. All she needs is time to grow into it." How the devil could he explain the further complication he'd come to discuss? He plunged ahead, since he was already treading over a field laid with explosives each time he talked with her. "The Winterses indicated in their invitation that they have a weekend guest."

"Yes, I recall Mr. Belford mentioning something to that effect."

"It's Reba Wilcox."

"Oh, dear."

"Yes, oh, dear," he echoed dryly. "Dear Geoffrey may not have the nerve to hire a poacher to kill you, but my dear countrywoman wouldn't hesitate for a moment, I can assure you. As to what her motive might be, I can't begin to guess."

"Perhaps she wanted to kill you because you've spurned her," she ventured.

Brand scoffed. "Spoiled and self-centered as she is, Reba wouldn't risk trying to kill me just because I snubbed her. Besides, the other attempts have clearly been on your life, not mine. All of this is related, and I mean to find out how."

"And you want to go on . . . reconnaissance, Major." Miranda considered the dangerous tangle and nodded. "Yes, I believe tea will be most interesting."

Unlike Brand's shabby manor house and neglected grounds, the earl's family seat was in pristine condition. Geoffrey Winters and his mousy little dumpling of a wife stood beneath the towering twelve-foot crystal chandelier in the entry foyer, both wearing false smiles of welcome for Abigail Warring, Lorilee and Miranda Auburn and the Rebel Baron.

Geoffrey's only genuine enthusiasm appeared in his greeting of Jon Belford. Old gambling and drinking companions since their rugby days, the two went into back-slapping orgies of reminiscence as Mrs. Winters primly ushered her unwanted guests into an immense sitting room where a row of servants filed in, each carrying a sterling tea tray laden with enough pastries, marmalades and watercress sandwiches to weigh down a good-sized dray horse.

"Mrs. Wilcox will be along shortly. She's only just returned from a ride with Mr. Winters. Please excuse her tardiness," the hostess informed the women as they took their seats in a small circle of Louis XV chairs. Her tone of voice indicated she would prefer the widow remain tardy for the duration of the weekend.

She poured from a silver teapot heavy enough to make her wrist ache, Miranda was certain. Her thin lips—the only thing about her that was—pursed in concentration as she offered delicate Sevres cups to the three women. It was quite clear that she had been coerced into this farce. Although Abbie was oblivious to the undercurrents, both Miranda and Lori felt a twinge of pity for her as she watched her husband usher the men across the cavernous chamber to a cabinet filled with ports, clarets and sherries.

"Mr. Winters always prefers a bit of wine to tea in the afternoons," Varinia said with obvious disapproval she dared not voice.

Miranda knew the man was well on his way to becoming an utter sot in addition to his other unfortunate vices. Smiling, she shifted the conversation to a neutral topic. "Your husband's family seat is lovely. I've never been in this part of Surrey. It's quite a beautiful spot. Unspoiled by industry and its attendant ills."

"But industry and all those little ole attendant ills are what's made you a rich woman, Widow Auburn," a drawling voice purred from behind them.

Miranda turned to the speaker. Reba Wilcox was dressed in brilliant robin's-egg-blue mull, tissue thin with scarcely a hint of undergarments to cover her lush charms. Ignoring the insult, Miranda remarked, "I understand you, too, have lost your husband . . . quite recently," she said, allowing her gaze to boldly rake the American hussy's highly unsuitable attire.

Both Lori and Abbie stared in open shock before regaining their composure, but, being debutantes conditioned to defer to their elders, neither said a word.

Most married women at London galas would think twice before wearing such a daring gown. For tea in the country, it was outrageously inappropriate. Every person in the room knew it. Mrs. Winters stiffened, nodding icily to her houseguest as she started to make introductions to the Auburns and Abbie.

Miranda gently interjected, "My daughter and I have already met the widow."

Mrs. Winters duly noted that Mrs. Auburn had not said they'd had *the pleasure of* meeting the widow. She gave Miranda a tight little smile as Geoffrey Winters rushed to Reba Wilcox's side with oily solicitude. Much to Abbie's distress, Jon did likewise, fairly drooling over her hand as he was presented to her.

"I believe you two are friends . . . from back in America," Geoffrey said as Brand sauntered over to make his obligatory bow.

He knew Miranda was watching him as he replied, "Yes, the Widow Wilcox and I are well acquainted. However, I wouldn't say we've ever been friends."

Reba put a dainty lace-gloved hand to her breast and made a moue. "How unkind of you, Brand. After all, we practically married."

When Lorilee gasped, the triumph lighting Reba's eyes reminded Brand of a fox bounding away from the coop with a chicken in its mouth. His smile matched hers as he answered, "And the Yankees put me in prison, but I escaped both fates."

Little did Reba know that Lorilee's heart was not fixed upon him. The revelation of their previous engagement would shock her but not hurt her. Miranda knew of his past with Reba. The devil of it was, he had no idea at all if it bothered her.

And he knew damn well that her opinion mattered to him. A great deal more than he would have ever imagined . . .

Chapter Thirteen

The afternoon went downhill from there, with Reba holding court while Geoffrey and Jon acted like a brace of slobbering hounds. Abbie Warring and Varinia Winters were scandalized by the lovely blonde's behavior and their men's reaction to it, but if Geoffrey hoped that it would arouse jealousy in Lorilee Auburn, he was doomed to disappointment. Miranda had never been prouder of her daughter. Lori ignored the ill-bred American's pointed barbs with an innocent charm that amused her mother and the baron.

Miranda was also pleased to note that Brand seemed impervious to Reba Wilcox's blandishments. And that his very indifference fueled the beauteous widow's determination to flirt with him. The only troubling matter was, oddly enough, that Lori seemed not to care about her suitor being stalked by such a creature. Now that Miranda thought of it, her daughter's behavior of late had been oddly inconsistent on a variety of occasions.

Never had she seen the girl act like such a flibbertigibbet, gushing vacuously about fashions and social events as she had done at Ascot. Perhaps it was the fault of time spent with Abigail Warring, but somehow Miranda doubted it. On the train ride to the country Lori had chattered with her friend about what they would wear to the Wayfields' ball, but today she was serenely level-headed while Abbie fumed with petulant jealousy.

Lori had always been horse-mad, but now that she was being courted by a man who was renowned for his race-horses, she never broached the topic. Whenever he spoke of his new foals and plans to turn his estate into a breeding farm for fine thoroughbreds as well as carriage horses, she showed only polite interest in the project, which Miranda knew was dear to his heart.

What is going on between them? Or, what was not? But surely after that romantic scene in the garden that Miranda had witnessed, Lori must have a tendresse for the baron. Of course, as far as he was concerned, Brandon Caruthers had not appeared overly attentive to Lori for the past few days either. If anything, his gaze seemed to fasten on her more often than her daughter. She assured herself it was only her imagination. It was also her imagination that made her envision ripping every last strand of golden blond hair from the Widow Wilcox's head.

"I understand you intend to enter the Ascot next year. A mare. Show those Englishmen what a Kentucky female can do," Reba drawled. "We're famous for our winning ways, after all." She stood closer to Brand than was socially acceptable, but then, neither was the glass of sherry she sipped the proper thing for a lady at teatime.

The gentlemen chortled at her not overly subtle double entendre—all but the baron. Picking up his neglected glass of port from a side table, he gazed at the hussy with cynical amusement glistening in his eyes. "Oh, my dear Mrs. Wilcox, I can assure you, I already know precisely what Kentucky females are capable of doing." With that, he raised the glass and polished off its contents, then set it down with a decisive clink and walked over to where Abbie sat forlornly near the piano.

"Would you favor us with some music, Miss Warring? I understand from Miss Auburn that you play quite well," he said with a charming smile.

Abbie's cheeks pinkened and she dipped her head, flustered by the baron's compliment. Murmuring assent, she took her seat and began to pluck out a lively Chopin piece. He then sauntered over to the settee and sat beside Miranda.

"Well done, Major," she said softly. Lori stood nearby, tapping her toe to the music, utterly unconcerned that her mother, not she, had been approached by her suitor.

"It was the only thing I could think to do to silence Reba . . . short of strangling her."

Miranda stifled a laugh. "You don't think she'd relish joining her dear Earl in the hereafter?"

"Not likely. She's afraid of fire."

"Ah, but I detect that you believe it's where she's bound anyway."

"No doubt in my mind, but she doesn't think that far ahead. The widow has plans for the here and now."

"They would certainly appear to involve you," she shot back more tartly than she had intended. Goodness, she was the one sounding jealous instead of Lori!

Brand chuckled. "She'd like nothing more than to become a baroness, or better yet a countess. Miss Warring had best look to Belford. The young fool's besotted."

"The Duke of Cumberland has an unwed heir. Mrs. Wilcox could aim even higher," Miranda said wryly.

"From what I've heard, he's also poxed. Remember, Reba has a fear of being burned," Brand whispered conspiratorially, waiting to see her reaction. Knowing she would laugh—or hoping she would.

"You are quite awful," she replied, unable to suppress a chuckle. Then she couldn't resist adding, "I have it on good authority that the young, ah . . . firebrand is not to be received at court in spite of his illustrious family name."

"Firebrand? Vulgar puns, Miranda?" He tsked at her with a lazy grin.

Suddenly she realized how much she enjoyed bantering with him. Even his use of her Christian name didn't upset her, although she knew it was not at all proper. Nor was it proper that they discuss socially taboo subjects, subjects she'd never consider speaking of with any female acquaintance, certainly no other man. Of course, he could infuriate her just as easily with his prickly pride and arrogant assumptions. She'd never met his like. *It's only because he's American,* she assured herself.

"You think she wants only a title, nothing more?" she asked, trying to divert her attention away from him and back to Reba Wilcox.

"Earl owned a good part of Kentucky and his family has banking interests stretching to the eastern seaboard. She has money enough to buy whatever her heart desires now."

"Except you." The moment she said the words, Miranda wanted to call them back. They were too personal. And a reminder that she was, in a sense, buying him for Lorilee. She had come to regret her peremptory "business proposition" to him when first they'd met. But he didn't appear to mind when he replied.

"I was young when I first met Reba. A fool. War has a way of making a man see things he never did before. She saved me from the biggest mistake of my life," he said with a smile.

"Marrying her?" Miranda knew the question was bold.

Brand shuddered just thinking of what hell on earth life with Reba would have been. "She would've been upset when I lost River Trails, but I can't even imagine what a shrew she'd have turned into after finding out she'd become a baroness without a sou."

"How fortunate for you both that she married Mr. Wilcox."

"Yes, it was. She made her choice . . . and I'll make mine."

Before Miranda could think of a reply to that cryptic remark, the music stopped and everyone clapped in perfunctory appreciation of Abbie's recital. Reba took advantage of the shifting attention in the room to slip over to where Miranda and Brand sat, draping herself languidly on a leather chair beside the baron.

"Geoff told me you had some little ole shooting accident at your place this morning," she said with a gleam in her eyes.

"Someone tried to kill Mrs. Auburn," Brand replied coldly. "It was no accident."

Reba's laughter was throaty as she eyed him. "Are you sure *you* weren't the target? You do have a way of making enemies, Brand, darlin'."

"Have you, perchance, been wandering about in the wood, Mrs. Wilcox?" Miranda inquired with a too sweet smile. She felt the baron's admiring gaze at her blunt sally.

Reba stiffened. "Surely you aren't accusing me of shooting at you?" she hissed, straightening up in the chair.

"Your marksmanship would explain why no one was injured," Brand said.

"Why ever would I try to kill *her?*" Reba gave Miranda a dismissive glance, then turned back to Brand. "If I still wanted you, I'd have to shoot her pretty child, now wouldn't I?"

A sudden lull in the conversation around the room left her words echoing so everyone heard them. An uncomfortable silence followed as the ladies and gentlemen stood in varying stages of shock and embarrassment.

Brand could sense Miranda's protective instincts for her daughter radiate like the light from a dozen suns. Gently he placed his hand over hers and squeezed it reassuringly, then said, "Mrs. Wilcox was just making an unfortunate jest. Everyone knows she isn't in the least interested in me."

Since the blatant opposite had been amply exhibited during the afternoon, there were a few coughs and titters. Then Mrs. Winters gamely announced, "There are more scones and marmalade."

"Do you think she hired someone to shoot at you?" Lori asked her mother as soon as they had returned to Rushcroft Hall. They were in Lori's room, selecting gowns for dinner that evening.

"As the widow pointed out, it would make more sense if she tried to harm you, not me," Miranda said, trying for wry humor but failing. There was a ruthless streak of steely hardness behind the Wilcox hussy's languid sensuality. Miranda had seen her like before in the drawing rooms of business associates with socially ambitious wives. Reba put the Englishwomen to shame. But what did she want? Surely she no longer harbored hopes for Brandon. He had made it more than apparent that he had no interest in rekindling their former relationship.

Lori voiced her mother's worst fears when she asked, "Do you think she'd harm me to spite the baron?" Before Miranda could respond, she continued, "That would make no sense whatever, since it has been you, not I, who's been the target of all these 'accidents.' "

"I must admit you're right." Miranda did not sound convinced. "However, just as a precaution, from now on you'll go nowhere without a pair of sturdy and loyal footmen to see to your safety."

"Only if you promise to do likewise," Lori countered. Her expression turned grave. "I know you've come within a hairsbreadth of being killed several times in London and now here. Please be careful, Mother," she admonished, grasping Miranda's hands in hers. "Stay close to the baron. He's used to such danger and can protect you better than anyone else."

Miranda knew that was true. She could still feel the bullets whizzing around them and Brand throwing her to the ground, covering her with his own body, then offering himself as a human shield while he helped her to the shed. The other feelings, when he'd lain on top of her, pressing her into the soft earth . . . those she pushed to the furthest recesses of her mind.

And now her daughter's trust made her feel horribly guilty.

Lori surprised everyone that evening by insisting on a picnic. Miranda's protests that such an outing might not be safe after the incident that morning fell on deaf ears as Jon and Abbie joined Lori's cause. Even the baron added his agreement, saying that if they invited the Winterses and Mrs. Wilcox, surely they'd be safe. Jon had given him an odd look at that point, but did not make any comment other than agreeing to send an invitation for the Sunday outing.

While the women gathered in the parlor after dinner, Brand left Belford to his own devices, which meant turning him loose on what remained of Rushcroft's badly depleted wine cellar. He wanted to talk with Sin and see what, if anything, his friend had learned through servants' gossip here in the countryside. Making his way across the garden en route to the stables and their outbuildings, he was surprised to hear Tilda's voice blended with St. John's.

Odd that she would walk out with Sin after the way the two of them had fought on the carriage ride from the railway station Friday afternoon. She actually sounded as if she were laughing! Was Sin winning her over? The man had charm enough to draw birds from the trees—but he was seldom motivated to employ it.

Brand waited in the shadows, not wanting to interrupt, but then he heard Sin protesting, "Now, love, don't be so starchy."

"You are beyond absurd, suggesting such an utterly ridiculous thing! And I am most certainly *not* your love," she huffed, spinning about on her heel and taking off toward the house, practically colliding with Brand, who jumped back to avoid her, impaling himself on the thorns of a privet hedge in the process.

She flew by in the darkness without even seeing the lord of the manor.

Wincing as he pulled his tattered shirt from the prickly branches, Brand muttered, "Another bloody tailor's bill."

"Eavesdropping to learn my technique?" St. John inquired dryly.

"Only if I decide to become celibate," Brand retorted. "What the devil did you do to set her off? I thought I heard laughter just before that explosion."

Sin shrugged, heading back inside the dilapidated stables to the temporary quarters he'd furnished for himself while they worked with the new foals. "Oh, she was laughing all bloody right. At me." He sounded affronted. "I merely suggested the cook could prepare a basket for the two of us and we'd have our own picnic on the morrow."

"Without benefit of chaperone?" Brand said. "I'm surprised she didn't slap your face for such impropriety."

St. John gave a broad grin, revealing a perfect set of teeth. "She was here *sans* chaperone, was she not? My Goliath will come around. And I'll have a feast for us to share. I've already spoken to the cook."

"Your self-confidence borders on the suicidal," Brand replied dubiously, picking a tiny thorn from his shoulder. "What have you heard in the village?"

"This is the first time since he's been out of knee britches that Winters has visited his father's seat except for grouse and fox hunting, which, as you know, take place during the autumn, not the heat of summer."

"You don't think it has anything to do with his precipitous marriage and its repercussions?"

"If by that you mean that he's without funds to spend in London, no. He's paid some of his creditors from the racetracks. The fellow has an absolute gift for choosing poor horseflesh, yet he has funds to indulge his misspent passion. Oh, still nothing on O'Connell. He's dropped from the face of the earth."

Brand stroked his jaw consideringly. "Winters is in debt, his father's cut him off, his new father-in-law keeps him on a tight leash, and still he has money. Where is he getting it . . . and why, if he has it, is he rusticating in the countryside?"

"Perhaps he's only deposited his unfortunate bride here and intends on leaving her after a decent interval?"

"With Reba on his arm? Somehow I doubt even poor Varinia Winters would stand for that insult. What do the gentry hereabouts make of my countrywoman?"

"Allow me to venture that she's not about to win over the vicar," Sin said dryly.

"Has she had any opportunity to hire someone locally who could've fired those shots?"

"I heard rumors about poachers in the vicinity, but I don't know if she'd have any means of employing them. One could scarcely summon them to Pelham Manor like interviewing footmen for positions."

"My gut tells me that either she or Geoffrey is behind the attempt to kill Miranda."

At Brand's Christian naming of Mrs. Auburn, St. John's eyebrows rose slightly. "Miranda?" he echoed, watching his friend's face darken.

"Ever since her daughter came to call . . . oh, hell . . . I've been thinking . . ."

Sin laughed. "Always a dangerous thing, especially when it concerns the female of the species."

"Then why are you so determined to woo her Amazonian maid?"

"When you grow as old and wise as I, you'll come to understand that there are some challenges a man must accept simply because they are there. No other reason at all."

Brand gave him a disbelieving snort and headed back to the house.

There he spent a restless night dreaming of Miranda Auburn's fiery hair spread across white sheets, her soft curves beneath his hands, her intoxicating scent filling his senses. Toward dawn he tossed away the covers and paced naked around the shabby room, wondering if down the hallway, the lady in question gave him so much as a thought.

A man accepts some challenges simply because they are placed in his path? Like feeling an impossible attraction for a woman rich enough to buy and sell him a thousand times over? After donning a robe, he took a seat at the window and watched the sun rise. What was he going to do once the danger to Miranda was over? Walk away from her?

"To use your own phrase, Sin, not bloody likely. Not bloody likely at all."

The day was cool and clear, the sun brilliant in an azure sky as the party assembled at the Rushcroft stables after Sunday church. In addition to Jon and Abbie, Miranda and Lori, the Winterses had been invited on the picnic. As an unavoidable courtesy, Mrs. Wilcox had also been included, but Varinia happily proffered their unpleasant houseguest's apologies that morning at the conclusion of worship. On impulse, Brand extended an invitation to the vicar's son and his new bride, a charming couple who lived in the village nearby.

One servant loaded baskets filled with roast pheasant and venison pies, peas in sherry butter, fresh raspberries with clotted cream, and crusty loaves of bread warm from the ovens. Another hefted ice-filled buckets of wine and even one with a luscious trifle of layered custard and fresh fruits. Although he could ill afford it, Brand intended that the revelers would feast like Her Majesty herself.

The Winterses and the vicar's son and his wife rode over while Sin oversaw the selection of horses for the houseguests. Lori cooed with delight at the dappled gray mare she was to ride, while Abbie and Jon were well pleased with their fine mounts from the baron's stables. Brand noticed Miranda standing back and recalled her reticence about riding that day in Hyde Park.

"I have the perfect horse for you," he said, even though she wore a simple cotton gown instead of a riding habit. "I guarantee Milky Way will treat you like the crown jewels. He's that gentle."

Miranda shook her head even as Lori protested, "Oh, Mother, this is the perfect opportunity to learn. I have another habit, and we're enough of a size that it would fit you."

Without allowing his gaze to move to Miranda's fuller breasts, Brand could see that otherwise she and her daughter were both slender and could well exchange clothes, although Lori's skirts might be a bit too short for her taller mother. "Go put on the habit while I saddle Milky for you. He's a pure white gelding and quite a gentleman," he coaxed with a winning smile.

"No, really, I've never been on horseback and ... well"—she leaned closer to Brand and whispered, "the great beasts terrify me. There, are you satisfied?"

With a soft chuckle, he threw up his hands. "All right, you leave me no choice then. I shall ride on one of the wagons with you."

"Don't be absurd. The other young people will ride well ahead of the wagons, and you don't want to miss all the fun," she pointed out.

"I ride at dawn every day. When I'm working I'm on horseback all day long. One afternoon off won't bother me a whit," he replied. "I'll drive one team and Sin shall drive the other, provided Miss Tilda will join him?" he asked, giving her a wink.

"Matchmaking, Major?" Miranda asked with a hint of a smile, uncertain what to make of the head stableman's pursuit of her lifetime companion. "Are his intentions honorable?" she teased primly.

"I doubt it, but having seen Miss Tilda in action, I can vouch she'll make certain he behaves himself."

They shared a laugh as Jon issued last-minute instructions for stowing his croquet set in the second wagon. A disgruntled footman rearranged several boxes in order to accommodate the bulky set. "Where does Mr. Belford think he'll be able to play out in this hilly countryside?" Miranda asked.

208

"The goats have cleared quite a patch of grass near the small lake where we'll picnic. While we were in church being sanctified this morning, he was out scouting the site," Brand replied.

"I'm sure you prayed for his soul," she said.

"That I surely did. Now who, I wonder, will pray for mine? I can assure you I'm in far greater need than any callow boy."

"Is that how you see them—callow in their youthful inexperience, I mean? I know none of the other young gentlemen have gone through the crucible of war as you have." She studied him as he helped her onto the spring seat of the heavy wagon, taking the reins from the stable-man standing patiently by.

"I'm older, yes. And war does things to a man. Not always for the better, I fear." His smile was sunny, but pain underlay what he said.

"I'll pray for you, Major," she replied quietly.

As the riders took off in a clatter of hooves and laughter, her eyes met his. And held. After a moment he said, "I need all the prayers I can get. Thank you, Miranda."

He had no right to use her Christian name. They'd been through this before, but somehow she could not summon her earlier indignation. Was it really indignation or a defensive wall she erected to hold him at bay? Today, with the sun warm on their faces, she could not bring herself to spoil this dangerous sense of camaraderie.

As the others vanished over the hill, Lorilee was in the lead. "She's a fine rider," Miranda felt duty bound to say, reminding them both of his obligations to her daughter.

"Yes, she is. You could be, too, if you'd let me teach you. Why are you afraid of horses?"

"It was nothing, really, just an unfortunate accident when I was a girl back in Liverpool. A team could have run me down."

"Ah, so you have always been accident-prone," he teased, slapping the reins so the horses set out at a leisurely pace.

"The driver was drunk, but fortunately, my father snatched me from harm's way before there was any real danger."

"I only wish these last weeks' events were that innocent."

"Do you still believe Mrs. Wilcox could be involved?" she asked.

He nodded. "Well, it seems rather a coincidence that she showed up the same time the attempts on your life began. I only wish Sin and I could find out what she's up to."

"At least she's not joining us today. I must confess to unchristian pleasure when I learned of her indisposition this morning," Miranda said.

Brand threw back his head and laughed. "Did you hear why she's indisposed? Seems, according to sweet little Varinia, that Reba switched from sherry at teatime to claret with dinner—a rather significant amount of claret. I imagine she's spending the day clutching a porcelain bowl beneath her chin."

Miranda's expression was positively gleeful. "I can think of no more suitable retribution. Oh, dear, there I go being unchristian again."

She did not look one bit penitent. "Do I bring out the devil in you, Miranda?" he drawled with one of those lazy grins.

He was altogether too close to the truth for her to be comfortable. "No—that is, I'm quite capable of devilish behavior on my own. Ask any of the men whom I've bested in business."

That wall again. She was rich and successful. He was poor and a failure. "We are different," he said gloomily.

"Everything you touch turns to gold. I've managed to lose my birthright in two countries."

Miranda sensed that she had opened an old wound with her defensive reply and regretted it. "You're the baron, and that can never be taken away from you, any more than can your good name. As to the war . . . I imagine it must have been terrible to return and find your home in ruins."

"It was all I had to keep me going in that hellish Yankee prison in Chicago."

"But you escaped. Not even the—dare I say it?—damn Yankees could bend you to their will."

He looked at her, trying to read those silver-gray eyes. What was she thinking? How much about his past did she know? Virtually all of it, he'd bet. "Your investigators were thorough. But I know virtually nothing about you. Tell me how you spent your childhood in Liverpool."

"It was quite boring, really. My father owned an iron foundry, and I was the eldest child."

"Siblings?" he prompted.

"A younger brother."

"Would your father have been proud of the way you've succeeded in business?" Brand asked, intuiting the answer.

"No. He believed women should remain at home and have children, not run commercial empires."

There was a wealth of sadness in her voice. How he wanted her to confide in him. Perhaps in time she would. Then again . . . perhaps not. *I'm a fool to even imagine . . .*

Ahead of them, Tilda sat stiffly beside Sin on the first wagon. Wishing to turn the conversation to a safer course, Miranda asked, "Why is Mr. St. John so intent on pursuing Tilda?"

Brand chuckled. "The challenge."

In truth, although her companion continually protested

her dislike of the horse trainer, Miranda feared that he was breaking down her resistance. Just as the major was breaking down hers. "Has he ever been married?"

"A confirmed bachelor. Until now."

"I thought you said that his intentions weren't honorable."

His eyes met hers, and his expression was very serious. "The right woman can change that for any man."

Suddenly all sorts of impossible ideas began tumbling about in her mind as she groped for a proper response. He meant Lori had changed him . . . didn't he? But then, he'd been engaged before . . . although she could understand how a woman like Reba Wilcox would sour a man on matrimony.

"I suppose you're right," she managed to reply, folding her hands primly in her lap to hide their trembling. Once they arrived at the picnic site, she must get away from him before she did something utterly unthinkable.

Brand cursed to himself. He'd frightened her. He was rushing his fences, and he knew better. How the hell could he and Lori end this tangle with their courtship and still allow him to spend time with her mother? It was time for the clever Miss Auburn to give him the boot.

After that . . . well, who the hell knew what would happen? He was not even sure what he wanted to happen. He desired Miranda Auburn. But did he want to marry her? More to the point, would she even for one moment consider marrying a penniless baron who had been willing to sell himself to her?

Chapter Fourteen

The pool was really more of a small lake in a picturesque setting shaded by tall oaks. Sin had instructed one of the servants to clean and repair the dinghy yesterday so the young couples could take turns using it. That way those who were unwed could spend time in private conversation while remaining in clear sight of the rest of the party.

Once the picnic gear had been unloaded and the guests were milling about, Brand took his friend aside, asking, "Has Tilda agreed to your own private picnic?"

"She's in on our conspiracy with Miss Auburn, old chap. I played that ace, and she agreed to make herself scarce. The rest is up to you and the widow's most clever daughter."

Looking at all the young people, Brand had his doubts but shrugged. "I'm not certain this whole scheme is wise. It seems to me you'll have a great deal more success with Tilda than I will with Miranda."

"Never underestimate a pair of women with a plan," Sin replied sagely. With that, he strolled over to Tilda and made an elegant bow, then assisted her back onto the wagon and drove away without a word.

None of the guests noticed them leave except Miranda, whose soft smile suggested to Brand that she approved of her maid's having a suitor. Behind that prim and businesslike exterior, did there beat the heart of a romantic? Somehow Brand doubted it, especially since he had nothing to offer her except himself. Could that possibly be enough?

As if trying to make up for his foolish neglect yesterday, Geoffrey insisted Varinia join him in a turn about the water while Jon supervised setting up the croquet game. When they began to play, Brand begged off and wandered over to the blanket beneath a large oak where Miranda was observing the activities.

"Why aren't you playing?" she asked.

"I never cared for lawn balls. I always lose," he replied, folding his long body gracefully to sit beside her.

"I cannot imagine you losing at anything you put your mind to." Those were loaded words, and the moment they escaped her lips, she knew it.

His smile was slow and insinuating, as if they shared a secret. "Don't be so certain. I lost the war. And it wasn't for want of trying, I assure you."

"That was hardly within the control of one man, Major, even one as formidable as you. You acquitted yourself very well on the battlefield."

"I keep forgetting how thorough your investigation of me was," he murmured, leaning back on his elbows to observe the progress of the croquet game. He was not in the least interested in it and wondered if she could tell. Or if she cared. He seemed to make her nervous. Perhaps that was a good sign. Or not. Blasted contrary female!

"I didn't investigate you out of prurient curiosity," she said defensively, and then realized how that sounded.

He looked up at her, grinning again. "Is that a blush, Mrs. Auburn?"

Somehow when he used her proper name in that tone of voice, it sounded even more intimate than when he called her Miranda. "Nonsense," she replied primly. "It's merely quite warm outdoors today."

In truth, it was pleasantly cool but he did not feel it would be politic to remark on that fact. Nor did he want to discuss the reason for her investigation—his intended marriage to Lorilee. Instead, he changed the subject. "The newlyweds look rather blissful from afar."

Miranda looked at Geoffrey and Varinia out on the lake. "He has a great deal to make up for to that poor thing. He's treated her abominably."

"A character defect, marrying for money," Brand said lightly, wondering why he'd brought it up . . . unless it was to see which way the wind might blow if he turned his attention from Lorilee to her.

"It's a time-honored tradition in English society. What matters is how a couple deals together after the marriage," she replied in a quiet tone of voice, as if recalling distant memories, memories that mixed the bitter with the sweet.

Before he could draw her out further about her mysterious relationship with Will Auburn, a loud squeal of delight from Abbie drew their attention to the croquet match, which Lorilee's friend was obviously winning— or being allowed to win.

As if reading his mind, Miranda said, "I wonder if Jon, too, is doing a bit of penance for his undue attention to the widow yesterday."

They shared a companionable laugh as the game progressed. Abbie did win and Jon beamed at all the ladies with patronizing good humor. By that time Geoffrey and Varinia returned from their lake excursion and Miranda was about to suggest the servants open the baskets for the feast, but Lori surprised her with another plan.

She hurried to her mother, trailed by the vicar's son and his wife. "Melvin and Alberta know of a perfect woodland glade near his father's church. It's across the other side of the lake and the deer come to browse there. I'd love to see it, and it's a wonderful day for a ride. Would you mind awfully, Mother, if we left you? It won't be for all that long," she cajoled.

Brand caught her eye and chivalrously offered, "I'd be more than happy to keep Mrs. Auburn company. I'm in the saddle altogether too much as it is."

"How kind of you, my lord," Lori gushed, barely giving her mother a chance to say anything before she headed toward the spot where the footmen were tending the horses. "Let's ride, then!"

Within moments the party was off, leaving Brand and Miranda alone with a pair of footmen. Food had been prepared for the servants, and he instructed them to take their basket and find a place to enjoy it in privacy. "When the young people return famished, you'll require all your strength, so refuel yourselves now. I'm certain you'll hear them without my summoning you," he added.

In a blink he was alone with her. Now what? "I don't know about you, but the aromas wafting from those baskets are quite distracting," he murmured, pulling back a white linen cloth and peering inside. "I see no reason why we should wait for the others to return."

"What of simple manners?" Miranda supplied.

He chuckled. "Just a small snack to tide us over. No harm in that."

"So said the serpent in the garden, if I recall my Bible."

"And I'm certain you do." His expression was wry as he looked at her sitting so very properly, her legs tucked to one side, skirts carefully covering all but the tips of her high-heeled boots. Her moss-green cotton dress softly accented the gentle curves of her body, and her hair was coiled in a soft chignon at her nape with wispy curls framing her face. If she didn't look exactly angelic, she certainly did look tempting.

To keep himself from reaching out to take the pins from her heavy hair and bury his hands in it, he inhaled deeply of the aroma wafting from the basket. "Ah, heavenly. 'Fresh bread and a jug of wine . . .' " He waited for her to pick up the poem.

" 'And thou beside me in the wilderness,' " Miranda supplied whimsically. "But it's not 'fresh bread,' it's 'a loaf of bread.' "

He shook his head in bemusement. "For a lady of business, you certainly know literature. When do you find time to read?"

She shrugged as he began to unload the bounty. "Actually, I don't have very much time anymore. When I was young—"

"And we all know how ancient you are now," he said with amusement as he expertly opened one of the chilled white wines.

"I'm considerably older than you."

"What? Five years?" He scoffed, then quickly went on without giving her a chance to respond. "I'll match you in terms of life experience and come out the winner. Want to make a wager?"

"I don't gamble, Major." Her tone was cool. Where was he going with this? She knew it was dangerous, but when he offered her a glass of wine, she foolishly accepted it and sipped. Ambrosial. Best to change the topic. "A lady never discusses her age . . . or her life experiences."

He took a long drink of his wine, and she watched the strong brown column of his throat swallow where he'd loosened his cravat. Somehow she intuited he was most comfortable working without a hat or coat, in shirtsleeves with his collar opened to the intense heat of his homeland, the sun beating down on his already bronzed face, streaking his shaggy hair paler gold. It was an arresting image and disturbed her greatly. She took another swallow of wine herself, then another.

"What's in that bowl?" she asked as he removed the lid.

"Looks like pheasant, and here are meat pies and fresh vegetables, even some fruit."

He had removed his gloves after they climbed down from the wagon. Somehow he always found a way to do that in spite of the impropriety. Her own sheer lace mitts seemed impractical indeed when he began tearing the tender meat into pieces. Then he uncovered the flaky pastries filled with spicy venison and placed one on a plate, along with a small pile of peas still in their crispy pods. To this he added a quarter of one of the pheasants and a chunk of bread, which he broke from the loaf.

"I shall require a knife and fork to cut the food," she said primly, trying not to look at his hands, those strong, scarred hands, elegant and powerful.

Brand heard the slight breathlessness in her voice. "I don't see any utensils," he said after making a very cursory search of the baskets. "Must've left them in the wagon."

He did not seem inclined to go in search of them. "I'll stain my gloves with grease." The protest seemed faint indeed, even to her own ears. She took another drink of wine.

"Then allow me to feed you." He took a sliver of tender juicy meat from the plate and held it in his fingers, offering it to her with a dare gleaming in his eyes.

Miranda had never felt so uncertain of herself, not even at her first ball as a sixteen-year-old girl back in Liverpool. Without allowing her bemused senses time to react with the natural caution she normally exhibited, she tilted her face toward his hand and opened her mouth.

Lordy, the lushness of those lips, so soft and sweet. Struggling not to tremble, he slipped the morsel into her mouth, being careful not to touch her. She closed her eyes and chewed, then washed the delicacy down with another sip of wine. When she opened them, he was offering her a pea pod. She took the crisp vegetable and felt the tang of sherry on her tongue.

"Mmm, delicious," she murmured.

"Yes, it is," he said, but his eyes were fastened on her, not the food. Twisting off a leg from the bird, he held it out. "Take a bite."

This is insane, a faint voice inside her head warned, but she leaned forward and bit into the rich succulent meat, so tender it fell from the bone. He caught the pieces easily in his hand and shoved them into his mouth with neat economy, then held out the bone for her once again.

"I . . . I need to hold it but I'll soil my gloves," she blurted out as her fingertips brushed against his hand.

"Then take them off. I won't tell."

Satan in the garden couldn't have been more beguiling. She took another sip of wine and placed the glass carefully on the ground, then yanked off her mitts and tossed them aside with a reckless flourish. When he offered her the bone again, she took one end in her fingers, touching his hand as she did so, and jerking back ever so slightly. Then she recovered, daring to reach out once more and seize hold of the prize.

Brand watched her take another bite. His mouth, filled with saliva from the juicy food a moment ago, went suddenly dry. He refilled their glasses, then offered her a crust from the bread. "This is my favorite part," he whispered, letting her pull at the slightly tough piece torn from the end. As it broke free, crumbs showered down over her

219

green dress and he dreamed of licking them, one by one, off the sweet curves of breasts and lower . . .

"May I have the wine?" she asked, daring to speak, afraid her voice would come out a raspy croak.

He handed her the glass he'd refilled and then clinked his own to hers in a toast. "Here's to a beautiful day . . . and many more to come." They both drank the golden liquid, as soft and sweet as the summer sunlight beaming down through their leafy bower.

Then he uncovered another bowl and removed a fat, ripe red raspberry. Dipping it in the heavy cream, he popped it into his mouth. "Umm."

"A gentleman would offer one to a lady first," Miranda reproved.

"So he would. But being a baron doesn't make me a gentleman, no matter what the House of Lords says," he replied with a grin. He anointed another berry and held it out to her.

There was no way she could take it from his hand without touching him. And she knew it. Knew he knew it. She opened her mouth anyway and let him slide it inside. *It must be the wine.* Somehow, of their own volition her lips closed around his fingers before he withdrew them. She sat back, aghast at her hunger, one she knew had nothing to do with food.

Brand watched as her eyes grew wide and her fingers flew up to her mouth. Her lips were stained bright red from berry juice, and they were just as plump and ripe . . . and oh, so kissable. Without thinking, he leaned over and took her hand away, replacing it with his mouth, brushing it softly against hers, back and forth, drinking the tart-sweet delight of raspberry and woman. Then their tongues touched, just the faintest hint of contact, but she drew away as if she'd never felt a man kiss her that way before.

And instantly he knew it must be true. Their formidable Queen had placed her Puritanical stamp on what was considered proper, even for married women. No lady was supposed to do more than her "duty" for her husband. For all he knew, Will Auburn had never truly kissed her at all—something Brandon Caruthers planned to correct immediately. His hands framed her face and his lips claimed hers more deeply.

They still sat discreetly apart on the blanket, leaning toward each other as he reached behind her head and buried his fingers in her hair, pulling the heavy mass at her nape free so that it tumbled down her back. Deep ruby fire danced in the dappled light filtering through the leaves. Her touch was unsure, exploratory as she let the tip of her tongue dart against his for an instant, then withdraw. She dug her fingers into his arms, feeling the hard flexing of his muscles.

He slanted his mouth at a different angle and guided her head, cradling it in one palm as he seized a fistful of lavender-scented hair and wrapped it around his wrist. She tasted of the fruit and more . . . oh, so much more. When he heard her moan softly against his mouth, he was lost. His tongue thrust deep and his mouth worked over hers hungrily, demanding response even as he tutored her in how to give it.

"I knew you'd be sweet . . . and tart . . ." he murmured against her lips as his hand glided down the long, silky column of her throat, over the indentation of her collarbone to the lush curve of her breast.

The fabric was sheer cotton and her undergarments were made of lace, her one feminine indulgence even in drab business attire. The abrasive texture of the lace teased her aching nipple as he massaged it. His words had not registered, but when he pulled her against him and they tumbled backwards onto the soft grass behind the blanket, Miranda came to her senses. With a muffled cry, she pushed free of him and sat bolt upright.

She saw with horror that one of the wineglasses had overturned in the midst of their passion, staining her skirt and his pantleg. What on earth had she been thinking? There were servants only a short distance away, and the young people could return at any moment. Her daughter could ride up and see her own mother lying with the man she intended to marry. Miranda moaned with disgust and placed her hands on either side of her head, trying desperately to gather her jumbled wits.

If only she had not consumed all that accursed wine! Feeling her hair loose about her shoulders, she began frantically searching for the pins to put it up. "I'm no better than that drunken tart," she sobbed, fumbling with the long, burnished mass.

Brand sat back, aching to take her in his arms but knowing to do so would drive her away forever. He also knew of whom she spoke. "You're nothing like Reba. Don't ever say such a thing." There was an undertone of anger that she should even consider such a comparison. "You're just human . . . a woman—"

"A woman who has nearly coupled with her own daughter's suitor!" She rounded on him like a wounded animal, cornered and desperate, letting anger purge away the guilt and shame . . . for the moment. She knew it would return later. Then she would have to deal with it, but not now. Dear God, not now. All she could think of was escape.

Trembling, she got to her feet somehow, refusing his assistance when he stood with effortless ease and offered his hand, the graceful lout. Jamming pins into her tangled hair as she twisted it into a knot at the back of her head, she said in the iciest voice she could muster, "I cannot be seen in this condition. One of the footmen will drive me back to your home. You will tell Lori and the others that I felt a sudden upset stomach—say the meat pies were tainted, the clotted cream was sour—say whatever you wish, only make them believe that was all that happened here!"

"This was my fault. I am deeply sorry I offended you, but you must know this has been a long time coming between us. We—"

"No!" she practically shrieked, holding her hands over her ears as if that would make him and his words—those terrifying, truthful words—vanish. "There is no *we!* Not now, nor ever will there be anything between us, my lord. Nor will you continue courting my daughter. If you possess one shred of decency—and I'm inclined to doubt it—you will allow her to—"

"Miss Auburn and I have already agreed we do not suit." Now it was he who interrupted as his temper boiled over. "Of course, she will be the one to break off our courtship," he replied tightly.

His words about Lori did not register with Miranda as she turned and fled to the wagon, climbing aboard the high seat with dogged determination, out of breath from far more than simply running.

All she called back to him was a frosty request that he summon one of the footmen to take her home. Cursing his stupidity, the wine, the woman and life in general, he trudged toward the pathway the servants had taken with their lunch to do as she asked.

Lori sat by herself in the isolated glade, watching a doe with her fawns frolicking across the open meadow. Behind her was a small stream that fed the lake on the baron's property. She smiled to herself. Things would be going swimmingly for them, alone at the picnic place. All Brand need do was dismiss the footmen on some pretext and get on with his courtship of her mother. It was such a romantic spot!

She had left the other couples laughing and flirting, feeling like an outsider since she was the only unattached one in the group. It would be nice to have a real suitor, but she had learned her lesson the hard way. Brandon Caruthers was in love with another woman, and Geoffrey Winters was in love with himself. Someday there would be a man right for her. She only had to school herself in patience until he came along. In the meanwhile, she was rather enjoying the role of matchmaker.

Surprisingly, Lori found that she actually enjoyed solitude, something she never would have imagined only a few short months ago. "Perhaps I'm finally growing up," she murmured to herself. Then she could not help wondering what sort of youth her mother had had. Or had not been allowed to have. At Lori's own age she was already a mother, wed to a man old enough to be her grandfather. Her reverie was suddenly interrupted by the sound of clumsy crashing through the elderberry thicket behind her.

"A ha'penny for your thoughts," Geoffrey Winters said with a charming smile as he strolled into view, sending the deer into flight.

"Where is Varinia?" Lori asked immediately. Suspiciously. She did not like the gleam in his eye one bit.

"Oh, she went to visit the village market nearby with Alberta and that foolish vicar of hers."

"Melvin is the vicar's son, a fact you'd know if you had come to church with us this morning," she chided.

Ignoring the rebuke, he took a seat on the fallen log beside her. "Don't be angry, puss. I was——"

Lorilee scooted away. "I am not your 'puss.' It is insulting in the extreme for you to address me so. For the sake of Abbie and Jon's friendship, I have overlooked your appalling past behavior, but do not presume any further, Mr. Winters."

"I realize I was . . . er, rather rash in my proposal to you at Ascot," he began, employing his most winsome smile. "I didn't intend to offend."

"Your proposal wasn't intended to offend me? What sort of a ninny do you take me for?" She stood up, too furious to think of anything but getting away from this vain popinjay.

"I take you for a beautiful woman who once enjoyed my kisses, a passionate woman. Here, allow me to show you just how passionate you are." He reached out and seized hold of her arm, trying to pull her into his embrace.

Lori was frozen with horror for a moment as she slammed against his chest, but when the smell of his macassar-slicked hair filled her nostrils, she nearly gagged. How had she ever fancied herself in love with such a narcissistic, faithless excuse for a man?

When he lowered his head to press his mouth to hers, she stomped with her full weight on his instep, using the sharp heel of her boot. Immediately he released her, crying out in pain. As he raised his injured foot, she caught him off balance and shoved his chest with all her might. He toppled backward over the log and into the creek beyond, where he landed with a loud splash in the icy water.

Lori could hear his curses echo through the woods as she strode quickly to where she'd left her mare. Let him explain why he was limping and how his clothing had become soaked.

The rocks in the creek had jagged edges on them, she thought vengefully as she rode back around the lake. Poor Varinia. Her husband would always be a skirt-chaser. How fortunate that Lori's own wise mother had prevented her from falling prey to him. Lori knew she would be far more careful selecting a husband.

She had learned a valuable lesson.

*   *   *

Miranda lay on the narrow bed in the guest room assigned to her at Rushcroft Hall with a cold compress on her aching head, trying to gather her scattered wits. When the party returned from the picnic, she must appear to be somewhat ill yet rally enough for them to catch the evening train for London. There was no way on earth she or her daughter would spend another night beneath that . . . that seducer's roof! It would entail quite an acting feat. Lori knew she'd never suffered a sick day in her life. Of course, there were the effects of the wine.

What had possessed her to drink so much of the blasted stuff? Normally, she was very careful of imbibing alcohol. She knew she had little better tolerance of it than did her daughter. How could she pretend she had an upset stomach, not a buzzing head? And what had the baron told them? Was it the meat pies or the clotted cream that had supposedly done her in? Drat it all, in spite of being cool and able to conceal her feelings in business, she had always been a terrible prevaricator when it came to personal matters.

How could she deceive Lori? Her daughter had been taken in by Pelham's pup and was now betrayed by the baron. There was no way she could allow Lori to marry that bounder, but neither could she explain the shameful seduction beneath the oak tree to an innocent like Lori. The poor child would be shocked and appalled that her mother had behaved no better than a woman like Reba Wilcox.

"No matter if I must disillusion her and lose her respect, I must save her from Rushcroft," she murmured to herself.

A soft knock on the door was followed by Tilda's entrance. The maid had a suspicious look on her face. Already Miranda knew she was in trouble, and Lori had not yet even returned.

"I heard you'd taken ill. Something you ate, according to the baron." The maid walked over and pulled the cloth from Miranda's eyes. "A little green about the gills, but you don't look to me as if you suffer from food poisoning. In fact, since Mr. St. John and I partook of the same food, I'm inclined to doubt there was anything wrong with it. I did note one empty wine bottle lying on the picnic blanket . . ." She waited a beat. When Miranda did not respond, she said, "You're faking."

"I am not," Miranda protested, sitting up and wrapping her arms around her bent knees, laying her head down on them. "I've never felt worse in my life." That at least was the truth.

"But it isn't your stomach that's hurting, is it?" Tilda's tone invited confidence now. "It's your heart."

Miranda's head snapped up. "Whatever do you mean?"

One black eyebrow arched in Tilda's narrow face. "I think you know."

Before Miranda could think of a reply to that disturbing remark, the door burst open and Lorilee rushed in. "Mother, the baron said you were taken ill! You're never ill." She took a seat beside her mother and reached up to press her hand against Miranda's brow, acting for all the world as if their roles had been reversed.

"Oh, she's sick, all right," Tilda said dryly. "Heartsick. And I'd bet my new brocade robe it's over the baron."

Miranda's jaw dropped. "Tilda, of all the impertinent, improper, ridiculous—"

"Methinks the lady doth protest too much," Lorilee said to Tilda with a cheeky grin. The maid nodded back in sage agreement.

Miranda looked from Tilda to Lori and back, utterly befuddled. "Since when do you quote Shakespeare to me, young lady?" she asked, knowing the quote was a bit off.

But for the life of her, she was unable to recall the precise wording.

"What happened between you and the baron, Mother? He appeared quite distraught."

As well he might! "We must go home. Once we're there, I shall explain everything. Tilda," she said, turning to the maid, "please help me pack our things. We must not miss the evening train to London." She began to pick up discarded garments, as frantic as a squirrel gathering nuts at first frost.

"Mother, I think there's something you should know," Lori announced. When Miranda did not stop throwing things in the trunk, the girl sighed and said, "I never intended to marry the baron. You chose him, not I. And for very good reason. You're the one who is in love with him, not I."

Miranda dropped the shirtwaist in her hands and turned to her daughter. Her mouth opened, but not a word came out. For the first time in her life she was utterly speechless.

Chapter Fifteen

The hour was late and everyone exhausted when the women arrived at their city house. Mercifully, the baron had remained behind in the countryside although he'd insisted Mr. St. John accompany them as protection, seeing that they were safely locked inside the walls of Will Auburn's mausoleum and surrounded by servants. Miranda's mind was still whirling from Lori's startling pronouncement, but they'd had no privacy to discuss it.

She had assigned the house servants the task of unpacking, ordered a cold collation for a late supper, although she had not the slightest appetite, then locked herself inside her office to collect her thoughts before summoning her daughter for a long and frank talk.

The only problem was that she had no idea what to say to the girl. The whole idea of herself and the baron—of him preferring her to a lovely young girl—why, it was so utterly preposterous she could not credit it.

But you hoped for it, that wicked voice inside her whispered.

She quashed it.

If Lori had decided he was too hard, too frighteningly uncivilized in spite of his superficial veneer of charm, that she could understand. After his despicable behavior this afternoon, she thought Lori wise to reject him—far wiser than she herself had been to arrange the match in the first place.

Miranda sighed as she paced back and forth across the spacious office. She had always been mercilessly honest in all her dealings, taking pride in her principles. Now was not the time to begin lying to herself. She shared the baron's guilt for the seduction. Oh, he was skillful, very practiced, no doubt about it, but she was scarcely some foolish twit barely out of the schoolroom. Even if she didn't have the experience of a tart such as Reba Wilcox, she had known where he was leading her. And she had allowed it . . . even if she had to fortify herself with alcohol in order to numb her conscience!

The baron—she refused to use any name more personal—had spoken about their mutual attraction. In the heat of anger, she had dismissed his claim, but now in the chill of remorse, she had to face the fact that it was frighteningly true. She, the plain, drab older woman, confident in her wealth and power, had been fascinated by him from the moment she'd laid eyes on him. Even though she'd hidden behind a wall of condescension, he must have sensed her weakness. He knew her better than she had known herself.

There was no way she could ever trust him. How mistaken she had been about his character, believing him a proud man of honor who would treat her precious daughter with kindness and consideration! Never in all her years of struggling to survive in this man's world had she been guilty of such a lapse in judgment.

And he'd used it, the rotter!

Her furious ruminations were interrupted by a soft knock on the door. Without waiting for a reply, Lorilee entered and closed the door behind her. Miranda could see her daughter was not as nervous as she. How had the tables been turned in their relationship? *The baron*, whispered a small, insistent voice buried deep inside her.

"We must talk, Lorilee."

Uh-oh. Lori knew things boded ill when her mother used her full name in that tone of voice. She fought the sudden feeling of being twelve again, caught eavesdropping while her mother discussed a very important business arrangement with Mr. Aimesley.

"Yes, we do," she replied with as much calm as she could muster. "Mother, I—"

"Since when do you perceive it your prerogative to interfere in my personal life, to deceive me and scheme with outsiders?" Miranda accused before she could stop herself. Lori's stricken look made her feel small, but the girl deserved a good dressing down for her part in this debacle.

Lorilee took a deep breath for courage and replied, "I never intended to deceive you. Lord Rushcroft is no more an 'outsider' than is Tilda. And, as to interfering in your personal life, I am your daughter. Who better has the right to be concerned about her own mother's welfare?"

That set Miranda back on her heels. She mustered every ounce of negotiating skill she'd honed over the years and went on the counterattack. "You presume too much, as does Tilda. I should fire her for this impertinence." At the shocked expression on Lori's face, she relented, adding, "But I will not."

"Well, thank heaven for that. This sort of hysterical reaction is precisely why I didn't explain my feelings toward the baron. And why I knew better than to suggest he suited you so well. You needed more time with him to recognize that for yourself."

"Hysterical!" Miranda practically shrieked before bringing herself under control. "The whole idea is absurd. I never intend to wed again." She turned and looked out the window at the dim glitter of gaslights on the pavement. "It would be disloyal to your father."

"Were you in love with him, Mother?" Lori asked, almost certain of the answer.

Miranda could feel her daughter's eyes on her and knew she could not lie. "I cared very deeply for him," she managed. "When you're young, you think being in love is the end-all and be-all of existence, but I can assure you it's not. I believed you understood about marriage for those of our class."

"I do, otherwise I never would've agreed to meet Lord Rushcroft in the first place. Marriage is based on more than"—her cheeks pinkened as she moistened her lips and said—"physical attraction." When Miranda's whole body jerked angrily, Lori backtracked quickly, intuiting that discussion would not work. She knew nothing at all about "physical attraction" beyond a few kisses bestowed by a fortune-hunting ne'er-do-well. Best leave that approach to Tilda, who was older and wiser in the ways of the world.

"I was given to believe that having things in common was the basis of a good marriage. Position in society, laughing at the same jokes, arguing about political matters and finding you really don't disagree as much as you thought you did. I've been watching the two of you together for weeks, Mother. You understand each other. You live in the same world. I'm just a schoolroom miss to him."

"A schoolroom miss who's taken a very great deal upon herself," Miranda said with asperity.

"Only because I care about both of you . . . and your happiness."

"Odd that I mistook your feelings for him that night in the garden when you kissed him." The moment she blurted out those foolish words, Miranda sucked in her breath, horrified at the petty jealousy they revealed.

Lori smiled like a kitten in cream. "I think of the baron as an elder brother, not a potential husband. And what you witnessed was long after we'd agreed that his courtship of me was over. Do you know what he told me when we had that discussion?"

"I have not the faintest idea," Miranda said sharply.

"That I would one day be like you. I consider it a high compliment."

"Has it occurred to you that he may be using you? That he's no better than Geoffrey Winters?"

Lori stepped back. "I've never known you to be cruel before," she said quietly.

At once Miranda felt contrite. "I didn't mean that as an aspersion on your judgment, dearheart. It's his fault, not yours," she said, reaching out to take Lori in her arms. "Please forgive me."

Lori could feel her mother trembling. She was as upset as Lori had feared she'd be when forced to confront her feelings for Brandon Caruthers. "No, it is not his fault that I decided the two of you should be together. He disagreed with me, too . . . when I went to his city house and—"

Miranda jerked Lori to arm's length. "You went alone to his home?"

Lori almost laughed at the horrified expression on her mother's face. "No—that is, I mean, yes, I did visit him, but I was not alone. I took Tilda along as chaperone."

"Is everyone involved in this insane conspiracy against me?"

"It is no conspiracy, and no one wishes you anything but happiness . . . happiness I don't believe you ever knew with Father." Lori knew she was trespassing into forbidden territory, but it was too late to call the words back.

"I was happy with your father. You have no right to say otherwise. And just what do you know of such worldly matters that would entitle you to sit in judgment on me?"

"None," Lori replied meekly. "I made a foolish mistake with Mr. Winters, but that doesn't mean I'm incapable of understanding what's been going on beneath my very eyes ever since the day Lord Rushcroft rescued you from the carriage crash in Hyde Park."

Miranda felt the guilt stab deeply. She, too, remembered that scene very well. "I'm sorry that you had to see such a sordid—"

"No! Never say such a thing," Lori protested, embracing her mother once more. "What I saw was two people trying desperately not to admit that they were attracted to each other."

Miranda broke away, shaking her head. How had her innocent child suddenly become such a keen observer of matters about which she was supposed to know nothing? "Whether or not the baron and I . . . that is, even if I were attracted to him, it signifies nothing. I'm an older woman. He's a younger man."

"He's closer to your age than to mine," Lori volleyed back immediately.

"So he once said to me, also," Miranda replied tartly. "No, it simply won't work. One cannot make mutton into lamb. That time in my life is over."

"But that's not true! You're only thirty-five—"

"Thirty-six," Miranda corrected her.

"As if that makes you ancient." Lori rolled her eyes in disgust. She knew that her mother's feelings of inferiority had something to do with her marriage. Well, the baron would have to sort that out, because she was certain her mother would never say anything against Will Auburn to his only child. "You have a whole life before you yet. Please don't let it slip away," she cajoled.

"I believe that should be my speech to you," Miranda said dryly, recovering her equilibrium a bit. "My life is full already. I have my work and, for a little while longer, I have you." She stroked her daughter's bright hair fondly. "It is more than enough, Lori. Much more than enough." Who was she trying to convince—her daughter or herself?

"You cannot send Lord Rushcroft away," Lori persisted doggedly. "Someone has been trying to kill you, and he can protect you until he finds out who it is. Why, even tonight he sent Mr. St. John to see us home. And he insists you not leave the house without a man to protect you." There, a possible trump card?

"I can easily afford to engage the services of a body-guard, dearheart, without the baron's assistance."

"He cares about you, Mother. I believe he loves you. And you love him. But for now, all I ask is that you not cut him out of your life."

Miranda shook her head. "This is one time when I cannot accede to your wishes, Lori. Please try to understand."

Lori had held her temper as much as her eighteen years allowed, but in the face of such intractable stubbornness, she gave in and stamped her foot. "You are the one who needs to learn understanding. I merely lack patience!"

Miranda watched her storm from the room and felt doubly desolate. She had made a fool of herself over a younger man and she had alienated her only child . . . all in the space of one wretched day.

Lori paced in her room, holding one of Callie's kittens in her arms. The purring animal did little to soothe her frustration. Tilda folded up Lori's discarded clothing, checking to see what required laundering and what did not.

"I tell you, she's impossible," the girl murmured.

Tilda arched one eyebrow. "Odd, but she's said the same about you from time to time."

"I had hoped once they . . . well, once he kissed her, she'd see that she loved him," Lori said forlornly, nuzzling the kitten for comfort.

"Like you believed you loved Mr. Winters after you kissed him?" Tilda reminded her gently.

Lori deflated, flopping ungracefully onto her bed. The kitten squealed and jumped away. "You know that was different. I was just a silly girl. What shall we do, Tilda?"

"Well, Mr. St. John has been instructed to see that the place is watched and someone accompanies your mother whenever she goes to the City. I suppose he could be our intermediary with the baron." She frowned then. "At least until this troubling matter of unaccidental accidents is straightened out."

"I tried to reason about that with Mother, too. It didn't work."

"Then I imagine we'll just have to leave it in the hands of Lord Rushcroft for the time being, won't we?"

Lori brightened, watching the kitten begin to bat at a tassel on her four-poster bed curtain. "If the baron finds out who's been trying to harm her, she'll be grateful and come to her senses. But in the meanwhile, Tilda, I have an idea . . ."

"I don't like it. We've paid O'Connell too much already and nothing's come of it," he fretted as he sawed off a large piece of steak and stuffed it into his mouth. The food in this abysmal hotel was not half bad, considering everything.

"What do you mean, nothing? Caruthers's mews nearly

burned down and he was frightened to death his precious horses were going to roast. And he believes that fool Winters was responsible," his companion argued, taking a small bite of meat, then shoving the plate away in disgust. The food here was truly awful.

"That was a good idea, using that Irishman to 'lend' money to Winters for his infernally unlucky gambling habit."

"I do have a good idea now and then. If only you could conclude your arrangements and have done with this mess."

"I told you, as long as Miranda Auburn is alive, that's impossible," he snapped.

"It isn't as if we haven't exhausted every trick in the book to change that! That harpy has the most incredible luck I've ever seen. But I have been thinking of another plan that will work."

He wiped his mouth with a napkin and looked across the table at his accomplice. "Now that all these so-called accidental attempts on her life have failed, she's being guarded like the crown jewels. All courtesy of Brandon Caruthers, damn his eyes. Just how do you propose to get to her?"

"By indirection. As you say, everyone is worried about the mother. So we'll take an alternate approach—through the daughter. If motherly love isn't greatly overrated, I suspect we'll have Miranda Auburn just where we want her. Dead and buried."

His eyes lit up. "Kidnap the daughter and lure the mother after her. . . . Hmmm, not a bad idea."

"I'll make the arrangements as soon as I speak with our source," his companion murmured with a cold smile. "Just give me a few days to work out the details." *What a fool you are. When I'm through, I won't just be rid of the*

Auburns, I'll be rid of you, too. And I'll control everything!

"Please, Mr. Aimesley, you must say yes. She'll listen to you. She's been working much too hard and needs to take time away from her office," Lori cajoled.

Kent Aimesley leaned back in the chair behind his large desk and sighed. As Miranda Auburn's senior associate, his was the largest office in the building, with the exception of his employer's. He studied the golden-haired young woman so earnestly asking for his help.

Miss Auburn could be most persistent when she got an idea in her head. "I fear it's no use. Until we complete the negotiations for the railway, your mother will insist on overseeing matters herself—and I must sail for America again within the week. With one of us on each side of the Atlantic, it will be impossible to prevail upon her to spend time away from here."

Lori looked around nervously. Although no one had seen her slip into Mr. Aimesley's office, she knew her mother was at the end of the hall. If Miranda caught her meddling this way in business affairs, she'd confine her to the house like a prisoner. There was no way to explain to this dull man the real reason she wanted her mother to stay home. One could hardly ask a former suitor to assist in her matchmaking.

She twisted her handkerchief and allowed the tears to well up in her eyes, deciding on a partial truth. "You don't know that several attempts have been made on her life, do you?" she asked.

"Good heavens! When? How?" Aimesley shot forward in his chair and stood up.

"Oh, dear, if Mother knew I'd told anyone, even you, Mr. Aimesley, she would be furious. But there have been several near misses. We were attacked at the opera by three street ruffians. And then there were two carriage crashes and even a shooting incident. . . ." She waited a beat, allowing him to digest what she'd said. If he still harbored the tendresse for her mother that she hoped he did, Lori felt certain she could win him over.

"Well, that does put the matter in a different light, I must agree," he said thoughtfully. "Perhaps I could convince her that she need not come in to the City, at least until I have to sail again. And I might put that off for a bit over a week, if I can make the proper arrangements. I shall see what I can do."

Lori beamed. "I knew I could count on you, Mr. Aimesley. Mother trusts you implicitly. If you assure her that matters are in hand here, you'll make my task of keeping her safe much easier."

"She's hiding from me, dammit," Brand muttered to himself.

"Turned you away at the front door, did she? Well, I suppose you could force your way past that feeble butler of hers and confront her, or waylay her as she enters her business offices, but somehow I don't think that would be quite the thing," Sin said dryly.

"I'm ever so glad you're amused," Brand growled.

"I believe a bit of subtlety and patience are called for—never your strong suit, old chap," St. John replied with a cheerful grin. He and Tilda had been in constant touch for the past several days since the weekend at Rushcroft Hall and the breaking off of his friend's courtship of Miss Auburn. "The lady's daughter has concocted a scheme or two. How do you feel about attending a ball at the Earl of Falconridge's city house tomorrow night?" From inside his jacket he pulled a heavy velum envelope sealed with the crest of Falconridge and handed it to Brand.

Caruthers tore it open and read while murmuring, "I've scarcely met Falconridge. He's a Liberal."

"And being a staunch Conservative, you avoid him in Lords as if he were a plague carrier." St. John chuckled tolerantly. "You are beginning to sound frighteningly English, m'lord."

Brand snorted. "Just because I make an innocent comment in passing, you needn't insult me for it." He returned his attention to the invitation. "How the devil did you get this?"

"Miss Auburn prevailed upon Mrs. Winters, who asked her father if he'd consider such a heresy as inviting you. He agreed."

"And I take it Miss Auburn has also prevailed upon her mother to attend?"

"How could she not when her daughter is once again out on the marriage mart? Of course, there will be a bit of gossip since Miss Auburn spurned you less than a week ago and now you'll both be present at the same function."

"It'll be a press of hundreds, if Falconridge's reputation as a host is to be believed. Not exactly the best way to speak to Miranda."

"I'm certain you'll think of something," Sin replied dryly.

The music was lilting, but Miranda felt no urge to tap her toe as she watched Lori dancing with the son of a young industrialist from Manchester. The cream of the peerage and the most wealthy commoners in the country filled the huge ballroom to overflowing. Falconridge was an earl, but his politics as well as the shipping firm his family owned brought him into contact with wealthy men of business, many of whom he counted as close friends. Being a woman in that men's arena, Miranda had not been extended the same privileges and had never before received an invitation to one of his countess's famous balls.

Lori had been thrilled when it arrived. She had apparently been truthful about having no romantic attachment to the baron, for she was dancing and laughing, the belle of the ball in a room full of eligible males. This was what Miranda had always wanted for her. So why did she feel so terribly unhappy? It certainly was not as if she harbored any dreams of dancing with a beau. That part of her life had ended before it ever began. She must live for her work and allow Lori to find joy in this world, a world to which she would never belong.

Thinking of her business and of long-forsaken dreams made Miranda wonder why Kent Aimesley had been so insistent that he could handle matters in the office this week and would not sail for Philadelphia as previously planned. She needed the refuge of hard work to occupy her mind and allow her to drop off to sleep in exhaustion at night. Otherwise . . .

No, I will not think of him.

"Would you honor me with this waltz, my dear Mrs. Auburn?" James Dunham inquired, bowing smartly.

He was an old family friend from Liverpool with whom she did occasional business. He was also well into his eighties, and she feared a brisk turn around the dance floor might just do him in, but there was no way to evade his unexpected invitation without appearing rude.

"I would be delighted, Mr. Dunham," she said with a smile, rising and allowing him to lead her to the floor, where the orchestra had just begun playing a Strauss piece with gusto.

As she was swept into the dance, she did not see her daughter standing at the side of the room with a sly smile curving her lips. Lori turned her head and winked at Brand, who was hidden behind a large potted palm.

Looking through the leaves, he watched Miranda dance.

Lord above, she was a delectable vision! Tilda had out-
done herself with that mane of fiery dark hair, piled high
in a welter of curls with a few tendrils trailing beguilingly
at her nape. Her gown was made of some satiny fabric
that caught the glitter from the myriad gaslights on the
chandeliers overhead. The cloth was deep orange shot
through with gold threads, colors one might have believed
would clash with red hair. Quite the opposite was true.

His mouth watered at the swell of milky white breasts
revealed by the low vee of the neckline. The skirt was
gracefully full but fell straight, not caught in one of those
infernal bustles. He could imagine the curve of her slender
hips and buttocks, indeed thought of grasping them and
plunging . . .

Shaking his head to clear away the deliciously lascivious visions which were raising his temperature, Brand
willed himself to concentrate on what he had to say to
her. Once he felt in control of his rebellious body, the
Rebel Baron strode boldly across the polished walnut of
the dance floor and made his way to where Miranda spun
in the elderly man's arms.

She was utterly unaware of his presence. He could
smell her scent, could in fact pick it out from any other
in this room filled with powdered and painted ladies. Miranda always smelled like lavender and sunshine, an essence uniquely hers. Inhaling it almost undid his
resolution not to think of sex. Almost. He took a deep,
calming breath and tapped Mr. Dunham on the shoulder.

"Eh, what?" the older man asked, turning in mid-stride
with a confused expression on his face. "Oh, Lord Rushcroft, good to see you." Then noting where the baron's
eyes were fastened in spite of the gentleman's nod to him,
he recalled what he had been asked to do. "Want to enjoy
this waltz with the lady, hey, what? I must confess to
being a bit old for dancing. My wind's not what it used

to be." He turned to Miranda. "It's been a pleasure, dear lady," he said with a courtly bow, handing her over to the younger man.

Before she could protest, Mr. Dunham was gone and she was in the baron's arms, being swept into the music.

Chapter Sixteen

Without creating a horrendous scene, there was nothing she could do but dance. The air around them was charged with more tension than an electrical storm. Miranda could feel the burning glances of curious onlookers who knew the baron had been escorting her daughter a scant week ago and that Lorilee had ended the courtship. What must they think now, seeing her mother in his arms?

"Shall we give them something to gossip about?" he dared her with a rakish grin.

"I believe we already have, courtesy of your ill manners," she whispered, trying to slip from his grasp without being obvious about it. "Release me at once."

"I don't believe I shall," he replied thoughtfully. "Having you back in my arms is far too enjoyable."

She stiffened angrily. "I have never been in your arms."

"I beg to differ. There was that day in Hyde Park after the carriage crash, then when I toppled you to the ground to escape flying bullets . . . and, of course, there was the picnic."

"If you were a gentleman—which you rightly deny being—you would never speak of such things."

"And that, I believe, is what the philosophers call a tautology," he said dryly. "Would you care to discuss philosophy? No? Perhaps politics? We always seem to have lively discussions about Parliament."

"I wish only to leave this dance floor as inconspicuously as possible," she hissed, knowing she was trembling and afraid that he, too, could feel the effect he was having on her.

"Too late for that. Look about you. We are the cynosure of all eyes. Ah, well, if we're not to have a civil discourse, then I suppose we'll just have to appreciate the music . . . and the feeling of being for a brief while in each other's arms. A reminder, Miranda, just a reminder," he said gently when she tried to pull away. "Can you deny you're enjoying this?"

When those golden tiger's eyes bored into hers so mesmerizingly, how could she even think, much less deny what they both knew to be true? She loved the feel of his tall, lean body moving in such perfect rhythm with her own. Her considerable height had been a plague all her life, and she had been happy that Lori was slightly shorter. As a girl in her one abortive season, she had found few dance partners tall enough to match her if she wore slippers with heels on them. But in Brandon's arms, she only reached his shoulder.

You're using his Christian name just as improperly as he does yours! Stop it!

She might as well command the tides to stop turning or the moon to stop orbiting the earth. Miranda could not deny she loved dancing with him. It seemed he was reading her mind when he said, "You've always been scrupulously honest . . . until we became involved. Now you even try to lie to yourself, don't you, Miranda?"

Damn the arrogant man! She forced herself to raise her head proudly and look into his eyes as she replied, "We are *not* involved.' "

"Then what would you call that kiss we shared at the picnic?"

"A most unfortunate mistake. One I shall never repeat," she said firmly.

He shook his head sadly. "Ah, Miranda, what must I do to convince you it was no mistake?"

"How about reversing the current of the Thames?"

"Or parting the Red Sea?" he replied with a faint trace of a smile. "I fear I can't claim any gift from the Deity enabling me to exercise such power. I'm only a man who has found a woman he wants above all others."

"Someone might overhear you saying such a shocking thing." Her eyes darted about the crowd, but everyone was busily laughing and talking over the sounds of the music. "I should slap your face and walk away."

"Threats? But you'd create a scene, and we both know how you detest scenes, especially when your daughter would be drawn into it."

"She knew you would be here, didn't she? She arranged for Mr. Dunham—"

"Don't give your daughter all the credit. Yes, she knew I was invited, but Dunham's my friend and I asked a favor."

"I thought he was mine," she said sourly. When Brandon threw back his head and laughed, her heart turned over. The lights caught in his hair, glittering on the sun-bleached streaks as a lock fell across his forehead. He was clad in a black suit as elegant as the one he'd worn to the opera that night, but this time he wore a deep green waist-coat. The small touch of color made his golden hair and tanned complexion seem exotic. Amid all the pale, narrow English faces in the room, Brandon Caruthers shone

246

brighter than the sun. Not a man could compare to him.

And he wanted her. Miranda simply could not believe it. Her head was spinning as he drew her nearer than was proper, uncaring about the gossip his behavior must be eliciting. But she had her reputation in the business community as well as Lori's future to think of. This had to end.

Before she could gather her wits to say so, the music stopped. He sketched a bow without relinquishing her gloved hand, then fastened her hand around his arm and led her from the floor, smiling wickedly at the curious glances they garnered along the way. Miranda wanted to choke the life out of him. But ending up in Newgate would cause even more scandal. She discarded the idea in favor of a diversionary ploy.

"There's your former fiancée from Kentucky. I'm certain you'll wish to say hello."

"And I'm every bit as certain I don't." He held their course for the open double doors leading to the gardens.

Miranda caught the narrowed eyes of the blonde. In spite of being surrounded by fawning males, Reba's attention was focused on Brand and Miranda. "I can practically hear the wheels churning inside her mind."

"Only if we heard rusty clunking sounds. Reba just acts, without any regard for the consequences," Brand replied as he swept Miranda past the woman without so much as an acknowledgment.

"Must be a trait of you Rebels. Perhaps the reason you lost the war," she snapped.

"Remind me to discuss it with Bobby Lee the next time I have occasion to chat with him," Brand said as the cool outside air hit them. "Now, you must admit it's right refreshing out here. You were looking a bit flushed inside."

"Only because you were embarrassing me."

"By dancing with you? No, darlin', that wasn't the reason your cheeks were pink . . . just as they're becoming once more."

Before he could lead her further away from the crowd and create even more juicy gossip, she had to put a stop to his smooth manipulations. "Speak your piece, Major, and have done with it." She planted her feet and stood her ground stubbornly at the edge of the steps leading down into the darkness of the garden.

"How about a small test? Hmmm, say another kiss, only this time you won't be able to run away and hide after it's done. Not with all the witnesses you'd have to pass on your way out."

"You are despicable," she hissed. "Of course I won't be lured into the darkness so you can do heaven knows what to me and everyone in the place will remark on our absence." She found it difficult to speak when his thumb was teasing lazy circles around the sensitive skin inside her wrist. Even through their gloves, she could feel the heat of his touch and remember the slight abrasion of his callused fingertips when he had caressed her bare skin.

Brand could see she was weakening. He was taking a terrible gamble. Her own passion might frighten her away from him for good. But she'd never known passion before. By its very nature it would frighten her. There was nothing he could do but persist. "Then I'll just have to kiss you right here in front of everyone."

The dare sparkled in his eyes. He knew she craved that kiss as much as she feared it. "If you do, I'll be forced to defend my honor by coshing you with that geranium pot," she replied, reaching toward the small stone vase on the patio railing.

"You probably would." He caught both of her hands in his and took a step backward down the stairs, pulling her with him. If she jerked one hand free, she'd have a perfect opportunity to brain him if she so chose.

Miranda knew he was gambling that she wouldn't do such an outrageous thing. And she admitted that she wanted him to kiss her again. "My heart will break when this is over." The words came out in a low, desperate whisper before she could stop them. She was horrified to reveal her weakness so openly. As if allowing him to lead her here had not already done so.

"I would never hurt you, Miranda," he vowed, pulling her into the darkness.

"You will whether you intend it or not," she said breathlessly. A part of her—the sane part—screamed for her to break free of his grip and flee for her life. But she kept step with him until they were behind the deep shadows of a dense topiary hedge.

Brand made no reply, but rather took her in his arms and cradled her head in his hand as his lips brushed over her eyelids and rained soft kisses over her cheeks and circled her mouth. The gentle assault was not what she had been expecting. But when she opened it to gasp with pleasure, she did just what he had hoped. He centered his lips over hers and pressed them together, letting his tongue tease hers, darting and flicking, letting her follow suit as he'd taught her.

She responded naturally, with passion as well as with her own inbred cautiousness, touching the tip of her tongue to his, then withdrawing, melding her mouth against his even as their bodies pressed together. The kiss at the picnic had not prepared her for the feel of his body, so long and hard, so powerful. She remembered that day when he had thrown her to the ground and covered her . . . this was like that, only different. The danger here was to her heart and soul, not merely her physical well-being.

The combination of his feverish kisses and the gentle rhythm of his hips moving against hers made her blood sing. Just as he had known it would. Then why had she come out here? What self-punishing urge had led her to disregard duty and propriety, to risk her reputation? To forfeit a lifetime of struggling to succeed in business, just to meet the dare of this fascinating, dangerous man? It could only end badly, but right now she didn't care.

Her fingers dug into the muscles of his shoulders, and her breasts and hips pressed into the hardness of his body. Although her times in bed with Will had been very different, she knew enough of marital relations to be aware of what the decided bulge in his trousers meant. He did desire her, incredible as it seemed. And she? She felt a hot, raw ache deep in her belly, a wetness in her woman's place that had never lubricated itself when she had performed her wifely duties. Duty was the farthest thing from her mind right now. She wanted to bed this man.

"Ah, Miranda, my love," he murmured against her hair. Brand fought the urge to pull it free as he'd done before, knowing there was no way she could return to the ballroom if he did. He could feel the painful heaviness in his groin and knew he had to stop soon. His point had been made. He dared not jeopardize everything by losing control now. Slowly, ever so slowly, he pulled back from her, planting light kisses along her jaw, cheeks and forehead.

But before he could say anything more, a catty voice purred, "Why, I declare, what a charmin' surprise. The mother's steppin' right into the daughter's shoes. Or do they pinch a bit?" Reba sauntered around the hedge with a malicious smile on her face.

Brand could feel Miranda's whole body stiffen with anger. Whether it was at him or at the intruder's rudeness it was difficult to say.

"I've always been quite comfortable in my own shoes— and my own skin. Something a woman of your morals would know nothing about, I'm certain," Miranda replied with icy disdain.

Seeing a real cat fight brewing as Reba's eyes slitted, Brand cut her off before she could reply, saying, "You always were a jealous vixen, Reba, but you used to be smart enough to know when it was time to give up and move on to the next man. You had no trouble back home when the Yankees were winning."

"But you weren't a baron then, Brand, honey," she said, licking her lips. "And I didn't have any money. Of course, I still don't have as much as Mrs. Auburn."

"The difference between us is far greater than our financial worth, Mrs. Wilcox," Miranda replied. "I earned my wealth by working in the iron and shipping industries, not on my back."

Reba lunged forward with a venomous oath, but Brand quickly stepped between the two women, seizing her hands and pulling her away from Miranda, whom he told, "I think it might be wise if you rejoined the revelers while I dispose of this small problem."

"Small problem? I'll be a great big ole problem if you don't let me go this minute," Reba hissed.

Utterly ignoring the American witch's outburst, Miranda gave a frosty nod to Brand. She could feel her cheeks burning with humiliation as she stalked silently back toward the house, head held high.

Brand watched her retreat, then muttered low in Reba's ear, "If you had as much grace and integrity in your whole body as Mrs. Auburn has in her little finger, I might've been willing to forgive you for Earl."

"What do you see in that dried-up old hag—besides all her lovely money?" Reba said, twisting out of his grasp and massaging her wrists. She tried one of her winsome pouts, which used to bring every man in Fayette County to his knees. It didn't work on Brandon Caruthers, now

Lord Rushcroft, damn his eyes. He looked at her with a weary sort of amazement, shaking his head at her as if she were a child having a tantrum—or worse yet, a recalcitrant horse he had to discipline.

"Everything in life always comes down to money with you, doesn't it, Reba? Well, as you've already told me, you have plenty now, so why don't you go and find yourself an earl or a marquess, even a royal duke, and see if you can charm him. I'm no prospect."

"But you loved me once, quite desperately," she whispered, moving closer. "Oh, I don't expect you'll want to marry me and have me holdin' the purse strings. I know you're too proud for that. It's why you broke off with that silly little blond child."

"Miss Auburn is more mature than you could ever imagine, and it was she who cried off, not I."

Reba smiled. "We both know better, Brand. But I don't care, as long as we can be together. I'll be your mistress, even if you marry that widow woman. You'll need some warmin' up after her cold bed. See how agreeable I've become?" she purred, raising her arms to encircle his neck.

"I wouldn't bed you if you were the last woman between Leipzig and Lexington," he said, taking her arms and shoving them back to her sides. "I'd rather sleep with a viper. In fact, there wouldn't be a hell of a lot of difference." He took her shoulders in his hands and held her at arm's length, glaring into her eyes to deliver his parting sally. "If you ever utter so much as one syllable against Mrs. Auburn or her daughter, I'll scrub your filthy little mouth out with sheep dip. Do you understand?" He punctuated his question with a sharp shake that loosened the pins in her elaborate hairdo.

With smoldering fury in her eyes, Reba nodded, too furious to talk. She stood rooted to the ground, glaring daggers at his retreating back until his long strides took him out of her line of vision. Then she set to repinning her hair. The wretched man had quite ruined it, and she had no maid to fix it for her! She stamped her foot with fury, only to send the yellow curls tumbling down in disarray once more. She stamped again and glared into the flickering lights in the direction which he had gone.

If looks could kill, Brandon Caruthers, the tenth Lord Rushcroft, would be a dead man.

Brand searched the room for Miranda without luck. When he saw Lorilee, he quickly approached her to see if she knew where her mother had gone.

"I'm afraid she pleaded a headache and made her excuses. She just departed, leaving me under the watchful eye of Mrs. Horton, who will see me home," Lori answered, a smile bowing her lips. "You must've made quite an impression out in the garden if her flaming cheeks were any indicator."

"I'm afraid it was Reba Wilcox who can claim the credit, at least for part of it," he said grimly.

"Oh, dear! You mean she had the temerity to go snooping after you and create a scene?"

"That's what Reba does best," he replied with a sigh.

"Well, the ball's just begun and supper won't be served until midnight. So, if you were to go after my mother, just to check on her well-being, you understand . . ." Lori let her words trail away suggestively. "Oh, yes, and Mr. St. John assured Tilda they couldn't possibly be home before then either."

He grinned at her in spite of himself. "Remind me never to get on your bad side, Lorilee. You'd put Machiavelli in the shade. Perhaps I should introduce you to some of my friends in Parliament so you could give them lessons on how to outmaneuver the opposition."

"Mother would flay me if I helped the Conservatives," she said with a conspiratorial wink. "Now do hurry along and you might just catch up with her coach before she can barricade herself inside our city house."

Miranda huddled against the heavy velvet squabs in her carriage, massaging her aching head as she tried not to think about what had just transpired in the garden. The scene with that Wilcox tramp was mortifying in the extreme, but the the woman's behavior was no worse than she expected of a woman of her character. It was how she herself had behaved that truly appalled her.

"How could I have followed him out into the darkness like some witless debutante and then . . ." She shuddered. If they had not been interrupted—indeed, if he had not had the sense to end that brief charge of passion—she would've done anything he wished, even fallen to the ground right there in the Falconridge gardens and let him take her.

But that had not happened. He'd regained control of his wits and broken the spell. Brandon had exercised restraint while she had not. The very worst of it was that she still wanted him! Miranda hugged herself and felt the bitter sting of tears caught in her lashes. What a fool she was to hope for such uncontrolled youthful passion. For romantic love at her age. Absurd.

That part of her life had passed by, and she had never had the opportunity to experience physical pleasure . . . if, indeed, there was any for a woman of decency. According to Her Majesty and all that Miranda had read, the lot of a respectable wife and mother was to endure her husband's touch as a duty. But she burned and ached in ways that she had never imagined before Brandon came into her life.

Brash, reckless foreigner, Rebel Baron from across the

Atlantic, he had awakened a side of her that had lain dormant since her seventeenth birthday . . . the day she was affianced to Will Auburn. She'd spent the years after that repressing the embers of her youthful curiosity. But Brand had fanned them into a raging fire with the intensity of his tiger-eyed gaze, his callused hands, his searing kisses.

She should be ashamed, but all she could feel was bitter regret for all she would never know . . . could never know, if she wanted to retain any vestige of self-respect. "But I don't care. I don't care anymore," she whispered brokenly, hugging herself, not quite certain what it was she did not care about. Her respectability?

Or the shame that would come after a night with the Rebel Baron? She blinked back tears. He'd been the one to come to his senses. There would be no night together for them. Whom was she deceiving? Only herself.

The silence inside her spacious carriage was broken by the soft clip-clop of the horses' hooves and the creak of heavy leather harnesses as the driver took her home. Home to that great ugly mausoleum, paean to wealth and influence. It would be cold and deserted. She'd given the servants the night off. Even Tilda had surprisingly accepted Mr. St. John's offer to attend a theater performance.

Steeling herself to enter the empty house, she rapped on the roof as the driver approached it. When he opened the trap, she said, "Just take the carriage around to the mews after you let me off by the porte cochere. You needn't wait, Ralph." She did not want him to see that she'd been crying. Servants did gossip, and she wanted no curiosity . . . or pity.

"Very good, ma'am," he replied as she closed the trap.

She alighted and stood for a moment as her carriage clattered down the cobblestones toward their mews off the back alley, putting off entering the desolate place where she lived. Then she heard the loud sound of another carriage approaching at a very swift pace. Turning, she was startled and somewhat alarmed when it swung into her drive and the coachman reined in. The major had warned her never to be out alone like this. But she'd been too upset to think of her own safety.

She was all alone in the shadows beneath the porte cochere, one foot poised upon the first step. Her latchkey was buried inside the foolish little beaded reticule she'd carried to the ball. She was so used to servants opening the doors for her that she'd not even bothered to take it out before dismissing the coachman. Frantically she began to dig to the bottom of the bag, fumbling in the darkness.

Then suddenly the coach pulled away. Miranda blinked and peered through the leafy darkness of the shrubbery as she grasped the key and extracted it from its hiding place beneath a silk handkerchief. That was when she saw his silhouette, tall and slim, a man dressed in formal evening attire but without a top hat. Even before he began walking toward her, she recognized him.

He moved with elegant grace, studying the pools of darkness behind the windows, searching the grounds, as if hoping she was still outside. He did not see her. She could slip to the side door and unlock it before he found her hiding place . . . if she chose.

Miranda stood rooted to the steps, the key digging into her fingers as she clutched it like a talisman. All she need do was will her feet to climb the stairs. Three more short steps. Then she heard his voice, soft on the warm summer air, drawling and sultry as the hot land from which he had come.

"Miranda, darlin', I know you're there."

And then he began walking straight toward her.

She stood perfectly still, not daring to breathe as he drew nearer. When he stood directly in front of her, she could make out the glow of his eyes, at the same level as hers since she was standing on the first step. "How did you know I was here?" The question sounded idiotic the moment she asked it. What did *that* matter now that she'd let him catch her?

"Your scent, darlin'."

"D-don't call me darling," she said, struggling to regulate her breathing. And failing utterly.

He ignored her admonition and took her by the shoulders, saying, "I've warned you about risking your life this way. What were you thinking, pulling a fool stunt like running off from the ball and dismissing your coachman before you were safely in the house—a deserted house at that?"

His tone was angry and his hands dug into her soft skin through her thin cloak. "Your concern for my safety is touching," she said, swallowing the bitter gall of disappointment. He'd come only to see that whoever had been attempting to kill her was not lurking about. Not for the reason she'd hoped. *No fool like an old fool.*

Miranda had almost said it aloud. Instead she added, "I've managed to take care of myself quite handily ever since my husband died. I shall do famously now as well."

When she turned sharply on her heel and broke free of his grasp, scurrying up the stairs, he followed in two long strides, cutting her off at the doorway. His tall frame filled it, blocking her entry. Before she knew it, she was in his arms and his mouth was crushing hers in a fierce, angry kiss.

The key clattered from her fingers as she clutched his broad shoulders and clung to him, letting him work the blistering magic his lips always conjured when they touched her flesh. He murmured something she couldn't make out, an oath of some sort, desperate and hungry as his kisses, which smothered the sound of his voice. The rapaciousness of his plundering gentled to slow, sweetly drugging caresses. His mouth moved over her lips, his tongue inviting hers to come out and play.

Miranda felt the world spinning and would have fallen to her knees if not for the strength of his embrace. Burying his face against her throat, he whispered softly between nibbling kisses, "Will you let me love you?"

It was up to her to decide . . .

Chapter Seventeen

She held him fast, her mind fuzzy with warmth, her body giddy with forbidden pleasure. Why should she not have this for one night? Perhaps it would not be any better than it had been . . . her mind drifted away from thoughts of Will Auburn's brief and infrequent beddings when Brand began an exploration of her breasts, opening her cape and letting his fingers skim over the soft mounds, rimming the low décolletage of her gown until her nipples tightened and ached almost painfully. She gasped.

"Miranda?" His husky whisper broke through the soft sounds of their breathing. Brand held his breath, waiting for her response.

"Yes, yes, yes," she murmured against his strong brown neck. Her mouth felt the slight rasp of golden whiskers as she caressed his jawline and worked her way back to his lips.

He growled something unintelligible and swept her into his arms, turning to carry her to the door.

The locked door.

"The key," she murmured dreamily, her arms wrapped securely around his neck.

"Where is it?" he managed to ask in a raspy voice.

"On the steps. I dropped it," she replied, almost giggling with delirious excitement.

Another muttered expletive. "Darlin', you do try a man and that's a fact," he said as he slid her to her feet, still holding her pressed tightly against his body while he stepped back to the stone stairs where the heavy brass latchkey glittered dimly in the patchy moonlight.

When he released his hold on her and bent down to retrieve the key, Miranda nearly toppled over his back. She was dizzy and breathless, and she'd had not one drop of alcohol all evening! Quickly he was once more embracing her, raining kisses all over her face and throat as he led her back up the steps and then turned to unlock the heavy oak door.

It was as dark as the ninth level of hell in the alcove surrounding the doorway. Brand fumbled with the key, trying to insert it in the lock. Threading a needle in a tornado would've been easier, he thought testily as he jammed the instrument of his frustration at its intended target over and over. Bloody lovely! Was this some sort of omen? He had to get her inside before her most proper English sensibilities forced her to reconsider what was by all standards a rash act of singular immorality.

Finally he felt the key slide into the well-oiled lock and turn. The door swung open, and he once again whisked her off her none-too-steady feet and carried her over the threshold. After kicking the heavy oak closed behind him, he jammed the key in the lock and turned it, assuring that no one would be able to enter and catch them unawares. The house was like a damned combination of a fortress and a tomb—and twice as dark.

He tripped over something darting in front of his feet.

From the size of the moving object—and the fact that he was not already minus a leg—Brand concluded he'd stumbled on Callie, not Marm, thank heaven for small favors! The mother cat scurried away silently as Brand stumbled against the carpeted steps leading from the side entry to the first floor.

He cushioned Miranda's fall by holding her above him. Although slender and fine-boned, she was tall for a woman and weighed enough to elicit a "Whoof" as the air rushed from his lungs.

"Have I broken your ribs, Major?" she whispered, concern edging her voice.

She tried to rise up off of him, but he caught her and pulled her back into his embrace. "I wouldn't know, and believe me, at this point I don't care," he said as he resumed kissing her throat and breasts. Then he felt the tickle of whiskers at the back of his raised neck. One of Callie's kittens was nibbling on him while he nibbled on Miranda!

Could Marm be far behind?

He dismissed that disquieting thought and shook the pesky little beast away as he began unfastening the ties of her cloak, a thin silk summer garment designed more for fashion than protection from the cold. But when he tried to toss it behind him, he felt little needle claws snagging it. Cursing silently, he rolled the silk cape in a ball with one hand, effectively cocooning the interloper, while he continued exploring Miranda's breasts. If she were going to cry off as she had the day of the picnic, she had better do it now or he could not guarantee how much of a gentleman he would be.

Rather than being upset by his intimacy, Miranda gloried in the feel of his fingertips and mouth skimming over the sensitive swells of her heated flesh. But the tingling, burning ache would not abate. It was pain and it was pleasure, all mixed together in a wash of longing for sensations she had never experienced before. Instinct made her arch forward, allowing him greater access.

Practice made him begin sliding open the tiny button loops down the back of her gown, eager to bare her treasures for his plundering mouth and hands. Almost at once, the gown's low neckline gaped and he was able to nuzzle his face in the deep vale between her breasts, now covered only by the delicate lace of her chemise and pushed up for his attention by the undergirding of corset stays.

Her moans of pleasure made her unaware of the tiny meows of protest emanating from the cape, but Brand could hear them. Persevering, he pulled away the sheer chemise to extract one rosy nipple, puckered and eager. He drew it into his mouth and suckled on it. This time when she gasped, he did not inquire if she was pleased. The very texture and hardness of the little nub told him all was good. But his backside pressed against the stairs was not good. Nor was the second kitten, who was now rubbing against the side of his face.

He had to get Miranda out of here and upstairs before she became aware of the voyeuristic little intruders and the spell would be broken. Slowly he levered himself up, continuing to kiss her as he helped her to her feet in the stygian blackness. "Is there a light in this place? It's right dangerous without any." With any luck, he could keep her occupied enough so she wouldn't notice a kitten or two along the way.

"Oh," Miranda murmured, bemused, realizing she had been sprawled on the stairs, lying on top of him without a thought for anything except what he was doing to her. "Yes, here," she said, groping along the wall until she found the fixture and turned it on as Brand struck a match and lit it. A dim flicker of pale golden light illuminated two pairs of stairs leading up and down. And one pair of kittens playing chase, heading in a mad dash to the lower floor. Miranda, still breathless and dreamy from his kisses, did not see them as they vanished into the darkness below.

Thank you, Lord! "Lucky we fell this way and not the other," he said, looking at the steep steps leading to the lower level. Without giving her an opportunity to consider that dangerous possibility, he took her hand and tugged her up the steps. "Show me the way," he commanded softly.

Cheeks burning, Miranda clutched his hand and guided him toward the main entry foyer. They fired low gaslights as they went. At every stop, he would gather her close and plunder her mouth with kisses, all the while continuing to work on the buttons of her gown. By the time they reached the grand staircase, the gown fell in a soft rustle of silk. Floating over another kitten!

Brand swept her quickly into his arms and nudged aside the mound of silk, which was now wriggling alarmingly. He ascended the steps, watching for more miniature "bushwhackers" waiting to attack. When they reached the top, he murmured hoarsely, "Which is your bedroom?" *Bolt the door and pray Marm is in the sitting room downstairs!*

"The third . . . at the end of the hall," she whispered, still unable to catch her breath. The feel of his arms carrying her as if she weighed no more than thistledown thrilled her. They were as hard as iron, yet living, flexing with strength and virility. Miranda felt herself shivering in spite of the flush suffusing her body. When he stepped into her bedroom, doubts assailed her. This was where Will had come to her in the darkness of night to perform his husbandly duties. Now she had invited a man not her husband to make love to her in that same dark bed.

But Brand would have nothing of darkness. Seeing the gaslight on the wall at the side of the door, he set her down and lit it as he shoved the door closed. Then he quickly picked her up again and carried her over to the large four-poster. Brand paused for a moment as his eyes darted around the room. No cats in sight. Did he dare hope?

Ever so slowly, he let her slide down the length of his tall body while they stood beside the bed. Still held fast, she surrendered to his kisses, only dimly aware that he was unlacing her corset strings. His warm fingers caressed the delicate bones at the curve of her spine. He shoved the silk and whalebone contraption over her hips, leaving her clad only in her chemise and stockings. Somehow en route her slippers had been lost.

She stood facing him, trying to cover herself, feeling suddenly shy. "I-I'm not a girl, Brandon . . ."

"You're a woman, the most beautiful woman I've ever seen," he murmured as his hands cupped her face and he lowered his mouth to hers, commanding, "Kiss me, Miranda."

She did, opening her mouth to his tongue and letting hers glide with it the way he was oh so skillfully teaching her to do. His hands slid back, long fingers digging into the heavy mass of her hair and massaging her scalp, loosening the pins holding her hair up until it spilled around her shoulders like a fiery cloud of deepest ruby red.

"I've always longed to do that . . . from the first time I realized how much of the beautiful stuff you had," he whispered softly, combing his fingers through the waist-length waves.

"It's just red hair, coarse and dark and not at all pretty like fine-spun golden hair." She'd always hated the unusual shade, the way it clashed with fashionable colors that blondes could wear. But Brand obviously was fascinated with its heaviness and the odd glints of fire in the highlights. He held it up to the light like a skein and let if fall through his fingers.

"It's magic, as changeable as you, dark and fiery, with deeply hidden secrets," he said as his mouth claimed hers again, while he held her against him with his fists buried in the tangles of her hair. Then he let it cloak her upper body as he began to pull on the drawstring of her chemise, working it down over her milky shoulders, totally baring her breasts.

"Lordy, you are a wonder," he rasped as he cupped a breast in each hand. They stood up, full and erect as any girl's half her age.

Feeling the chemise slipping down below her navel with only the curve of her hips to cover her most private place, she whispered, "Please . . . the lights."

"The light's just fine. You don't savor a vision of beauty in the dark," he replied as his hands encircled her slender waist. He cupped her buttocks, raising her up so he could bend his head to feast on her breasts once again.

The suckling heat of his mouth made all modesty flee as the burning ache turned into a keen, tingling pleasure. She arched against him, pressing her hands against his chest and pulling off his cravat, then tugging at the studs in his shirtfront until they began to pop free. He shrugged off his jacket and tossed it carelessly onto the floor, then resumed kneading her bottom and feasting on her breasts.

Now Miranda was eager, desperate to feel his bare flesh, answering some primal instinct—was it one of those deeply hidden secrets he spoke of? She only knew that she had to touch him, feel the heat of him. She whimpered as his rapacious mouth moved between her breasts, taking one, then the other and circling the areola with his tongue, flicking the hard, nubby tip of a nipple before drawing it into his mouth.

She was lost in passion. He realized this was all completely new to her. He must go slow. Ah, but that would be hard . . . hard as the throbbing member between his legs clamoring to delve into her warm, sweet flesh and find surcease. He could not allow that until she was ready. And she was ready, at least to be placed on the bed so he could finish undressing.

Brand reached over and yanked the coverlet down, then let his hands slide over her hips until her chemise slid off. Shushing her small gasp of embarrassment, he knelt before her and began to peel down the garter from one long, elegant leg, kissing his way from her thigh to her ankle.

The room spun crazily, and Miranda could do nothing but collapse back onto the edge of the mattress behind her as Brand tossed away one stocking and set to work on the other. He even kissed her toes! Who could ever have imagined that having one's foot caressed and kissed could be so erotic? Before she realized what he was doing, he had positioned her up against a pillow and was sitting beside her on the bed.

She could feel his hot tiger's eyes raking up and down her body, following the path of his hands as they traced the curves and valleys of her flesh. She was a mature woman, had borne a child, was too tall and angular . . . all the doubts and insecurities of her life flooded suddenly back into her consciousness. "Brandon, I—"

Knowing what she was trying to say, he murmured, "Don't say anything. You're perfect." His hand skimmed across her flat, silky belly.

"I have stretch marks." The instant she said it, she blushed beet red. No lady ever mentioned such a thing!

He chuckled softly, bending to dip his tongue into her navel. "If you do, they're fine enough to be invisible." Planting another kiss on her belly, he trailed his lips up to her breasts while his hand slowly glided down to her mound. He could feel her stiffen ever so slightly when he touched her most secret place. Deep red curls guarded it as his fingers carefully worked their way toward where her hot, slick honey waited to be tasted . . . later. That would shock her innocent sensibilities too much for the first time. Gritting his teeth, he pulled back from that invasion, forcing himself to allow her to set a slower pace of discovery.

Miranda ran her hands over his shoulders, shoving his shirt down so she could touch his skin. The sinuous ripple of lean muscles over his shoulders and arms fed her craving. She grew bolder when he leaned back to shrug off the shirt, then bent down to resume caressing her. The abrasion of his chest hair teased her already sensitive breasts. She reached between their bodies and buried her fingers in the pelt of golden fur, tracing the pattern of it as it narrowed down to a thin arrow vanishing below his belt buckle.

His heart pounded as she pressed her palms flat against the muscles of his chest. Did hers beat out the same frantic cadence? Most certainly so, if her breathlessness was any indicator. She ached with wanting, writhing beneath his hands and mouth. Her hair tangled around her shoulders and spilled across the pillows. She could feel it against her bare back. The realization dawned: She was completely naked, lying spread across her bed in a lighted room.

"Brandon, the lights," she managed to get out between little whimpers of pleasure as he kissed and petted her body, making it sing with a longing she could never have imagined.

He raised himself up over her now, looking down on her flushed face, the luscious pink spreading lower to heat her breasts and belly. "If I turned off the lights, I couldn't see how beautiful you are," he whispered tenderly, then added as he stood up, "and you couldn't see my body."

He knew positively that Auburn had never entered her chambers with the lights on. The old fool probably wore a nightshirt. "Aren't you just the least bit curious, Miranda, love?" he cajoled.

His hands were poised at his belt buckle, and the breath whooshed from her lungs. She should be shocked, appalled, outraged . . . but every fiber of her being cried out, *Yes, yes, I am!* Was she brave enough to admit it aloud? Cowardice bred into her by generations of repression made her answer only with her eyes.

Hungry eyes, glowing with silver fire in the dim light.

Ever so slowly, his hands, those beautiful, tanned and callused hands, began to unfasten the belt. Her eyes darted down to the bulge at his crotch. She knew what that meant, but she wanted to see even that! What a depraved creature passion and her major had made her. She could hear his soft chuckle as he noted her trespass, but all he said was, "Shoes first."

Miranda watched as he sat on the small dressing stool in front of her vanity and slipped off his shoes and hose. How large and masculine and utterly out of place he appeared on that flimsy little chair. Yet at the same time, he moved with such elegance that it did not matter. When he stood and stepped back to the edge of the bed, she could not help moistening her lips with the tip of her tongue in nervous anticipation of what came next.

Brand could feel her eyes on him and smiled at her as he began to unfasten the buttons of his fly. He ached so much, he feared he'd spill his seed before he could rid himself of the damned tight britches! Her eyes were round with wonder and as hot as molten silver, adding to his misery . . . and his pleasure. Odd, how the two seemed to go together in making love.

When he completed his task, he took a deep breath, trying desperately to calm himself, then slowly eased down his pants and underwear, freeing his engorged staff. The cool air did nothing to dampen the burning pulse of it. He watched her watch him and was pleased. She did not shrink away, although he knew she had to be frightened by the newness of this.

Although she'd never seen her husband's member, she knew it had not been this large—could not have been. Brand's staff jutted from the dark gold thicket at his groin as if possessing a life of its own. She should have been terrified, but instead she was mesmerized. Mesmerized by the sheer male beauty of him, long-legged and broad-shouldered with cunning patterns of light gold hair glistening on his forearms, and that heavier pelt on his chest. Now she could trace the course of it to its ultimate destination.

Without giving her time for modesty—or second thoughts—he placed one knee on the bed and took her hands in his, pulling her up to kneel with him in the center of the bed. Burying his fingers in her hair, he cradled her head and kissed her deeply, pressing the lengths of their bodies together without the barrier of clothing, allowing her time to get used to the sensations before he pressed her into the mattress and covered her.

Miranda could feel his heat encircle her, and her bones seemed to melt. His body was hard and sinuous while hers was soft and pliant. She loved the raspy scratch of his beard as he pressed kisses to the madly beating pulse at the base of her throat and moved lower to her breasts once more. Her fingers burrowed through the hair on his chest, glorying in the pounding of his heart. When he raised his head and kissed her again, she opened to him, allowing her tongue to glide out to meet his, boldly making forays into his mouth, twining with his as she ran her hands up and down his back, even daring to dig her nails into his steely hard buttocks.

Then she felt his hand move between their bodies and cup her mound, but she was too awash with excitement to stiffen or pull away. The moment his fingers found the wetness drenching her woman's place, a bolt of raw pleasure lanced through her and she arched against him, whimpering and wriggling her hips. He explored briefly and elicited more little cries of ecstasy from her, which she was unaware of making.

Brand knew she was ready. And he was desperate. Gritting his teeth to keep going slowly, he lowered her to the mattress slowly and propped his weight on his elbows as he continued kissing her. With one knee he gently parted her thighs, then poised himself to enter her. "Miranda, love," he murmured as his aching staff nuzzled against the portals of paradise. She was so slick and ready that the head pressed in with ease, but when he tried to go deeper, he found her incredibly tight.

It's been over a dozen years since she's received a man, he reminded himself as he stopped, waiting impatiently for her body to adjust to the invasion.

Her earlier worries about how they would fit returned, but were quickly pushed aside as the delicious pressure of his flesh inside her made her ache for more. With a longing denied for a lifetime, her body arched to pull him deeper, deeper . . . until at last he was fully seated, stretching her and filling her. She bit her lip and felt the tears sting her eyes again, but this time they were tears of joy and wonder, not sadness and loss.

To be joined this way—utterly, with no impediment of clothing or darkness between them—this was the way nature had surely meant the union of man and woman to be. Then he began to move, ever so slowly, gently, his hips rocking against hers as he stroked. Her nails dug into his back, urging him on. When he rasped out a command that she wrap her legs around his body, she complied and he plunged even deeper.

Sweat beaded his forehead as he tried to hold back the pace, but when he felt her silky thighs tighten around his waist and her hips arch in response, he was lost. He rode her hard and deep, waiting desperately for the signs that she was ready to join him. Brand was certain she had never come to completion before. He would not rob her of that.

She was drowning in the pleasure, greedy, needy, wonder-filled beyond her wildest dreams. The sweetness of it overwhelmed her, yet left her hungry for something elusive. She hovered on the brink of some sort of discovery she could not imagine. She craved it. But she never wanted this to end. Still, she was unable to stop her body's demands as it arched and writhed wildly against his.

Then it swept over her, swamping her senses with such intense, pulsing pleasure that she cried out his name and clawed at his back like a wild thing. Just when she was certain she'd die right then and there if the ecstasy did not abate—surely it could not go on—his whole body stiffened and his staff swelled even more deeply inside her. Another drenching wave of ecstasy crested in her with his release.

She held fast to him as he murmured her name and collapsed on top of her. Their bodies were slick with perspiration as they lay in the coolness of the night, panting together, sated. Gradually their breathing returned to normal, and he started to roll away, but she held him fast.

"I'm crushing you," he said.

"No, I don't mind," she replied softly. What she really meant was that she never wanted this to end ... even though she knew it must. But she would not think of that now. Now she only wanted to feel the solid warmth of his body joined with hers, to revel in the newness of an experience she'd never had before.

And could never have again.

But then he gave that sad thought the lie when he began to move inside her once more. Ever so slowly, he stroked her quivering flesh, rousing her again to passion. The task was not a difficult one. Miranda gave a mewl of joy and arched against him, her fingers digging into his shoulders, her legs clamped tightly around his hips. They danced yet again that most ancient and beautiful dance of love, but this time he held back ever so long, eliciting moans and pleas from her for release from the sweetest torture.

Miranda was incoherent with pleasure. He was like strong wine or some exotic drug from the East, and his body gave hers delights more potent than anything she could ever imagine. When the second cataclysm began, it seemed to last far longer, wrenching everything from her, body and heart and soul. What would be left of her when this was done? Feeling his body once more joining hers in oblivion, that worrisome thought faded away.

Gradually they both came back from their distant journey.

He nuzzled her throat and planted a kiss on her nose. Then as he raised his hand to brush a tangled curl from her cheek, he noticed traces of tears. "Miranda?" His voice held a note of distress. "Have I hurt you, darling? I know you haven't . . . haven't been with a man for—"

She placed her fingertips over his lips, caressing them as she silenced him. "No, you have given me nothing but the greatest pleasure I could possibly imagine. I never . . . that is, Will never . . ." Her words trailed away. It seemed disloyal to lie in the same bed she'd shared with her elderly husband and speak ill of him. "It was not like this," was all she was able to manage as he gently rolled off her and pulled her to his side.

"You've never spoken with anyone about why you married a man three times your age," he prompted, stroking her shoulder, waiting to see if she would confide in him. That would be a good beginning.

Miranda hesitated. "I—I never have. Will was . . ."

"I know, he was kind to you and you feel loyal because of that, as if it would be a betrayal if you said anything else about your relationship."

His insight was phrased with such concern that she sighed. "What a remarkable man you are, Major."

"A little while ago you called me Brandon," he said with a gentle smile, touching her chin with his fingertips. He watched her blush.

"Yes, well, I was scarcely myself then, was I?"

"Perhaps that's the real Miranda—the woman who wants what she's been denied all her adult life."

"I've led a life of considerable privilege, from childhood on," she replied defensively.

"Your childhood ended rather abruptly, or I miss my guess." His eyes searched hers.

Well, if she were ever to unburden herself to anyone, this man knew her best—and not only in the biblical sense of the word, she thought with a flush heating her cheeks. Suddenly she felt the need to speak of what had happened so long ago. Perhaps one kind of catharsis led to another. That only made her blush all the more.

In the dim light, he simply held her and waited, combing his fingers slowly through her hair, untangling it, making no demands. Then he placed a soft kiss on her forehead, as if sealing a pact between them, a pledge that whatever she said in this room would never be carried outside it.

Perhaps that was what made her begin the journey to so long ago, a remembrance that was bittersweet in the extreme . . .

Chapter Eighteen

"My father was a successful businessman in Liverpool. He owned a large iron foundry and had invested in some shipping interests as well. I was his only daughter. I had a younger brother, Albert, who it was assumed would one day take over the business, but I was the apple of Father's eye. Both he and Mother spoiled me quite outrageously."

Brand smiled, thinking of the imperious Miranda as a schoolroom miss ordering her governesses about, but he said nothing, just waited for her to go on.

"Just before my first season, I met a young man and became quite infatuated. His father was the vicar of St. Alban's, a prestigious parish in Liverpool, but still, scarcely a position of wealth comparable to my family's."

"Your parents objected to your marrying him because he was poor?"

She shook her head. "No, they approved of Mr. Aimesley, but my mother wanted me to have a real season first, just so I would be certain I was making the right choice. Father spent a considerable amount on that come-out, but the night before a large ball given in honor of my seventeenth birthday, he came home from the foundry ashen-faced. He and my mother were closeted away in his study for several hours, and when she emerged, she was in tears, although she assured me all was well.

"I knew it was not. Within the week the newspapers carried the story about a shipping firm being insolvent. It seemed that Father had taken all the profits from the foundry and sunk them into that shipping business. He was on the verge of total ruin. But an old family friend, Will Auburn, had advised him against doing what he did, and now offered him help."

Brand stiffened, but Miranda quickly assured him, "It was not the way you think. Will had been widowed several years earlier and his wife had never been able to provide him an heir. He doted on Bertie and insisted on loaning my father a small fortune so our family did not lose the foundry, even though it was a competitor of his. I think he intended that Bertie should inherit his holdings as well as our father's one day. But then my brother died in a cholera outbreak, and Father became despondent. He fell ill, and Will took over running the business.

"By that time he was almost a member of our family. We had survived so much grief together."

"What of your suitor?" Brand asked.

"We couldn't marry during a period of mourning, of course, although we still expected to eventually. But when it became apparent that Will would have to care for my parents and me for the rest of their lives . . ."

"That was when he made his offer."

"It sounds so calculating, as if he somehow knew that Bertie would die and Father would fail. He wanted desperately to have children to inherit his life's work, and I was young and healthy and had grown up knowing him.

Whom better might he ask? A woman near his own age could never give him his heart's wish."

"But you did."

"What else could I do? Marry Kent Aimesley and leave the care of my aged parents to Will Auburn? That would scarcely have been fair."

"It certainly was not fair for you to have to sacrifice your whole future for an old man's dream." Besides the tinge of anger in his voice, there was also a bit of admiration. "But you did it anyway."

"I did it, yes. I won't say it was easy at the time ... but over the years, I've come to realize that I was never really in love with Mr. Aimesley."

"Aimesley? Isn't he—"

"My business associate? He is, and a more trusted and loyal employee neither Will nor I could ever have asked for. Mr. Aimesley came to my husband and asked for work several years after we were married and Lori had been born. He was educated and ambitious, good with sums. Will took him on and never had cause to regret it."

"A remarkably charitable man," Brand said softly. She had cared for the old devil. He felt petty for being jealous.

"He was remarkable in many ways. When Lori was only three, Will's health began to fail. Within a year, he was bedfast, although his mind was still keen. I nursed him and he tutored me. Since we would obviously never be able to have a son, he decided a woman could be just as capable as a man of running a business."

"And you proved him right."

She flushed under his admiring gaze. "I learned everything from him about the iron industry and the new steel-making hot air blast furnaces. He was visionary and intuitive about investments and taught me well. As he grew more ill, he allowed me to assume more and more responsibilities, although his business associates were horrified and attempted to dissuade him. Several of them actually tried to have him pronounced incompetent in court, but the effort failed.

"That fight cost him dearly, for within a fortnight of the judgment in our favor he was dead." Her voice was flat and bitter as she continued, "I took over his foundries, the shipping firm and two banks . . . and I saw the men who attacked him go bankrupt for their trouble." She looked into his eyes and asked levelly, "Does that frighten you?"

"After our first meetin', darlin', it doesn't even surprise me," he replied with a smile. "You did what you had to do to survive in a man's world. But you also paid a price. Why didn't you ever marry again?"

"Shortly after Will died, so did my father, then my mother. I was in mourning for nearly three years. And I had a young daughter who had lost her father and grandparents. Will had only distant cousins back in Liverpool, and everyone in my family was gone. I was all Lori had. So I devoted my time to her and to expanding my business ventures, especially in banking. That, and all the sad memories in Liverpool, were the reasons I moved to our London house that Will had just built. I never really had time to think about marriage . . . and honestly, most of the men of my class were quite put off by me."

"They were fools, Miranda. I'll never interfere with your work."

His words shattered the bond of closeness between them. Miranda was suddenly aware that she had made a terrible mistake. She pushed against his chest and slipped out of his arms, rolling quickly to the side of the bed before he could protest. Then she realized she was naked and saw the stream of clothing scattered hither and yon about the room.

She was trapped. She could not leave, but he must.

Despair and shock filled her breaking heart. She pulled the sheet up to cover herself and burrowed back into the pillows. He remained lying on his side, watching her with one arm bent at the elbow, propping up his head. The sheet that she had pulled up draped carelessly over his hip, leaving his upper body bare.

"What's wrong, darlin'?" he asked, his voice very quiet. He knew, and his gut clenched, but he was damned if he'd make it easy for her.

Miranda swallowed hard and tried to frame the words. All she could manage was, "You'll have to go now."

"That's it? I'm dismissed?" He waited, biting down on the churning anger mixed with hurt. He'd known the risk and taken it anyway. "Darlin', I'm not a stallion to be put to stud and then led away," he said when she would not look at him.

The indelicate remark made Miranda's eyes widen and her face flame. He was sitting up now, heedless of the sheet which barely covered his sex, this lean and hard man with whom she'd lain. Her lover. "There is no need for crudity, Major," she said, and instantly realized how prim and cold it sounded after what they'd just shared . . . what he'd just given her.

The anger boiled over, scalding him. "You've found out what it is to be a woman for the first time in your life and you're afraid of it—of me! That old man never really made love to you, did he? All he did was his *duty,* and you did yours. What we did tonight went way beyond duty."

Her voice was cold as ice. "That *old man*, my lord, was my husband, and I honor his memory."

He was hot with pain. "By letting another man into the bed he shared—however inadequately—with you?"

She turned her head as if he'd slapped her. "The guilt

is mine, not yours, but you're right, he could not . . . make me feel as you have. I'm very grateful—"

"I don't want your gratitude, Miranda. I want your love," he said, gentling his voice as he reached for her hand.

She jerked it away. "I can't give you that, Brandon. It wouldn't work—I'm older than you and set in my ways. Besides," she rushed on, "I have Lori to think of. Oh, I know she has some romantic notion of playing matchmaker between us, but she's too young to understand the way the world works."

"Please explain it to me," he replied, struggling for patience.

"There would be a terrible scandal if . . . if we were to become involved."

"And you think this isn't 'involved'?" he asked quite reasonably, his arm gesturing about the rumpled bed

She looked away, unable to bear the pain. "I—I cannot give up my work. It's all that kept me sane after Will and my family died, leaving me alone with a child to raise—a child I knew would one day leave me."

"And you're afraid I'd be one of those overbearing men who insist a mere woman can't run the very businesses she built with her own hard work." He was puzzled, hurt and struggling desperately to understand.

"No, I suspect you would not," she replied quietly.

"Then what? Are you afraid I'd leave you for a younger woman?"

The question struck closer to the truth than she could bear to admit. She dared not let him know how very insecure she was. The dream was impossible. The scandal unthinkable. "No, but as I said, there would be gossip."

"Why would a woman as strong as you be afraid of a little gossip, Miranda?"

"It would not be me but Lori who'd pay the price. I

cannot have that. Surely you can understand," she said beseechingly.

She had never intended to let this happen. All she'd asked for was one night. *But will one night be enough?* an insidious voice deep inside asked. Miranda rubbed her aching temples, and her hair fell in tangled waves over her shoulders, offering further proof of her wanton desires.

"No, I don't understand," he said. "You're wrong about Lorilee. Your daughter is stronger than you give her credit for being. She's right about us. We do belong together." He damned himself for a fool, but he wouldn't give up. He touched her shoulder ever so softly. "I'll give you time to think about it, Miranda."

"There's nothing to think about," she said with weary resignation. She could hardly bear to look at his splendid body, the lean muscles, the golden hair covering his chest. Now she knew the feel of him, the taste of him, the most intimate things . . . beyond anything she'd ever been able to imagine. She had hurt him. But he was young and titled and wildly attractive. The Rebel Baron would have no shortage of women in his life. She was doing him a favor, actually.

At least that was what she tried to tell herself as she watched him slide from the bed and begin gathering up his scattered clothes, then donning them with inbred grace in spite of his anger. He was just tucking his shirt into his britches when she broke the silence. "Now that you and Lori won't be marrying, you'll have need of funds for restoring Rushcroft Hall. It's an excellent investment, and my bank—"

He whirled on her with fire in his eyes, the scar on his cheek white with fury. "So that's it! You think I'm still trying to marry for money. Why marry the daughter and settle for a portion of the prize when I can marry the mother and have it all!"

"No, Brandon, I didn't mean—"

"Yes, I believe you did. That's what this is really about—not gossip, not Lori—just all that cold, hard cash you worked so hard to amass. You know, I was wrong," he snarled as he scooped up his jacket and swung it over his shoulder. "You and Reba have a great deal in common. You measure every man you meet in pounds and pence."

Miranda blinked, utterly speechless as he stormed out of the room. She sat frozen in the bed, listening to the echo of his footsteps down the stairs until the outside door slammed in grim finality.

Brandon Caruthers was gone for good. She had accomplished what she'd set out to do . . . or had she?

Since her clothing lay strewn from the side entry stairs all the way up to her bedroom, Miranda donned a night rail and robe, then gathered up the incriminating evidence. It took longer than she imagined, for not only were her garments there, but so were her hairpins, scattered in a trail down the hall. Worst of all, the baron's shirt studs had flown across her bedroom when she'd ripped the shirt from his body! Retrieving them all required a most diligent search. What gossip would follow if one of the upstairs maids found a man's jewelry lying beneath her bed?

When Tilda and Lori returned later that night, Miranda feigned sleep and neither tried to awaken her, although she heard the soft murmuring of their conversation in the next room. No doubt speculating about whether or not the baron had whiled away a few hours with her before departing.

No one must ever know. She repeated that over and over

as she lay in her lonely bed staring up at the ceiling in the darkness. How could she have made such a terrible mistake? Opened such a Pandora's box of hurt . . . and need? Before, she had only guessed about what she'd missed, but now she knew. And with the knowing came the wanting. Small wonder the Church and Her Majesty both exhorted women of good morals to abstain from sex whenever possible.

It was as addictive as opium!

She tossed and turned all night, exhausted but unable to sleep, for every time she drifted off, she dreamed of the major and how he'd made love to her. And awakened, aching for him to carry her to that far place of wonder again and again.

In the morning, Tilda entered her bedroom with coffee and an inquisitive expression on her face. To head off her questions, Miranda said, "Please have a bath drawn, good and hot."

"Feeling a bit achy, are we?" Tilda asked with a hint of a smile.

"No, 'we' are not. I did not sleep well last night—"

"I can imagine you didn't," came the impertinent reply as Tilda turned and yanked on the bell pull, summoning an upstairs maid to set up the bath.

Miranda could've bitten her tongue for giving the clever Tilda such an opening. She counterattacked, asking, "How did your evening with Mr. St. John go? You came in quite late."

"You would know, since you didn't sleep a wink last night." Now Tilda smirked.

"What do you expect? To find the baron hiding beneath my bed?" Miranda seethed with indignation.

"Oh, I don't think His Lordship spent any time *under* the bed," she replied.

Her mistress was spared thinking of a retort when the

upstairs maid entered and Tilda instructed the girl to fetch fresh towels, then draw a bath in the chamber adjacent to the bedroom.

Dismissing them both, Miranda lay back in the large claw-foot tub and let the perfumed heat soothe her, for she did indeed ache in places unused for many a year . . . and in places never used at all before last night. Her attempts to relax were rudely interrupted when Tilda returned bearing a letter.

"It's from him," she said, laying it on the marble-top table beside the tub.

As if "him" were self-explanatory. Miranda dismissed Tilda more sharply than she should have but made no effort to open the letter. It leaned between two bottles of bath scents, a heavy velum envelope bearing the Rushcroft seal. Taunting her.

Finally the bathwater grew cold and she could not bear sitting in it or looking at the unopened letter a moment longer. Without ringing for help, she stepped out of the tub and rubbed herself dry, not bothering to use lotion, but quickly pulling on a robe and belting it before she tore open the envelope.

She should have taken a seat before reading the terse words he wrote, for they made her whole body quake.

My dear Mrs. Auburn,
Because of last night, there is one matter of exceeding urgency upon which we must confer. After that is resolved, I shall not trouble you further. I shall call upon you at ten. Do not think to turn me away.

B

What could he possibly want? It was quite obvious that he was still killingly angry with her. Had he reconsidered her offer of a loan? No. She had grievously offended his prickly pride by offering it. What had made her do such a foolish thing? A man such as Brandon Caruthers truly could not be bought. He did not want her money. But neither did the note sound as if he intended to plead his case for continuing their impossible relationship.

Mystified, she selected a dress and readied herself without summoning Tilda, who would insist she wear something fetching and want to fix her hair in a flattering style. She donned one of her gray business suits and braided her hair, putting it up in a tight coil at the back of her head. When she turned to look at herself in the mirror, her face crumpled.

She was old. Dark smudges beneath her eyes accented her awful pallor, and with her hair parted down the center and pulled back tightly, every tiny line in her face was magnified. Well, best that he see her as she really was—and as she would all-too-quickly become in a few brief years, while he was still young and virile, with every woman in London ready to fall at his feet.

She splashed her face with cold water to wipe away the traces of crying. He must never know that she hurt even worse than he did. He would recover. Somehow, Miranda did not believe she ever would.

It was difficult to face him in the harsh reality of daylight, but she was not a coward, she told herself as her hand froze on the doorknob. Yes, she *was* a coward. Wasn't that the greatest part of the reason she'd sent him away in the first place? Miranda refused to pursue that line of thought. She had to get this over with immediately.

When she opened the door, the major was pacing like a caged tiger in the front parlor where the butler had asked him to wait. He turned and stared at her as she closed the door securely behind her. It would not do to have servants overhearing whatever it was he had to say.

As if reading her mind—a disconcerting trait of his—he smiled bitterly and asked, "Afraid someone might eavesdrop?"

"It would serve neither of us well if someone did," she snapped. "What is it that is so urgent?"

"I know what a busy woman you are, so I'll try not to detain you." His voice was heavy with irony.

His knuckles whitened as he clenched his fists at his sides. As usual, he'd shed his gloves somewhere along the way. She could not bear to look at how splendidly handsome he was in a dark gray frock coat. One lock of sun-bleached hair fell across his brow, and he combed it impatiently away as he resumed pacing.

"Pray continue," she prompted when he seemed unable to frame the words for what he intended to say.

"There could be a child. I'll not abandon my own flesh and blood."

She sank onto a chair, too stunned to speak for a moment. "A child?" she echoed dumbly. "No, that's not possible—I mean, that is, it took nearly a year before I became p-pregnant," she stumbled over the horribly indelicate word never uttered in mixed company. "With Lori," she finished in a hushed voice.

His eyes pinned her to the chair. "I'm not a seventy-year-old man, Miranda. And you're scarcely the ancient crone you're trying to be." He looked from her hair to her dress and back with disgust. "It isn't likely after just one night, but it could've happened, and if so, I mean to be a father in that child's life."

"Do you expect me to marry you on the chance that I might be carrying your child? Or to have—"

"Don't even think it!" he snapped, so furious he wanted to stride across the room and choke her. But the stricken look on her face made him realize that she would never visit an abortionist, no matter how much scandal ensued.

"I apologize, Miranda. I had no right to accuse you of such a thing."

"As I had no right to assume you wanted to marry me. So we are at an impasse."

He smiled sadly. "No, not yet. You have to let me know when your next courses come. Then everything will be over between us."

The look he gave her indicated he did not believe that any more than she did. Her face must look a perfect fright. Bright scarlet did so clash with dark red hair. "Very well. I shall do so. Thank you for your concern, Major," she added softly as she rose on shaky legs and moved toward the door.

"I still insist on guards to watch over you until we find out who's trying to kill you. Sin and I will continue to investigate. In the meanwhile, don't leave this house without carrying the Adams revolver I gave you. Sin says you know the basics of how to fire it now. I'm sending over two guards—"

"You need not concern yourself—"

"Yes, I do. Nothing will change that. The men are professionals and they know how to protect you. Do you think whoever's tried unsuccessfully four times will just give up?"

She shook her head. With everything that had happened since yesterday, the attempts on her life were the very last thing she'd considered. "I shall use due caution, Major. Thank you." With that, she opened the door and fled down the hall to the sanctuary of her office.

She always found solace in work.

Having done his duty after the preceding evening's folly, Brand felt an almost suffocating need to get out of London. Did he hope for the unlikely possibility that Miranda carried his child? She had said she would not marry him—

but such a circumstance might cause her to reconsider. Of course, it would not augur well for their relationship. She might resent the child. She would certainly resent *him*. He did not want her on those terms.

But damn, he did want her! So bloody much he ached just thinking of how she'd looked last night with all that dark, lush hair tumbling over her creamy skin, the glow in her eyes as he caressed her, the way she responded to him—and he to her. After they had made love, when she had told him about her first marriage, he'd dared to hope for a chance to win her.

And she'd thrown money in his face instead.

Proud, prickly and utterly impossible female. Competing in a man's world had hardened her and made her suspicious of everyone's motives, most particularly his. If he had a lick of horse sense, he'd pack himself off to the country and stay there.

But before he could do that, he had several matters which required his attention. Spurning Miranda's insulting offer of a loan had been essential to his self-respect, but it did leave him in even more desperate financial straits than he'd been the day he arrived in England. Oh, the sale of several foals had held his creditors at bay, but he did not have the time or resources to develop a breeding program that would bring in a substantial income.

In the library at Rushcroft Hall, however, he had stumbled upon what might prove to be his salvation. That was what led him to visit Herbert Austin Biltmore once again. The unpleasant little solicitor had not been entirely truthful in revealing all the details regarding the entailments of the Rushcroft title. There was one way the baron could raise enough money to see him through until he could get the stud farm and his racing stables established.

And he meant to put the punctilious little solicitor to work on it immediately.

Chapter Nineteen

"You simply cannot mean to sell such a home," Biltmore sputtered. "Why, it's in one of the finest locations in all of London."

"All the more reason it should fetch a pretty penny," Brand shot back.

"B-but you'll have no city residence. Parliament is in session. If you sell the Caruthers home on St. James Square, where will you live—in some shabby rental?"

Brand shrugged. "Frankly, I don't care. Now that Disraeli has manipulated the Conservatives' voting reforms through Parliament, the current session will be over before you can finalize a sale. I'll worry about lodgings next year. I intend to spend most of my time in the country improving my land. And for that I shall require the cash this will generate. Fortunately, my cousin never studied the document of entailment or even the house would be gone by now." He gave the solicitor a harsh stare, which set the little man to rustling papers furiously as he nodded.

"Very good, my lord. If you are certain—"

"Yes, Mr. Biltmore, I am quite certain," Brand cut him off impatiently. "Please keep me apprised of offers. I want to sell expeditiously, but I also expect to receive what the place is worth in spite of its, ah, shall we say, depleted condition."

Once he left the stuffy office, one burden seemed to slip from his shoulders. At least he would have a small margin of cash with which to hold the wolf from the door—or the stables, in this case. Smiling grimly, he was about to raise his hand to hail a hansom, when one already carrying a passenger pulled to a halt directly in front of him.

"I was hoping to catch you before you left the solicitor's," Sin said as Brand climbed into the carriage. "I trust all went according to plan?"

Brand knew Sin was referring to more than the arrangements to sell the city house, but he did not wish to discuss his meeting with Miranda. His friend was certain he had become her lover, but Sin could never guess just how wrong things had gone after their first night together. The baron had no intention of enlightening him.

"We should realize enough from selling the old wreck to keep us afloat for another year or two."

St. John frowned. "That's cutting right to the bone. Reiver will have to work especially hard," he replied, winking at the humor of having the stallion put to stud so often. He looked over at the baron guilelessly.

The thought of his own "stud" services caused Brand to scowl. All business, he asked, "What brought you chasing after me at Biltmore's office?"

"I have at last run O'Connell to ground. Thought you might like to go with me when I confront him."

Brand nodded grimly. "Lead on, McDuff."

"Now, why do Americans insist on misquoting—"

"I've had my use of Shakespeare denigrated enough," Brand snapped.

"I cannot imagine by whom," Sin replied with a grin but said nothing more. He recognized the look in his friend's eyes and decided to quit while he was ahead.

They rode through the squalid streets of the East End as factory smoke belched over an already sullen day, tinting the gray clouds a bilious yellow. As summer's heat warmed the filth pouring into it, the Thames gave off an overpowering stench. Tumble-down buildings sat row upon dark row like coal scuttles strewn amidst the narrow twisting streets, and the foul air weaved its way around them.

"How can society allow people to live like this?" Brand asked, shaking his head. "This is the richest nation on earth."

"Wait until we reach Seven Dials. It gets worse," Sin replied.

Brand only shook his head, disgusted and heartsick, eager to return to the clean fresh air and purifying labor of the countryside. He'd never been a city man.

The driver refused to enter the notorious section of the city, one so fearsome that even the Peelers would not patrol there. Brand and Sin offered him a sizable bonus if he were at the post when they returned. He agreed, although they were not certain whether it was the casual mention that St. John's employer was a member of the House of Lords or the clink of coins that convinced him. His cooperation was essential, since they might have to leave Seven Dials in a hurry.

"I do trust you're armed?" Sin asked. He himself was carrying a sword-cane and two Webley revolvers, one in his jacket pocket, one in his waistband.

"Never since that night at the opera have I gone unprepared for the worst in this hellish city. I've got an

Adams and my 'toothpick,' " Brand replied, eyeing the denizens of the area warily.

"Only one Adams. Pity you gave the other to Mrs. Auburn," Sin said, testing the waters as they walked. Brand made no reply, but the tight set of his mouth spoke volumes.

A fellow with blackened teeth leaned against a crumbling brick wall, paring his dirt-encrusted nails with a tiny stiletto as they drew near. His eyes, pale yellow and slitted like a serpent's, sized up the unlikely duo. The smaller fellow was wiry and well armed. His companion was much larger and had the look of the peerage about him. The narrow scar on his cheek indicated he was no stranger to a good fight.

So desperate were the street toughs of Seven Dials that they'd kill just for a new suit of clothes. "Help ye, gov?" the man asked, making an obsequious bow before the tall swell. "Name's Lionel Biggs, but them hereabouts calls me Lion, they does. Whot ye lookin' for? A woman?"

Suppressing a shudder at the thought of what sort of woman this fellow might produce, St. John replied, "Our thanks, Mr. Biggs, but we know our way."

"Hospitable ole boy," Brand said dryly as they turned the corner. "Somehow I don't imagine we've seen the last of him."

Sin only grunted his agreement. "This is the corner and that must be the place."

Brand inspected the rabbit warren of twisting alleyways surrounding the shambling decay of a soot-blackened brick building with more mortar missing than holding the masonry together. "Cutthroats aside, we're risking our lives just walking inside that place. It could tumble down around our ears with one good sneeze. You're certain your source is reliable? This is where O'Connell lives?"

St. John smiled evilly. "After I threatened to geld him

right there on the stable floor, I believe he told me the truth."

"Quite a come-down for a man who was placing thousand-pound wagers at the races a few weeks ago."

"It wasn't his money," Sin replied.

"Then let us see just whose it was."

Inside they went, following the stink of boiling cabbage and rat offal as they climbed some rotting stairs to the third floor. Rather than knock on the door at the end of the hall, Sin tried turning the rusty knob. With a loud creak, it opened, revealing a dank, tiny room with one window, the panes partially broken out, the jagged edges so encrusted with grime they impeded the small shaft of light glimmering through the narrow gangway between buildings. Its pale rays shone down on splintery wood floors and a rickety pair of chairs facing a table with a broken leg. In the darkest corner, lying on what looked like a pile of rags, a figure stirred upon hearing the sounds of footsteps.

"Hoo are ye?" a scratchy voice asked. The nasal cockney accent did not belong to O'Connell.

"Friends of the Irishman's," Brand said. "Where is O'Connell?"

The filthy figure scuttled up from the bed of rags like a crab emerging from beneath a pile of slime-encrusted rocks. He squinted at the tall stranger with his one good eye. "Don't know no bloody Irishman."

"You're sharing his domicile," St. John said, withdrawing a gleaming blade from the concealment of the carved walking stick he carried. He flourished it menacingly. "Where is the Irishman?"

"You'd better tell him," Brand advised. "He gets right testy when someone doesn't answer his questions—truthfully, mind."

"I don't want no trouble, gov, honest I don't," the man

whined. " 'E ain't got no more need o' this place, and it be safer than the street. Rent's paid till end 'o the week."

"What do you mean, he doesn't need it?" Brand asked as Sin held the business end of the blade pointed directly at the little man's chest.

" 'E left 'ere last night. Said 'e 'ad a job whot paid real good. Wouldn't 'ave to live in this 'ere muck no more."

"What kind of job? Working for whom?" Sin prodded.

"Some swell. Dressed like ye," he replied, gesturing to Brand. "All's I know is Connie was bound for Surrey. Somethin' er other about some nobleman's 'orses."

"Rushcroft Hall. My stables," Brand said grimly.

When the tall one with the odd accent said "my stables," the little thief blanched and began backing away. "Ain't 'ad nothin' to do wi' it, gov."

Ignoring him, Brand said to Sin, "If he left last night—"

"That doesn't give us much time. There's a train on the quarter hour, if I remember the schedule. Otherwise we'll have to wait until noon for the next one."

"Can we make it?" Brand asked as Sin pulled out his pocket watch.

"Perhaps if we sprout wings and fly. But greater miracles have happened," he replied as they dashed for the stairs.

The moment they were gone, Benbo followed. His gnarled bones did not allow him to keep up with them, but he knew Lion would be interested in the expensively dressed pair. There might be a farthing or two in it for his trouble.

Concluding the same thing, Lion had already assembled his crew of cutthroats. When the tall man and his small companion rushed from the building, the human wolves attacked, hoping to use the element of surprise to overcome superior firepower. But the strangers were prepared for the worst. When the first of Lion's men leaped out of the shadows, knife slashing for his throat, Sin impaled him on his sword, kicking the blade free of the dying man with his boot.

"Watch out behind you," he warned the baron, who was already crouching and spinning about, his pistol drawn. Sin fired and the second man went down, but not before the Adams revolver was knocked from Brand's hand by a third man. A fourth sank his blade into Brand's arm. It was difficult to maneuver in the narrow alleyway surrounded by a veritable mob intent on killing them. Ignoring the searing pain in his arm, Caruthers slipped his own blade from his boot and used its greater length to wicked advantage.

As one attacker tried to retrieve Brand's pistol, Sin fired, hitting him square in the back. He fell with the weapon buried beneath him. Sword and pistol clutched in his hands, Sin murmured to the baron, "Pull the Webley from inside my waistcoat."

"I'm . . . occupied at the . . . moment," Brand managed to reply as he slashed an attacker's hand and kicked another man back into the fellow holding his blood-spurting fingers.

Lion stood back, letting his boys do the dirty work, but it looked as if they might not be able to handle the job. Pity. Ten of them against the two swells, and one of those barely larger than a circus midget! As his victims made a break for it, leaving the bloody remnants of his gang swarming after them, he faded into the shadows. If his boys were able to subdue their prey, he would be at the kill to claim the largest share of the bounty they stripped off the foreigners.

Lionel Biggs was not called the Lion for nothing.

The chase was on through the labyrinth of rookeries, where old mansions collapsing in decay abutted shanties erected with rotted, mismatched boards pried from fallen-down fences, even pulled from the slime and mold of the Thames. The inhabitants were the living dead: thieves, beggars and those too near death to be either one any longer. One newspaper had written that Europe's grandest mansions were flanked by its worst graveyards.

Now all Brand and Sin wished was to not end up in this one. It seemed that as soon as they evaded one group of armed rabble, they were cut off at another intersection by a new band. "We're well and truly lost, I fear," the baron said as they hid in a tumbled-down ruin of what had once been the mews of the towering three-story home fronting it, now overgrown with weeds and vines.

"No, I've kept my bearings . . . I believe."

"That's reassuring," Brand replied dryly. "Because I think I hear beaters moving this way."

. Sure enough, a group of men was thrashing through the house, asking the inhabitants if they had seen two rich fellows, one of them a blackamoor. The subjects of their inquiry made a dash out of the mews and down the cob-blestones, slippery from a brief summer rain.

"Damn, they're gaining on us. Can't you run any faster?" Brand asked.

"Only if I had a horse beneath me," Sin panted. "Your . . . bloody . . . legs are twice . . . as long as . . . mine."

"We still on course?" Brand surveyed the end of the narrow passageway they were in and thought he saw a streetlight. Civilization! "Only a few hundred yards farther," he urged his small companion.

Gradually the footfalls began to grow fewer as more of the cutthroats gave up. Their victims were indeed approaching a thoroughfare. When they reached it, a huge grin split St. John's face.

"There's the hansom. Didn't I tell you I'd kept my bearings!"

* * *

Lori approached the door to her mother's office, determined not to be put off for one more moment. Miranda had been closeted all day with Mr. Aimesley, who had arrived around noon with urgent business papers for her to look over and sign. They had not even stopped to take luncheon, and Lori's pleas to be allowed to speak with her had been ignored.

As soon as she heard Aimesley in the foyer, accepting his hat from the butler, Lorilee raced down the hall at a most unladylike speed. She tapped, then stepped inside without waiting for permission to do so, lest her mother turn her away. Miranda was hunched over her desk, staring at a sheaf of papers laid out across the surface, her head cradled between her hands. When she looked up, Lori gasped.

"Mother, you look dreadful! Oh, I did not mean—"

"I thank you for your kind words of reassurance after the grueling afternoon I have just spent," Miranda interrupted, rubbing her temple as she reached for a pen and began tapping it against the polished walnut desktop.

"You know it's not this afternoon but last night I wish to know about. Tilda told me the baron called on you early this morning . . . again." She waited expectantly.

Miranda sighed and shoved back the contracts. For a few brief hours the problems of the American railway investment had held at bay her sense of desolation. Now she would have to face it. But the pain was too private to share, even with her only child. "As to last night, what was between the baron and me is none of your concern," she said as gently as she could manage.

"Was between you?" Lori picked up on the nuance immediately. And did not like it. "He left the ball almost as soon as you did. I know he followed you home."

"You know nothing of the sort," Miranda snapped indignantly. "And I will not have this conversation with a young lady just out of the schoolroom. It—it isn't proper."

"Oh, bother what's proper. Did you quarrel?" Lori asked impatiently. "Is that why you dressed like a Billingsgate fishwife to greet him this morning?" She tried for a teasing tone but could see at once by the stubborn set of her mother's chin that all she'd succeeded in doing was making her furious.

Miranda stood up and stopped herself at the last second from smoothing the wrinkles from the horrid gray monstrosity. "This is one of my best dresses, scarcely what a 'Billingsgate fishwife' could afford." She was unable to keep the sharpness from her tone. "But that is neither here nor there," she said, taking a deep breath. "You will not question me any further about the baron or my wardrobe again. I am a woman of business, and this is how I must appear to conduct it."

"Does that also apply to wearing your hair in a ratty knot that I know Tilda did not braid and having dark circles beneath your eyes?" Lori asked, genuinely concerned about her mother's exhausted appearance. She rounded the desk and before Miranda could stand up, Lori knelt and threw her arms around her, laying her head in her mother's lap. "Oh, please don't let us fight. I did not mean to hurt you."

Miranda stroked her daughter's silky hair and felt the tears building up behind her eyelids. She squeezed them back, fearing that once the floodgates opened, there would be no stopping . . . ever. *I'm too old to behave like a girl Lori's age.* "I did not mean to speak so harshly to you, but this has been a . . . difficult time for me. Mr. Aimesley brought even more bad news regarding the railway venture. Another bidder in America is trying to force his way in—some banker who is holding up the entire project for us."

Work was a safe topic. But not one she normally discussed with her daughter.

"I'm sorry that has not gone well, but it's only money," Lori replied.

"Spoken like one who has never been forced to do without it," Miranda said with equal parts humor and sadness.

"It's your *happiness* I worry about, not your pocketbook."

"Alas, the two are all too often linked together. Someday you may find it to be true, but I hope not. In the meanwhile, I believe there is a recital at the Wimberlys' tonight that you would enjoy attending, is there not?"

Realizing that the subject of the baron was closed—at least for the present—Lori sighed in resignation. She would enlist Tilda in arranging to meet with him. If her mother would not explain what was wrong, surely he would. One way or the other, Lorilee was determined to see this misunderstanding, whatever its cause, straightened out.

She gave a sniff and wiped her eyes, noting her mother's were also suspiciously damp, and said, "Terrance Wimberly is a crashing bore and his sister Hortense will only torture us with her harp music. I believe a relaxing evening at home and some rest for you would be best."

Miranda regarded her dubiously. "Are you certain?"

"Quite," Lori replied, giving her a quick peck on the cheek. "Now, I'm going to have Cook fix a hearty supper for us, to make up for your not eating a bite all day."

Miranda watched Lori hurry from her office. Her intuition told her the girl was up to something, but then she looked down at the paperwork on her desk and became distracted. Best to go over the figures again so she could have a restful meal with Lori and get some sleep tonight. She'd be all right in the morning, she assured herself.

But could not make herself believe it.

"I tell ye, Yer Lordship, if not for me rheum'tism acting up, every horse in the stable would have to be put down." Wiggins, an elderly groom, squinted through his rheumy eyes and spat into the hay. "I forgot 'n left me lin'ment here in the feed barn. Coshed me pretty good, they did."

Brand asked, "How do you feel now?"

"Oh, I got a right nasty bump on my head 'n some cuts and bruises. Cook wanted to send for the doctor in the village, but I told him he's a better healer. Got lots of practice. Young Mathias come running from his place when he heard the commotion, but it were too late. I'da done better, but they was half me age. Got off a shot with me blunderbuss, I did, though." He spat again, then added, "Missed 'em, blast it all."

"What did those fellows look like? Can you describe either of them?" Sin asked the old stableman, who obliged.

Brand and his friend exchanged a look. One was certainly O'Connell.

"Caught 'em at the granary, door wide open and them loading a cart," Wiggins said, picking up his story once again. "They already had the feed bins overflowin' inside the stables. Reiver, all his mares and the colts was just startin' in to eat."

"And they would have continued to eat until they were foundered," Brand said grimly, realizing how close this saboteur had come to ruining him. If turned loose with unlimited grain, most horses would die of ruptured intestines. He and Sin would have been fortunate to save even a few of his prize breeding stock.

Brand instructed Wiggins, "As soon as the sheriff arrives, send him directly to the house."

Of course, by the time the sheriff rode in and the hue and cry went out around the local countryside, the culprits had vanished.

Brand and Sin shared a late supper in the kitchen of the old manor house, discussing the day's events. The first time the baron had said he would share a meal with his stablemaster, the cook and house servants had been scandalized that a peer would eat in the kitchen. Even worse, he would dine with an employee, a blackamoor! Perhaps since St. John spoke as if he were a peer himself, that was why His Lordship treated him thus. There was simply no understanding the aristocracy.

"Most probably O'Connell's back in London, trying to collect his pay from whoever sent him," Brand said glumly, stabbing a potato with his fork.

"I don't doubt it, but if I catch the morning train, I may be able to run him to ground again," Sin replied hopefully.

"He won't return to that stinking hole in Seven Dials if he's got coin enough to find better accommodations."

St. John nodded in agreement, dabbing his lips with his napkin.

"But who would pay him without first verifying that my stables have indeed been ruined? After all, he botched the first attempt with the fire at the mews. Why hire an incompetent for a second attempt?"

Sin put down his napkin and shoved away his plate, appearing thoughtful for a moment as he murmured, "Unless it didn't matter whether or not he succeeded, only that he made the attempt."

Brand's eyes narrowed. "What do you mean?"

"Even if we hadn't found out O'Connell was headed here, we'd have received a wire immediately after this debacle . . ."

"Which would send us rushing pell-mell to the country," Brand finished St. John's thought, recalling how they'd jumped on board the train as it was pulling from the station, in hot pursuit of O'Connell.

"All the better if we had sick and dying horses to tend, but perhaps even one night out of London would be enough."

"Miranda!" Brand cried, shoving his chair back from the table.

Both men were up and reaching for their coats, food forgotten as they realized they had fallen into a trap and an innocent woman would pay the ultimate consequences.

"Be quiet, Tilda, else you'll waken Mother," Lorilee whispered as the two conspirators tiptoed down the servants' stairs at the back of the house. Dinner had seemed interminable as Lori had waited for Miranda to finish her dessert and linger over coffee, but she had not wanted to arouse her mother's suspicions by seeming to rush her off to bed.

Tilda had gone through her usual ritual of brushing her mistress's hair a hundred strokes and pulling back the covers, even bringing a book of Lord Tennyson's poems for Miranda to read in bed.

"If anything should put her to sleep, *that* will," Lori had murmured. She was no admirer of Her Majesty's poet laureate.

When they heard no sounds stirring in the dark house, the two women set out, but Tilda still worried. "I sent a note to Mr. St. John and have received no reply. It is not like him to fail to answer an urgent letter. Perhaps the baron does not want to discuss what went on between them any more than does your mother."

"Nonsense. Just because they act like fools, that is no reason we should accept it. Anyway, we can leave a message if, for some reason, Lord Rushcroft is not at home."

"I still don't like this," Tilda groused as they slipped into the alley and began walking to the next square. "It's late. What if we cannot hail a hansom driver?"

"Then we shall walk," Lori said determinedly.

"All the way from Kensington Gardens to St. James Square!"

They did not see the man in the shadows as they closed the back gate. He smiled to himself. This was going to be even easier than he could have imagined. He glided through the cover of the shrubbery and emerged on the next street. A hansom driver waited for his instruction.

"She's coming to us, a right obligin' colleen," O'Connell said.

"Out alone this time of night?" the driver asked incredulously.

"Not alone. She has the maid with her. We'll have to nab the two of them. All the better to convince the widow she'd best be cooperating."

"If ye say so," the driver replied, looking about the street as if expecting a Peeler to pop from the bushes at any moment.

"Just drive around the corner, boyo. They're afoot. Sneaking off to see himself or I miss me guess." O'Connell chuckled. "All we have to do is offer them a ride. They'll jump right in."

Chapter Twenty

"We're in such luck," Lorilee whispered excitedly as she sighted the hansom turning the corner. "Imagine finding a public vehicle so easily at this hour."

Tilda reached out and gripped her charge's arm, eyeing the hansom warily. "It almost seems too convenient. I expected to have to walk to the square at the least before we encountered anyone."

"It's a hansom, Tilda, for goodness' sake." Her tone of exasperation turned to concern as she realized why the maid was being so cautious. "You're thinking about whoever tried to harm my mother, aren't you? Why would they send someone after—"

"Back to the house," Tilda declared as some deep instinct from her horrific childhood in India flared to life. She grabbed Lorilee's hand and began dragging the girl after her, picking up her skirts as she ran.

Lori did likewise and the two women darted back down the alleyway to cut through the mews. Choosing the dark route proved unwise. The carriage pulled up to the end and blocked it. As they raced in the opposite direction toward the safety of home, a large figure suddenly materialized from behind the adjacent mews, blocking their path. He was tall and broad-shouldered with shaggy hair that stuck up at odd angles from the sides of a tattered billed cap whose brim obscured his face.

To Tilda and Lorilee he looked like the devil incarnate as he walked toward them in a slow, ambling gait. Like a wolf stalking lamed prey, he was in no hurry. The women were caught between him and the driver of the hansom, who was shorter but quite stocky. He moved in behind them, carrying a nasty truncheon in one hand.

Scandal be damned! Tilda opened her mouth to scream, but the hiss of the big man's voice stopped her—that and the gleam of the pistol he held in his hand as he said, "If you make a sound, I'll be shootin' the girl. Not to kill, mind, just to cripple."

Lori stood frozen, mute with horror at what she had done. Now not only had she endangered her dear Tilda, but perhaps her mother as well! She tried to think as the two men came at them. Suddenly from the corner of her eye she spied the narrow gangway directly to her left leading into the Reardons' garden. It was overgrown with shrubbery where they could hide and cry an alarm before these thugs could shoot them.

Without taking time to consider, she gave Tilda's hand a warning squeeze and then yanked on it as she whirled and dashed toward the only possible escape. The taller fellow let out a snarled oath, but did not fire his weapon. He dared not for fear of alerting the Peelers. Hope bloomed as she cried out for help.

"Thieves! Kidnappers!" Tilda joined in as they scurried through the narrow passage, but all the houses were dark, and servants, the only ones near enough to the rear of the houses to hear them, might not wish to become involved.

After all, what decent women would be out at this time of night?

Lorilee saw the shrubs of the garden, but her hopes sank at once. She'd forgotten that the Reardons had a high oak fence partitioning the garden—and its gate was locked. Frantically she grabbed the latch and yanked, yelling, "It's Lorilee Auburn! Please help me!"

Not a light came on. No one appeared. Except the big man with the Irish brogue who seized her roughly by the throat, choking off her cries as he pulled her against his smelly body. He reeked of horses, tobacco and gin.

Lorilee saw the gleam of the knife blade in front of her eyes and ceased her struggling. "That's a smart colleen."

Tilda started to jump on him in an attempt to free her young charge. "If you move, I'll be cutting her," he almost crooned.

By this time the second fellow was there, seizing the maid and menacing her with his truncheon. "One more peep 'n I cosh ye, unnerstand?" he rasped in a garlicky slur.

The two women were dragged down the alley and shoved into the dark interior of the hansom. The big Irishman joined them while the driver whipped the team into a brisk trot.

The only sound breaking the stillness of the night was the clop of hooves over the cobblestones.

Miranda could not sleep. She had lain awake for hours staring at the ceiling, wide-eyed in the darkness. Every time she closed her eyes, visions of Brandon intruded. How could she ever sleep in this bed again after sharing it with him? She had instructed the upstairs maid to change the sheets this morning, two days ahead of schedule. The servants might gossip, but there was nothing she could do about it. She certainly could not lie down enveloped in his scent.

But clean sheets had done nothing to erase the memory of his touch, the feel of his mouth on her breasts, his hands roaming over the curves of her hips, pulling her to him, burying himself so deeply inside her. She shook her head and continued pacing the floor. But refusing to even look at the bed won her nothing. He was inside her head . . . and her heart.

What a terrible mistake her craving for one night of passion had been. If she had never known what she was missing, she would have had regrets, yes. But regrets could not possibly hurt as badly as this. She cursed herself for a fool. And her major? He was scarcely innocent in the matter of the seduction. He'd stalked her, followed her home and caught her in a moment of self-pitying weakness. Taken advantage of her, that's what he'd done!

Miranda shook her head and massaged her temples, feeling the weight of her unbound hair as it glided around her shoulders and fell to her waist. Even that was a reminder of him and how he'd praised the beauty of what she'd always thought of as ugly coarse red hair. He'd urged her to let it down.

With a muttered oath, she sat at her dressing table and began to put her hair into the usual plait she wore for sleep. But the springy stuff stubbornly fought her, tangling and refusing to braid. Tilda normally did it, but Miranda had not felt up to enduring her questioning eyes and softly voiced innuendoes, so she'd dismissed her as quickly as possible, saying not to bother with the plait.

"It would serve her right if I awakened her from a sound sleep just to fix my hair," she muttered to herself spitefully.

But then she broke down and sobbed. She was blaming her own irresponsible actions on the baron, Tilda, even

Lori, when it was she herself who was guilty. That was the code by which she'd lived all her life. Miranda Stafford Auburn did not pass off responsibility for her deeds.

And those deeds could have profound repercussions. What if Brandon was right? She could be carrying his child. Her hand clutched her flat stomach, as she remembered how she'd felt when she was expecting Lori. Then she had been respectably married and performing the duty for which Will had chosen her. She had loved Lori with her whole heart from the moment of her conception.

This was so utterly different. She was now an older woman, a widow with vast social and economic responsibilities, and a daughter in the midst of her debut season. If she had conceived, the scandal would ruin not only her but innocent Lori as well. She should hate such a baby, dread the very thought of carrying it beneath her heart.

But she did not. Could not. An odd, fluttery sort of joy infused her mind, until she quashed it. This was a serious matter which required logic and planning, not emotion. "I may be borrowing trouble. I'm too old to conceive after only one night," she whispered, trying to reassure herself and kill the impossible dream.

But then she remembered how Brandon had taken her . . . twice, his long, shuddering releases so unlike the brief spasms her husband made. Yes, as the baron had reminded her, he was young and virile. And conception was all too possible. He'd also insisted he would be a father to his child, regardless of whether or not she would marry him.

But he had never asked her to marry him. She'd perhaps assumed too much last night when they talked, when he spoke of their future. Her fear of continuing their dangerous liaison had made her lash out at him and insult his pride in the worst way imaginable—by offering him money. At that moment she had indeed felt as cheap and mercenary as Reba Wilcox.

The damage was done. The relationship between them had ended. She would not marry ever again out of a sense of duty. If she learned she was carrying a child, she would make arrangements for Kent Aimesley to take over her affairs and then she would retire to the country. Someplace far away. Scotland, perhaps. She'd always fancied seeing Edinburgh. She could assume another identity to protect the child, pose as a reclusive widow.

But what of Lori's season? She would have to speak with Elvira Horton, who had some social stature. Surely Elvira would be willing to oversee her daughter's future and make certain she chose a suitable young man.

The thought of leaving Lori made tears well up in her eyes. She had always detested weepy women. Was that a sign that she was indeed enceinte?

"I have no idea if it is even true yet. I must stop borrowing trouble since there is more than enough on my plate right now." With that pronouncement, she turned and looked at the rumpled bed. Did she dare return to it and try to sleep?

Hopeless.

Instead, she lit a small kerosene lamp and made her way downstairs in her robe and slippers. There was a mountain of work sitting in her office. She might as well put this time to some good use. Her resolve was interrupted by a loud pounding on the front door just as she reached the bottom of the steps. Knowing it would take their elderly butler several moments to dress and answer the summons, she approached the door cautiously.

Who could be here demanding entrance at this ungodly hour? Then she heard Brandon's voice and almost dropped the lamp. Quickly walking to the stained-glass window at the side of the heavy door, she peered through and saw that Mr. St. John was with him. Only slightly reassured, she opened the door, and the baron rushed inside.

"What on earth are you doing here in the middle of the night?" she asked as he seized her in an embrace.

"Miranda, thank God!"

"Let me go," she hissed, glancing red-faced at the small man who stood behind them, looking discreetly down at the floor as she wriggled from the major's arms, her head spinning from the warmth of his touch.

"Why did you throw open the door that way? Where are the servants?" Brand demanded, knowing he was acting idiotically now that she was obviously safe.

"I happen to be the only one awake. Please lower your voices before you rouse the whole household and create a horrible scandal."

"It might be wise if we were to step inside the parlor for some privacy," Sin suggested quietly.

Miranda nodded. Of course he was right. With a bit of luck she could find out what had occasioned this outburst and send them on their way without anyone being the wiser. She led them into the small entry parlor with as much dignity as she could muster while dressed in a robe. Her hair was only half braided and askew, and she was wearing carpet slippers on her bare feet! Oh, the gossip this would create!

Seeing that his Miranda was her old stubborn self, Brand felt a wave of relief flood over him before he could stop himself. *His* Miranda. He grinned at her, the hurt of her earlier words forgotten for the moment as he asked, "Couldn't sleep? Maybe a glass of warm milk might help."

She could sense the undercurrent in his solicitude and stiffened her back. "I was working on the railway contracts, as a matter of fact."

"In the middle of the night, dressed like that?" he asked disbelievingly.

"We're behind in closing the deal. I often do my best work at night." That was an inappropriate choice of words.

"So do I," he replied, grinning innocently as he added, "Foals usually come at the most inconvenient times, don't they, Sin?"

Knowing there was a good deal going on here to which he did not wish to be privy, St. John merely said, "Quite so."

"I don't think this is an appropriate hour to discuss our respective work habits, my lord." She stood with her arms crossed protectively over her chest, but stiff-backed, chin high, with one slippered foot tapping irritably on the Brussels carpet. "So I repeat, what is the reason for barging into my home this way?"

"We were lured back to Rushcroft Hall this afternoon. Sin ran O'Connell to ground in Seven Dials, but we just missed him. He was busy trying to kill all my horses."

At her incredulous expression, St. John explained about the granary and the possible outcome if old Wiggins hadn't stumbled upon the scene.

"First your mews, now this. It would appear, my lord," she said, "that someone is trying to ruin you."

"And to kill you, which is far more significant," Brand replied. At her puzzled look, he continued, "Don't you see? We were lured away, leaving you unprotected. If the horses had really gotten into that grain, we'd have been overwhelmed with trying to save them, and if you needed help . . ." His words faded away as he studied her, all amusement gone now.

Miranda could feel his concern touch her heart across the space separating them and knew it was genuine. In spite of everything, he did still care for her. *Or is it for the child you might carry?* That insidious thought leaped inside her mind unbidden and caught her off guard. She stepped back, one hand clutching the lapels of her robe as she realized what a sight she must be.

"As you can see, I am quite unharmed. I do appreciate your concern, my lord, Mr. St. John, but this house is built like a fortress."

"With a gate you open quite readily," Brand replied in exasperation. "I'm convinced there is a tie between what's been happening to my horses and the attempts on your life."

"You don't think Geoffrey Winters—"

"No, he's an idiot. After spending a weekend in his company, I'm quite certain he hasn't the nerve to kill anyone. But someone who knows her way around horses and has a strong dislike for you has nerve to spare."

"Mrs. Wilcox." Miranda could easily believe her capable of it. "But I don't understand what she would stand to gain by killing me."

"I don't know, but I intend to find out. In the meanwhile, you remain here surrounded by servants—armed servants."

When she started to bristle at Brand's peremptory command, Sin said quietly, "Mrs. Auburn, this O'Connell is a very dangerous fellow. We have a witness who can identify him as the man trying to kill the baron's horses. He'll come for you next. Most probably while you're en route to the City this morning. It would be wise if you stayed at home. I'll alert the men watching the front and back doors."

Miranda nodded. "I thank you both for your help."

Although she included Brand in her thanks, she looked only at St. John.

*   *   *

They rode in the dark for nearly an hour, the coach twisting and turning around street corners, its window cover-
ings drawn down so that the women had no sense
whatever of where they were. The only thing they could
tell was that they had not left London, since the clop and
bounce over cobblestones still continued.

But the silence of the empty streets was eerie. In the
posh residential district where they lived, the quiet was
broken by shrubbery rustling in the summer breezes and
the soft cry of an occasional night bird, or the noise raised
by passing carriages. But here, all that was discernible
were faint echoes of emptiness. Then, faraway sounds
from the river broke the stillness.

The big Irishman made no attempt to molest the
women, and for that Lori was grateful as she and Tilda
huddled together on one side of the cab while he sat
across from them. When he'd drawn the blinds, he'd also
made a point of locking the doors and placing the key in
his pocket. One tiny kerosene lantern illuminated the
cramped, filthy old hansom, which reeked of stale smoke
and unwashed bodies, as well as the peculiar combination
of horse and sawdust that emanated from their captor.

Lori was almost certain he must work around a racetrack. She'd certainly not encountered him at Ascot. The
very thought of it almost brought forth a bubble of hysterical laughter. The most elegant racing venue in all the
world—what would rabble such as this kidnapper do
there? She needed to know more about him if they were
going to outsmart him.

Mustering her nerve, she said, "My mother is a very
shrewd woman of business. If you harm us, she won't pay
you a farthing."

Tilda tried to shush her, but Lori met his narrowed pale
eyes with courage that she knew must be foolhardy.

He barked an ugly laugh. "Oh, she'll dance to whatever

tune we pipe, colleen, and niver give us a lick of trouble."

Us? Somehow Lori intuited he did not mean the brutish driver. "Whom do you work for?" she blurted out, then wished to call back the words.

"Lorilee, hush!" Tilda cried out.

He nodded in her direction. "She's right, ye know. If I was to tell ye that . . ."

The nasty threat hung in the air for a moment before the hansom jerked to a halt. He leaned forward, fished the key from his pocket and unlocked the door. Then he reached out one large meaty paw and grabbed Lori's arm as he stepped out of the cab.

"Get your hands off me. I can walk," Lorilee said with more bravado than she felt.

He ignored her, jerking her roughly against him so she tumbled out the door into the darkness. Still holding her by one arm, he called in to Tilda. "Come along now, ye blackamoor bitch, else I'll be forced to put a few bruises on yer charge."

At the terrible slur, Lori hissed furiously and, without thinking, sank her teeth into the meat of his hand, biting down as hard as she could. He let out a string of oaths as he grabbed her hair and pulled so hard, tears sprang to her eyes. But she did not release her bite.

"I could be usin' a wee bit of help here, boyo," he called out to the driver, who had climbed down from his perch and seized hold of Tilda as she tried to pound on the taller man who was hurting Lorilee.

Both women continued to struggle, Tilda crying out into the darkness for help while Lori's teeth drew blood from her captor. The sounds of the fight echoed through the deserted streets. They were in an industrial district, closed down for the night, except for one dim light emanating from a window several dozen yards away. The battle was an uneven contest, quickly lost as both women were knocked unconscious.

The kidnappers began carrying the limp bodies toward the light as a figure in a frock coat hurried out to meet them. "What on earth have you done? I'm surprised Scotland Yard hasn't heard the uproar! Hurry," he commanded, looking up and down the empty street. "Bring them inside. You had better not have harmed the young lady."

The sunrise came with its usual accompaniment of coal soot and sulfur fumes spewing a gray miasma over London. A bit early for Reba to be awake. Brand smiled grimly. All the better to catch her while her wits were clouded by sleep. He knocked sharply on the door of the elegant city house she was renting from the Marquess of Ellenswick.

When the butler answered stiffly that the mistress was not receiving, he brushed past the old man, saying imperiously, "She'll damn well see me. Downstairs, dressed, or upstairs naked."

The old man studied the unshaven, dangerous-looking man with a scar on his cheek and decided he meant business. "Whom shall I say is calling, sir?"

"Lord Rushcroft, an old friend from Kentucky."

After the butler scurried off, leaving him to cool his heels in a sitting room, Brand wondered if it might not have been best to head directly for her. He wouldn't put it past the woman to slip out the back way. Then again, Reba always did love a challenge.

What would be the best way to approach her? He felt gut-deep that she was involved in the botched attempts to kill Miranda and to destroy his racing stock. The latter he could almost understand. He had spurned her, and Reba did not take rejection well. But to want Miranda dead?

Reba could not know how involved he and Miranda had become . . . could she? He recalled that scene in Falconridge's garden and reconsidered.

The butler returned, stiff with disapproval. He doubtless had a great deal about which to disapprove since Reba had taken up residence here, Brand thought wryly. "Mrs. Wilcox will see you in her upstairs apartments. If you will come with me, milord."

Brand followed the old man up a steep staircase and down a long, narrow hall. The house was small but well appointed. When the servant announced him, Brand stepped into a small sitting room adjacent to Reba's bedroom, the double doors of which stood ajar. She was posed languorously across a fainting couch, dressed in a robe of scarlet silk that fell artfully open, revealing the curves of her lush breasts, covered only by red lace.

"Well, to what do I owe this unexpected pleasure?" she purred.

"There won't be any pleasure when I finish with you, Reba," he said, closing the door behind him.

"Are you certain, darlin'?" She stood up slowly, allowing a generous amount of long white leg to slip out from her robe before demurely straightening it and tightening the belt to emphasize her tiny waist.

When she reached him and raised her arms, placing them around his neck, he let her, then pulled her roughly against him and savaged her mouth. He was disgusted at the way she responded like a cat in heat, immediately plunging her tongue into his mouth and writhing her lower body against his as she dug her fingers into his hair. He pulled away and peeled her off his body.

He felt as if he needed to gargle with his granny's home remedy of boiled water and black-strap molasses. "Now that we have that out of the way, we can talk."

Her eyes blazed with startled surprise, then slitted furiously.

"You're more practiced at that than you were back in Kentucky," he said. "Maybe I sold ole Earl short . . . or you had other teachers." She tried to slap him, but he was too quick for her, seizing her wrist and squeezing it painfully.

"I'll scream if you don't let me go."

"I doubt it."

"You're hurting me," she said, pouting. When he released her, she rubbed the reddened marks he'd left. "What makes you so cussed mean, Brand?"

"I think you know. First, the mews at my city house were nearly burned down. Then yesterday a fellow named O'Connell tried to kill Reiver and all my broodmares and colts at the Hall. Would you happen to know him? A real charmer, he is, full of Irish blarney."

"Don't be ridiculous, Brand. Why would I consort with racetrack trash?"

"I never said he worked the racecourses," he replied flatly.

"I didn't say I hadn't heard of him—just that I didn't consort with him." Reba always recovered quickly, he'd give her that. "What would I have to gain by ruining you?" she asked oversweetly.

"Revenge." He studied her face and read calculation. Guilt. How in heaven's name had he ever been stupid enough to think he loved her? "Perhaps revenge against Miranda Auburn, too. Someone's been trying to kill her, as well."

Reba let out one of the trilling laughs that used to charm all the men in Lexington. "I declare, I still can't imagine what you see in that old woman except her money. And you despise me for being mercenary and marrying poor Earl."

"Miranda and Earl are nothing alike and you know it."

"Well, I don't know a thing about anyone trying to kill her—or your silly ole horses. And you can't prove that I do."

"She's not only rich, Reba. She's powerful and has the ear of men high in the government. So do I. Here you're just an American intruder, while I'm a peer. I wouldn't tangle with us if I were you. You're right likely to end up in Newgate. Ever seen the place? No? I hear it's even worse than that Yankee prison in Chicago."

"You can't threaten me. Get out." Her voice was icy now, and she stood by the bell pull, ready to use it if he did not comply.

Brand shrugged. "I've learned what I needed to know, Reba." As he closed the door behind him, he heard the sound of a Meissen vase shattering against it. Ellenswick would have to bill her for it.

Miranda sat down on the chair, the room going black before her eyes as she read the contents of the almost illegibly scrawled note. Biting down on her lip to keep from crying out, she pulled the bell and a maid quickly entered her office. "Please go upstairs and check on my daughter and Tilda. I fear they've overslept."

No, it could not be true. It must not be true!

Moments later, the puzzled servant returned. "They are nowhere to be found, ma'am. Shall I turn out the staff to search?" Her young voice quavered when she watched her usually calm mistress go stark white and tremble.

"No! That is, there is no need. This note explains everything."

Chapter Twenty-one

They said to come alone. Miranda was certain there had to be at least two of them. Her brave daughter and fiercely loyal maid would not have fallen into the vapors and allowed themselves to be whisked away without a fight. "Please, God, don't let them be hurt," she murmured, shuddering and swallowing back her tears. There was no time for such weakness. The note's instructions had been most explicit.

She was to take her private coach and ride along the Strand during the mad rush at day's end when everyone in the City was leaving. A public hansom driver would approach and offer her a ride. She was to dismiss her carriage and go with the man. God only knew what the destination would be. But to reach Lori and Tilda, she would ride through the very gates of hell.

The note had explained tersely that if she failed to follow the instructions, she would never see them alive again. She was to bring no one with her. During several moments of rash panic, she had considered sending for

Brand. He and Mr. St. John knew that someone was trying to kill her and they were investigating. Perhaps they had learned something since last night, but she doubted it. Perhaps they might be able to help her rescue Lori and Tilda, but she doubted that, too.

The only thing certain was that whoever was behind this had gone to considerable trouble to see that the baron and St. John were otherwise occupied. If she involved them, it would surely endanger Lori and Tilda. She simply could not take the risk.

Of course, she could not be certain that the kidnappers would free the hostages even if she complied. The only thing she knew was that they intended to kill her, even though the note did not say so. But why? Who? Somehow Reba Wilcox must be involved, but Miranda could fathom no earthly reason for the woman to wish her dead. Even if Reba knew about the baron's spending the night in her bed, that could not explain it. This went far beyond mere jealousy.

There was only one way to get to the bottom of the mystery and to have a chance of saving her daughter and her companion. She must handle it alone. After a lifetime of dealing with adversity by herself, she would have to overcome this greatest challenge alone. However, the note had said nothing about coming unarmed. She was certain that was because the kidnappers had no idea she even owned a gun.

But after the disastrous outcome of her first shooting lesson at his country house, Brand had insisted that Miranda take one of his Adams revolvers and learn to use it. Mr. St. John had given her a few brief lessons and seemed satisfied with her progress. Now she knew from which end of the weapon the bullets issued. At close range she was even a passable shot.

Carefully removing the Adams from its rosewood case,

she checked to make certain it was loaded. Good. She sat down at her desk and clutched the gun in her hands, trying desperately to think of a plan, but none came to her. If only she knew where she would be taken. Whether Lori and Tilda would truly be there.

Perhaps there was a way . . .

The sooty skies of London blended their yellowish gray industrial pollution with the first hints of twilight as Mrs. Auburn's carriage pulled away from her house and headed toward the City's press of vehicles and swarms of humanity and livestock. She was too preoccupied to notice Mathias crouched hidden in the shrubbery. Mr. Sin would have his hide if she slipped away undetected.

He and Major Caruthers had been so worried about Mrs. Auburn, they had summoned him from the country to help watch her. The youth was there to check on the men hired to safeguard the lady, then report to the baron. But neither of the two guards was at his station. Mathias had made inquiry at the mews and found that one had been sent to deliver some business papers to her office earlier that afternoon and the second fellow had been lured into the kitchen by a comely tweenie who was currently feeding him freshly baked peach tarts.

It was apparent to the clever youth that the lady had deliberately slipped from her home without allowing the men to do their job of protecting her. Her safety was up to him. Without further hesitation, he dashed after the carriage and leaped agilely into the boot, concealing himself beneath the canvas.

Soon the carriage was enveloped in a giant press of humanity and animals. Ragged beggars bumped shoulders with somberly dressed clerks while a herd of goats stopped the flow of traffic along the Strand, baaing loudly as they were driven past irately cursing hansom drivers.

Mrs. Auburn's driver held his temper when a cart overflowing with potatoes cut directly in his path, causing him to jerk on the reins. He stopped his carriage and waited for the cart to bounce past.

Then another vehicle, a battered hansom, pulled from an alley across the way and slipped neatly around the cart, which did not move. In a flash, a man jumped from the old hansom and rapped sharply on the door of Mrs. Auburn's carriage. As Mathias watched, the lady climbed out and instructed her driver to return to the city house without her.

The youth observed as the servant protested leaving his mistress alone with such a disreputable sort. Indeed, the stranger was filthy, with long, stringy hair. Even from a distance, his clothes smelled of Billingsgate's fish markets and looked the worse for it. But Mrs. Auburn repeated her instructions in such an imperious tone that her driver quickly subsided.

As soon as she followed the grimy little man into the hansom, the cart pulled away, clearing a path for her carriage to proceed on its way. The hansom headed in the opposite direction. Mathias had only a moment to jump clear and grab a hold on the rear of the conveyance containing his charge. The hansom slipped down yet another narrow alleyway, vanishing into the gathering darkness.

Miranda was disoriented as the vile-smelling little man closed the curtains, blocking out the view just when the hansom rounded a corner. She tried to keep track of the twists and turns but within moments gave it up as hopeless. Equally hopeless was her effort to communicate with her companion. Using crude hand gestures, he indicated that he could not speak. Then he followed this by opening his mouth wide, revealing a set of badly rotted teeth . . . and the scarred stump of a severed tongue.

When he leered nastily at her, she paled but refused to give him the satisfaction of further showing her fear. Her hands clutched her reticule as if she held receipts for the royal treasury inside it, but he did not demand she give it to him. Yet.

Why bother? He'll probably take it and strip the jewelry from my body after I'm dead.

She gritted her teeth as the hansom began to slow at last. Miranda was relatively certain they were somewhere along the Thames. The noise of river traffic in the distance and the growing quiet as the horses' hooves echoed off tall buildings indicated that they were in the warehouse district. While inspecting her shipping interests from time to time, she had always noted the distinctly cavernous sounds made when a carriage passed between such large structures after they had closed down for the day.

When the hansom pulled to a halt and the mute scrambled out the door, opening it for her with a grotesque flourish, she was shocked. The sign hanging over the small side entrance to the warehouse read: Auburn Shipping, Ltd. Miranda whirled and looked up at the driver, saying, "I own this place. Why have you brought me here? Where are my daughter and her companion?"

Then a voice spoke from behind her. "You need not worry about Miss Auburn, my dear. As for yourself and that blackamoor maid, I fear the circumstances are quite different."

When she turned to face him, Miranda felt her knees weaken with shock. All she could manage to blurt out was, "You!"

"I'll be relievin' you of that pretty little pouch," the driver said in a nasal Irish accent as he jumped lithely to the ground and snatched her reticule. "Niver know what a foolish female might take it in her head to do. Shoot Yer Worship, mayhap?"

Miranda turned between the two men, never having felt so betrayed or so confused in her life.

"You simply have to believe me, Brand. Why would I make up somethin' as crazy as this?" Reba batted her lashes at him and affected a dramatic sigh. "He's utterly ruthless."

He stared at her perfect heart-shaped face with its wide, guileless eyes and pouty red lips. How appearances could deceive. Reba was quite a convincing little actress, but this was the most bizarre tale she had ever concocted. Was it just wild enough to be true? "This could be a ruse to get me out of the way while you have O'Connell make another attempt on Miranda's life. Why should I believe you?" Brand countered.

Reba began fishing in her reticule and withdrew a crumpled piece of paper. "Do you recognize the writing?" she purred.

"I'll go with you," he said after a quick examination. He seized his hat and yelled for the footman, instructing the lazy servant to fetch Sin.

"No need, old chap. I'm here. Would you mind lowering your voice to a roar? The whole of St. James Square can hear you as well as I." Sin and Reba exchanged hostile glances—his sardonic, hers seething.

"Come on, Sin. We're off to see a man about a horse."

"O'Connell?" St. John asked with relish.

"Not quite. You're not going to believe this . . . unless you're considerably more spiritual than I ever imagined."

After arming themselves, the men escorted Reba to the carriage she had arrived in and Brand assisted her inside. As she arranged her skirts, she glared at St. John, daring him to climb in after her. He ignored her, instead jumping agilely to the driver's box and shoving the elderly coachman aside.

Brand took the seat opposite her, saying, "He'll get us there a lot faster."

"You'd actually sit beside a nigra, wouldn't you?" she sniffed, knowing the nasty reference would infuriate him. She intended that.

Brand paid her no heed, too deep in thought to consider her provocation. The pieces of the puzzle were beginning to fall in place now that he understood why Miranda had been targeted for death. But just as the carriage lurched ahead, a cry caused Sin to rein in and leap from the driver's box.

Brand stuck his head out the window and saw Mathias sprinting up the street, waving frantically as he called out to them. The youth was gasping for breath, too winded to speak as he collapsed in Sin's arms.

In an instant, Brand jumped out and joined them. "What is it? Miranda?" he asked, struggling to hold his fear in check as Mathias nodded, still unable to speak.

"He's run quite a distance," Sin said, lowering the sweat-drenched youth's slight body to the weed-infested grass in front of the house.

Still gasping, Mathias said, "I followed . . . the lady. She left . . . without the g-guards and—"

Brand cursed, knowing someone must've lured her away. His quickly exchanged look with Sin confirmed it. "Where did she go?"

Just as Mathias started to answer, Reba's carriage shot away from them, the old driver whipping the horses as if the very devil were on his trail. Sin dashed after it, jumping onto the back of the conveyance just as it picked up speed.

"Can you take us to where they're holding Mrs. Auburn?" Brand asked Mathias.

He held his breath until Mathias replied, "Yes, it's down by the river—a big warehouse."

"Deserted this time of evening," Caruthers muttered, refusing to give in to the blind panic clutching at his heart. Miranda in the hands of men who intended to kill her! Brand helped Mathias to his feet. "You game to go after them, son?"

"Always, Major," Mathias replied with a grin, wiping the perspiration from his eyes, ignoring the misery of his sweat-drenched body.

By this time Reba's carriage was pulling to an abrupt halt at the end of the street. St. John had climbed over the top and used his pistol to convince the driver it was wiser to listen to him than to the woman inside, who was now shrieking at him for stopping.

"She was making sure we were diverted while they seized Mrs. Auburn," St. John said when Brand and Mathias caught up to them.

"No doubt. Come on. We've no time to waste. I'll guard Reba while we ride," Brand said as he climbed inside the carriage. Mathias and Sin jumped onto the driver's box, leaving the old man standing in the street as they took off in a mad dash toward the warehouse district.

Miranda stared at Kent Aimsley as if she'd never seen him before in her life. "Why are you doing this?" she blurted out when he entered the small office in the warehouse where she had been confined for the past hour.

"Why, indeed," he replied rhetorically. "You certainly weren't naïve enough to believe I was still carrying an unrequited tendresse for you after all these years? No? Well, then, why do you suppose I went to work for the man you married and stayed to work under a woman when he died?"

The contempt in his voice and the sneer twisting his mouth made him look like a man she had never known . . . a dangerous, evil stranger. "Will and I paid you well and advanced you to a position of great importance," she replied numbly.

He raised one pale eyebrow and looked down on her with open scorn. "Oh, you paid me well enough—for a bloody glorified clerk! I slaved for you. Without me, that foolish old man—not to mention a mere female—would never have been half as successful as you've been. Now at last I'll receive what is due me."

Though it was patently untrue, Miranda knew that Aimesley believed his rantings about how he, not she, was responsible for the vast empire she had built. "Where are Lori and Tilda?" she asked, trying to focus on him so she could figure out how to proceed. "If you've harmed them, I swear—"

"They're here. A bit uncomfortable amid the boxes and bales, but safe for the nonce. I wouldn't dream of seeing harm come to my new ward."

The words were clipped and cold. Miranda's heart froze. "You intend to kill me and Tilda, then take over my business? Become Lori's guardian?"

"Who else? You're estranged from what little family Auburn left in Liverpool. Only a few distant cousins and an elderly uncle, as I recall. I'm confident the courts will see that I should be her guardian. After all, who better to oversee the young lady's assets . . . and choose her husband? A nice irony for Will Auburn's daughter after he took you away from me."

"You know I had no choice in that," she replied before realizing what she was saying.

He stiffened angrily. "You had one after the old man died! But even then you made it quite clear that you had never cared for me."

"All you wanted was my money. Not me." Her voice was flat. How sad that everything in her life seemed to turn on her own inadequacy as a woman. But there were more important things than her fate, she realized as Aimesley gave a hollow laugh. She had to save her daughter from this monster. God only knew what sort of man he'd force Lori to wed. Someone he could control. Someone who would care no more about Lori than Kent Aimesley did about her.

Miranda felt the big Irishman's malevolent presence behind her. The ruffian leaning against a filing cabinet in a corner of the room had taken her reticule and searched it. Satisfied with the decoy "weapon"—a letter opener he had found—he had not attempted to search her person further. The gun felt heavy, hidden in the folds of a pocket in her full skirt. She might be able to get both men into her sights, but what of the mute? He'd vanished into the interior of the building through another door. Were there more of Kent's employees inside?

As if in answer to her question, a short, fat man nattily dressed in a gray suit came bustling through the door. "Good. You've got her. After Mrs. Auburn's sad ole drowning accident, the railway contract will come to me."

He was an American, but Miranda had never before seen the fellow. "Who are you?" she asked, wondering if she dared to stand up and try moving to get the three men in her sights.

"You wouldn't believe me if I told you," he drawled with a nasty snigger. "Fetch her along, O'Connell. Nutter is bringing the old nigra female. You two," he said, turning to Miranda, "are going on a boat ride . . . only you ain't comin' back."

"We can't ride up and alert them," Sin warned as they neared the building where Mathias had seen the men take Miranda. He eyed Reba speculatively. "And we'd be wise to keep her bound and gagged while we set about rescuing Mrs. Auburn."

327

"You wouldn't dare touch me," she hissed.

"He won't have to sully his hands with you," Brand replied, pulling a handkerchief from his pocket and twisting it into a strong bond with which to tie her hands. When she opened her mouth to let out a warning scream, he stuffed the handkerchief instead into her mouth, then pulled her roughly across the seat. "Don't tempt me to wring your neck, Reba. I'll do it in a trice if anything happens to Miranda."

Before she could spit out the gag, Sin offered him a length of leather from the coach's tack with which to bind her wrists and another to secure the gag. They worked quickly, then locked her inside the carriage and set Mathias as guard and lookout while they walked around the corner to search for a way to enter the warehouse undetected. In moments they were inside after utilizing St. John's skills as a lockpick.

"Comes in handy now and again," was all he said, shrugging, when Brand lifted one eyebrow in surprise.

Feeble beams of moonlight glowed through small, high windows. Towering piles of crates, barrels and boxes filled the vast building, giving off the aromas of spices, leather and other exotic goods. Whispering softly, they agreed to split up and circle the room in search of Miranda.

Halfway around the circuit, Brand came upon a narrow slit of light issuing from beneath a closed door. He moved forward and waited for Sin. As soon as the little man reached him, they decided Sin would create a diversion to draw out whoever was inside while Brand waited to jump him.

St. John knocked over a large pile of tea crates, creating a fearful clatter. A stocky man brandishing a truncheon flung open the door with an oath and bellowed, "That you, Dusty? Didn' take long to drown the wenches, did it?"

Brand seized him around the neck in a choke hold that sent the club flying. "Now," he said as he tightened his hold until the man's eyes began to bulge, "where is Mrs. Auburn? Tell me and be quick about it or I'll turn my friend loose on you."

St. John advanced, the long blade of his sword-cane gleaming evilly in the dim light as he jabbed it in the man's gut. "Best heed him, old chap."

"T-they took 'em b-both," he stammered.

"Both?" Brand asked tightly.

"The lady 'n the bla—" He cut himself short, noting Sin's dark color, then gulped, "the maid."

That's when Sin looked past Brand and their captive into the room from which he had emerged. Lorilee sat bound and gagged, tied to a chair. "It's Miss Auburn!"

Brand shoved the man into the room so hard, he fell to the floor. While Sin continued holding him at sword's point, the baron took the gag from Lorilee's mouth. Now he understood why Miranda had dismissed her guards and driver and had come here alone. "I should've thought of this," he said angrily. "Have you seen your mother?" he asked.

"No," she replied, coughing from the dirty rag stuffed in her mouth for so many hours. "Do they have Mother, too? I was so afraid that's what would happen. I haven't seen anyone except the two ruffians who abducted us. But an awful little man who couldn't talk came and took Tilda just a few moments ago."

"Where did they take the women?" Sin asked the man on the floor. "You're not mute, but I can arrange it so you will be if you don't tell us," he said, raising the point of his blade to the man's mouth.

His captive paled. "The river. There be a barge out back, off the wharf." He scooted away from the menacing tip of the blade as he spoke.

"And you're going to show us the way," Brand said as he freed Lorilee from her bonds. "Wait here. Lock the door behind us and don't come out until we return," he instructed the terrified girl.

They took off at a run, shoving the huffing kidnapper before them as he led the way down to the wharf. A lonely whistle blew in the distance, and the stench of phosphorus and sewage wafted up from the lapping water as they dashed over the wooden planks. The place seemed utterly deserted.

Were they too late?

Miranda and Tilda exchanged signals as the men led them toward a barge tied at the end of the long pier. Tilda's bonds had been removed, but her circulation had been cut off for so long that she had difficulty walking. In spite of it, Miranda knew she would be a fierce fighter in the struggle to come. The fat man and Aimesley led the way, while O'Connell and the mute walked behind them. The Irishman had appropriated the hansom driver's truncheon. He kept slapping it in his hand as a reminder of what the women could expect if they gave their captors any trouble.

I have a gun in my pocket, Miranda mouthed silently to Tilda when she was certain the men behind them could not see. Tilda barely nodded, then flashed her eyes toward the barge, indicating that it would be best to wait until one or two of the men climbed aboard before attempting anything. Now Miranda nodded. Unaware, the conspirators discussed the railway contract.

"We'll sail for home tomorrow, but I'm relyin' on you to take care of everything on this end," the fat man said.

"With Miranda Auburn found drowned, no one will question my taking over her business affairs," Aimesley said. "I'll quietly withdraw our offer to the Union Pacific

330

for the loan and the shipping contract. Everything. I shall be prostrate with grief, of course."

"You wretched miscreant," Miranda hissed.

"Never fear," he said, turning back to her, "I shall take excellent care of your daughter."

"I imagine you have a suitable husband already picked out. One who'll do whatever you say." They neared the barge. She held her breath as O'Connell walked around them and began to untie the heavy ropes securing it to the pier. The little mute stayed in the shadows like a jackal.

"Rest assured I have the perfect husband in mind," Aimesley said in a pleased tone of voice. "You were going to marry her to an older man. A pity I don't have a title like your Rebel Baron, and I am a bit older than he—but not as old as Will Auburn when he wed you."

"You wouldn't dare! Lori would never consider—"

"She has no idea I'm involved in this 'unfortunate accident.' She'll be prostrate with grief and rely on me. Anyway, I'll give her little choice in the matter."

He was gloating, but Miranda reined in her temper, reinforced by a gentle nudge from Tilda, reminding her that this was their only chance. The women exchanged hand signals indicating that Tilda would attack Aimesley while Miranda jumped free so she could pull her weapon from its hiding place.

The Irishman grunted as he struggled with the ropes. In a moment the ropes would be loose and he would close in on them again. It was now or never. Tilda lowered her head suddenly and ran at the tall, thin man, butting him squarely in the stomach so he flew back against the edge of the barge, which was bobbing waist-high in the water. The fat man reached out with an oath, his fist swinging at Tilda while Miranda stepped back. She could see

O'Connell out of the corner of her eye, jumping up to aid his employers as she started to pull the revolver from her pocket.

It caught in the folds of her skirt.

Chapter Twenty-two

O'Connell was upon her and they struggled until he clipped her jaw with one meaty fist and tossed her over the edge of the barge. He remained unaware that she had a gun. Miranda landed on the hard metal bottom and struck her head a glancing blow. Everything went black for a moment as she struggled to remain conscious. She could hear the curses and shrieks as Tilda vented her wrath on their would-be killers. At the same time she heard other voices echoing down the pier from the wharf above.

Did one voice sound like Brandon's? Surely the blow to her head was causing her to imagine things! Miranda seized hold of a crude wooden bench and tried to regain her footing so she could withdraw the wretched gun from where it was caught in her skirt, but the world spun crazily around her.

Then she saw his beloved figure through the fog-drenched light, running down the pier with St. John at his heels. As if they'd rehearsed it, the baron and St. John each chose a target after the major used the butt of his pistol to crack their "guide" on the head, crumpling him to the pier. O'Connell fired at Brandon, eliciting a scream from Miranda, but the Irishman missed.

Not daring to use his Remington because the women were in his line of fire, Brand took advantage of the diversion Tilda was causing to duck and dodge as he closed on the big Irishman. Sin engaged the mute, who leaped agilely at him with a wicked blade drawn, an inarticulate, growling cry coming from his mutilated mouth.

Caruthers connected with O'Connell, tackling him so they fell to the rough wooden planks with a deep thud, rolling and twisting. Brand smashed his foe's hand against the splintery edge of a piling, and the gun went flying. But the Irishman had a knife in the other almost instantly. The two of them rolled dangerously near the edge of the pier, wrestling for control of the blade.

Although Tilda had been struck on the left shoulder by the fat man's fist, she shrugged away the pain and rounded on Aimesley just as he withdrew a small pistol from his waistcoat. Sin watched Tilda from the corner of his eye but then was forced to turn his full attention to the deadly little mute, who held the long stiletto in one hand while a small derringer instantly materialized in the other. Using his sword-cane to slash neatly across the mute's wrist, he disposed of the gun, but the little man ignored his bleeding left hand and began weaving in a deadly arc with his blade while evading St. John's longer weapon.

"That's for Miss Lori," Tilda cried as her good arm came crashing down on Aimesley's wrist when he fired at Sin's back. The shot went wild, splintering the wood of the pier. "And that's for Miss Miranda," she added, raising her skirts for good aim as her long leg flew upward and the tip of her pointy-toed boot connected solidly with his genitals. Kent Aimesley collapsed in an ungainly heap.

Brand and the Irishman were evenly matched in size and strength. O'Connell fought like the cornered rat he was, but the baron had an even more desperate need. He had seen this man raise his fist to Miranda. The ruffian would pay dearly for that. Coming up on top of his foe, Brand held O'Connell's knife hand at bay while smashing the Irishman's face.

Miranda watched the deadly battle, blinking hard to clear her vision. The big thug once more rolled on top of Brand. Suddenly, sausagelike fingers bit painfully into her upper arm as the fat man jerked her against him. Giving up on aiding Aimesley in his battle with Tilda, he had clamored aboard the barge to use his last desperate bargaining chip.

"I'll kill the woman," he yelled just as Brand's fist once again landed a thundering blow to O'Connell's throat. The baron was on top again and pummeling the Irishman insensate. Sin had just succeeded in disarming his foe. He realized the danger to Miranda before Brand emerged from the killing haze enveloping him.

"For once in her life, Reba told the truth. I say, you look remarkably well for a dead man, Wilcox . . . a bit bloated perhaps." St. John studied the pudgy man holding Miranda in his grasp with a gun jammed in her side.

Earl Wilcox was trembling so fearfully, he could barely hold the weapon to her side. Rivulets of foul-smelling sweat ran down his face, soaking into his starched collar. Miranda remained perfectly still as Brand climbed up and took a step toward them. "No, Brandon, don't—"

"Yes, Caruthers, you bastard, please do. I'd love to shoot your woman in front of you—almost as much as I'd love to shoot you."

"If you harm her in any way, Earl, you'll die like the cowardly pig you are, choking on the vomit of your own fear while I gut you," Brand ground out. But he did not move. "This is between you and me. You've always hated me. Coveted everything I ever had. Why not settle it now? Shoot me and be done with it."

"No!" Miranda shrieked, knowing what Brand intended. If the fat man moved his gun to fire at Brandon, she could wrench free and St. John could shoot him. With O'Connell out cold and Aimesley lying moaning on the pier, everyone would be safe. Everyone but Brandon.

"Right temptin' offer, Brand, but I think I'll play it safe," Wilcox replied. His hand was steadier now and he was gaining some confidence. "Take their weapons, Nutter. Oh, by the way, y'all know why he's called 'Nutter'? Use your imagination." Earl chuckled at the little mute, who was standing several feet from Sin, with his good hand clamped tightly around his bleeding wrist.

At once Nutter moved toward St. John. Miranda knew she had to act now or they would all die. Mimicking Reba, she gave an appallingly theatrical sigh and went utterly faint in his grasp. He cursed and tried to hold her up, but the barge was rocking on the current and he lost his balance. They both went down. Miranda managed to roll away from him. Without time to remove her Adams from its hiding place, she aimed at her large target and fired.

The kick of the gun jolted her and the smell of powder and burned cloth filled her nostrils. Miranda coughed. Earl Wilcox died.

Intent on reaching her, unable to see who had fired, Brand let out a roar as he raced to the barge, paying no heed to O'Connell. Sin and Tilda, too, were transfixed by the battle between Miranda and Wilcox. Nutter almost got past Sin. Almost. But Tilda saw the American reaching for the derringer he'd been forced to drop and cried out a warning. St. John swept up his blade just as Nutter tried to shoot him. Coming in low, he sent the tip of it up through the mute's heart.

While no one was looking, O'Connell figured his chances. Wilcox and Nutter were down, but Aimesley was coming around and might be of some use. The Irishman lunged for his gun and rolled up, shaking away the blurry vision caused by the beating he'd just taken. A lifetime of street brawls had made him incredibly resilient. He took aim on Brandon Caruthers's back and squeezed the trigger.

Miranda was still clutching the gun with which she'd killed Earl Wilcox, unable to grasp the enormity of what she had done when the shot rang out. Brandon pitched forward at the side of the barge, her name on his lips as he went down. Then she saw the big Irishman standing behind him, aiming once more at his fallen enemy. Without a thought, she raised her weapon and fired before he could get off a second shot.

A bright red splotch bloomed on his left shoulder, and the force of bullet sent him spinning around as he fell to the pier. Sin was on him in a trice, while Tilda scooped up his gun and leveled it on Aimesley.

Miranda would never remember the unladylike way she scrambled over the side of the barge, skirts hiked up and legs showing. She jumped to the pier and knelt at Brandon's side, dropping the gun without realizing she had done it. The sound of police whistles shrilled in the distance, drawing nearer, but she was oblivious to them as she cradled her major's head in her lap and bent her head to hear his whispered words.

"You're a natural shot, darlin'," he murmured. A faint smile tugged at his lips, which looked bluish in the dim light.

"Shh, my darling, don't try to talk. We have to get you to a doctor," she whispered. She could feel the wetness of his blood soaking through her skirts. O'Connell had shot him in the back. Miranda knew that if a lung had

SHIRL HENKE

been punctured, his chances of surviving were slim to none. She prayed as she tore away the bottom ruffle from her soft cotton petticoat and rolled it into a wad, pressing it against the wound.

"Damned if that doesn't hurt almost as bad as the last time my father thrashed me . . ." he said on a low moan.

Miranda bit her lip when he started to slip into unconsciousness. "You will not dare to die on me, Major," she commanded in her steadiest voice. Then more softly, as she stroked a lock of dark gold hair from his forehead, she murmured, "Please, my darling."

Brand heard Miranda's voice, strong and determined as ever. But had she called him "my darling"? Then the pain seared him when she adjusted her makeshift bandage around the hole in his back and everything faded into blackness.

"The baron is a very fortunate man. The bullet missed his lung by a fraction of an inch. Nasty business digging it out, though," Dr. Torres said as he replaced his instruments in his bag.

"Will he be all right?" Miranda whispered, looking from the young doctor to Brandon's pale face. He was well dosed with laudanum but resting fitfully.

"If fever doesn't set in . . . or an infection. I subscribe to the germ theory of disease. You must keep the wound clean. That's absolutely essential for the healing process. Try to get fluids down him, and keep him sedated so he doesn't toss about and reopen his injury. I'll be back tomorrow."

Miranda had used Dr. Micah Torres's services ever since Lorilee had come down with a mysterious fever as an eleven-year-old girl. He was considered one of the finest physicians in England, coming from a long line of healers practicing in London for generations. The young

338

doctor possessed a reputation for being willing to implement new research from the Continent and even America. He had saved Lori when all the other so-called experts had said she would die.

If only he could work a similar miracle with Brandon.

"I shall oversee his care personally. He and his friend saved our lives," she added. Her face flushed pinkly even though the doctor gave no indication of interest in why a prominent woman of business such as she would take an injured peer into her home, much less place him in her deceased husband's bed and nurse him herself. Let the gossips be damned.

The fever Dr. Torres had feared did indeed come. Miranda spent the next three days at Brand's bedside in the large room adjacent to her own, allowing herself time to fall exhausted into her own bed for only a few hours here and there while Tilda spelled her. Lori, who had come through her ordeal with surprising aplomb, helped shoulder her mother's business responsibilities by acting as a liaison with Mr. Timmons.

With Kent Aimesley in Newgate awaiting trial along with Reba Wilcox, Dustin O'Connell and his accomplice, Miranda's secretary and Lori had worked together to finalize the railway loan, iron contracts and shipping arrangements with Dr. Durant of the Union Pacific. Lori brought the sheafs of documents to the sickroom where the baron lay hovering between life and death. Distracted, Miranda would have signed anything placed before her. She did not even bother to read what Lori and Timmons asked her to look over.

The details of the elaborate negotiations had just been completed when Lori tiptoed into the baron's bedroom on a sunny summer afternoon. It had been her father's once, but she had been too young to have much memory of that. Now she thought of it as belonging to Brandon Caruthers. Just as her mother so obviously did. All she had to do was make Miranda admit her feelings, a formidable task indeed.

"You look a fright. Tilda says you haven't slept in days."

Miranda looked up from sponging Brandon's face. "Such flattery. I do thank you for your kind words, but I have matters on my mind a bit more pressing than getting my beauty rest."

Lori studied the dark circles beneath Miranda's eyes and the ratty braid of hair hanging over one shoulder. Her mother was wearing the same wrinkled gray dress she'd had on yesterday. "What good will it do the baron if you fall ill yourself?" Lori asked logically. "Then Tilda and the servants shall have double the duty and I'll be left in charge of Auburn Enterprises. The bank and shipyards, too," she added impishly.

"I feel fine, and missing a bit of sleep isn't going to harm me. Br—the baron's fever isn't contagious."

Just then he stirred in his sleep and she turned back to him, once again wringing the cloth in cool water and bathing his face with it. She started to pull down the covers so she could use it on his upper body but became aware that her maiden daughter was in the room. "It isn't proper for you to be here, Lori," she said decorously.

Lori let out a most indecorous snort. "That's precisely what Mr. Timmons said to me when I first walked into your office. You won't scandalize me by pulling down that sheet. It really covers very little."

"Honestly, Lorilee," Miranda huffed, but just then Brandon's hand grazed hers. She returned to her task, ignoring her stubborn daughter.

"The doctor believes the fever's about broken," Lori ventured. "His color does look markedly better."

"He was awake for a few moments this morning," Miranda said hopefully.

"Oh? What did he say?" Lori asked innocently.

Miranda's face turned pink. "That, young lady, is none of your concern. Now, please go. I shall ring for help if I require it."

"Very well, I shall leave you two alone . . . again," Lori replied, suppressing a chuckle as she imagined what Brand had said to elicit a blush from her mother.

Brand heard the door close. He'd been drifting in and out of sleep for the past day or so—it was difficult to discern the passage of time when one was fever-shot. He knew that from old wounds suffered during the war. He also knew that Miranda had bathed and examined every scar on his body during this illness. She'd crooned to him and caressed him.

Hell, she'd saved his life when O'Connell had downed him! But when he'd tried to tell her how he felt this morning, she'd run off like a scalded cat. All he'd been able to get out was that he was grateful she'd learned to fire the revolver, and she was gone. He hadn't had the time to tell her how proud he was of her courage.

Or that he loved her.

Perverse woman. He knew that if he opened his eyes again, she'd leave him to the care of servants. And he craved her touch. Ever so gently, as if he were still unconscious, he inched his hand to where the curly end of her braid dangled on the side of the bed. Twining his fingers in the shiny hair, he marveled at its thickness, savoring the way it tickled his skin. She leaned over him and adjusted the wrappings around his upper body. Of course, the accursed hole in his back still ached abominably and he was weak as a kitten.

That thought almost elicited a chuckle. Yesterday the little horde had escaped from the kitchen and two of them had found their way up to his room. One had been licking his face when the horrified tweenie had rushed through the door and scooped it up with profuse apologies. Tilda had pried the other miscreant from the draperies.

"You may stop faking now, Major," Miranda said crossly, pulling her hair free of his grasp. "I can tell you're awake."

He opened one eye. "Promise you won't run off?"

"I shan't *run* anywhere. But I do have other matters to attend to now that you've begun your recovery." She started to scoot off the edge of the mattress.

He tried to hold on to her wrist but was too weak. She slipped from his grasp. "We have to talk, Miranda."

"We have nothing to discuss, my lord, other than for me to express my gratitude to you for saving my life as well as the lives of my daughter and Tilda. We've already proffered our thanks to Mr. St. John," she hastened to add.

"Are wedding bells in my friend's future?" Brand asked.

A small smile broke over her face. "I fear they are. He was so impressed by the way his 'Goliath' handled Kent Aimesley that he proposed right there on the pier while the Peelers were arresting the kidnappers."

"Did she agree?"

"Not until he picked her up and threatened to dunk her in the Thames."

Brand laughed, but the pain quickly stopped him. "And what about us?"

Her heart seemed to stop beating. Why was he asking? Because of some misguided sense of duty toward a child she might or might not be carrying? Surely he could see how ill suited they'd be. She was too old. She had too much money. And she had hurt his pride by trying to bribe him with it. He would never be able to forgive her for that. She could not forgive herself.

The words hung between them for a moment more. Then Miranda could see that his strength was ebbing as his eyelids drooped. "You need to rest. We'll discuss matters later," she said and quickly fled the room.

"Why are you avoiding the baron, Mother? He's been asking for you for two days." Lori confronted Miranda in her office, where she'd sequestered herself ever since Brand began to mend.

"I've been busy. He's managing famously without me. Mr. St. John intends to take him home within the week," Miranda replied, keeping her gaze fastened on the pages before her.

"Pish! You have little to do. The contracts with the Union Pacific have all been signed. Mr. Timmons and I have taken care of everything. You're hiding from Brandon because you're in love with him and don't have the courage to face him."

Upon hearing her daughter use the baron's Christian name, Miranda's head snapped up. "How dare you be so impertinent?" she demanded angrily.

"It's only the bald truth, and we both know it. He wants to marry you, and you want to marry him."

"Life is not that simple, dearheart," Miranda replied with a sigh, all the anger of a moment ago gone as she sat back and wearily rubbed her aching forehead. "The baron is younger than I, and what is worse, he was your suitor. If we were to . . . to marry"—she could hardly get the word out—"well, think of the scandal it would create. Your season—"

"Oh, bother my season! I don't give a fig about silly old Society. I've learned a great deal over the past few months. So much has happened. Being kidnapped and nearly murdered in cold blood can make a woman reconsider what is important in her life. I have. Think of that poor little mouse Geoffrey Winters married, and how shallow Abbie is to stomach Jonathon Belford just because he'll one day be an earl. I don't want a life such as that, Mother. In fact . . . I'm not at all certain I wish to marry."

Miranda blanched. "You cannot mean that! It was your dearest wish—"

"No, Mother, I fear it was *your* dearest wish. You wanted for me what you never had for yourself—and I am grateful, truly I am." She walked around the large desk and took Miranda's hands, squeezing them in her own as she bent to press a kiss to her cheek.

"I did want to be accepted by the other girls in my schools, to have friends, but as to marriage . . . well, I'm not ready. In fact . . ." Lori paused, letting Miranda digest what she said, giving her mother time to consider what she was going to propose. Kneeling earnestly at Miranda's knee, Lori looked up into her troubled face. "I have found over the past week that I possess a good head for business. And I really enjoy it! Even Mr. Timmons has started to give me grudging compliments. It must be something I inherited," she said with a grin.

"Timmons did say you handled the contracts as well as Mr. Aimesley could have—had he ever intended we sign them," Miranda replied, still a bit dazed by this turnabout.

"Well, you must know by now that I'm not at all the fluff-headed fashion doll I pretended to be while I was matchmaking between you and Brand."

"I wondered why you were suddenly so maladept," Miranda said dryly.

Lori worked up her courage and pressed on. "I would like to go to America and take over the assignments Kent Aimesley had. Mr. St. John and Tilda have agreed to go with me," she hastened to add. "I know I can do it, Mother. I'll make you proud of me. And who knows?

Perhaps one day I'll meet a suitable man there. One who won't give a fig about society. A man like Brandon Caruthers," she added softly. "So, you see, the scandal doesn't matter to me at all—nor to him. Does it to you?"

Did it? Miranda had survived firestorms before, created simply because she'd assumed her husband's place in industry. All her attempts at propriety had been made with Lori in mind. No, she did not care about scandal if it did not harm her daughter. But she had wed one man for a child he wanted. She would not do it again. She could feel Lori's eyes studying her earnestly.

"You have given me much to consider, dearheart. I need time to think," she replied.

"Very well, but not for too long. Brand will be joining us for dinner tonight."

There was no way she could face him across a dining table before they had settled matters between them in private. Perhaps once that had been attended to, he would leave and she would not have to worry about dinner conversation. With that disturbing possibility firmly fixed in her mind, Miranda knocked on the door of the master suite and he bade her enter. She straightened. Perhaps she should have freshened up first, changed into an afternoon gown instead of the business suit she had donned that morning.

What was she thinking—to fix her hair the way he liked and powder her face in hopes of seducing him? Miranda shook her head and opened the door.

She was girded for battle. He could see it in the severe gray suit and the tight bun confining her hair. He leaned back in the easy chair with his legs stretched out on the ottoman before it. "You'll forgive me if I don't get up, but I might disturb him." He stroked Marmalade's dark orange fur, and the grizzled old tom purred loudly. Brand positively loved the way her eyes widened and her mouth formed a small "O" of astonishment.

"B-but you're terrified of cats—especially him," she practically squeaked.

"Remember when you saw me with the kitten in the garden? Well, it all started with Callie. She's really quite affectionate. While I've been confined to this room convalescing, the little invaders and their mother have visited me. Then this old fellow wandered in a time or two. As you can see, we've reached a detente."

"I'd say it's considerably more than that," Miranda responded tartly as the tom dug his claws into Brandon's heavy velour robe and kneaded in utter contentment. "He's never taken to a man before." The implications of that foolishly blurted out remark were not lost on either of them, but she rushed on, changing the subject. "I understand you will be joining us this evening for dinner. Do you think it wise to strain yourself so soon?"

He grinned at her. "Why, Miz Auburn, ma'am, I'd thank you for your kind solicitude if I didn't know you were itching to get me out of your house."

"That's not true! You were shot while rescuing Lori, Tilda and me. I would hardly be so ungrateful as to turn you out before you'd made a complete recovery."

"Is that what this is all about—gratitude?" he asked softly. "Come sit by me, darlin'." He patted the side of the huge ottoman and scooted his legs over to make room for her.

Miranda forced herself to stand her ground and not back away. If she did as he asked, she would be lost. She could not dare draw that close to him again. Ever again. "I shall be most comfortable here," she said stiffly, perching on the edge of an uncomfortable chair with an occasional table between them.

"Coward," he murmured as his gaze met hers and held. "I want to marry you, Miranda."

"No, you do not. You feel it's your duty to marry me, my lord. I won't ever again marry out of duty."

He could feel the cold finality in her words. "I'm not Will Auburn, Miranda." He could not keep a note of frustration from his voice.

"No, you're less than half the age he was when he proposed."

"What is it? Five years—or all of six between us? Age difference has nothing to do with this, darlin'. Neither does duty. Nor money."

"Ah yes, my money. The filthy lucre with which I offended your noble pride." She seized on the hurt she'd done him, hoping he would remember how angry he'd been then and spare them both. But he would not be diverted.

"That dog won't hunt!" Unfastening the cat from his robe, he set the tom on the chair and stood up, stalking over to her as he said, "I love you, Miranda. And you will marry me."

She stood up, vainly trying to escape before he reached her. She was not quick enough. He embraced her, pulling her against his chest.

"No, please. Let me go."

She struggled ineffectually as he lowered his mouth to her neck and pressed a soft kiss against the delicate column, murmuring, "Now be gentle, mind. After all, I am a wounded man." Then he captured her lips, cradling her head in his hand so she could not turn away.

Her legs melted like butter in the sun. She could not fight this . . . fight him. Not when he kissed her with such searing beauty. Her hands fastened around his shoulders and she returned the kiss, opening her mouth at the insistent dance of his tongue as it rimmed her lips. They both

groaned when he plunged inside. She could feel the un-
mistakable proof of his arousal pressing at the juncture of
her thighs and arched into it.

"Woman, what you do to me," he whispered between
kisses. "You will marry me." Before she could react, he
forced himself to release her, holding her at arm's length
as his eyes stared intently into hers. "But first we're going
to get some things straightened out." He loved the muzzy-
headed way she looked at him, still dazed from the kiss,
her heart's emotion so painfully visible in her eyes.

"I can't," she murmured in a faraway voice. "This is
what happens . . ."

He grinned. "Yes, it always is. Always has been ever
since the first time I saw you as a desirable woman riding
that train to Ascot. But I don't just desire you, Miranda,
I love you. For your courage, your honor, your sense of
humor. For the keen intelligence of your mind, and your
willingness to work your fingers to the bone to achieve
your dreams. When I thought I was going to lose you—
that Wilcox and O'Connell were going to kill you—I was
more frightened than I'd ever been in my life."

She looked deep into his eyes and read the truth there.
He truly believed he loved her . . . now. "But what if I'm
not with child? What if I'm too old to give you children?
You deserve so much more, Brandon. It's your duty—"

"Will you please leave off talking about duty, my love?
When I came to see you the morning after I stormed out
of here, I was still hurting pretty bad. You did deal my
pride a fearsome blow, I won't deny it—and," he hurried
on, "I wanted to hurt you back. Oh, I convinced myself
that I had to make certain any child of mine had my name,
that I'd be responsible for it, but in my heart I knew that
what I really wanted was for you to love me. I would love
giving you children, Miranda, but if I can't do that, I don't

care. You already have Lori, and I think of her like the little sister I lost. We can be a family.

"All I need is you—not your money. In fact, I've made financial arrangements to keep the Hall going for another two years. By then I'll have my stud farm and racing stables up and running. I don't want a farthing from you. Won't take it. All I want is your love. Is that too much to hope for?"

Tears shimmered in Miranda's eyes. She was too overcome with emotion to speak, so she shook her head—and realized that her hair was brushing against her back. He'd undone the pins while he was kissing her, the rogue, and she'd not even been aware of it! "I love you, Brandon," she finally managed. "With all my heart. But I've never learned how to show this kind of love before. You'll have to teach me."

"Never had a more apt pupil," he murmured, tipping up her chin with his fingers. "It'll be my greatest pleasure, darlin'." Reverently he lowered his mouth to hers and sealed their vows.

From his perch on the ottoman, Marmalade observed them and purred contentedly.

Epilogue

Spring, two years later

"I've just received a letter from Lori," Miranda said excitedly as she tore into the envelope, which was watermarked and much the worse for wear during its crossing of a continent and an ocean.

She looked delectable in a green-and-white-striped dress that accented her slender figure and brought out the clear silvery color of her eyes. Her husband inspected the glow of happiness on her face as she made her way across the newly built training yard to where he was working with Golden Girl, one of Reiver's best two-year-olds.

Handing the reins to Mathias, he said, "You're the one who's going to ride her. Put her through her paces some more."

The young man, who had become legendary on the English racing circuit in the past two years, grinned. "Yes, Major, pleased to do it."

Miranda watched Brand approach, once again struck by

how unbearably handsome he was, how in his element here. He wore muddy high boots and buckskin breeches and his shirt was open at the collar with sleeves rolled up, revealing his tantalizing golden body hair to her hungry eyes. Her gaze took in his long-legged stride and watched as a fresh breeze ruffled his sun-bleached hair, once more badly in need of barbering. *All the better for me to get my hands into*, she thought with a small thrill of pleasure.

She spent most of her time at Rushcroft Hall since their marriage and was growing to enjoy the clean air and sedate pace of country life as much as he. With telegraphs and Timmons helping her, it was not all that difficult to run her businesses without fighting her way into the City, except on rare occasions. Often weeks went by when she never saw London.

She did not miss it.

Brand met Miranda in the middle of the soft green turf and swept her up in his arms, swinging her around in a circle until her hair, loosely coiled in soft curls at the back of her neck, lost its pins and flew out in a dark reddish skein that floated to her shoulders when he finally stopped.

"Brandon, put me down. The servants will talk," she said without really meaning it. She laughed huskily as he bent and planted a kiss on her nose.

"Now, what has our world-traveling young lady to say?"

"She's someplace in the Far West called Wyoming. It sounds terribly primitive at this railroad camp." She began to read:

Dear Mother and Brand,

The scenery is quite spectacular here—mountains to the north, and incredibly wide open plains that seem to go on forever. Were it not for the railroad towns dotting the Union Pacific route (dare I tell you these quickly put up and torn down villages are called "hells-on-wheels"?), there would be nothing out here but wild red Indians. Tilda takes great exception to the American custom of naming these New World tribes after her own ancient civilization!

I have met the most remarkable man. General Jubal McKenzie is contracted by Dr. Durant to be the general manager of the railway, or railroad as the Americans call it. A shrewder and more demanding man of business I have never met. I am learning a great deal from him. His chief of operations is a fascinating young man, half red Indian and devastatingly handsome in a dangerous sort of way—but have no fear that I shall run off with him, as he is married to the general's granddaughter!

Tilda and Sin have leased a comfortable house in Denver and intend to spend summer there because baby Tilly is teething and too uncomfortable to endure the rigors of a rail camp. I, on the other hand, am flourishing. The Union Pacific expects to meet its counterpart from the west somewhere in Utah by early summer.

Dr. Durant has seemed most pleased with my progress reports and suggestions. I hope it is not just because my family has such a large interest in railway stocks!

The morning whistle just blew. I must be off to work. Give my baby brother a big hug and tickle him for me. I miss you all terribly and plan to be back in Denver by fall. Perhaps you will take that long-promised trip to America then? This is a hint, Mother. Brand, please see that the three of you visit before year's end.

Much love,
Lorilee

"I don't think she need worry about how seriously the Union Pacific people are taking her work. She's been invaluable to them," Brand said as Miranda finished reading. "What do you say to sailing for America in August?"

"Profane railwaymen and wild red Indians?" Miranda gave him a wide smile. "Your homeland sounds like a dangerous place."

"But you miss Lori so much you'll risk the trip." He could tell by the happy gleam in her eyes that she was already looking forward to seeing her daughter. "Besides, America is no more dangerous than the streets of London."

"You've been doing more than your share to remedy that in Parliament, my lord," she replied, drawing him down for another quick kiss.

"That's 'my lord major' to you," he growled, deepening the kiss as he swept her into his arms and began carrying her toward Rushcroft Hall.

The old place still required considerable refurbishing, but the sale of his city place had fetched a tidy sum, which he'd immediately plowed into the development of his stud farm and racing business. Profits were increasing exponentially as word spread about his superior stock, both race horses and carriage horses. Although he refused to use any of his wife's wealth, the baron had already been able to begin renovations on the lovely old manor house. Within another year or two it would be the showplace it had been a century ago before his profligate ancestors had let it go to ruin.

"Johnny will awaken from his nap within the hour," she cautioned. The year-old, tow-headed boy was the pride and joy of both their lives, named for Brand's father. She had been overjoyed to learn that she was at last with child after months of trying unsuccessfully to conceive. The Caruthers name would be carried on, and if she had any say about it, there would be many more brothers and sisters for John Shelby Caruthers. As her husband carried her up the stairs past tittering servants, Miranda felt certain she need not worry about accomplishing that goal.

Kicking the bedroom door closed, he allowed her to slide slowly down the length of his tall, lean body. They stood facing each other, locked together and leaning against the door. "Remind you of anything?" he drawled as he began unfastening the buttons down the back of her gown.

"You mean our wedding night when we never made it to the bed before you tore my clothing off and ravished me?" she asked on a breathless sigh as he nuzzled her throat.

"As I . . . recall . . . madam," he said, punctuating his words with kisses as he worked, "you had me stripped . . . to my unmentionables . . . before I had your . . . corset unlaced."

"Unmentionables!" Miranda, busy pulling open his shirt, let out a gusty laugh. "If there is anything you've taught me over the past two years, Major, it's that nothing is unmentionable between lovers. Besides, men's garments are easier to unfasten than women's—and we did finally make it to the bed," she added saucily, slipping his breeches down after she'd deftly unbuttoned his fly. "Your encores were wondrous."

"Aaah," he gasped as she reached inside and took hold of his rigid staff with one small, skillful hand.

"A pity we don't have time to test that remarkable American stamina now," she murmured. "Perhaps tonight?"

"Insatiable woman," he crooned, then rotated his hips in rhythm with her strokes. "But you've forgotten one important rule—boots first."

"Only if we plan to get as far as the bed," she answered

reasonably. "Johnny will be awakening soon, remember?"

He had somehow managed to slide her soft cotton gown off her shoulders and shove her camisole down to free the tips of her breasts, which were hardened into tight little buds. The heat of his mouth on them nearly made her dissolve. She arched up, letting him flick the nipples with his tongue, then suckle on them. The lovers slowly crumpled together onto the soft carpet.

He spread her hair out around them like a fiery mantle, taking one long curl and binding her to him by wrapping it about his neck. "Miranda, my love, my life," he whispered as her lips parted and joined his in a deep, searing kiss.

She could feel his callused hands—those wonderful, long-fingered hands—stroking up her calf toward the sensitive skin of her inner thigh while he pulled her skirt and petticoats up. She arched her hips, allowing him easy access to slide down her pantalets. When his hand cupped her mound, it was Miranda who cried out.

"Please, Brandon, my love, now—now!"

He obliged her as she spread her legs, positioning his staff and sliding it deep inside her welcoming heat. At once her thighs tightened around his hips and she arched against him. He felt the tug on his scalp when her hands seized fistfuls of thick blond hair and guided his head to her breasts once more. As he suckled her, she moved in perfect sync with his thrusts, crying out in unabashed pleasure.

This austere woman of business who coolly ran banks, iron foundries and shipping yards was his and his alone at moments such as these. Miranda was wild and abandoned, caring nothing for what servants might gossip or Society say about her Rebel Baron of a husband who raced horses and refused to dance to the tune piped in London. This was real. This was all that mattered.

SHIRL HENKE

They rolled around on the floor and Miranda came up on top, her skirts ruched up about her thighs as she rode him like a Valkyrie. Brand reached up and cupped a breast in each hand, using his thumbs rhythmically on the nipples until she threw back her head and moaned. Knowing the end was near, he once again tumbled her beneath him, driving fiercely into her as if this were the last mating on earth.

He felt her reaching her peak and looked down with awe at the bright pink blotches that stained her face and traveled over her throat to her breasts. Such a lovely sight on her fair silky skin. But when her body began to spasm in bliss, she wrung from him the last vestiges of his control and he, too, gave in to the ecstasy.

She could feel him stiffen and swell even more as his shuddering release poured into her, sending her into yet another climax of her own. When they made love, it was difficult to tell just where one of them began and the other ended, as every nuance of their wild joinings elicited such mutual bliss. He collapsed on top of her, sweat-soaked from their exertions, even more than he had been from working under the warm spring sun.

"I'm afraid I've quite ruined your lovely dress—and now we both smell of horses."

He did not sound the least bit apologetic and she did not the least bit care. Burying her face in the springy hair of his chest, she inhaled deeply. "You smell of male and I like that."

"I was riding a filly," he said with a lopsided grin.

"Human male, not horse, you dolt, and you did just ride—but I'm far from a filly."

"Fishing for compliments, are you, darlin'?" he said, pressing kisses on her eyelids, nose and cheeks before centering his attention on her mouth. "You are the most beautiful woman in all of England."

Between kisses, she said dreamily, "Only England?"

"Well now, to be certain it's all the world, we'll have to start with that visit to America this fall, won't we? But I'm sure you'll still hold the title if we circle the globe."

"I'm not so certain." She looked up at him with a blaze of joy on her face. "You see, I'll be growing quite fat by the end of the year."

Comprehension dawned and he beamed at her. "Lordy, darlin', I'm supposed to be running a stud farm for horses, not children."

"Let's work at beating Reiver's record—but mind you, always remember that your stable of mares is a stable of one," she said with mock severity.

Brand chuckled. "Woman, that is one condition you won't ever have to negotiate."

Acknowledgment

I first conceived the idea of an embittered Confederate cavalier who had lost everything in the war and then found the English title he inherited was as bankrupt as his lost plantation in Kentucky. The concept seemed rather dark for the American Lords series, which was intended to be comic as well as romantic. Lorilee Auburn, not her iron-willed mother Miranda, was to be his leading lady. But how to put a light touch to the story? My husband Jim came up with a twist—have Lori become matchmaker for her mother and turn the tables on Brand. All sorts of possibilities for humor followed. So did Gideon Hercules St. John, "Sin" to his friends. If he reminds you a bit of his very English counterpart Alvin Francis Edward Drummond, "Drum" from *Wicked Angel, Wanton Angel,* and *Yankee Earl,* I also owe Sin's character to Jim.

After writing three books set during the Regency, I was a bit at sea when I moved into the Victorian era. My good friend and colleague Karyn Witmer-Gow, a.k.a. Elizabeth Grayson, lent me a large canvas sack of reference books which were a lifesaver, guiding me across the Atlantic into mid-nineteenth-century England. It is so much easier on a writer when the "lending librarian" has no due dates stamped on her books.

I hope you have laughed and cried with Brand and Miranda, as you did with Jason and Rachel in *Yankee Earl.* Next on deck will be Josh and Sabrina in *Texas Viscount.* Somewhere in the near future, how could I resist a story for Lorilee? After losing a hunk like Brand, she certainly deserves a hero of her own. Let me know what you think.

Happy reading!

Shirl Henke

www.shirlhenke.com

*Another American Lord comes to
claim his birthright and the Englishwoman
he is destined to love in . . .*

SHIRL HENKE's
THE TEXAS VISCOUNT

THE BRIT

Staid, starchy Sabrina Edgewater, teacher of deportment, first encounters her nemesis in a dockside brawl that earns him the nickname of "Texas Viscount." To the very proper Englishwoman he is the "Texas Visigoth." She gives the ruffian a good dressing down, never imagining that the lout would turn out to be the Earl of Hambleton's heir. His devilish good looks make her heart beat madly, but she tells herself that Joshua Cantrell is . . .

THE BARBARIAN

Raised in a Texas bordello, Josh becomes a self-made millionaire in the cattle business before he's turned thirty. He only agrees to become a viscount because his Rough Rider commander, now President Theodore Roosevelt, asks him to ferret out an international conspiracy. The last thing he expects is to lock horns with a prissy little schoolmarm, even if she is cute as an acre of speckled pups . . .

THE BLACKMAIL

Josh packs a six-shooter and swills whiskey straight from the bottle. Lord Hambleton implores Miss Edgewater to teach his heir the social graces. When she refuses, the wily earl blackmails her with money enough to open her long dreamed of school for indigent girls. But dare she risk her heart to achieve her heart's desire? Or is her heart's desire . . . *The Texas Viscount*?

Coming in October 2004. Watch for it!